TWO
SERPENTS
RISE

■ ■ ■

ALSO BY MAX GLADSTONE

Three Parts Dead

TWO SERPENTS RISE

Max Gladstone

TOR®

A Tom Doherty Associates Book

NEW YORK

TWO SERPENTS RISE

Copyright © 2013 by Max Gladstone

A Tor Book
Published by Tom Doherty Associates, LLC
175 Fifth Avenue
New York, NY 10010

www.tor-forge.com

Tor® is a registered trademark of Tom Doherty Associates, LLC.

Library of Congress Cataloging-in-Publication Data

Gladstone, Max.
    Two serpents rise / Max Gladstone. — 1st ed.
        p. cm.
    "A Tom Doherty Associates book."
    ISBN 978-0-7653-3312-4 (hardcover)
    ISBN 978-1-4668-0204-9 (e-book)
    1. Paranormal fiction.   I. Title.

PS3607.L343T96 2013
813'.6—dc23

                                              2013006325

Tor books may be purchased for educational, business, or promotional use. For information on bulk purchases, please contact Macmillan Corporate and Premium Sales Department at 1-800-221-7945, extension 5442, or write specialmarkets@macmillan.com.

First Edition: October 2013

Printed in the United States of America

0 9 8 7 6 5 4 3 2 1

Book One

■ ■ ■

CLIFF
RUNNING

1

The goddess leaned over the card table and whispered, "Go all in."

She hovered before Caleb, cloudy and diaphanous, then cold and clear as desert stars. Her body swelled beneath garments of fog: a sea rock where ships dashed to pieces.

Caleb tore his gaze away, but could not ignore her scent, or the susurrus of her breath. He groped for his whiskey, found it, drank.

The cards on the green felt table were night ladies, treacherous and sweet. Two queens rested facedown by his hand, her majesty of cups (blond, voluptuous, pouring blood and water from a chalice), and her majesty of swords (a forbidding Quechal woman with broad face and large eyes, who gripped a severed head by the hair). He did not have to look to know them. They were his old friends, and enemies.

His opponents watched: a round Quechal man whose thick neck strained against his bolo tie, a rot-skinned Craftsman, a woman all in black with a cliff's face, a towering four-armed creature made from silver thorns. How long had they waited?

A few seconds, he thought, a handful of heartbeats. Don't let them rush you.

Don't dawdle, either.

The goddess caressed the inner chambers of his mind. "All in," she repeated, smiling.

Sorry, he thought, and slid three blue chips into the center of the table.

Life faded from him, and joy, and hope. A part of his soul flowed into the game, into the goddess. He saw the world through her eyes, energy and form flowering only to wilt.

"Raise," he said.

She mocked him with a smile, and turned to the next player. Five cards lay faceup before the dealer. Another queen, of staves, greeted the rising sun in sky-clad silhouette—a great lady, greater still when set beside his pair. To her right the king of swords, grim specter, stood knife in hand beside a struggling, crying child bound upon an altar. The other cards struck less dramatic figures, the eight and three of staves, the four of coins.

Three queens formed a strong hand, but any two staves could make a flush, and beat him.

"Call," said the man in the bolo tie.

"Call," said the Craftsman with the rotting skin.

"I see your raise," said the woman, "and raise you two thousand." She pushed twenty blue chips into the pot. The goddess whirled, a tornado of desire, calling them all to death.

"Fold," said the creature of thorns.

The goddess turned again to Caleb.

Did the woman in black have a flush, or was she bluffing? A bluff would be brash against three other players with a possible flush on the board, but Caleb's had been the only bet this round. Would she risk so much on the chance she could drive three players to fold?

Calling her bluff would take his whole reserve. He'd have to give himself to the game, hold nothing back.

The goddess opened her mouth. The black within yawned hungrily. Perfection glinted off the points of her teeth.

You can win the world, she said, if you're willing to lose your soul.

He looked her in the eye and said, "Fold."

She laughed, and did not stop until the black-clad woman turned over her cards to reveal a king and a two, unsuited.

Caleb bowed his head in congratulations, and asked the others' leave to go.

Caleb bought another drink and climbed marble stairs to the pyramid's roof. Dandies, dilettantes, and high-society corpses clustered near the edge, glorying in the panorama of Dresediel Lex by night: gleaming pyramid-studded city, skyspires adrift like crystal scimitars above, the ceaseless roll of the Pax against the western shore. A ceiling of low clouds confronted the metropolis with its own reflected light.

Caleb was not interested in the view.

A carved black stone altar rose from the center of the roof, large enough to hold a reclining man, or woman, or child. From the iron fence around the altar hung a bronze plaque embossed with a list of dates and victims' names.

He didn't read the plaque. He knew too much history already. He leaned against the railing, and watched the old altar. Dew rolled down his whiskey glass and wet his hand.

Teo found him twenty minutes later.

He heard her approach from the stairwell. He recognized her stride.

"It's been a long time," she said, "since I've seen you leave a game that fast. Not since school, I think."

"I was bored."

In modest heels, Teo was Caleb's height and broader, built of curves and arches. Her lips were full, her eyes dark. Black ringlets framed her round face. She wore white pants with gray pinstripes, a white vest, a ruby shirt, a gray tie, and an expression of concern. Her hand lacked a drink.

She joined him at the rail.

"You weren't bored." She turned her back on the altar, and looked east over the city, toward the gleaming villas atop the Drakspine ridge. "I don't know how you can spend so much time staring at that old rock."

"I don't know how you can look away."

"It's bad art. Mid-seventh dynasty knockoff, gaudy and over-ornamented. Aquel and Achal on the side look more like caterpillars than snakes. They didn't even sacrifice people here often. Most of that happened over at our office." She pointed to the tallest pyramid on the skyline, the immense obsidian edifice at 667 Sansilva. Caleb's father would have called the building Quechaltan, Heart of the Quechal. These days it had no name. "This place did cows. The occasional goat. People only on an eclipse."

Caleb glanced over his shoulder. Dresediel Lex sprawled

below: fifteen thousand miles of roads gleaming with ghostlight and gas lamps. Between boulevards crouched the houses and shops and apartment buildings, bars and banks, theaters and factories and restaurants, where seventeen million people drank and loved and danced and worked and died.

He looked away. "We have an eclipse every year, a partial or a lunar. For a full solar like the one this autumn, the priests would work through all the prisoners and captives they could find, throw in a few innocents for good measure. Blood and hearts for Aquel and Achal."

"And you wonder why I don't look? It's bad art, and worse history. I don't know why Andrej"—the bar's owner—"keeps it around."

"You wouldn't have thought that way seventy years ago."

"I like to think I would have."

"So would I. But your grandparents, and my father, they weren't born different from the rest of us, and they still fought tooth and claw to defend their gods back in the Wars."

"Yeah, and they lost."

"They lost, our boss won, kicked out priests and pantheon, and now we all pretend three thousand years of bloodshed didn't happen. We put a fence around history and hang a plaque and assume it's over. Try to forget."

"What's put you in such a good mood?"

"It's been a long day. Long week. Long year."

"Why did you fold, at the table?"

"I catch hell from the goddess, and I need to explain myself to you, too?"

"The goddess doesn't know you like I do. She's reborn every game. I've watched you play for eight years, and I've never seen you cave like that."

"The odds were against me."

"Screw odds. You had to know the lady in black wasn't suited."

He turned from the altar. Southwest winds bore the sea scent of salt and death. "Can't you go stalk some girl fresh from university or something? Leave me in peace?"

"I'm reformed. I am no longer a dirty old woman."

"Could have fooled me."

"Seriously, Caleb. What's wrong?"

"Nothing," he said, and patted his pockets for a smoke. Of course nothing. He quit years ago. Bad for his health, the doctors said. "The odds were against me. I wanted to get out with my soul intact."

"You wouldn't have done that four years ago."

"A lot changes in four years." Four years ago, he was a fledgling risk manager at Red King Consolidated, recovering from a university career of cards and higher math. Four years ago, he was dating Leah. Four years ago, Teo still believed she was interested in boys. Four years ago, he'd thought the city had a future.

"Yes." A tiny copper coin lay at Teo's feet, a bit of someone's soul spooled up inside. She kicked the coin, and it tinged across the roof. "Question is, whether the change is for the better."

"I'm tired, Teo."

"Of course you're tired. It's midnight, and we're not twenty-two anymore. Now get down there, apologize to that table, and steal their souls."

He smiled, and shook his head, and collapsed, screaming.

Images burrowed into his brain: blood smeared over concrete, a tangled road into deep mountains, the chemical stench of a poisoned lake. Teeth gleamed in moonlight and tore his flesh.

Caleb woke to find himself splayed on the sandstone floor. Teo bent over him, brow furrowed, one hand cool against his forehead. "Are you okay?"

"Office call. Give me a second."

She recognized the symptoms. If necromancy was an art, and alchemy a science, then direct memory transfer was surgery with a blunt instrument: painful and unsubtle, dangerous as it was effective. "What does the boss want with you at midnight?"

"I have to go."

"Hells with her. Until nine tomorrow, the world is someone else's responsibility."

He accepted her hand and pulled himself upright. "There's a problem at Bright Mirror."

"What kind of problem?"

"The kind with teeth."

Teo closed her mouth, stepped back, and waited.

When he could trust his feet, he staggered toward the stairs. She caught up with him at the stairwell.

"I'm coming with you."

"Stay here. Have fun. One of us should."

"You need someone to look after you. And I wasn't having fun anyway."

He was too tired to argue as she followed him down.

2

Moonlight shone off the streak of blood on the concrete path beside Bright Mirror Reservoir.

Caleb watched the blood, and waited.

The first Wardens on site had treated the guard's death as a homicide. They scoured the scene, dusted for fingerprints, took notes, and asked about motive and opportunity, weapons and enemies—all the wrong questions.

When they found the monsters, they began to ask the right ones. Then they called for help.

Help, in this case, meant Red King Consolidated, and, specifically, Caleb.

Dresediel Lex had been built between desert and sea by settlers who neither expected nor imagined their dry land would one day support seventeen million people. Down the centuries, as the city grew, its gods used blessed rains to fill the gaps between water demand and supply. After the God Wars were won (or lost, depending on who you asked), RKC took over for the fallen pantheon. Some of its employees laid pipe, some built dams, some worked at Bay Station maintaining the torturous Craft that stripped salt from ocean water.

Some, like Caleb, solved problems.

Caleb was the highest-ranking employee on site so far. He had expected senior management to swoop in and take charge of a case like this, with death and property damage and workplace safety at issue, but his superiors seemed intent to leave Bright Mirror to him. At the inevitable inquest, he would be the one called to testify before Deathless Kings and their pitiless ministers.

The RKC brass had given him a wonderful opportunity to fail.

He wanted a drink, but could not afford to take one.

For a frenzied half hour, he'd ordered junior analysts and technicians through the routines of incident response. Isolate the reservoir from the city mains. Pull some Craftsmen out of bed to build a shield over the water. Find a few tons of rowan wood, stat. Check the dam's wards. Cordon off the access road. No one comes in or out.

Orders given, he stood, silent, by the blood and the water.

Glyphs necklaced Bright Mirror Reservoir in blue light. The dammed river ran glossy black from shore to shore. He smelled cement, space, the broad flatness of still water, and above all that a sharp ammonia stench.

Two hours ago, a security guard named Halhuatl had walked along the reservoir, casting about in the dark with a bull's-eye lantern. Hearing a splash, he stepped forward. He saw nothing—no night bird, no bat, no swimming coyote or bathing snake. He scanned the water with his lantern. Where the light touched, it left a rippling trail.

That's strange, Hal must have thought, before he died.

A chill wind blew over the water, producing no waves. Caleb stuck his hands deep into the pockets of his overcoat. Footsteps approached.

"I grabbed this from the icebox in the maintenance shack," Teo said, behind him. "The foreman will miss his lunch tomorrow."

He turned from the water and reached for the parcel she held, white wax paper tied with twine. "Thank you."

She didn't let go. "Why do you need this?"

"To show you what's at stake."

"Funny." She released the package. He undid the twine with his gloved hands, and opened the paper. A frost-dusted slab of beef lay within, its juice the same color as the blood on the concrete.

He judged the distance to the water, lifted the beef, and threw it overhand.

The meat arced toward the reservoir. Beneath, water bulged

and reared—a wriggling, viscous column rippled with reflected stars.

The water opened its mouth. Thousands of long, curved fangs, stiletto-sharp, snapped shut upon the beef, piercing, slicing, grinding as they chewed.

The water serpent hissed, lashed the night air with an icy tongue, and retreated into the reservoir. It left no trace save a sharper edge to the ammonia smell.

"Hells," Teo said. "Knife and bone and all the hells. You weren't kidding about teeth."

"No."

"What is that thing?"

"Tzimet." He said the word like a curse.

"I've seen demons. That's no demon."

"It's not a demon. But it's *like* a demon."

"Qet's body and Ilana's blood." Teo was not a religious woman—few people were religious any more, since the God Wars—but the old ways had the best curses. "That thing's living in our water."

Her voice held two levels of revulsion. Anyone could have heard the first, the common terror. Only someone who knew how seriously Teo took her work with Red King Consolidated would detect her emphasis on the word "our."

"No." Caleb knelt and wiped the meat juice off his gloved fingers onto the ground. "It's not *in* our water. It *is* our water." Stars glared down from the velvet sky. "We've isolated Bright Mirror, but we need to check the other reservoirs. Tzimet grow slowly, and they're clever. They could be hiding until they're ready to strike. It's blind luck we caught this one."

"What do you mean, it *is* the water?"

"The Craft keeps our reservoirs clean: wards against germs, fish, Scorpionkind larvae, anything that might pollute or corrupt. Charms to curb evaporation. The reservoir's deep, with dark shadows at the bottom. When the sun and stars shine, a border forms between light and darkness. The Craft presses against that border. If there's enough pressure, it pokes a tiny hole in the world." He held his thumb and forefinger an inch apart. "Nothing physical can fit through, only patterns. That's what these Tzimet are." He pointed to the reservoir. "Like seed crystals. A bit of living night seeps into the water, and the water becomes part of the night."

"I've never seen a crystal with teeth." She paused, corrected herself. "Outside of a gallery. But that one didn't move." She pointed to the blood. "Who was it?"

"Security guard. Night roster says the guy's name was Halhuatl. The Wardens thought this was a homicide until the reservoir tried to eat them."

Gravel growled on the road behind: the golem-carts arrived at last. Caleb turned. Exhaust puffed from joints in the golems' legs. RKC workers in gray uniform jackets walked from cart to cart, checking the rowan logs piled within. Two junior analysts stood beside the foreman, taking notes. Good. The workers knew their business. They didn't need his people interfering.

"Horrible way to die," Teo said.

"Quick," Caleb answered. "But, yes."

"Poor bastard."

"Yeah."

"Now we know Tzimet are in there, we can keep them from getting out. Right?"

"They can't get into the water system, but to keep them imprisoned we need better Craftsmen than we've been able to get out here so far. Those glowing glyphs hide the reservoir from animals that want a drink. We've inverted them to hide the outside world from the Tzimet. They can't hear us or smell us, but they could kill us no problem if they knew we were here."

"You sure know how to make a lady feel safe."

"The Craft division's woken Markoff, Billsman, and Telec; once they arrive, they'll build a shield over the water. Feel safe then."

"No way Telec's sober enough for work at this time of night. And Markoff will be trying to impress the shorefront girls with his rich-and-sinister routine."

"Dispatch found them all, and claims they're up for it. Anyway, the Tzimet aren't a big deal in the meantime, long as they don't get into the pipes."

"Glad to hear it." She grimaced. "I think I'll lay off tap water all the same."

"Don't let the boss catch you."

"I said I'd stop drinking it, not selling it. Can this kind of infection happen any time?"

"Technically?" He nodded. "The odds of Tzimet infestation in a given year are a hundred thousand to one against or so. We didn't expect anything like this for at least another century. Poison, bacterial blooms, Scorpionkind, yes. Not this."

"So you don't think it was natural?"

"Might have been. Or someone might have helped nature along. Good odds on the latter."

"You live in a grim universe."

"That's risk management for you. Anything that can go wrong, will—with a set probability given certain assumptions. We tell you how to fix it, and what you should have done to keep it from happening in the first place. At times like these, I become a hindsight professional." He pointed at the blood. "We ran the numbers when Bright Mirror was built, forty-four years ago, and thought the risks were acceptable. I wonder if the King in Red will break the news to Hal's family. If he has a family."

"The boss isn't a comforting figure."

"I suppose not." A line of golem-carts rolled past behind them.

"Can you imagine it? A knock, and you answer the door to see a giant skeleton in red robes? With that flying lizard of his coiled on your lawn, eating your dog?"

"There would be heart attacks." Caleb couldn't resist a slim smile. "People dying with the door half open. Every personal injury Craftsman in the city would descend on us like sharks when blood's in the water."

Teo clapped him on the shoulder. "Look who's got his sense of humor back."

"I might as well laugh. I have another three hours or so of this." He waved over his shoulder at the carts with their cargo. A bleary brigade of revenants in maintenance jumpsuits lurched by, bearing rowan. They stank of grave-musk. "I won't leave until three, maybe four."

"Should I be worried that it takes demons to break you out of your funk?"

"Everyone likes to be needed," he said. "I might be late to work tomorrow."

"I'll tell Tollan and the boys you were out keeping the world safe for tyranny." She fished her watch out of her pocket, and frowned.

"You late for something?"

"A little." She closed the watch with a click. "It's not important."

"I'm fine. I'll catch up with you tomorrow."

"You're sure? I can stay here if you need me."

"Fate of the city on the line here. I have my hands full. No room for self-pity. Go meet your girl."

"How did you know there was a girl?"

"Who else would be waiting for you at two in the morning? Go. Don't get in trouble on my account."

"You better not be lying."

"You'd know if I was."

She laughed, and retreated into the night.

The maintenance crew poured ten tons of rowan logs into the reservoir. Revenants did most of the hands-on work, since they smelled less appetizing to the Tzimet. Soon, a smooth layer of wood covered the water. Caleb thanked the foreman as his people slunk back to their beds.

The rowan would block all light from stars and moon and sun. The wood's virtue poisoned Tzimet, and deprived of the light that cast their shadows, the creatures would wither and die.

Overhead, Wardens circled on their Couatl mounts. Heavy feathered wings beat fear through the sky, and Caleb felt serpents' eyes upon him.

By sunrise, every executive in Red King Consolidated would be knocking on Caleb's door, demanding to know how Bright

Mirror was corrupted. Craftsmen could bend lightning to their will, cross oceans without aid, break gods in single combat, but they remained human enough to hunt scapegoats in a crisis. Sixty years after Dresediel Lex cast off the gods' yolk, its masters still demanded blood.

So Caleb searched for a cause. Bright Mirror had been built with safeguards upon safeguards. If a mistake was made, what mistake, and who made it? Or was there some force at work more sinister than accident? The True Quechal, or another group of god-worshipper terrorists? Rival Concerns, hoping to unseat Red King Consolidated as the city's water source? Demons? (Unlikely—the demon lords made a hefty profit from their trade with Dresediel Lex, and had no reason to hurt the city.)

Who would suffer for Halhuatl's death?

Rowan logs bobbed on the still reservoir. Caleb's footsteps were the only breaches in the night's silent shell. City lights glowed over the dam's edge, as if the world beyond was burning.

He walked the shoreline, searching for a sacrifice.

3

By the time Caleb reached the far side of the reservoir, he was so exhausted he almost didn't see the woman.

He had not found his cause. All the equipment and wards seemed to work. No barbed wire was severed, no holes cut into the fence. No drums of poison stood empty beside decaying chemical sheds. He spied no pitons or carved handholds on the cliffs above the water.

When he closed his eyes and examined Bright Mirror as a Craftsman would, he saw an enormous web spun in three dimensions by a drunken spider. He could make no sense of that weave, let alone tell if it was broken.

He opened his eyes again. The dam's edge cut the world in half, water and rowan below and sky above. To his right stood a dormitory shack, windows dark, inhabitants lost in sleep and demon dreams. Caleb was alone.

He blinked.

Not alone.

A woman leaned against the shack, arms crossed, one knee bent, her heel resting on the wall.

She did not seem to have noticed him. He engraved her on his memory: slender, and tense as a bent blade. Short black flames of hair blazed from her head. Thin lips, with sharp edges. She wore calf-length pants the color of sand and rock, a white sleeveless shirt, and dark gray close-toed sandals with leather straps that wrapped around her ankles and calves. She looked as if she had no business anywhere near Bright Mirror Reservoir.

She rubbed her bare arms, and shivered from the cold.

Either the woman had not seen him, or didn't think he could see her. If the former, she'd see him soon enough; if the latter, no sense demonstrating she was wrong. He surveyed grounds, sky, water, and shed, as if she did not exist. Step by nonchalant step, he drew closer. She glanced at him, and smiled a self-satisfied smile. She did not greet him, nor did she speak, which settled the matter to Caleb's satisfaction. She thought she was invisible. Fair enough.

When he came within range, he sprang.

He pinned her arms to the wall. She did not curse or struggle, only stared at him with wide startled eyes of a brighter black than he'd known eyes could be.

He was lucky, he realized, that she didn't try to fight him. Her arms felt strong, and his groin was exposed to her knee.

"Who," she asked, "are you?"

"That's my line."

"You don't look like a Warden. Is this your hobby, jumping unarmed women in the middle of the night?"

"What are you doing here?"

"I'm taking the air," she said with a smile. "Waiting for a nice man to accost me. Only way to get a date in this town."

"Give me a straight answer."

"I fell from the sky." She was beautiful, he thought, as weapons were beautiful. No. Focus.

"I work for RKC. This reservoir has been poisoned. The water's infested with Tzimet. One of our workers is dead. I'm not here to joke."

Her smile broke. "I'm sorry."

"Who are you?"

"You first."

"I'm Caleb Altemoc," he said before it occurred to him not to answer.

"You can call me Mal," she said. "I'm a cliff runner." Caleb's eyebrows rose. The rules of cliff running were as simple as the rules of murder: runners chose a starting rooftop and a destination, and met at moonrise to race, following any path they chose so long as their feet never touched ground. "I train in these mountains at night. I've come every evening for a couple months, but usually no one's awake. Between the Wardens, the zombies, and the carts, I had to stop and watch."

"Months. Why haven't we caught you before now?"

Her eyes flicked down. A shark's tooth pendant hung from a cord around her neck. The tooth was etched with the Quechal glyph for "eye," capped by a double arc that signified denial or falsehood. Eye and arc both glowed with soft green light. A strong ward against detection. Expensive, but cliff running was a sport for idiots, madmen, and people who could afford good doctors.

"Why should I believe you?"

"If I'd poisoned this water, would I wait around for someone to discover me?"

"That's for the Wardens to decide."

"I haven't done anything wrong."

"Trespassing is wrong. And they'll want to talk to you even if you're innocent. If you've been here every night for the past few months, you might have seen something that could help us."

"I won't go with the Wardens." She pushed against his grip, to test him. He did not release her, and shifted to the side to bring his groin out of range. "You know how they feel about cliff runners. Ask me what you want, but keep them out of it."

"I'm sorry."

"I'm sorry, too," she said, and hit him in the face with her forehead.

Caleb stumbled, and caught himself against brick. Blind, he turned, following her footfalls. His vision cleared in time to see her leap out over the reservoir. He cried a warning she did not seem to hear.

Claws of black water burst up to pierce and catch and rend. She fell between them all, landed on a thick rowan log, and sprang from it to the next. Talons sliced through the air behind her. Mal fled toward the dam, trailing a wake of hungry mouths.

Caleb had no time to call after her. Four thorn-tipped columns rose from the water, arched above him, and descended. He dodged right, hit the ground hard, lurched to his feet and sprinted along the water's edge. The Tzimet could not see him, but they knew humans: where one was, others would be also.

Out of the corner of his eye he saw Mal run and leap, now an arc, now a vector.

He did not wonder at her, because he had no time. He ran with fear-born speed.

Iron stairs led down to catwalks crisscrossing the dam's face. Caleb reached the stairs seconds ahead of the Tzimet, clattered down the first flight, and crouched low on the landing. The dam plummeted three hundred feet beneath him to a broad valley of orange groves. Miles away, Dresediel Lex burned like an offering to angry, absent gods. He pushed all thoughts of height and falling from his mind. The iron landing, the dam, these were his world.

Wards at the dam's crest stopped floods during the winter rains. They should hold the Tzimet.

Emphasis on "should."

He swore. Mal (if that was her real name) was his best lead, and she'd be dead soon, if she wasn't already. One misstep, a log rolling wrong underfoot, and she would fall into a demon's mouth.

He waited for her screams.

A scream did come—but a scream of frustration, not pain, and issued from no human throat.

Mal dove off the dam into empty space.

Once, twice, she somersaulted, falling ten feet, fifteen. Caleb's stomach sank. She fell, or flew, without sound.

Twenty feet down, she snapped to a midair stop and dangled, nose inches from the dam's pebbled concrete face. A harness girded her hips, and a long thin cord ran from that harness to the crest of the dam.

Blue light flared above as Tzimet strained against the wards. Iron groaned and tore. A claw raked over the dam's edge. Lightning crackled at its tip.

Mal pushed off the concrete and began to sway like a pendulum, reaching for the nearest catwalk—one level down from Caleb. He ran to the stairs. Another talon pressed through the dam wards, scraping, seeking.

At the apex of Mal's next swing, he strained for her. She clasped a calloused hand around his wrist, pulled herself to him, wrapped a leg around the catwalk's railing, and unhooked her tether.

"Thanks," she said. Sparks showered upon them. Fire and Craft-light lanced in her eyes.

"You're insane."

"So I've heard," she said, and smiled, and let go of his arm.

He grabbed for her, too slowly. She fell—ten feet back and down, to roll and land on a lower catwalk, stand, run, and leap again. She accelerated, jumping from ledge to ledge until she reached the two-hundred-yard ladder to the valley floor.

Caleb climbed over the railing to follow her, but the chasm clenched his stomach. His legs quaked. He retreated from the edge.

Above, demons clawed at the emptiness that bound them.

The Wardens would catch her in the valley, he told himself, knowing they would not. She was already gone.

4

An hour and a half later, a driverless carriage deposited Caleb on the corner of Sansilva Boulevard and Bloodletter's Street, beside a jewelry shop and a closed coffee house. He hurt. Adrenaline's tide receded to reveal pits of exhaustion, pain, and shock. He'd told the Wardens he was fine, he'd make it home on his own, thanks for the concern, but these were lies. He was a good liar.

Broad streets stretched vacant on all sides. The carriage rattled off down the empty road. Night wind brushed his hair, tried and failed to wrap him in a comforting embrace.

He remembered lightning-lit eyes, and a tan body falling.

He'd given the carriage the wrong address, and stumbled a block and a half to his destination, a ten-story metal pyramid built by an Iskari architect mimicking Quechal designs. Over the door, a plaque bore the building's name in an art deco perversion of High Quechal script: the House of Seven Stars.

He exhaled. It was this, or home.

"You've come up in the world," said a voice behind him, deep as the foundations of the earth.

Caleb closed his eyes, gritted his teeth, and counted in his head to ten and back in Low Quechal, High Quechal, and common Kathic. By the time he finished (four, three, two, one), the flare of anger dulled to a familiar, smoldering rage. His nails bit into his palms. Perfect ending to a perfect day.

"Hi, Dad," he said.

"Either that, or you've abandoned that rat-trap house in the Vale to live off your friends until they kick you out."

"It's a long way home. I've been working."

"You shouldn't work so late."

"Yeah," Caleb said. "I shouldn't. I wouldn't have to, either, if you'd stop trying to kill people."

"I don't know what you're talking about."

Caleb turned around.

Temoc towered in the darkness beyond the streetlamps. He was a man built on a different scale from other men: torso like an inverted pyramid, arms as thick as his legs, a neck that sloped out to meld with his shoulders. His skin was a black cutout illuminated by glowing silver scars. The same shadows that clouded his body obscured his features, but Caleb would have known him anywhere: last of the Eagle Knights, High Priest of the Sun, Chosen of the Old Gods. Scourge of the Craftsmen and right-thinking folk of Dresediel Lex. Fugitive. Terrorist. Father.

"You're telling me you don't know anything about Bright Mirror."

"I know the place," Temoc said. "What has happened there?"

"Don't play dumb with me, Dad."

"I play at nothing."

"Tzimet got into the reservoir. We're lucky they killed a security guard before the water cycled into the mains this morning. Otherwise we'd have thousands out already, crawling in people's mouths, spearing them from the inside."

Temoc frowned. "Do you think I would do that? Consort with demons, endanger the city?"

"Maybe not. But your people might."

"We stand up for our religious rights. We resist oppression. We do not murder innocents."

"Bullshit."

Temoc lowered his head. "I do not like your tone."

"What about when you ambushed the King in Red five months back?"

"Your . . . boss . . . broke Qet Sea-Lord on His own altar. He impaled Gods on a tree of lightning, and laughed as They twitched in pain. He deserves seventeen-fold vengeance. I am the last priest of the old ways. If I do not avenge, who will?"

"You attacked him in broad daylight, with thunder and shadow and incendiary grenades. People died. He survived. You knew he would. No one who can kill gods would go down that easily. All you did was hurt the innocent."

"No one who works for Red King Consolidated is wholly innocent."

"I work for RKC, Dad."

An airbus passed overhead. Light from its windows cast the pavement in alternating strips of brilliance and shade. The light revealed Temoc's face in slivers: jutting cliff of jaw, heavy brow, dark, deep eyes, Caleb's own broad nose. A dusting of white at his temples, and the firm lines chiseled into cheeks and forehead, were his only signs of age. No man in Dresediel Lex could say how old Temoc was, not even his son—he had been a hale young knight when the gods fell, which made him eighty at least. He nurtured the surviving gods, and they kept him young, and strong. He was all they had left—and for twenty years, they had been his only companions.

Caleb looked away. His eyes burned, and his mouth felt dry. He massaged his forehead. "Look, I'm sorry. It's been a long night. I'm not at my, I mean, neither of us is at his best. You say you don't have anything to do with the Bright Mirror thing?"

"Yes."

"If you're lying, we'll find out."

"I do not lie."

Tell that to Mom, he could have said, but didn't. "Why are you here?"

Caleb's father might have been a statue for how little he moved—a bas relief in one of the temples where he had prayed before the God Wars, where he prayed and cut his arms and legs and dreamed that one day he would tear a man's heart from his chest and feed it to the Serpents. "I worry about you," he said. "You have been staying out late. Not sleeping enough. Gambling."

Caleb stared at Temoc. He wanted to laugh, or to cry, but neither impulse won out, so he did nothing.

"You should take better care of yourself."

"Thanks, Dad," he said.

"I worry about you."

Yes, Caleb thought. You worry about me in those last raw hours before nightfall, before you try to tear down everything we who work in this city build during the day. You worry about me, because there's no more priesthood, and what are kids to do these days when there are no more reliable careers involving knives, altars, and bleeding victims? "That makes two of us," he said, and: "Look, I have to go. I have work in four hours. Can we talk about this later?"

No response.

He turned back to his father, to apologize or to curse, but Temoc was gone. Wind blew down Bloodletter's Street from the ocean and sent a small flock of discarded newspapers flapping into the night: gray beasts old the moment they were made.

"I hate it when he does that," Caleb said to nobody in particular, and limped across the street to the House of Seven Stars.

Teo had an apartment on the seventh floor, a corner room she'd bought with her own soulstuff. The day she signed the contract she'd drunk a half-gallon of gin with Caleb in celebration. "Mine. Not my father's, not my mother's, not my family's. My soul, my house." When he observed that she was technically part of her family, she'd thrown a napkin at him and called him a bastard.

"You know what I mean. My cousins are all tied to the purse strings. Not one of them has even the poorest excuse for a career. They live in those damn beach houses up the coast, or circle the globe on Pop's ticket, three weeks doing coke off the naked back of an eighteen-year-old boy in one of those nameless ports south of the Shining Empire, a month ogling sentient ice sculptures in Koschei's kingdom. Lunch in Iskar, dinner in Camlaan, a romp in the Pleasure Quarters of Alt Coulumb, and none of it earned. This place, this is mine." She put a fierce edge on that word.

"And what's yours," Caleb replied, drink-slurred, "is mine."

"I'll hang the most absurd pictures on the wall, and keep a shelf of single malts, and polish the counters so they reflect themselves a hundred million times. Never will there be a single book out of place or a single picture crooked."

She was drunk, too.

"Can I visit?"

"You may call on me for the occasional bacchanal and revel."
She glared down her nose at him like an empress from her throne.
"In exchange, if I am out of town on business, you must feed
Compton," meaning her cat, a treacherous calico.

"Sure," he said, and took the key she offered.

He leaned against the lift wall and watched the floor numbers
tick up to seven. Phantoms filled his skull: Temoc, father, rebel,
murderer, saint. The goddess whispered in his ear. Blood. Stars
reflected in dark water. They all faded into vacant, expansive
night, the night after the death of the world.

The night of his mind shone black. Mal curved before him
like a blade.

The lift's bell called Caleb back from the ocean of her eyes to
a white-carpeted hallway hung with dull oil paintings. Vases of
silk flowers stood on teak tables heavy with ornamental bronze.
He shuffled down the hall, and searched his jacket pockets for
Teo's key.

His thoughts were chaos and blood and fire as he slid the key
into the lock. Chaos, blood, and fire; flood, poison, riot, ruin. Mal
didn't seem the poisoning type, but what was the poisoning type?
Why linger at Bright Mirror if she wasn't involved? She should
have snuck away the moment she saw Wardens. Perhaps she
trusted her shark's tooth to keep her safe. Flimsy defense, since
Caleb could see her. Then again, the Wardens lacked Caleb's scars.

He needed a bed, or a comfortable couch. He'd catch hell from
Teo in the morning for stumbling in unannounced, but her
apartment was closer to the office than his, and he had stashed
clothes in her closet—clubbing clothes, yes, but he could salvage
an outfit from them for work.

He pushed the key home, turned the knob.

Light stung his eyes, and for a confused moment he thought,
good, Teo's still awake. He stepped into the living room.

Thirty seconds and a shriek later he staggered, eyes closed,
out into the hallway. The door slammed behind him. His cheeks
burned. From within, he heard two women's voices raised in argument. He waited, eyes still shut, until Teo's words assumed

the weight of finality, and the other woman retreated toward the bedroom, cursing.

The latch turned and the door opened.

"You can look now," Teo said.

She'd wrapped herself in a plush white bathrobe, hair a tangled mass on her forehead. Compton wound sinuously between her bare feet, and licked sweat from her ankles. Over Teo's left shoulder, Caleb saw a blonde wearing white cotton briefs and nothing else stagger into the apartment's one bedroom and slam the door. "She seems nice," he said, lamely. Teo didn't respond. He tried again: "Sorry. I'll go."

She assessed him with a glance: clothes in disarray, hair standing up, tie crooked and loose. "What happened?"

"The Bright Mirror thing went south. There was a girl there, and she woke the Tzimet up. I have to be in the office early, but I need sleep. Hoped I could use your couch." I didn't realize you were using it, he thought but didn't say. "Sorry. Dumb idea." He didn't want to go home. "I hope I didn't screw up anything for you."

She sighed. "You didn't screw anything up. Quite the opposite, in fact."

"I'm sorry."

"Don't worry about it. Sam's emotional. An artist. She'll be fine in the morning. The couch is yours, if you want it."

"I shouldn't."

"I can't let you stumble back out into the night looking like a half-strangled puppy. I'll tell her you're one of my idiot cousins or something. Don't make me regret it."

"Too late," he said, but she had already turned her back on him.

Lights off, he lay on Teo's couch in the dark, staring up at the terrifying cubist landscapes that adorned her living room. A panorama of the Battle of Dresediel Lex hung over the couch, burning pyramids and torn sky, spears of flame and ice, bodies impaled on moonlight sickles, warring gods and Craftsmen rendered in vivid scrolls of paint. One corner of the painting showed

Temoc locked in single combat with the King in Red, before he fell.

Caleb's eyes drifted shut. Tzimet towered above him, reaching toward the cold stars. Compton dug claws into his leg. He rolled onto his side. Leather creaked.

He drifted to sleep, drowning in a black sea.

5

Dreams of knives and blood on stone woke Caleb to the hard harsh morning, to the light beyond Teo's windows and to the crick in his neck. He pulled himself off the white leather couch like a man pulling himself out of hell, and staggered for her bathroom, rubbing one hand over the scars that webbed his torso.

A long shower later, he dripped across Teo's living-room carpet to the hall closet. His nightclub suit would do, a sharp pressed gray with a white shirt, so long as he left the vermilion vest and spats and cravat behind. Yesterday's shoes were scuffed, but serviceable. He'd have them polished on the way, and find a toothbrush, too.

From Teo's spare pantry he scrounged a bowl of polenta, and two eggs, which he scrambled. On the table as he sat down to eat, he found a note written in her sharp hand.

> *I'd say help yourself to breakfast, but I know you already have.*
> *See you at work. The door will lock behind you.*
> *Sam's pissed, by the way. No surprise. I'll work my way back into her good graces, but you owe me coffee, at least.*

The signature was an uppercase *T* in pen strokes so deep they dimpled the thick parchment.

The wall clock read 9:47 A.M. Caleb ate a hurried breakfast under the baleful stares of bloodthirsty paintings, washed his plate and the frying pan, and left in a rush, realizing only after Teo's door clicked shut behind him that he had left his hat on her coffee table.

Dresediel Lex crushed him in a cacophonous embrace. Carts and carriages and wagons clogged the street outside Teo's building. Drivers shouted at pedestrians, horses, and other drivers as if they could break gridlock by inventive language and the threat of violence. Couatl, buzzing optera, airbuses and simple balloons tangled in the flat blue sky.

Heat ruled the city, dry dominant heat like a god's gaze or the breath of a forge. All bowed before the heat; buildings prostrated themselves, and people slouched nearly naked beneath the beating sun. By this hour Craftsmen, bankers, brokers, and all others who dressed for work were safely ensconced in air-conditioned offices. Actors and students and night-shift workers walked the streets in shorts, light shirts, miniskirts, tunics, sleeveless ponchos. Caleb caught himself following the long bare legs of three young women down the sidewalk, and closed his eyes. A sharp smile surfaced from the confusion of his memory: the woman, Mal.

He bought a newspaper from a corner stand for two thaums—cheap enough, but his head ached from spending even a little soulstuff. Hangover, had to be. He'd won a good chunk of soul the night before, shouldn't need to visit the bank for a week or so. The newspaper held no news about Bright Mirror Reservoir, a good sign. The King in Red did not control the press directly, but news of a crisis like Bright Mirror had to be managed.

Caleb walked two blocks to the airbus station and caught the next dirigible downtown. The bus moved west and north, threading around and beneath skyspires toward the 700 block of Sansilva, where eighty-story pyramids rose to worship the sun.

No real worship had taken place there since Liberation, of course. Still, the pyramids impressed.

The air lost its haze, and the sky retreated from the earth. Craftsmen and Craftswomen drew power from starlight and moonlight, though they could also drink from the sun, or from candles, fires, living beings. Smoke and exhaust from the city's wagons, factories, and cooking stoves would not disturb simple, day-to-day Craft, but the Concerns of the 700 block brooked no interference with their dark and delicate work. They burned their sky clean.

In the depths of winter, when rain washed sweat from the city's brow and flash-flood rivers coursed down alleys, the sun still beat down on the 700 block. At night, sorcerous clouds covered the poorer districts, Skittersill and Stonewood, Monicola and Central and Fisherman's Vale, reflecting light back to earth so that, in dark Sansilva, even the faintest stars would hang exposed to hungry Craftsmen.

Caleb got off the bus a half-block from RKC's headquarters, the obsidian pyramid at 667 Sansilva. True Quechal protesters stood outside, chanting and waving clapboard signs: NO DEMONS IN OUR WATER. THE GODS DEFEND. NO WATER WITHOUT BLOOD. Half wore modern clothes, slacks and shirts and skirts, and half garments even Caleb's father would have thought clownishly traditional: white dresses hemmed in silver cord for the women, and cotton kilts for the men, their bare and unscarred torsos covered with Quechal glyphs in red paint. Four black-uniformed Wardens watched the crowd, arms crossed. Sunlight glinted off their badges, and off the silver planes of their faces.

As Caleb approached, a soapbox preacher pointed to him with one gnarled finger and cried, "Flee this place! Traitors walk here, traitors to blood, traitors to Gods and their own kind!"

Caleb ignored the man and edged around the crowd. No sense wondering how the True Quechal had learned about Bright Mirror. Their noses were better than vultures' for smelling rotten meat.

"If you will not flee," the old man called, "then join us. It is not too late. Stand against the blood-betrayers, the worse-than-dead! Take up the cause!"

"Get lost," Caleb shouted in High Quechal as he walked past.

The old man's face twisted in confusion. He probably didn't know High Quechal, beyond a handful of half-remembered words from some underground religious service. Few spoke the priests' tongue these days. Caleb only knew it because his father had taught him.

He walked through the protest. Behind, the chants and slogans swelled again to crescendo.

Caleb stepped off the lift at the pyramid's twenty-third floor, into the silence of men and women working.

He wound through cubicles toward the Director's corner suite. Tollan would want to see him before he drowned in the sea of paperwork no doubt already covering his desk. Much as it pained Caleb's boss to admit, some truths could not be conveyed in the blanks of official forms.

He saw her office door, and slowed.

Tollan's door was a pane of frosted glass—a source of comfort to the whole department, because from her general position in the office they could tell her mood. If she was at her desk, the world was at peace; if pacing, at war; if tending her peace lily, best hide and wait for the axe to fall.

Caleb could not see Tollan, or her desk, or her peace lily. A black blade had cut her office from the universe. Terrible things moved in that blackness, and few of them were human.

The door crept open.

Caleb ducked into the nearest cubicle, startling its blocky, middle-aged occupant from his work.

"Sorry, Mick."

"Caleb? Where have you been? The boss is looking for you."

"I'll talk to Tollan when she's done with—"

"Not the boss," Mikatec whispered. "The *boss*."

Caleb knelt behind the cubicle wall. Mick had papered his workspace with pictures of his younger, sleeker self, playing ullamal, holding athletic trophies, screaming triumph. Caleb crouched beside his coworker's memories, and listened.

Quills scratched paper. Chair wheels squeaked. Fingers drummed on a desk. An actuary the next row over coughed.

From the darkness beyond Tollan's door came a voice like the end of the world: "I hope our trust in you is not misplaced."

Color faded from the pictures of Mick's glory. Ghostlights overhead flickered and died. Someone—a new hire, had to be—cursed, and someone else shushed her. The noise of pens and chairs and drumming fingers stopped. The risk management department grew still.

Tollan's door swung shut.

Three distinct, sharp taps trespassed on the hush, then three more, then the thud of a bronze-shod staff on stone. The noises repeated. A heavy robe swept over the stone floor.

Caleb held his breath.

The King in Red moved among the cubicles, wreathed in power. The taps were his triple footsteps: the bones of his heel, the ball of his foot, the twiglike toes striking in sequence. "As you were," he said. No one stirred. Sixty years ago, the King in Red had shattered the sky over Dresediel Lex, and impaled gods on thorns of starlight. The last of his flesh had melted away decades past, leaving smooth bone and a constant grin.

He was a good boss. But who could forget what he had been, and what remained?

The footsteps receded, and light seeped back into the world. An elevator bell rang. When the doors rolled shut, Caleb exhaled, and heard others do the same. A thin layer of sweat slicked his brow.

He patted Mick on the shoulder, loosened his collar, and walked to Tollan's office.

Tollan paced behind her desk, cradling a glass of mescal. She took a sip, and shook herself. Her long black hair was up in a tightly coiled braid, which left her face severe and thin.

"Where have you been?" she asked when he closed the door.

"Sleeping."

"Sleeping." She laughed without humor, and looked down as if surprised to find herself holding a drink. "Once in a while I convince myself I'm used to him, I can handle him. Then I see him angry." She squeezed the glass as if to crush it, reconsidered, and set it on her desk.

There was no need for her to say whom she meant.

Caleb waited. At last, he said: "I was at Bright Mirror until half-past four. If I arrived earlier, I would have been too tired to help you or anybody."

Tollan kept pacing. He had expected her to shout at him. Her silence was worse.

"Bright Mirror is under control," he continued. "Nobody was hurt. The Tzimet are contained. They'll die slowly, but they will die. We can keep the water flowing. He shouldn't blame this on you."

"That's your professional opinion?" Her shoes ground against the floor when she turned.

"Isn't it yours?"

"We took every precaution," she said in a tone contemptuous of precautions.

"We use high-energy Craft in those waters. Something was bound to slip through sooner or later."

"You don't believe that any more than I do. Or any more than he does." She jabbed a thumb toward the ceiling, and the King in Red's penthouse office sixty floors up. "Someone screwed us."

"It's possible."

"Possible." She spat the word. "The worst part is, the boss isn't angry for what we've done, or didn't do. He's angry because this puts the Heartstone deal in jeopardy."

Heartstone was a dowsing company, water development, energy. "What does that have to do with Bright Mirror? We're buying Heartstone straight out."

"Only if Alaxic, their mad old chief exec, decides to sell. Bright Mirror has him worried. The King in Red says, that Alaxic says, that he won't go through with the deal unless someone convinces him this wasn't our fault. Face-to-face."

Caleb shrugged. "So someone should do that."

"The boss wants you."

"Me? I'm no good at that sort of thing. Send Teo. She's Miss Contract Management. They gave her a parking space and everything."

"The boss doesn't want to send you because you're a good negotiator. He wants to send you because of who your father is."

Caleb didn't say anything. Many replies leapt to mind, none of them polite.

"Old man Alaxic used to be a priest. He studied the Craft after the God Wars, started his own Concern, but to him, the

King in Red is still the guy who killed his gods." Tollan's eyes were fierce, and narrow as her mouth. "Will you do this? Go to Heartstone, and explain what happened?"

"I will," Caleb said. "But I'd rather the King in Red use me because he thinks I'm good at my job than because of who my father was. Is."

"Tell him that yourself, the next time you see him. And if you're still alive after, tell me how it goes." She flipped through her day planner. "I'll work with Heartstone to set up an appointment. What will you say to Alaxic?"

"That we've contained the problem. Either there was a freak malfunction, or the reservoir was poisoned. We'll monitor the system, step up security, and keep him in the loop about whatever we find."

Tollan frowned. "It's not enough."

"It's the truth."

"I wish we had something more substantial. The Wardens said you saw an intruder, who ran. Any details you can add?"

Black eyes, and a smile like a bared knife. Long, taut muscles, dusky skin. Laughing. Taunting. "I have some leads to follow up, that's all."

"Nothing concrete? Nothing we can give Alaxic, or the King in Red?"

He saw Mal spinning through space, as demons' claws clutched after her.

"No."

6

"No?" Teo's shout echoed through Muerte Coffee. The listless girl behind the register snapped shut the novel she'd been browsing, and scanned the tables in panic.

"Quiet," Caleb hissed. The coffee shop was almost empty, but small. Anyone might be listening—the man in the pinstriped suit pretending not to read a tabloid's swimsuit issue, the woman walking a pen through her fingers, the girl at the register. Only the garish yellow skeletons that adorned the walls seemed to be watching him, but you never knew.

"Are you out of your mind?"

"The Wardens already know there was a runner. It's not as if I'm hiding that."

"But you didn't tell them the runner was a woman. Or that you spoke with her. Or that you know her name."

"Part of her name. I don't even know which part. She could have been lying."

"That's not your call."

He shrugged. "I kept the information to myself because I thought Tollan should be the first to know—the crime hurt RKC more than the city."

"But you didn't tell Tollan, either."

"No."

"Concealing something like this from her, from the Wardens, from the King in Red—one of them will kill you. Or they won't. They'll make you beg for death, and hold it back."

"I know I'm playing a dangerous game."

"You can't imagine how dangerous."

"What do you think will happen to this woman if I tell them

about her? Some Wardens will hunt her down, lock her in a cell, and tear her mind to shreds."

"Isn't that the point? She's a poisoner."

"I don't think so."

"That's a huge comfort, you having so much experience with this sort of thing."

"She moved like a cliff runner. She was telling the truth about that."

Teo dumped two spoons of sugar in her coffee and stirred. "So she's a suicidal thrill-seeker who can evade our security. Sounds like an upstanding citizen."

"Upstanding, maybe not. But I don't think she's a terrorist."

Teo rolled her eyes. "You think she's cute."

"I think she stumbled into the middle of something way too big for her. I empathize."

"And you think she's cute."

The bell over Muerte's door rang six times to herald the arrival of a small pack of bankers, broad-shouldered men whose over-muscled arms strained against their jacket sleeves. Their hair spiked up from their skulls, and all their vowels converged to a dull schwa. As the bankers ordered triple espressos, Caleb changed the subject: "Tell me about Sam."

Teo frowned, but knew better than to talk sensitive business in a crowded room. "It's a new thing." She stirred her coffee again, though the sugar was already dissolved. "She's impulsive, smart, impractical. My type."

"Actor?"

"Painter."

"That's a change."

"Not all blondes are actors," Teo said.

"Most of them are, around here."

"The theaters think blondes are hot. I don't make the public taste, even if I happen to agree with it."

"Always with the foreign devils. Whatever happened to finding a nice Quechal girl and settling down?"

"You sound like my grandmother: 'Teotihual, if you must be an altar maid, at least stay within the pale of your own kind!' "

Caleb stifled a laugh. "She still says 'altar maid' for women who like other women?"

"What do you expect from the older generation? Sensitivity training?"

"Pretty offensive, though."

"Toothless. No one comes hunting for sacrifices these days."

"Not too clear what 'pale' means, either, sounds like."

"Give her a break. Low Quechal's her first language; she only speaks Kathic with me and my brothers because our Quechal's so bad."

The bell over the door rang again, and a wave of hot air ushered the bankers out. Through the window, Caleb watched them saunter into the pyramid next door. The air above the street shivered. He thought about thirst.

"You won't tell Tollan about this girl," Teo said after the door swung shut.

"Mal."

"About Mal."

"Correct."

"What will you do, then?"

"I told you about her."

"I mean what will you do next."

He sipped his coffee. Teo's eyes narrowed.

"You told me because you're about to do something stupid, but you don't know how stupid. You trust me to stop you from going too far."

The coffee tasted like black, dense earth, and burned his throat on the way down.

"I'm not your conscience, Caleb."

"I'm not asking you to be. I just want to talk things through. And I want someone to know what I'm up to, in case it all goes wrong."

"You have a plan."

"I do."

"Tell me."

"I want to find her. That's the only way to know I'm right. Find her and learn who she is, what she saw."

"No."

"It's not that bad an idea."

"It's not even possible, that's how bad an idea it is. You've seen her once, and you might know part of her first name. Do you have any idea how many people live in the greater DL metro area?"

"Seventeen million, give or take a few hundred thou."

"And how many of them have names that contain the syllable 'Mal'?"

"Mal's probably short for Malina."

"Don't think I've heard that one before."

"It's a kind of cactus flower. Very traditional name. Your grandmother would love her."

"So you have a name, possibly fake. What else?"

"She's a cliff runner. She's good, and rich enough to afford some High Quechal glyphwork. That narrows the range. Other runners should be able to lead me to her."

"That's assuming she told you the truth, about her name or about being a runner." She frowned. "You're interested in this girl."

"Woman."

"You're interested in this woman."

He might have lied, if there had been any chance of fooling Teo. "I'm interested. I'm interested, and I don't want to sic the Wardens on her. I've seen what they do to people when they want answers. She was afraid last night."

"Why would she be frightened if she wasn't guilty?"

"I won't dignify that with a response." He stared out the window into the heat. "I don't want someone else to burn for something my father or his cronies did. And she will burn, if the Wardens get their hands on her. They'll crack her skull, pull the memories out, sew her back together again. Meanwhile, my father escapes unscathed, like always."

"He told you he didn't have anything to do with this one. Why would he lie?"

"Why tell the truth?"

"That's not an answer."

"No," he admitted. "You remember university?"

"What do you think I've forgotten?"

"You remember when you told me you'd decided to break up with Ivan, that you'd met a girl. That you needed to do this, that it was a part of you. I asked you why you'd come to me. You said you had to know you were telling the truth to yourself, and the only way to know that was to tell it to someone you trusted to know when you were lying."

She tilted her head to one side. "Do you think this is the same thing?"

"As coming out?" He put up his hands between them. "No. Of course not. Shit. Sorry."

"Apology noted."

"But this could kill me. I'm not being figurative. The Wardens will want my head for lying to them. I'm maybe obstructing justice, aiding and abetting who knows what. It's not like I'm above suspicion, either. Tollan has been good to me, but I doubt she ever forgets who my father is. So I want to know—am I telling the truth? Is this something I need to do? Or am I about to commit suicide because I want to get in this woman's pants?"

"I said I wouldn't be your conscience."

Caleb drained the last of his coffee, and stood. The shop felt too small. Skeletons mocked him from the walls, waving their arms in an obscene dance. Fire built inside him, fed by words he didn't remember how to speak. Teo bit her lower lip, teeth showing white against her dark skin. Weighing scales shifted in her eyes.

"Do it," she said at last, as if passing sentence. "Find her. But if you don't manage it in two weeks, I'll go to Tollan myself. She will kill you for keeping this from her, and I'll never work in this city again because I waited to tell her. I'll have to throw myself on the tender mercies of my family, and be cursed to wear nice dresses and glad-hand Craftswomen at parties, or else join my cousins in the hedonism tango. I'll hire a Craftsman to raise you from the dead once Tollan's done with you, just so I can kill you again. I'll do that whenever I get bored. And life with my family is so. Very. Boring." She emphasized each word with a tap of her forefinger on the table.

"You're serious."

"I am serious."

"Why let me look for her at all? Why not go to Tollan right now, or force me to?"

"Because four years ago you would have gone all in with two queens in hand and a third showing, rather than let yourself be bluffed out of the pot. Because you used to have fire, and you've got scared. You're becoming a risk manager in truth as well as title, and it's hard to watch. This is a stupid idea, but I won't stand in your way. In fact, I'll lay you a soul and a half that you won't be able to find her and learn what she knows before my two week deadline's up."

"Three thousand thaums." Two months' payment on his house. Buy-in for one hell of a high-stakes game. "Odds?"

"I'll give you two-to-one against. I don't want to bankrupt you."

"You sure you can cover it? I don't want to send you running back to Mama when I come to collect. I know how uncomfortable your family makes you."

"You should talk."

"You're on."

They shook. The yellow skeletons grinned.

He grinned back at them.

7

The next day's dawn clawed at Caleb's eyes. He tugged his hat brim low, and climbed the gravel path that wound up the sandy hill toward Heartstone's headquarters. The driverless carriage that had brought him rolled away into heat and haze.

Caleb felt about sunrise the way he felt about RKC's accounting department: necessary, and best kept at a distance. But Alaxic, Heartstone's chief executive, was a busy man, and when he set the meeting early, Caleb hadn't argued—he needed this talk to end well. If Alaxic took pressure off the King in Red, the King should relax his grip on Tollan and the Wardens, leaving Caleb free to search for Mal. If not, Caleb's chances for finding her dwindled to nothing. Especially if the Wardens decided to peek inside his head for any details about the runner he might have missed.

Dry dwarf pines rustled beside the path. Caleb turned to look, and a slender blade settled against the swell of his throat. He froze. Sharp points and edges pressed into his back. A needle breathed over his right eyelid. He heard the silence of something large standing still, and near.

"State your name and business," said a voice like chalk on slate.

"Caleb Altemoc." He swallowed. His throat pressed against the security demon's claw. "I'm from RKC, here to see Alaxic." Slowly, he reached into his pocket, and slid his badge out of his wallet. "I have an appointment."

The claw did not slide across Caleb's throat, nor did the spines of the demon's chest impale him. This was probably a good sign.

Caleb waited.

The Tzimet in Bright Mirror Reservoir were to proper demons what a monkey was to a man: similar in shape, sometimes even stronger, but pale imitations with regard to intellect and cruelty.

Minutes passed. He waited on the hillside, millimeters from death.

Footsteps. He tried to turn his head, but the thorns at his cheek prevented him.

A woman entered his field of vision: skin a shade darker than Teo's, face round, red-tinged hair pulled back in a bun. She wore a khaki suit with a knee-length skirt, and carried a clipboard. She glanced from his face to the clipboard, and held out her hand. "You must be Caleb. I'm Allesandre Olim. Mister Alaxic is eager to meet you."

Claws, blades, and thorns released him. One moment, a sneeze would have driven ten spikes through Caleb's skull; the next, he stood free on the path. Caleb accepted Allesandre's hand and shook it. Her grip was firm, and she did not smile.

"Apologies for the security. Our work here is delicate, and dangerous. This way, please."

"You have effective guards," Caleb said, and would have turned to look behind him. Allesandre shook her head, and he stopped. "The demon's still there, isn't it?"

"Will you follow me?" she said, and left the path.

Caleb followed. The hillside where they walked looked rocky and uneven, tangled with sagebrush and weeds, but he felt a smooth stone walkway under his feet.

Allesandre led him to a circle of standing stones. With a wave of her clipboard she slid a five-hundred-pound altar aside, revealing a rough-hewn tunnel into the earth, and rock steps descending.

They climbed down the steps for a long time.

At first the tunnel felt warm as desert noon, then warm as a baker's oven. Dim red light illuminated wall carvings of the Hero Sisters, eagle-headed gods, and of course serpents: the ancient Quechal who dug this passage had etched a double bar of stylized scales under each graven figure.

"This," Caleb said, "is a strange place to work." The Quechal carvings reminded him of childhood, of nights listening to his father chant holy tales of blood and murder. He remembered some of these designs from the walls of his father's temple in the Skittersill, before it burned. "You don't see carvings like these anymore."

"The bas reliefs are authentic," Allesandre said. "Five hundred years old, give or take a century."

Caleb lifted his hand from the wall. "Trying to save on real estate?"

"Hardly," she replied. "Sites like this are vital to our work."

When he first heard the voices, he took them for wind through fissures in the rock. Deeper, deeper he followed Allesandre, and the whisper rush resolved to words in an obscure form of High Quechal, a jumble of nouns, adjectives, and verbs from which he caught snatches of meaning: Serpent. Flame. Lost. Burn. Make. Mold. Crush.

Stinging sweat ran down his cheeks, the line of his jaw. His shadow and Allesandre's, melded, stretched long and thin behind them, a road into the darkness from which they had come.

The passage opened onto a broad, black stone ledge on the lip of a vast cavern. Light from the depths cast the world crimson. Stalactites hung jagged overhead, twined round by metal pipes. Chant braided with the rhythm of machines.

Men and women crowded the ledge. They wore loose white linen, and tool belts girded their waists. They worked at stone altars and plinths, adjusting bee-carved dials, pulling levers shaped like snake's heads. Burning motes danced in the air before their faces. The technicians chanted as they worked, heads bobbing to keep time.

The words and carvings were High Quechal, but this place lacked the trappings of ceremony: no priest, no priestess with bone flute, no Mat-Keeper with blade upraised. Modern, angular Craftsman's glyphs glowed from every surface.

An ancient man in a black suit stood by the railing at the platform's edge. Hands behind his back, he stared down into the cavern. Scraps of thin white hair clung to his scalp. His body stooped, as if it could no longer bear his strength.

The white-robed crowd parted for Allesandre. Caleb followed

in her wake. She stopped behind the old man, and said: "Sir, I've brought Caleb Altemoc, from RKC. Caleb, this is Mister Alaxic."

Caleb swallowed, for reasons that had nothing to do with the heat.

"Altemoc," said the old man, chewing the syllables of the name. His voice was high and spare. "Not Temoc's boy by any chance?" There was no question which Temoc he meant.

"Yes, sir. My father and I aren't close."

"Hard to be close with a wanted felon."

"I don't approve of his life choices, and he doesn't approve of mine. We have an equitable arrangement."

Alaxic did not turn. "Strange that the most stalwart of the True Quechal would give his son a foreign name."

"When I was born, he thought there was a chance for peace. He and my mother chose my name as a sign of that peace."

"You were born before the Skittersill Rising."

"Yes," Caleb said.

"Dirty business." Though Alaxic's hands remained clasped behind his back, his fingers worked and twitched as if playing an invisible instrument. "Men standing to defend their rights. Killed by Wardens who should have protected them."

"That's one way to put it."

"And the other?"

"I'd be less generous."

"Humor me. Speak freely."

"I'd say the rioters were fanatics who wanted to sacrifice their neighbors to bloody-minded gods."

"You don't share your father's faith."

"I don't respect murderers, as a rule. However they try to justify themselves."

"Ah." Alaxic turned from the ledge. He was not wrinkled, but worn, skin stretched thin and drum-tight. One eye stared white and sightless from his face, and a puckered, twisting scar bent the right side of his mouth into a smile. His remaining eye glittered, cold, black, and sharp. "A modernist."

"I suppose." Stop this conversation, he told himself. Don't let yourself get dragged in. "I don't imagine you asked me here to talk politics."

"Politics and security," Alaxic said, "are two sides of the same parchment." He raised his hands, and tried to spread them. His fingers crooked in like claws, and quivered. "Dark writing on one side may be read from the other. Once, we sacrificed men and women on Quechaltan to beg rain from the gods. We do the same today, only we spread the one death out over millions. We no longer empathize with the victim, lie with him on the slab. We forget, and believe forgetfulness is humane. We fool ourselves. Your organization is founded on that foolishness."

Don't chase the bait. "Sir. The Bright Mirror infestation is an isolated incident. We're studying what went wrong, so we can guard against it."

Alaxic shook his head. "You don't understand why you've been called here. You think your purpose is to soothe me to sleep. To convince me to sell my life's work to your master."

The engines of Caleb's caution thrilled to motion. He felt as if a careful player had just glanced at his cards, then raised. "Why am I here?"

"Yesterday, Red King Consolidated sent me more documents about Bright Mirror Reservoir than I could read in a thousand years. But papers can lie. I want someone to stand with me face-to-face, and tell me I can trust your master."

The air pressed close, heavy with chant and heat. "What do you mean?"

Alaxic beckoned him to the railing. "Look down, son of Temoc."

Caleb almost refused on principle, but principle had no place on company time. He stepped to the platform's edge, leaned out, and looked down.

Liquid fire filled the pit, rolling, burning, boiling, red and yellow, orange and white and blue. A tremor traveled from one side of the fire to the other, like a twitch on a horse's flank.

Following that tremor, Caleb saw the eye.

What he had mistaken for an island in the molten rock was in fact an enormous eye ringed by scales of lava—an eye bubble-lidded like a snake's, if a snake were large enough to swallow worlds.

A serpent lay coiled beneath them, a serpent larger than the cave, larger than the pyramids of Sansilva. Its immensity shattered all concepts of size. Uncoiled and rearing to strike, this creature would cast a long shadow over Dresediel Lex.

Sweat chilled on the back of Caleb's neck.

That serpent had a sister. Caleb knew their names.

"That's Achal," Alaxic said. "Aquel's in the depths now. They turn and move in their slumber, as we do. They're bigger than we are, though."

"Guard and shield us from the fire," Caleb whispered in High Quechal. The words came unbidden to his lips.

"Well." Alaxic smiled. "I see you have some religious sentiment after all."

"That." He tried again to speak. "Do you have any idea what that is?"

"We know exactly what she is. Better than anyone in history." Alaxic stared down into the pit. "At the beginning of time, the earth trembled and split, and many men and gods died. The twin daughters of the Sun descended into the depths, seeking the cause of the tremors, and found two massive serpents, larger than mountains, older than the earth. Once, they had slithered between the stars.

"Demons danced around the serpents, inciting them to tremble, to riot. The sun's first daughter tore her heart from her chest, and threw it into the first serpent's mouth; the serpent gained her wisdom, and her name—Aquel. The demons tried to prevent the sun's second daughter from doing the same, but she threw her heart over them into the second serpent's mouth, and the serpent gained her wisdom, and her name—Achal. Aquel and Achal took pity on gods and men, and chased the demons from their fiery domain into the cold of space. They slept, then, but sleeping they forget. When the sun dies, the demons return, and the Serpents wake, and we give hearts and souls to remind them we are their children."

"Not anymore, we don't."

"As you say."

"And I wasn't talking about myths."

"Neither was I," Alaxic said.

"We fed those things on our flesh for three thousand years. They're not gods. They're animals, if that. Congealed power. We used them as weapons once, and broke this continent in half. Destroyed a dozen cities. Millions died."

"Millions died because, in the darkness of our ignorance, we dared try to control the Serpents. We have learned, in the centuries since the Cataclysm. For thousands of years the Serpents fed on us. Now it's our turn to feed on them."

Technicians chanting. Quechal carvings marked with Craft. Steam pipes in the heat. "You're drawing their power."

"The hungrier the Sisters grow, the hotter they burn. We use their soulstuff to power our Craft, and they burn more fiercely. We harness that heat to drive thaumaturgical engines. At this moment, we can only pull a few hundred thousand thaums a day before they start to toss in their sleep. Their dreams are the seeds of earthquakes."

"The King in Red isn't buying you because of your waterworks," Caleb said. "He wants the Serpents."

"RKC needs our water, but the lakes and rivers we have harnessed will not sustain Dresediel Lex for long. Your master believes he can use the Serpents' heat to purify the ocean, like your system at Bay Station. Pull saltwater into these caverns, let it evaporate, collect and cool the steam. The prospect of nearly unlimited power also intrigues him, of course."

"Gods."

"No." Alaxic smiled, slightly. "But close. And your master wants them. I do not care for him. When he conquered our city, I strove against him in the air, and fought him on the earth. I learned his dark arts after the War, hoping to cast him down with his own power. But I am tired now, and I refuse to let the Craft carry me on to skeletal immortality. Do you understand?"

Caleb did not understand, but he could not think of anything to say.

"Craftsmen hedge risks, gird themselves against worst-case scenarios. But the worst case here far outstrips any hedge you can secure. If your master mismanages Aquel and Achal, there will be no second chance, no insurance, no recovery. If the Sisters wake, the city will burn. If the King in Red wants my Concern, he must guarantee that RKC will preserve the Sisters' slumber before all other priorities, even his own life. I want a contract written and signed in blood, or the deal is off."

"We can't give you a blanket guarantee."

"You can. And you will. Your master needs my Concern more than I need to sell."

Caleb remembered Tollan pacing her office, and the black anger of the King in Red. He looked over the platform's edge, and envisioned the Serpents towering above Dresediel Lex with diamond fangs bared.

"I don't have the authority to agree to those terms."

"Pass them along. Or do not, and let the deal fall through. I leave this in your hands: do you trust your master to put our people's safety before his own?"

The sleeping serpent twitched. A groan of tormented rock rose from world's root.

"I do," Caleb said after the echoes died.

Alaxic nodded, once. Caleb could not tell if he was satisfied. "Allesandre will show you out."

8

When Caleb delivered the message to Tollan, she cursed for three straight minutes. Contract revisions so late in a deal were expensive, and precarious. For two days, a trio of senior Craftsmen corralled Caleb in his office, asking question after repetitive question about his conversation with Alaxic. They forced him to complete forms in triplicate, in cuneiform, in blood.

He emerged from those days in a wandering fog. He drank to soothe himself to sleep, but talons of black ice haunted his dreams. Visions slunk out of darkness into day. Once, he looked up from his paperwork and thought he saw Mal walking past his office door.

On the wager's third day, Caleb left the office before eight for the first time since Bright Mirror. Rather than hopping an airbus home over the mountains, he ate a quick dinner at an expensive Sansilva bistro and headed downtown to the glowing neon strips of the Skittersill.

As he traveled east from the pyramids, streets narrowed and buildings hunched low to the earth. Lamplight flickered in the mouths of painted demons in shop windows. A pair of eyes sculpted from glowing transparent tubes glared down from an optician's billboard. Sour smoke wafted from an open club door. A blind man played Quechal airs badly on a three-string fiddle. Far above, Wardens circled. Their mounts' wingbeats thudded in Caleb's breast.

Drunks crowded the sidewalk. An airbus landed on a nearby platform and unleashed a deluge of students: sharp young men with slick hair, eager women in halter tops and short leather skirts, their smiles all printed by machine.

Dresediel Lex had been one of the first cities liberated in the

God Wars, but not all the city's rulers perished with their gods. Priests poured out their blood on battlefields, true, but some noble Quechal families laid down arms. They were neither rewarded nor punished for their surrender. They sunk into the earth—and into the Skittersill, where they thrived, feeding off the city's sin.

Teo's family came from that stock. These days they owned manufacturing and shipping Concerns, but her grandfather had been a slumlord, and worse. And when his children went straight, others took their place.

Caleb came here to play cards, when he wanted easy money and didn't mind extra risk. A careless winner in the Skittersill was as likely to leave his table dead as wealthy.

Tonight, he had a purpose. Mal claimed to be a cliff runner, and her skills bore out her boast. Running was a select hobby. Even in a city the size of Dresediel Lex, most runners would know one another. So he had to find a runner.

Caleb knew little about the cliff-running community, but runners were addicted to risk. That addiction should carry into other arenas.

His usual tables were too rich for players who jumped off rooftops in their spare time. Cliff runners needed every thaum they could scrounge to buy charms of speed, strength, and balance from booze-tinged back alley Craftsmen—and to buy doctors when those charms failed. A cliff runner who gambled would look for cheap, vigorous action.

He tried six bars before he found the right game: four angry children in spiked leathers, and a woman with a long white scar running from the crown of her skull down past her ear. The skin around the scar looked slick from recent regrowth. She played with contempt for her companions; she did not smile, or laugh, or even speak. She wanted to be anywhere but here.

She wasn't the only one. The goddess above their table listed from player to player, a staggering, tired jade.

Caleb bought in. The players suspected him at first—he handled the cards well—but he drank more than they did, and played with careful abandon. His soulstuff flowed freely, and the others relaxed. Over an hour he dared his companions into riskier play, and the goddess quickened in the table's center. She touched each player with a chill like cold water on skin; she demanded worship, and they knelt.

Flames quickened in the scarred woman's eyes.

Caleb lost several small hands, doubled up through a member of the leather brigade, and rose at game's end slightly richer than when he sat down. When he thanked them all and made his way to the bar, the scarred woman joined him. She bought his drink, and waved off his protests. "I'm Shannon," she said.

Caleb introduced himself. "You play well for a newcomer." He raised his whiskey to the light, and watched the room through its amber lens.

"What's to say I'm new?" She knocked back her shot, and ordered another.

"You're comfortable with risk in general but you're not used to poker. You took a ten and a seven to the flop, but you scared off three hands better than yours."

"A woman has to get her thrills somehow," she replied with a crooked smile.

"Where did you get yours before you started to play cards?"

"Cliff running." She leaned back against the bar. "I was a good runner. Skill matters to a point and after that it's how much you're willing to bleed. Three months back, I bled too much." She swung her hand through a plummeting arc, and turned her head to show him the scar.

"Looks bad."

"It was bad," she said. "I was out for almost a month, and when I woke my balance was twisted. I train when I can. During the week I come here, and hope the game will keep me from growing scared."

"Doesn't it bore you, after what you've done?"

"Sometimes. Sometimes, it surprises me." She shivered as she downed her second shot. "What do you want with a washed-up runner?"

"Pardon?"

"This isn't my game, but it is yours. I can tell. Even this dive has two tables that play for higher stakes. When I ran, I never went to a course that wouldn't challenge me. You joined our table for a reason, and I don't think it had anything to do with those kids."

"You're not a humble person."

"Humility is a vice of which I have never been accused."

"I'm looking for a runner," he admitted, "named Mal. Malina, maybe. Quechal woman, short hair, about my height. I hoped you could help me."

Shannon sucked air through her teeth. "Crazy Mal."

"That sounds like her."

"She's good. You won't know what to do with her when you find her."

"I'll worry about that when I do."

She laughed, a blunt sound heavy with alcohol. "I can't help you much. Mal keeps apart from the rest of us, and I've been away too long to know where she runs now. The courses change." She finished the drink. "Walk me home," she said, and limped through the crowd toward the door.

He escorted her down long straight streets below signs ghostlit in colors no god ever made. They turned off the Corsair Parkway onto a lane of small clapboard houses nestled against the foot of the Drakspine. Craftsmen's palaces gleamed on the mountain peaks, and clouds and skyspires shone with the city's light. Shannon's house was dark. As they reached the stoop he heard within the sound of laughter and muffled conversation.

"Roommates," she said. She laid a hand on his arm. Her eyes reflected the city like still pools. "Do you want to come inside?"

"Yes." He didn't move.

She sank onto the stoop, and looked up at him. "But."

"I'm on a quest, I think," he said, not having realized this before. "Or something like one."

"Those went out of fashion a long time ago."

"Maybe. Maybe that's the problem. I'm sorry."

She bent her legs, crossed her arms over her knees, and let out a long-held breath. "It's better this way. I'm drunk."

"You're strong," he said. "You'll be running again soon."

She smiled.

"Where can I find her, and when?"

"She used to run on Sixthday, in the border between Skittersill and Stonewood. You'll find a trace of her there, if anywhere. Look for the fire. Balam can help you—he's a fat man, with a smiling face." Shannon tapped the back of her head. "Here. He trains runners. He'll know more than I do."

She uncurled back against the steps, and waited below him, considering. A carriage passed on a side street. The jangle of tack and harness faded, and so did the laughter inside the house.

"Go, then" she said at last. "If you won't stay."

He thanked her, and left her there, and wondered at himself the whole way home.

9

Dresediel Lex had worse neighborhoods than the Skittersill. Some places were too dangerous for the dangerous, and one of these was Stonewood.

Before the Craftsmen came, the petrified forest to the city's southeast stood barren, uninhabited and uninviting. After Liberation, refugees flooded in, hoping for new lives, jobs, family, free of gods. Some found what they sought, and others—drunk, mad, or simply poor—pitched their tents in Stonewood, and banded together in loose clans for protection against the giant spiders that spun steel webs between dead and ancient trees.

The people of Stonewood were less organized than the Skittersill mob, but jealous of their territory. Every few years, some enterprising hoods ventured south from Skittersill to stake a claim among the poor and lost. Their bodies were never found. The bodies of men and women from Stonewood who crept north to work or beg or whore appeared often indeed.

Ten acres of shattered buildings and blighted land separated the two districts, and preserved them from constant bloodshed. During Liberation, a god had died there, draining life from soil and air in his desperate bid for survival. After sixty years, living beings still walked uneasy on those streets. Beggars who slept on the broken roads did not wake, or woke transformed by nightmare visions. No one visited the borderland, save cliff runners who came to drink and dance in the ruins.

Caleb waited for Sixthday, when, Shannon said, Mal came to run. He suspected she was a high-pressure professional of some sort, Craftswoman maybe. Cliff running was her passion and escape, hence the late-night trips into the mountains, the precautions against being seen.

At dusk he donned denim pants and caught a driverless carriage through the Skittersill. When the cab refused to take him farther south, he paid the horse and walked.

The Skittersill ended in a jagged row of abandoned buildings, and the border began: rubble, ruined stone, rusted steel, the skeletons of shops, temples, towers broken by the dying god.

Two blocks in, he saw firelight rise from the roofless wreckage of a warehouse. Caleb approached the ruin, and ignored the shadows that detached from rock and fallen wall to follow him.

He met no sentries, only men and women lying drunk near fallen statues, smoking weed as they reclined against the foreheads of dead kings. Marks covered every surface, painted warnings and boasts in arcane calligraphy. Runners flitted between broken towers above, or scaled walls, spiders racing spiders.

One wall of the warehouse lay collapsed, felled by time or a flailing divine limb. Cliff runners gathered inside, corded with muscle, covered with scars and tattooed on arm and chest and neck.

A collection of pillars to the rear of the warehouse had once supported a lofted office, long since gone. Runners tested themselves there, jumping between pillars. Some landed and leapt again with ease, and others fell into packed dirt. A thick middle-aged man in a leather jacket shouted encouragement and abuse to them from below. A yellow tattooed face grinned on the back of his shaved head. This had to be Balam. Older by at least a decade than any of the other runners Caleb had seen: a survivor, fortysomething and ancient in a young man's endeavor, his peers long since retired or dead.

Caleb approached, waited for a lull in Balam's tirade, and said, "Excuse me."

The man turned to him with thin-lipped surprise and contempt. Caleb had dressed to blend in, but jeans and leather jacket left him several pints of ink and a handful of piercings away from looking like he belonged. He'd debated dressing to show his scars, and decided against it; the scars would earn him respect, but also the wrong sort of attention. Who knew where the Wardens had informants? So he endured scorn, and pressed on: "Shannon said you could help me find Mal."

"Maybe I could." Balam spoke slowly, as if his words were tough meat he had to chew for flavor. "But why would I?"

A semicircle of runners gathered. Their leathers and spikes were uniforms of a sort, Caleb thought, sure as ancient Quechal paints and piercings.

"Mal challenged me to find her. I've traced her here." He sounded more confident than he felt.

Balam's stomach protruded from his jacket, a swell of muscle beneath a thin layer of flesh. His skin glowed roundly in the firelight. "You can't catch her." He looked Caleb over, examining the thin arms under his jacket, the slender legs inside his trousers. "Might kill you even to try."

"She challenged me."

The trainer rested his thick fingers on the mound of his belly. "Mal runs like there's something after her with teeth and something ahead brighter than gold. If you go against her, you will fall, and you will shatter. Do you understand?"

"Yes," Caleb said. I just want to talk with her, a small part of him railed. He ignored it.

"You like the ground too much. Run from it, and it'll break you." Balam turned back to the pillars. The runners there, who had paused to watch the conversation, sprang once more to motion. The audience on the ground remained, because Caleb remained. Balam ignored them. His fingers tapped his stomach like a drum. He smelled of leather, and smoke, and animal sweat.

"I'll find Mal." Don't blink, Caleb told himself, any more than normal. Count your heartbeats. This is no different from bluffing any player at any table in the world. "Or I'll tear the city apart looking for her." Or the Wardens would.

"Best get started."

Caleb had almost decided to leave when he noticed the runners beside him staring into the southern sky. Beyond the pillars rose the warehouse wall, and on top of the wall a woman stood silhouetted against the gray night. Caleb recognized her, even before wind fanned the flames behind him and threw flickering red light on her face. She was a blaze of sunset wrapped in skin: hands on hips, elbows out, head back. She wore tan trousers, thin-soled boots, a sleeveless shirt and brown gloves, all worn, all torn.

Caleb recognized her, and ran. There were no ladders, no stairs leading up the wall, but a few pillars rose nearby. From those he could leap and reach the wall, grip the edge, pull himself up. She could escape before he reached her, but if she wanted to escape why show herself at all?

Long use had worn handholds into the nearest pillar. He climbed. She watched him. The other runners paused.

He reached the top of his pillar. Monkey-fear seized his gut as he sought the next: five feet away. Five feet, easy, he told himself, you used to jump from rock to rock in your back yard all the time, five feet apart give or take. Nothing to worry about, only tense and go.

He landed before he realized he had jumped, and the shock shot through his body, every cell screaming: never do this again. He might have listened, but his balance was too far forward. Stopping wasn't an option.

He leapt to the next pillar. Fear pounded through his veins instead of blood. Three more pillars, two, one, and then only the gap between pillar and wall. He was moving too fast to stop, and airborne above broken stone.

He struck the wall chest-first. The world inverted, and he coughed up dust and dry rock and coppery blood. He didn't fall.

His arms splayed out atop the ruined wall, and the rest of his body dangled over the drop. Legs flailed for a foothold in pitted brickwork. His fingers slipped and found no purchase.

He tried to pull himself up, but his left arm was a solid bar of pain, an exploding universe contained in the shoulder joint. Broken? No, that would hurt more. Dislocated, maybe. Damn.

Footsteps on brick. Brown thin-soled boots stepped between his arms, and she knelt. He saw the curve of her calf, and remembered her jumping, twisting, falling from Bright Mirror Dam into night. The closed-eye pendant dangled around her neck, but it did not glow. She cocked her head to one side like a bird either curious or about to strike. Her eyes were wide, her eyebrows raised.

"If it isn't the policeman," she said.

"I'm no Warden. I'm not trying to arrest you."

"Then why are you here? You've gone through a lot of trouble to find me."

"I need to talk to you. For your own safety."

"You do know how to make a girl feel safe," she said, and: "A week from tonight, on top of the Rakesblight Center, at ten. Come. Race. If you catch me, then we'll talk."

"I'll catch you."

"Let's see." She touched the back of his right hand with her fingertip, cool and smooth and hard-polished from gripping rock. He closed his eyes, consciousness slipping; when he opened them again, she was gone.

He fell, right arm wheeling and left jutting at an odd angle from the socket: an angel with one wing broken. He struck something heavy and round and human, and thick arms set him gently on the broken ground. Caleb looked up into Balam's blunt face. Other cliff runners peered down, astonished and confused. They crowded him with warmth.

"You still want to catch her?" Balam asked as Caleb struggled against his body's weight to rise.

"Yes."

The trainer didn't reply.

Caleb closed his eyes, and thought about Mal, and about this strange massive man, old in middle age, and about Shannon and her scar. Who was Mal, to have this hobby?

He levered himself into a sitting position, and the pain from his arm almost made him vomit.

"You love the ground too much," Balam said. "Or it loves you."

"Where's the nearest hospital?"

All told, once he escaped the god-shattered wasteland, once he staggered into a hospital waiting room, once the doctor looked down over the gold rims of her glasses and reached through his skin to set his shoulder from the inside, once he woke from the swoon of pain and soul-loss, he judged the evening a success.

Seven days. More than enough time to heal, and prepare.

When Teo met him in the hospital, she looked so worried he almost didn't tell her the story.

"I suppose you'll call the whole thing off now," she said as he tested his mended shoulder's strength. "Hand her over to the authorities."

"I can't quit now." He reached for his pants. "I've almost won our bet."

10

Two days later, wounds healed and mind unsettled, he stalked Teo's office.

"What do I have to do," she said, looking up from a pile of paperwork, "to get you out of here so I can focus?"

"Thanks for your support. I'm in trouble."

"What happened to the cocky attitude? I've almost won, all that stuff?"

"I have almost won."

"But you're pacing."

"I'm so close. It's this last little part that's the problem."

"The part where you have to beat a runner at her own race."

"That's the one."

"You know what you should do. Tell Tollan, fall on your sword and"—she waved the quill tip of her pen at the door—"walk away."

"Would you give up, if our situations were reversed?"

"Of course."

"I think she's innocent."

"You're infatuated."

"I'm not. I want to help her."

"Because she's pretty."

"Because it's the right thing to do," he said. "And pretty is not even the right word. She burns. She's a verb."

"You're an idiot."

"You fall for people all the time."

"Fall is certainly the operative word in this case." Teo returned her pen to its copper stand with an exasperated click of quill on metal. "I've never dated a key suspect in an ongoing investigation. As far as I recall, and feel free to correct me, I've never come back from a date with anything worse than a hangover. How many bones did you break last week?"

"That's beside the point," he said, though it wasn't. He studied one of the paintings on her office wall: a canvas awash with orange and brown and splashes of blue. A city rose, or fell, from the angry brushstrokes—a city suspended between two hells. "Would you rather I fold?"

She crossed her arms and reclined in her chair. Leather creaked to cradle her. "That isn't fair."

"I'm not blaming you. You're right. I never would have let that hand pass four years ago. I got scared, got tight. I'm afraid of losing my job, my house, the shreds of soulstuff I've squirreled together. But this woman doesn't deserve to be handed over to the Wardens just because she doesn't listen when the world tells her where she can and can't go."

"She's dangerous."

"She's amazing," he agreed.

"I don't think you get my point."

"I don't think I care."

Teo leaned forward. Caleb steeled himself against whatever she was about to say.

A bell rang, interrupting them both. She grimaced and pressed a button on her desk. A tiny door opened in the baseboard behind her wastebasket. Two hesitant red eyes peered out from the shadows.

The white rat stepped cautiously into the room, nostrils flaring. Satisfied of its immediate safety, the rat darted up Teo's desk and sat atop her paperwork. It wore black velvet barding blazoned with a silver spiderweb; a leather scroll case the size of a cigarette hung around its neck. Teo opened the case with a flick of her forefinger, and tapped a parchment scroll into her palm.

The rat accepted a few thaums of her soul in payment for the delivery, sketched a mechanical bow, and darted back through its hidden door, which snapped closed. Teo unrolled the scroll, read the message there, and swore.

"Heartstone?"

"Heartstone," she confirmed. "This deal will kill me, or else I will kill every single person involved in it."

"Please don't. That would include me."

"I might kill you anyway," she said. "They want all our customer complaints for the last year, to prove some damn thing or other about our service. As if I didn't have enough on my mind."

"I have five days to figure out how to run faster than the best cliff runner in the city."

"Practice." Teo grabbed a pen and scrawled a list on a spare palimpsest.

"Their practice almost killed me."

"Then cheat."

He raised one finger and opened his mouth. Ten seconds passed, twenty, and no words came out. A sun rose in his mind.

"Teo, you're a genius," he said, and left.

Caleb couldn't beat Mal if he played by her rules. He was neither Craftsman nor athlete. His skills lay at the card table.

But Mal had challenged him to catch her, not to win. If he cheated, she might not talk, but since he couldn't win by playing fair, he would lose nothing by stretching the rules. Balam would not approve, but Caleb didn't need his approval.

Cheating at a footrace was difficult. There were no cards he could hide in his sleeve, no tricks of shuffling or sleights-of-hand. Fortunately, Caleb had other alternatives.

He descended winding stairs into RKC's basement library, a labyrinth of twisting paths built centuries before as a ritual maze for the priests of Aquel and Achal. After the God Wars, the King in Red used the paths and dead-end chambers to store the millions of contracts by which the city maintained itself in the absence of divine grace.

This library held no Iskari romances, no histories of the Atavasin Empire or treatises on gardening or the cultivation of dreamweed. Shelves strained to support ledgers, pacts, scrolls, codices of souls collected and paid. These documents, and the Craft they anchored, were RKC's meat and blood.

No windows opened onto the library. No candles burned.

Ghostlamps offered the only light. Attendants wandered branching paths between high walls lined with forbidden tomes.

After a half hour's search Caleb found the Sub-Basement of Honorable Confusion and Folly, which held the industrial contracts. From the third oversized shelf in the fourth bookcase he removed a hand-bound sheaf of documents, spine embossed with "Rakesblight" and illuminated in gold leaf. He recognized this book, its prim, stiff binding and the green marble cover paper: he had written most of the reports inside. Rakesblight had been one of his first projects.

He flipped through pages of contracts and graphs and sigils until he reached the glossy pictures at the book's heart: plans of the Rakesblight Center, with lines of Craft drawn in blue. He sketched a copy of the diagram in a small notebook he carried, and stared at his sketch as if to drink its lines off the page into his mind. He made a small correction, and retrieved a larger book, labeled North Station in heavy letters, from the oversized shelf.

North Station surrounded Rakesblight and its neighboring properties on three sides. The people of Dresediel Lex paid RKC and other Concerns for their lights, water, and food in slivers of soul. In North Station, Craft engines smelted this soulstuff into power free of memory, affection, or moral content. That power in turn set the city's lamps ablaze and pumped its water down miles of pipe.

Caleb laid the book open on a wooden table that creaked with its weight. North Station's physical schematics were almost illegible below the blue lines drawn above and around them. Near North Station, the Craft twisted into thick ropes of obligation and interest and torment. Those ropes moved like belts in a machine.

Perfect.

Closing the book, he stood alone in the sub-basement. It was lunchtime, and the architects and students and junior Craftsmen who usually worked here would not return for an hour at least.

The library dripped with Craft. Mystic bindings and filaments clogged the narrow avenues between bookcases. Craft lines tangled and knotted until only scholars could tell a consignment order from a service contract, a statement of work from a record of accounts receivable.

Not so different from the air around North Station.

Caleb pulled his chair into the center of the room, and stepped onto its seat. The legs wobbled, but did not give. He slid a handkerchief from his jacket pocket, unfolded the cloth and held it before him at arm's length. The fabric hung limp in the dry basement air. He spread the fingers of his free hand beside the handkerchief, but felt nothing. He raised both handkerchief and hand above his head. No change. Carefully, slowly, he searched the air. At last he found the right spot: the handkerchief did not move, but a cool breeze blew against his hand. No. Not a breeze. More like a stream of water, if water were invisible, and not precisely wet.

Caleb traced the invisible flow for a few feet in either direction. He closed his eyes, and at first saw only the black behind his eyelids. A world emerged: the library outlined in lightning and blue flame. His body was a tangle of wires, his hand a skeleton's hand. A silver line passed through his palm. Light flowed along its length. The scars that spiderwebbed his forearm tingled and awoke. The Craft-line became solid to his touch.

He opened his eyes, framed his mind in an attitude he would not have recognized as prayer, and jumped.

11

The sun died, devoured by the rolling ocean. Dresediel Lex bloomed from its death, like a flower on a grave. Pyramids and skyspires cast light into darkness. The arteries of commerce glowed. In an office atop the obsidian pyramid where he once broke the gods, the King in Red sipped coffee and watched the city his power made possible, the city his radiance illuminated.

The lords of the earth and the bums in rags and tatters hid from that light, under ratty blankets or in the perfumed caves of nightclubs and dance halls. Across town by the shore, five students doffed their clothes and ran naked into cold dark water. Dresediel Lex by night was a brilliant menagerie. The animals trapped inside scraped at the bars of their cages.

Caleb arrived early at the Rakesblight Center, a black square box a thousand feet on each side and four stories tall. Animals were bought here, butchered, and sold—unsuspecting pigs herded a hundred at a time into rooms that smelled nothing at all like death, so well did the center's Craft scrub away the stench and spiritual taint of slaughter. From those rooms the pigs' corpses moved to wheels and metal jaws and conveyor belts. By the time their meat reached the sale floor, it had become cold flesh in a small box, nothing left to suggest it once squealed or rooted in muck.

Two years before, the King in Red had bought the place from Illyana Rakesblight, the Deathless Queen who designed the center to replace the fallen Goddess of Plenty. After the purchase, Illyana retired to an island she raised from a distant ocean, and the King in Red assumed her role. Each knife and abattoir became an extension of his power. Caleb's job had been to review the plant and ensure RKC would profit enough to offset operating costs. The center was a good investment, he decided after weeks of waking up shivering from nightmares of nothing-wrong, of smiling as he was flayed alive by sharp, spinning wire; the King in Red agreed. Caleb earned a promotion from his nightmares, never entered the Rakesblight Center again, and renounced all meat for seven months after the deal cleared.

He skirted the edge of the center's parking lot. No true night ever fell in Dresediel Lex, but there were shadows enough to hide. Soon he reached the alley between the center and the warehouse next door, which belonged to a demon-summoning Concern. He found a fire escape set into the center's wall and began to climb.

Cliff runners flitted across the gap between the buildings above, silent as falcons falling, so swift he might have missed them between blinks.

He climbed faster, and tried to calm his heart. Reaching the top of the ladder, he clamored to the roof and stopped, amazed.

The runners waited, arrayed for war.

Some stood and some crouched on the flat black roof, uniform in their lack of similarity. Short hair and long, thick and thin, skin tattooed or clean or pierced, dressed in basic black or strips of multicolored cloth, armored with chain or girded by soft leather. Caleb felt underdressed in his denim pants and cotton shirt.

The runners did not speak to him or to each other. Noise might attract Wardens and other undesirables. They communicated through gesture and glance.

Fifty curious gazes turned to him. He ignored all but one.

Someone had chalked a white line on the roof from north to south. Beyond that line the city rolled over buildings and below skyspires, to the black ocean and the cold sand.

Mal stood on the line, arms crossed, waiting.

As he approached her, the air grew warm. She'd slicked her hair back against her scalp, and bound it with a leather strap.

"I'm glad you made it," she said.

Rooftop gravel ground beneath his feet as he approached her. "Why are you chasing me?"

"I'm trying to protect the city." He took another step. "And you."

The cliff runners watched.

Ten feet. Five.

"You're the one who needs protection," she said.

Three. Two. One. He smelled sweat, sandalwood, and leather. "I'll take my chances." He reached for her.

He blinked.

When his eyes opened, Mal was halfway across the roof already and gaining speed. Caleb had no time to drop into a crouch: he fell forward, caught himself with his leg, and pressing off the ground he fell and caught himself again, tumbling more than sprinting after her.

Mal reached the roof's edge first, and leapt to an outbuilding a story lower than the warehouse. She landed with a roll as Caleb launched himself into the yawning gulf.

12

The world opened beneath Caleb, six stories' drop onto solid gray asphalt. Emptiness and wind tore at his mind, but he landed on the neighboring roof, and rolled. His knee throbbed. Adrenaline dulled the pain, and he staggered to his feet and ran again.

Mal had already reached the outbuilding's edge and leapt, this time across a twelve-foot chasm toward a stockhouse that supplied the Rakesblight Center with victims. Caleb gaped in disbelief. The distance was too great. Not even Mal could make such a jump—nor did she.

She struck the wall feet-first, caught the ledge overhead by her fingertips, and pulled herself onto the roof. How had she learned that? If her first try had not been perfect, she would not have survived for a second.

No time to speculate. Caleb jumped, and closed his eyes.

Dresediel Lex was built of stone, glass, and contracts—promises stronger than steel, tying the city together by pledge and payment. Bonds of contract were invisible, unless you looked at the world as Craftsmen learned to look, with eyes closed and mind open.

The black behind Caleb's eyes came alive with blue-white webs, strands several feet thick, as if woven by pyramid-sized spiders. The contract lines stretched to the horizon. They bound building to building, tied skyspires to the earth, lit streetlamps, pumped water through subterranean pipes, cooled hallways and made the desert city livable. Ahead, these lines converged on the nova palace of North Station.

Falling, Caleb grabbed a silver cord.

Scars all over his body burned as they woke and drew on the

cord's power. He shot forward, dragged by a line of lightning. Cold fangs sank into his arm. His eyes snapped open from the speed, and the visible world resolved blue around him again. The contract cord had carried him almost a hundred feet; he flew over the stockhouse's rooftop. With a shout of triumph, he released the cord and fell to the gravel, landing with knees bent. The chemical stench of close-kept pigs enveloped him; wards burned off most of the stink, but not all.

Mal sprinted ahead of him, toward North Station. With eyes open, Caleb could no longer see the station's burning soul, the blaze of contracts—only its colossal physical form, a sprawling complex of cooling towers and thick pipe, lit by ghostlight and gas flame, and surrounded by a barbed wire fence.

Once Mal crossed that fence, alarms would sound, and Wardens would arrive. She'd be caught, and his work to find her, to learn what she knew and keep her free of the Wardens' hands, would be meaningless.

He could not let that happen.

Bloodstained aprons, sheets, towels fluttered on clotheslines at the far end of the roof. Mal left a wake in sanguine cloth. He followed her, reached the roof's edge steps behind, jumped.

Lava coursed in his veins and melted his muscles. Every exhalation broke upon a rushing indrawn breath. He gripped the reins of Dresediel Lex and they scorched him with their chill. Already his hand felt frozen. His flight, like everything, had a price. These cords took his soul as they carried him. Soon they would drain him completely and he would fall.

Mal landed on the fence, climbed without apparent concern for the barbed wire—another cliff runner's trick, maybe, or else enchanted gloves—and dropped to a service shed on the other side. As she landed into North Station, the sky erupted in red light. A banshee shrieked, and others around the station perimeter cried out in answering alarm. Mal paused atop the shed like a locust on a blade of grass, then sprang onto a thick conduit and ran toward a cyclopean cooling tower at the station's heart.

He landed on the conduit behind her. The noise of his impact caused her to glance back. Her eyes widened; she fled, and he followed. As they ran through the forest of vents and ducts and pipes, he called to her, panting: "We need to talk."

"You're persistent." Her voice was even, conversational.

"It's a virtue."

"How are you flying?"

"I made a gamble."

"I hope you didn't risk anything valuable." She ducked under a chest-height conduit; he vaulted over it and struck his shin on a jutting metal bar. His pants tore.

"Only my soul." He grabbed for her, but she sprinted ahead, reached the coolant tower, and began to climb.

From the pipe she leapt to the lowest rung of an access ladder, climbed that and jumped again, this time to a duct that ivied around the tower. She moved from handhold to handhold easily as a guitar player changing chords.

Groping blind, he found a line of Craft that spiraled up the tower, and gripped it with both hands. Chill fingers clawed at him as he rose. His heart beat to burst the cage of his ribs and rain blood on the city.

More banshee cries shivered through North Station as other cliff runners crossed the fence. Wardens would come soon, Couatl mounts beating terror through the night sky. A Couatl could outpace Caleb in the air, read a newspaper three miles away in the dark, track a rat in its nest or a man in a mob. Even if Mal could evade them, he would not.

Red warning flares cast a hellish pattern on the balloon of an airbus approaching the tower—lower, and nearer to North Station, than an airbus should fly. Irrelevant. The world was an incandescent maze. Chest heaving, brain blood-battered, Caleb approached the lip of the cooling tower.

He let go of the line, and, for a moment, flew.

Momentum thrust him skyward. He tumbled toward stars and skyspires, and at the apex of his flight let out a whoop of triumph that turned to fear as he began to fall.

There was no time to think. The stone tower thrust at him, a sword point with the world's weight behind it.

Rock struck him hard in the chest, in the legs, and everywhere else. After a few seconds, he realized he was still alive, prone on the lip of the tower, boiling steam to his left and void to his right. Hot air and sulfurous fumes engulfed him. Arms splayed, he embraced the stone.

He was alone.

He sat up, teetered, and nearly fell into seething smoke.

A gloved hand crested the tower, followed by the rest of Mal. Her hair was a black nimbus, her face and arms sweat-slick. Fierce eyes stared at him through smoke.

"Hi," he said.

"Couldn't think up a better line"—she gasped for air—"on the way up?"

Caleb couldn't think of anything to say, and anyway he could not speak for his lungs' heaving. He edged toward her around the precipice.

"So what happens now," he said when he drew near.

"Now." She stood, and fixed him with a broken glass grin. "We see how much farther you're willing to go."

He lunged, too late. She dove off the tower's edge.

The force of her leap carried her clear of ducts and ladders and platforms. She fell, spun, tumbled—and landed, on the balloon of the airbus passing below. Gray silk dimpled around her body.

Sirens wailed. A fresh breeze feathered Caleb's brow.

He jumped after her.

Sharp wind buffeted him. Falling, he strained with fingers, arms, and tortured shoulders for the contract-cords that guided the airbus. Cold talons tightened around his heart.

He clutched at nothing.

Blue fire tore through his arms and chest.

Caleb halted two feet above the gray balloon. Pain jolted his eyes open. Mal lay beneath him as if on a pillowed mattress.

"You made it," she said, shocked.

"Couldn't think of a better line on the way down?"

"You're an interesting man."

He was about to say something inane about living in interesting times, when a thousand suns exploded over Dresediel Lex.

His shadow fell across Mal. Light bellowed through his body.

A woman a thousand feet tall, four-armed and six-winged, emerged from North Station like a swimmer from a shallow pool. She opened many mouths and roared.

Flame and figure both vanished in a heartbeat. The city's million lights went dark. Night closed around Caleb like a warm fist.

The canvas struck him in a rush. Blinking galaxies from his eyes, he scrambled on the slick fabric, found no grip, and started to slide.

The more he fought, the more he slipped. He heard Mal call for him; he reached for her and slid farther. Fingers brushed his grasping outstretched hand and she was gone, and the balloon was gone. He tumbled into the sky. Dresediel Lex wheeled below, above him, and he saw North Station's towers fallen. Fire clung to broken rock.

He fell for hours, or seconds, until something struck him hard in the chest. Darkness rushed in, writhing with terrible dreams.

13

When Caleb woke, he was staggering through a familiar hell. Ixaqualtil Seven Eagle ruled a realm of darkness where fire shed no light and no stars shone, a vast vacant universe that resounded with the cries of dying and damned, with demonsong, with the crackle of flame and the slither of invisible blades on invisible whetstones. Within that cacophony Ixaqualtil crouched before the Sun's empty throne, feasting on all who dared approach his master's perilous seat.

The Sun-God was dead, slain by the King in Red during Liberation, but His servant yet awaited the unwary, two hundred fifty six dagger-teeth bared in a hungry smile.

In Ixaqualtil's hell one did not move for fear of stumbling into a hidden pit, a black fire, a beast's waiting mouth, yet Caleb was moving. Walking. Each step poured sharp pain down his side. He tried to stop, but could not. His left arm was wrapped around a woman's shoulder, her arm around his back. When his feet faltered, she pulled him along.

Caleb saw only suggestions of shape within the velvet dark, but he knew Mal walked beside him.

"You shouldn't be in hell," he said.

She started at the sound of his voice. So did he: cracked, hoarse. "You don't know me well enough to say that. I'm not, though, yet."

"What happened?" He struggled to place one foot in front of the other. Clouds of noise and flame obscured his mind.

"You fell. I caught you."

"Caught me how? You were lying"—he remembered—"on top of the airbus."

"It would have been bad manners to let you fall." In the

distance, he heard the subsonic roars of Couatl. Wardens, hunting. Still alive, then. Probably. No doubt there were Wardens in hell. The Couatl roared again; Mal flinched beside him, and spoke, as if to block them out: "I don't know why I saved you. If I thought about it, I might not have. I rolled off the balloon, caught the airbus's rudder, and grabbed you with some Craft."

"You're a Craftswoman?"

"A bit of one."

Caleb remembered a rush of wind, and a winged, sun-bright woman. When he closed his eyes he saw her in negative.

"I remember a woman of light."

"You faced the blast," she said. "I saw its reflection, and the darkness after. At first I thought the light had blinded me. Then I realized the power was off."

He blinked, and saw their hell with clear eyes. Darkness grew texture and depth; hints of black and red and violet adhered to brick, to glass and pitted pavement, pipe and cobblestone and palm tree. They staggered down an avenue walled with stores and small restaurants: Salamanter's Deli, Cusko & Sons, a Muerte Coffee franchise. Shards of broken shop windows covered sidewalk and street; they should have caught streetlamp light like diamonds on a jeweler's cloth, but there were no streetlamps. No lights in the shops, either, or the upstairs apartments. Neither stars nor moon relieved the darkness.

Caleb saw by firelight reflected off the belly of the clouds. The city was burning.

"We're in the Vale," he said. "My home isn't far."

"I know. I found your address in your wallet."

"I have no secrets from you now."

"I wouldn't say that."

"You saved my life."

"It does look that way."

He tried to laugh, but his ribs hurt. "The other runners, who ran into the station after us . . ."

"I don't know." He thought at first she might say no more, but she continued: "We won't learn anything tonight."

"I hope they escaped." He imagined Balam's reaction to his students' death. The ground will break you, he had said.

"So do I."

Terror passed overhead on beating wings. A roar below human hearing shivered him. The Warden swooped away toward the fire, and Caleb could move again.

"Gods."

"Watch your language," she cautioned.

"What else could it be? An explosion that powerful, with blackout and riots just after. Gods," he repeated, less a curse than an expression of wonder, "and their faithful. They hit North Station. One of the True Quechal must have smuggled a god inside somehow. Or a goddess."

His foot slipped on a stone. Her grip tightened around his waist, and pain flowered in his ribs. He recovered his balance, and they walked on.

"This is me," he said when they reached Three Cane Road, and they turned onto it together. Caleb barely noticed the road's gentle slope on his morning commute, but it was a mountain path tonight.

Fresh black paint disfigured the houses here. Some gang of fervent amateurs had scrawled scenes of scripture and sacrifice on the pale adobe walls: Aquel and Achal devouring the Hero Twins; Qet Sea-Lord giving his body to the deep.

After ten minutes' agonizing climb they reached Caleb's squat two-story. A small gang gathered on his lawn, three men and two women bearing paints and brushes and knives. The tallest man had defaced Caleb's front wall with a crude, violent cartoon of Aquel chasing demons from the earth.

"Hey!"

The painters turned. In darkness Caleb could not see their faces. They might have been his neighbors. Paint glistened like blood on the wall.

"Get the hell away from my house," Caleb said.

The tall man set down his brush. His shoulders were broad, his steps heavy.

Caleb twisted free of Mal to meet the man's advance.

"We have a right to be here," the man said in High Quechal, his vowels round and broad, consonants knife-sharp. He spoke as if each word were a boulder he had to lift and let fall. He'd learned the tongue from books. "The dark is sacred. We glorify the Gods."

"The gods," Caleb said, and the tall man recoiled, for Caleb also spoke in High Quechal, swiftly and without accent. "The gods spit on your offering. They don't notice such small gifts. Count yourself lucky. If you met them face-to-face, your heart would burst and your brains boil." The painters stood sharp and at bay, like surprised rats. Did they understand him? "Leave my house," he added in Kathic. "Scuttle back to your holes." He shook, and hoped they took his tremors for rage rather than exhaustion and injury.

"Who are you?" the tall man asked.

"My name is Caleb Altemoc." For the first time in years, Caleb put the accent on his father's name. "Leave me in peace."

One of the shorter men took a slow step back. The others followed. That first step taken, the second followed faster, and the third faster still. They retreated into the Vale.

Caleb watched until they were no longer people or even rats but insects, ants, disappearing into the deepening dark. Night overcame him and he slumped against the side of his house. Bloody paint smeared across his cheek.

Through the shifting world he saw Mal sheathe a knife.

With her aid, he shuffled along the wall to his front door. He searched his pocket and after a brutal interval found his keys. "In the last blackout some kids, same ones maybe, painted half the houses two blocks over. Paint sinks into the adobe. You have to redo the whole wall to get it off. Public nuisance."

She watched him fumble with the lock and miss the keyhole twice. "Need help?"

"I'm fine."

"What if they didn't run? What if they wanted to fight?"

"They believe in the old gods, or claimed to. Anyone who believed in the old gods, and liked to fight, died a long time ago."

The latch clicked open, and he stumbled into his living room. Mal followed him, and he closed the door behind her.

Caleb lived alone in the Vale, no girlfriend to impress, no pets save a four-foot iguana he kept to chase the larger spiders away. What did such a life require? In the living room, a couch, two secondhand chairs, an unlit brazier, a shelf full of books on poker and bridge and a few cheap Iskari romances, the kind with dashing swordplay and dark Craft and men who raced to save the world from doom. A low table by the couch bore a five-story house of cards. Caleb was almost glad for the blackout: darkness made the room look like the chaotic abode of a dangerous mind, rather than a chamber cluttered with a young man's junk.

Mal waited by the door. Caleb searched the table for a match and lit the candles scattered on shelves and tabletop. "Sorry." With a wave he indicated the mess. "I didn't expect guests."

Mal turned a slow circle on the carpet. Fire painted the room orange and black, and her the same. "Why all the candles?"

"I like candles more than ghostlight. They feel authentic. Besides, lights aren't reliable in this part of the city, especially in summer."

"Is that so?"

"You must live on the west side," he said, meaning: you're richer than I thought. She didn't respond, not that he expected a response.

"Do your lights die so often that you need to leave candles out?"

"No." He looked away from her, at the shadow she cast on the wall. "My father comes to visit sometimes. Craft tends to break when he's around."

She leaned against the couch. "Your father." Head lolled back, mouth open, she reminded him of a sacrifice in an old engraving, curled around the blade plunged into her stomach, crying out in pain or rage or ecstasy. She whispered: "Caleb Altemoc," accenting his father's name.

"I told you when we met."

"There are names and then there are names. I didn't think you meant *that* Temoc, of all the Temocs in Dresediel Lex."

"Temoc Godhaven. Temoc Last-Standing, Temoc who strikes as an eagle from the heights. Priest of All Gods. Tormentor of Dresediel Lex. Yes. That Temoc."

"He really is your father?"

Caleb nodded.

Her eyes were dark as the inside of her mouth. "Why did you chase me?"

"That's not the question you should ask."

"What is?"

"Ask why I didn't tell the Wardens you were at Bright Mirror."

She blinked. "Why?"

"Because if I told them, they'd have thought you poisoned the reservoir. If I tell them what you did tonight, they'll accuse you of blowing up North Station."

"I didn't."

"I believe you. But they wouldn't. If you'd gone with me two weeks ago, they would have asked you questions—that's all. Now, they're eager, and desperate. They'll tie you to a rack, pull your memory out through your eyes and slice it with silver knives until they find the truth."

"And they'll learn I'm innocent. What do I have to fear?"

"Pain."

"Pain doesn't hurt."

"This kind does. It changes people. Bright Mirror wasn't your fault—it was my father's, or the fault of those who follow him. Dad's hurt too many men and women, by his own hand and by proxy. I don't want him to hurt you, too."

Candlelight soaked her hands in blood. "What do you want from me?"

"Tell me what you saw at Bright Mirror. Give me something to go on, some angle to chase."

"Nothing. Moonlight on the reservoir. Your guards. The Tzimet."

"No sign of a poisoner? Nothing incriminating?"

"No."

"I need more."

"I have no more to give."

He walked around the couch toward her. Flames danced in her eyes. The shark's-tooth pendant hung from her neck. He touched the pendant, lifted it between thumb and forefinger. His hand grazed her chest, and she twitched as if he had shocked her.

"How did you get this?" he asked softly.

"I bought it."

"Old Quechal workmanship. You didn't find it at a Craftsman's boutique."

"I have sources."

"In the Skittersill."

"Yes."

"You must have paid a small fortune." He turned the tooth over. Intricate carvings covered its back.

"A lady never tells."

"I can help you," he said. "If you give me the pendant."

"Why?"

"You use it to sneak into places you shouldn't be. That brought you to Bright Mirror two weeks ago, and to North Station tonight. Someone's playing you for a patsy. If I take this, maybe I can find out who."

She didn't respond. Slowly, he lifted the pendant over her head, and slid it into his pocket.

When he looked up, she was watching him.

"You ran after me," she said, "even though you might have died, because you wanted to help. And you won the race."

"I didn't win. I cheated. I fell."

The curves and planes of her face were red and yellow and black. "If you hadn't won, I wouldn't have caught you."

Like water she flowed toward him. Her small blunt nose touched his, and her leather slacks pressed against the inside of his thighs. Her dried sweat smelled of salt and sea and flesh. She kissed him. Her lips were cool, the rest of her body warm.

He tossed inside her kiss like a splinter in a flood. Too soon. Too strong. A crashing kiss, a kiss with death at the bottom. He thought of his dark room upstairs, where there were no candles to light their bodies turning on fine cotton sheets. Drowning, he breathed her in, and she filled his lungs instead of air.

Their lips parted, and he saw himself reflected in her eyes.

"Well?" she said after a moment.

"No," he replied. A knife lifted from his throat. The gates of heaven swung shut.

Her right eyebrow crept up, and her head tilted to the side— puzzled, not disappointed. "Why not? Because I kissed you before you kissed me? Because you don't want this?"

His mouth was dry. Words formed slowly, heavy with regret. "Because I do. But if we go upstairs now, it will be over tonight. We'll lie together, and you'll disappear."

He lived in her scent. He struggled to master himself, and at last stepped back.

He recognized her expression from countless card tables, from Craftsmen and snakelings and demons and human beings judging their cards and judging him.

"Do you want me to leave?" she asked at last.

"It won't be safe outside until morning. You can use my bed. I'll sleep down here, on the couch." He sidled toward the stairs, but did not take his eyes from her, so he tripped over the coffee table and scattered the house of cards. "I just need to go upstairs and get a few things, first."

Cresting the stairs he found his bedroom door closed. He stepped inside, and pulled the door shut after him, blocking out the candlelight from below. The bedroom was not dark: a dim blue radiance shone within, the color of the Sansilva sky at night.

"Dad," he said in High Quechal. "You need to leave."

14

"You knew I was here." His father's voice rumbled like an avalanche. "How?"

"I don't make card towers, Dad. My hands shake."

Temoc lay on Caleb's bed, reading a book on contract bridge. The bed was made, corners tucked in military fashion, though Caleb had left the sheets in disarray that morning. Temoc must have made it before lying down.

Caleb's father was girded for battle, his skin black as empty space. Jagged patterns of moonlight gleamed from his forehead, his cheeks, his chest and arms and stomach.

"Don't you ever wear a shirt?" Caleb asked as he approached the bed.

Temoc dog-eared his page in the book, closed it, and sat up. "I was waiting for you."

"Whatever you have to say, I don't want to hear it."

"I can see you're angry."

"I'm not angry," he snapped. His father shrugged. "I'm not. Do you have any idea how many people you killed tonight? I was almost one of them."

Temoc stood. Shadows melted into his skin. Mazes of silver light dimmed and died, leaving a network of scars across his body and face.

Caleb's father had fought for sixty years. Stone and lightning and time could not defeat him. His was a losing war, against knowledge and truth and undead hordes, but he refused to die or surrender. Songs were sung of his exploits in the God Wars and down the decades since, bloody violent odes chanted by drunken hoodlums in the Skittersill.

"I didn't do it," Temoc said.

"Someone tried to break the city tonight, using a god for a weapon. Who might that have been, do you think? Mom? The Wardens? The godsdamn King in Red?"

"Believe what you will. Speak to me in whatever tone you think yourself entitled to use. I did not cause this blackout. I would swear this to you on the gods, if you believed in them."

Caleb shook his head.

"I do not lie."

"Who else could have convinced a god to do something like that?"

"Goddess," Temoc said, and stopped, and closed his eyes. Caleb waited, and soon his father found words again: "The figure burning in the sky was Ili of the White Sails. She is no more."

Caleb wanted to put a hand on his father's shoulder, and throw him out the window. "Fine. Feel sorry for a goddess, not for any of the people killed tonight in the blackout, in the hospitals. In the riots. Every True Quechal dope who throws a beer bottle at a Warden this evening and has his arms broken for the privilege is on your conscience, whether you admit it or not. Either way, find somewhere else to hide. I need this room."

Glass broke two streets away, shattering the bedroom silence. "I did nothing," Temoc said. "My people did nothing. The Wardens attacked my hiding place soon after the blackout. I fought my way free, lost my pursuers, came here. Call me murderer, terrorist, call me whatever they've taught you to call those of us who keep the faith, but I had no part in tonight's attack. I am innocent of this attack, and of the death of Ili of the White Sails."

"Why should I believe you?"

"I'm your father."

"That's no answer."

"I have to go. The Wardens will be here soon."

Caleb scanned the sky outside his window for Couatl, and listened for the beat of their wings. He saw nothing, and heard only the distant riot.

"We have a few minutes left before they catch my trail."

Was that patch of darkness a cloud, or a Warden's mount? "The blackout won't last."

"Of course not. One power station was destroyed, a single link in the chains that bind our city. Lights will return within the hour. Breaking your master's grip would require more than a single explosion."

"Which of course you know, because you've spent seventeen years planning this kind of attack."

Temoc did not answer.

"You claim you're innocent of the whole thing?"

"I do."

"Why did you come here?"

"I wanted to see you."

Caleb closed the drapes, but did not turn around. "Liar."

"They'll be hunting me now, more hungrily than they have for years. I won't be able to visit as often. They might come for you."

"I won't tell them you were here."

"No. Tell them. They'll know if you lie, and you'll be in more trouble than I've made for you already."

"If you say so."

"Who's the girl?"

"She's, you know." Caleb laughed bitterly. "I never told you there was a girl."

"I heard the two of you downstairs."

"She's . . . wild."

"I'm glad to hear it. You need more wildness in your life."

Staring into the drapes, Caleb thought back seventeen years to the Skittersill Rising. Poor men and women had clutched their charnel gods like beggars wrapping themselves in threadbare cloaks. The protest revolved around Temoc. He was the movement's sun, its shining center. Ten years old, Caleb had watched his father in awe: the last true priest, the paladin of fallen temples.

Temoc swelled with his people's need, and his family crumbled around him.

At last, the great man made his choice. Caleb woke to screams and blood. His mother cradled him and cried hot, fierce tears. His father was gone.

"Thanks, Dad," Caleb said.

A gust of wind answered him.

When Caleb turned, he saw an empty room. His bedroom's second window stood ajar. Night breeze brushed the curtains.

Temoc could have closed the window behind him, and vanished without leaving any sign. This was his form of courtesy, the nearest he could come to saying good-bye.

Caleb placed the book about contract bridge on his nightstand, and left the page dog-eared. He straightened the comforter, patted the mattress to remove all trace of Temoc, and went downstairs to guide Mal up to bed.

15

Caleb woke to an empty house. The bed upstairs where Mal had slept was carefully made. A bowl and mug rested drying beside the kitchen sink. When he returned to the living room he saw a cream-hued envelope atop the piled books and playing cards on the coffee table. The envelope bore his name in a sharp, angular hand. Within, he found a note:

> *Caleb—*
> *Thank you for the race. You're an intriguing man.*
> *We will see more of one another.*
>
> *—M*

He showered briefly, keeping his tender left side away from the pounding water. He dressed in loose slacks, and winced when he raised his arms to don a thick cotton shirt. He'd visit a doctor in the afternoon. Clinics would be crowded all morning with every hypochondriac working stiff who bumped his head in the blackout.

For now, he needed a meal and twenty or so cups of coffee.

He shrugged into a tan corduroy jacket, slumped downstairs, opened his front door, and collided with a silver statue wearing a black uniform.

"Caleb Altemoc," the Warden said in a voice with its serial numbers filed off.

Like all Wardens, the man before Caleb was literally expressionless. A quicksilver pall encased his head and neck. Dark blots on the metal suggested a brow, two eyes, nose, mouth, features that blurred when Caleb tried to focus on them. An enamel badge glinted from the left breast of the Warden's jacket: an ebon skull with the number "5723" in crimson on its forehead. "What?"

"You are Caleb Altemoc," the Warden repeated.

Caleb memorized the number. It was the only name he would ever know for this Warden. Upon joining the force, each recruit had a number etched into her bones, scored into her soul. A Warden's mask could not be worn without a badge, and each badge reported its wearer's number; a Warden who abused her power could be identified by that number and cast out.

At least, in theory.

"That's me," he said.

A scalloped shadow passed over them both. Caleb looked up. A beast half serpent and half bird crouched on his roof, wings flared. The Couatl had a snake's face, a crest of red and yellow and green feathers, and a vulture's all-encompassing black eyes. Another Warden sat in a saddle on the creature's sinewy neck.

A second Couatl, no doubt belonging to the Warden at his door, coiled and preened on Caleb's front lawn.

"Please come with us," the Warden said. "We have questions."

"Are you arresting me?"

Smooth silver darkened where the Warden's brow should have been. "You're not in any trouble, sir. You will answer our questions, and be free to go."

"I have a right to know why I'm being taken," Caleb said, though he knew, or at least suspected, the answer, "and where," which he did not know and about which he knew better than to guess.

"I can't tell you." Perhaps the Warden did not know, yet. That quicksilver mask was a means of communication as well as a disguise. Orders passed through it, and commands. "Will you come?"

Caleb had little say in the matter: Craft augmented Wardens' speed and strength, and their mounts were swift and hungry. Even if he could escape, he had nowhere to run.

He closed the door behind him, locked it, and tugged on the lapels of his jacket. "Well. Can we travel by carriage, at least? I hurt my ribs in the blackout last night."

"You'll ride with me," the Warden said. "My mount flies steady."

Caleb was not reassured, but he followed anyway.

This was not his first interview with the Wardens. They sought him out after Temoc's attacks—the ambush in the 700 block, the attempted sabotage of Bay Station a few years back, all the rest. So accustomed were the Wardens to debriefing Caleb that they'd questioned him after the zombie revolt two years ago, though Temoc played no part in that.

They only came for him once the action was over. Temoc must have eluded his pursuers.

How long had this Warden waited outside Caleb's door? How long had his partner's mount coiled on the roof? Had they seen Mal leave? Did they let her go?

No sense worrying. She could take care of herself. Nothing incriminating about a woman spending the night at a single man's house. He hoped.

The serpent's emerald neck was as tall as Caleb's waist. The Warden mounted his saddle and motioned for Caleb to climb on behind.

As he settled against the warm scales, invisible cords lashed his arms to his sides and his legs to the beast's back. He relaxed into the spectral bonds. The more he struggled, the tighter they would grow.

"I thought I wasn't under arrest?"

"Not arrest," the Warden said. "Protection."

"Feels similar."

The Couatl's muscles surged, and in a thrashing, horrible instant the creature rose into the air. Two massive wingbeats bore them past the housetops. The Warden on Caleb's roof goaded her own mount to flight, and together they wheeled south, toward the bustling cancer of downtown Dresediel Lex.

When they crested the mountains, Caleb saw the damage from above. Skittersill had born the brunt of the riots. Shattered windows, burnt-out shops, and broken bricks marred the streets—as if giant children had played there, careless of the lives they crushed.

Set beside the Skittersill, the wealthier districts' scars seemed affectations. Repairman teemed Sansilva, replacing windows in boutiques and jewelry shops. Even the finest looted gems would not be lost for long: Sansilva stores cursed their wares pre-sale. Over the next week the thieves and fences of Dresediel Lex would suffer insanity, depression, catatonia, and violent disfigurement until the stolen merchandise returned to its owners. Grocery stores lost more from riots and looting than did fashion houses: few grocers could afford curses or insurance, and their stock was perishable.

Couatl circled the crater where North Station used to be, keeping watch, a funeral guard over a goddess's corpse. Couatl had once been sacred birds, before Craftsmen claimed and changed them. Caleb wondered if the Wardens' mounts remembered their old masters.

The Couatl that bore Caleb turned from the crater and flew west, toward the black pyramid at 667 Sansilva.

Caleb swallowed. Powers lurked inside that pyramid, powers that could turn a man inside out, or trap a woman in agony until the sun burnt to a cinder and the planet fell to dust—powers ancient and implacable. He knew those powers. They paid his salary.

The Couatl descended toward the pyramid's peak, a black glass slab carved in concentric spirals: ancient Quechal versions of the circles modern Craftsmen used. Here, in ages past, high priests worked miracles. The priests were gone, but their patterns and tools remained.

A crystal dome forty feet across stood in the center of those spirals. The Warden landed them beside the dome. Couatl claws clicked on obsidian.

The beast lowered its head. Caleb's bonds disappeared, but he did not move.

"Go on," the Warden said.

Caleb dismounted and almost fell. When the world ceased to pitch and yaw, he walked toward the dome, and through.

Crystal pricked his skin like a million needles. Upside-down the world was, and back to front, inverted in eyes and mind. Gasping, he breathed infinity. Panic seized him, but when he next inhaled, cool air filled his lungs. He coughed, shivered, swore, and stumbled forward onto a glass floor.

The dome was transparent from within. Morning light streamed from the cloudless sky onto a red Iskari carpet. An unoccupied and richly furnished room lay beneath the crystal: two plush leather couches, six unoccupied chairs, three freestanding bookcases packed with arcane tomes, and a tall desk of the same black glass as the pyramid, but stained a faint crimson.

"Hello?" he asked, and received no answer.

Warily, Caleb approached the desk. It was seven feet long, four feet wide, and cluttered with papers, pens, small clockwork toys, thick volumes of Craft, scrolls that murmured in tongues dead or yet to be invented. A sepia painting the size of a playing card rested in a heavy silver frame at one corner of the desk, beside a fist-sized depression in the glass.

Each corner of the desk bore a similar depression, and from them deep channels ran to gargoyle-mouth spouts in the desk's sides. Quechal priests killed by removing the heart, but they drained blood before each sacrifice: blood loss induced euphoria, and brought victims closer to the divine.

"It would have been a waste to throw the thing out."

Caleb turned from the altar.

A skeleton in a crimson bathrobe stood behind him. It held a steaming mug of coffee in one hand, and a folded newspaper in the other. A circlet of red gold adorned its skull, and two ruby sparks glittered from the pits where its eyes would have been.

Caleb snapped to attention, hands at his sides, chin up. "Sir."

Lord Kopil, the King in Red, Deathless King of Dresediel Lex and Chief Executive of Red King Consolidated, did not acknowledge Caleb's salute. "Obsidian isn't porous, you know. It's not physically possible for sacrificial blood to have colored that altar. Your gods—our gods, I suppose I should say, or the Quechal gods—made this possible: their hunger pulled blood into the glass, stained it like coffee stains teeth."

With a bony index finger he indicated his own pale yellow cuspids.

"They were no gods of mine," Caleb said.

"Your father's gods, then," Kopil allowed. He released his newspaper, which floated across the room to the cluttered desk. "Two drops, three, entered the stone for each sacrifice. Think about the millennia of full moons and midsummer's days and eclipses that stone represents, thousands of deaths offered to the Hungry Serpents and Qet Sea-Lord and the rest. They have gone before—and none will come after." The bones of his feet clicked like a crab's claws against the floor. "You've worked for me for three years, six months, and two days, Caleb, yet we've only spoken a handful of times. Why do you suppose that is?"

Because you're the most powerful Craftsman in Dresediel Lex, Caleb thought, and I'm a peon. "We don't have much in common," he said at last.

"The professors who recommended you to my service claimed you were intelligent and ambitious. I would like to think those are traits I share." The skull possessed no lips to smile, nor did his tone convey any trace of humor.

"That's not what I meant."

"Tollan says you're talented. Yet you've remained content with a mid-level position in risk management."

"I've done well there." He paused, expecting his boss to interrupt, but the King in Red only sipped his coffee. "It's exciting work."

"It's not."

"Excuse me?"

"I wouldn't expect a soldier to call a guard shift at our front desk 'exciting,' and I don't expect you to say the same about your current role in risk management. It's good work, not exciting."

"I like control: bets I can win, situations I can manage."

"If you like control so much," the King in Red asked, "why are your ribs broken?"

Caleb's mouth went dry. "I fell."

"Your soul is frailer than it was when you left this building two days ago." Red sparks shone in the black holes of Kopil's eyes. "You have used, or borrowed, much power in the last twelve hours. You may have fallen, but you flew first, I think. Nor is this your only recent injury: last week, you drew on the Company's medical policy to heal a dislocated shoulder, and a hairline fracture of the collarbone." Shadows shifted on the skeleton's face. "For three years you've worked for me, confident, competent, unassuming, a perfect, invisible employee. On the night of the gravest assault against our company in three years, you suffer severe and mysterious injuries. How did you come by those injuries, I wonder."

The King in Red's voice was conversational and cold. Its chill seeped into the air, and stung Caleb's skin.

"To what end have you bent your intelligence and ambition, Caleb? Not to glorify yourself in my service, I'm sure. Have you plotted with your father to destroy me? To destroy everything I have built?"

Caleb did not blink, did not show his fear. A pit yawned at his back, and the slightest misstep might send him tumbling without Mal to catch him. "No, sir."

Kopil laughed, a chattering, unsettled sound of bare branches blown by wind. The sun faded and the sky bruised to gray. Silver glyphs glowed about his eye sockets.

An invisible serpent circled Caleb and lifted him from the floor. Scales pressed his arms to his sides. Cold carrion breath hissed against his neck.

"No?" Kopil said. "You were at North Station last night. Tell me why."

Words skittered from Caleb's grasping mind. "I was chasing a lead. A woman who snuck into Bright Mirror. A cliff runner."

"Your report," the King in Red noted absently, "made no mention of a woman. Only an intruder, of indeterminate gender and appearance."

"If the Wardens tried to hunt for her, she would have disappeared. The cliff runners look after their own. She was innocent—a catspaw. She needed help, not an arrest party."

Ruby eyes burned into his soul. "That was not your decision." The invisible serpent tightened its grip. He gasped at the pain in his ribs.

"She had a pendant. It's in my pocket. Take it out."

The shark's-tooth pendant twitched, wormed free of his pocket, and floated to eye level, revolving in the half light. Kopil regarded it. The closed-eye glyph glowed dull silver on the tooth's surface.

"She thought the pendant kept her hidden. But that's not all it does, I think."

The King in Red snapped his fingers, and Caleb fell silent. No sound trespassed on the darkness.

At last, Kopil spoke. "A charm to track and observe the wearer. Well-hidden by the obfuscating ward. Clever, in a base fashion. Quechal Applied Theology—a modern Craftsman wouldn't see it unless he knew how to look."

"Someone found a cliff runner who likes to go where she doesn't belong, gave her that pendant, and followed her until she led them to a place where they could hurt us. They tricked her into showing them how to sneak in, and sneak out again. They used her to poison Bright Mirror and blow up North Station."

"The Wardens will find the person who made this, and the truth of your story." Kopil slid the tooth into the pocket of his robe. "But your situation has not changed. You show me a talisman and claim a woman you will not identify wore it when she broke into our facilities—a fact you hid from Tollan, and from me. I find your testimony less than compelling."

"I'm telling the truth."

"We know your father was in your house last night. We traced him there, and lost his trail after."

The serpent's coils compressed his broken ribs. He gasped. "Temoc was in my house when I came home last night. He told me he didn't plan the North Station raid. After that, he left."

"A strange claim."

"It's not a claim. It's a message."

Kopil cocked his head to one side. "What do you mean?"

"The Wardens attacked Temoc last night. How did they find his hideout?"

"An anonymous tip."

"An anonymous tip. Which they needed, because they haven't been able to find him for twenty years. But they traced him to my house. Do you think he got sloppy while running for his life? He wanted you to talk to me, because I would tell you I think he's innocent of the attack."

"Why?"

"Because I'm the last person who would believe his innocence."

Kopil did not respond.

"People died on that altar," Caleb said. "My father killed them, and his father, our whole line as far back as memory. Temoc took his first life when he was seven years old. If Craftsmen hadn't freed Dresediel Lex, I would have done the same. I'd fight him until the sun burned black. So he came to me, and told me he was innocent, knowing I was the least friendly witness he could find."

"Do you believe him?"

"I don't know. He seemed sincere."

"You're lying."

"I'm no Craftsman, but I'm no terrorist, either."

"Where do you stand, then?" asked Kopil.

"On my own side."

"Your side hurts."

"Yes," Caleb said when he realized what the King in Red meant. "It does."

Kopil crossed the red rug and stood before Caleb, six feet tall and slender in his crimson robe. He radiated cold power. His skin had rotted decades past, sinews and muscles crumbled, heart shriveled into dust. He endured. A cold wind blew between them.

"Let's fix that," Kopil said. Darkness rolled out from him to drown the world.

Caleb could not flinch or flee. Five arrows struck him in the chest—no, five fingers, and they did not pierce his skin but passed through it as if dipping into a pool of water, water that could feel, and think, and scream. He opened his mouth, and shadow crawled past his lips, over his teeth, wriggled down his throat to nest in his lungs. He could not breathe, but he did not die, and the King in Red began to work.

A second skeletal hand joined the first in Caleb's chest, hot as hatred and cold as love. If not for the shadow filling his mouth, he would have ground his teeth to powder, bit through his tongue. His broken ribs were two arches of jagged glass. Kopil's hands moved over that glass, smoothing and joining. Pain rose in a fugue, variations on a theme of agony.

The music stopped. Light returned. Kopil drew his hands from Caleb's chest. Bits of tissue and spare red drops clung to his skeleton fingers. The mortal refuse smoked, boiled, and burned from the King's pale bones.

Caleb could move again. He touched his side, and found it whole.

The King in Red shook his hands as if to dry them. "Lift your arm. Do you feel any pain?" Caleb did, and felt none. "Inhale." Sweet air filled his lungs. His muscles trembled, and laughing he breathed again.

"How do you feel?"

"Like I just ran here all the way from Fisherman's Vale. Tired in the bones. My stomach's cold."

"Eat well tonight. You almost killed yourself yesterday; I took as little power from you as I could for the healing, but you're weak as if you haven't eaten in days. Go to a restaurant tonight. Order enough for three men. Drink plenty of fluids."

A wrenching, horrid screech erupted from the floor behind the King in Red. Black glass warped open to reveal a staircase that spiraled down into the pyramid.

"Go," the skeleton said. Caleb attempted to walk, staggered, and caught the edge of the altar-desk. He steadied himself, tried another step, and made it halfway to the stairs before Kopil's voice stopped him.

"I know what it's like to be on no one's side but your own."

The King in Red had lifted the picture in the silver frame.

"Sir?"

Kopil opened his palm as if setting a bird free. The picture slid through the air. Caleb caught it, and looked for the first time at the image: an old-fashioned sepia miniature. Two men embraced at the foot of a black pyramid. They were young and smiling and obviously in love, both dark as magisterium wood, one shorter than Caleb, the other tall for a Quechal man, six feet at least and thin, with narrow sloping shoulders. His eyes were black, and his smile looked familiar.

Thin, Caleb thought, so thin he could almost see the bones of the tall man's skull.

Kopil stood beside the desk, beside the altar, his finger bones spread on bloodstained glass. His shoulders were narrow and sloping, and his smile had not changed.

"Eighty years," Caleb guessed.

"More than that."

"What was his name?"

"Timas."

"I'm sorry."

"They took him for the sacrifice to the Hungry Serpents." Kopil tapped the surface of the altar. "He's still here. A piece of him, at least. Two or three drops."

"Why are you telling me this?"

"We all think we're on our own side, until the time comes to declare war."

Caleb released the picture. It flew back and settled on the desk beside the King in Red.

"Go," Kopil said, and Caleb descended into the office building that was once a temple.

INTERLUDE: FLAME

The lake of fire coruscated red and blue and orange. Alaxic, lost in thought, traced the patterns and colors of heat.

Magma breathed sirocco in his face, dried his parchment skin. "I could remain here," he said, "until lava cured me into dust. That would be better, I think."

"You'll like retirement," said the woman at his side: Allesandre, his patient, loyal student; his sacrifice. "Or maybe you won't, but it's for the best. We'll take everything from here. Don't worry."

"I have spent six decades worrying." The old man lifted his hands from the railing and placed them into his pockets with care, as if his bones were porcelain. "Since the God Wars. Since the Skittersill Rising. My life lies down there."

"Don't worry," she said, and gripped his shoulder. "We will finish what you started."

Alaxic felt her strength, and wondered at time, distance, and the wheels of age that grind the great to powder.

Calm and quiet, he left the cave.

Book Two

■ ■ ■

SEVEN LEAF LAKE

16

Serpents covered the gallery wall, asps and vipers, hooded co-
bras, slender finger-wide coral snakes and bulge-bellied anacon-
das. Writhing, they ate each other.

Caleb watched close up, his nose inches from rippling scales.
A diamondback rattler devoured a garden snake; a fat flat-headed
serpent from the jungles of southern Kath ingested the rattler's
tail in turn. Hisses filled his ears.

"Grotesque," he said, and shivered. "I don't know what you
see in Sam's work."

"Grotesquerie," Teo said from behind him.

"That's what I said."

"Not what I meant. That's the name of the piece. Urban Grotesquerie."

"I see where it comes from. This is sick." The rattlesnake
wriggled forward, as if by devouring prey it might escape the
jaws behind.

"It's art. If you're looking at it, it's working."

Caleb turned away.

Teo's gallery was floored in varnished wood and lit by tall
windows facing south. Sam's work hung on the white walls:
twisted, inhuman creations, sculptures of men devouring the
entrails of other men in a cannibalistic network, bas reliefs of
cities that had never been and would never be. On the exhibi-
tion's opening night three weeks before, as Teo chatted up do-
nors, buyers, and benefactors, Caleb had spent twenty minutes
staring at the only thing on the walls that qualified, as far as he
was concerned, as a painting: an image of two triangles interlaced, in oils on unfinished canvas.

Those triangles haunted his sleep for ten days afterward,

towering yet so small he could hold them in his palm. In dreams he tumbled into that painting, his soul stretched long and thin—a thread in rough canvas. Around him he heard other threads, men, women, children, falling forever and screaming as they fell.

Teo sat beside a small table upon which rested an open bottle of champagne and Caleb's empty glass. She drank from her own glass, and smiled as she swallowed. Caleb poured more wine, and offered Teo the last drops, which she refused—"You need good fortune more than I do!" He sat down facing her.

"To fortune," he murmured. They touched glasses and drank together. He watched her as she watched the snakes. A trick of Craft projected their hisses out into the room, so that no matter how Caleb shifted or where he stood, serpents seemed to hover at his back, forked tongues flicking the saddle ridge of his ear. "That's uncomfortable," he said, swatting at empty air.

"It's art," she repeated. "Supposed to be uncomfortable. Makes you think."

"Makes me think about getting eaten by snakes. I saw a snake eat a deer once, out in the Badlands. The deer had been paralyzed, maybe stung by the Scorpionkind or something. This big viper wriggled out of a hole, wrapped the deer up, killed it, and ate it. Some of my nightmares look like that."

"What do the other ones look like?"

He pointed at the wall of serpents.

"This doesn't speak to you? Thousands of snakes, pressed so close together they have to kill one another to eat?"

"You think she's talking about the city."

"Of course she's talking about the city."

"It's different."

"How, exactly?"

"Well. The snakes eat one another," he said, but when she smiled at that he tried again. "People in Dresediel Lex aren't so close together," but that was a difference of degree, and he wanted a difference of kind. "Gods, I don't know. That, though"—he waved vaguely at the wall of snakes—"isn't everything. What about compassion? Love?"

"We get those all the time from cheap romances. Only a true artist can show us this."

"You don't believe the world is that bleak any more than I do."

"I don't have to agree with Sam to like her work."

"Especially if you're sleeping with her."

"Exactly." Teo sipped champagne. "Speaking of which, how is love working out for you so far?"

He looked away from her. "Love has nothing to do with Mal."

"The hell it doesn't. Love, lust, whatever you want to call it. Why else would you almost die trying to protect her?"

He grimaced, and remembered the agony of healing. "To the King in Red."

"To Lord Kopil," Teo said with a jaunty toast to Caleb and the snakes. "Long may he burden my soul with unearned thaums."

"The Heartstone bonus came through this week, I see."

She tapped the curved Iskari lettering on the champagne bottle. "You think I'd pay for a Hospitalier '83 on my salary?" Despite her family's wealth, Teo tried to live within her personal means. The soulstuff her parents pressed on her, she threw into the collection, curation, purchase and sale of art. "The bonus cleared last week. You haven't seen your share?"

"Not yet. Not that I'm hurting for thaums after winning our bet."

"You're lucky I'm the trusting type. I never saw evidence of your victory."

"To your unwarranted faith in my honesty." He drank, and closed his eyes, and the serpents' hisses became the sound of steam in the cave beneath the world, the groan of shifting rock as Aquel and Achal tossed in their sleep. "I'm worried about this deal."

"We've done seven months' due diligence. The King in Red wanted every avenue checked. You personally reread whole sections of that contract."

"I did. Sections. The thing is seventy thousand pages long. They folded space to fit it in one conference room for the signing. It's not even all on paper: some paragraphs are carved on stone plinths, some on the pyramid itself. Nothing that complex is safe."

"Every morning you walk into your bathroom, put your hand to the tap, and fresh water flows out, courtesy of Red King Consolidated. That's a complicated system, and you trust it daily."

"Pipes, filters, pumps I understand. It's easy to tell when they're broken. The Heartstone deal isn't about water. It's about Craft: power pledged on the promise of more power, demonic pacts, bargains with beings beyond our reality. Some of its clauses depend on the going price of souls in the Abyss." An exaggeration; he'd been to some of the nearer hells on business trips, but their denizens did not seem so interested in the soul trade as stories claimed. "The structures of Craft involved are so complex even their creators barely understand them. We've fixed all the problems we can find—it's the problems we can't that worry me."

"That's Sam's point." Teo waved at the snakes on the wall. "This city is stranger and more alien than we can conceive— snakes wriggling over one another, feeding on one another." She interwove her fingers and twitched them.

"Don't remind me."

"Think about it this way," she said. "Look at the snakes again."

"No."

"Do it."

They slithered, devouring but never satisfied: a twist of Craft allowed the serpents being eaten to writhe out of their predators' gullets unscathed, only to be consumed again.

"I'm looking."

"Imagine you were a snake."

"I'd rather not. Especially in this context."

"Imagine you were a snake," she repeated, and he did. He wound over and around himself, forever hungry, consuming as he consumed, his world a matrix of pain and fear. "All you see are snakes, and the world makes no sense at all. But from a distance we see the pattern of which the individual snake is only a piece."

"So you think I should stop worrying about the fact that I can't see how Heartstone fits together?"

"I think you should realize that the world isn't all cut to your scale. Sam's gallery openings and premieres and patrons keep these serpents alive, even though their little snaky brains can't comprehend that stuff. RKC, Heartstone, they're so big they might as well be gods. We shouldn't expect to understand them entirely."

"What about the King in Red? Or Alaxic? Do you think they comprehend what they're doing?"

"They're Deathless Kings. Their minds aren't bound by brains and fleshy bits anymore. Maybe they think differently from the rest of us."

He remembered a small picture in a silver frame, and the way the King in Red leaned against his desk, shoulders slumped and head bowed. "Maybe." Teo glanced at him, curious, but whatever she wanted to ask, she changed her mind.

"Regardless," she said. "May more deals like Heartstone leave us rich in soulstuff and good wine."

"I'll drink to that," Caleb said. On the wall, vipers hissed in a reptilian hell.

17

When Caleb and Teo reached the pyramid at 667 Sansilva, the giant auditorium was already crowded with RKC employees in work robes and formal dress. Snakelings wound about the pillars that supported the balcony, long bodies glistening. Humans, skeletons, and well-preserved zombies, a scattering of Scorpionkind, brass giants bearing the vision-gems of distant Craftsmen, and all the other rabble of RKC crowded in the seats and aisles.

Caleb and Teo shouldered between a golem and a paunchy balding man in a skullcap. The speeches had begun; they could not see the stage, but the vaulted ceiling threw the King in Red's voice down upon them.

"The last three months," Kopil said, "have been a time of trial. Together we spilled gallons of ink and blood. Together we moved mountains. Together we suffered grueling meetings in the Abyss." The crowd murmured assent. Teo had ventured into the Abyss herself during the negotiations, painted in henna and silver wards against the odd intelligences that lived there. "Heartstone Holdings has remade the Craft of dousing and well-drilling in its own image. An analyst at Traeger Matins Laud once suggested that Heartstone might supplant us as provider of water to this city. For a few years, I almost believed they could do it."

The King in Red pitched that line as a joke, and was rewarded by a few uneasy chuckles. Shedding the confines of the flesh had not improved Kopil's sense of humor, but people laughed anyway. Vast power made even bad jokes funny.

Caleb squeezed past a young woman with blue skin and a zombie carrying a brain in a bubbling jar.

"We decided that together we would be greater than either of us apart. Red King Consolidated, of which we are all limbs"—the young woman with blue skin touched her forehead, throat, and heart, as did others scattered through the crowd—"began the dance of union with Heartstone Holdings. Today, we achieve our goal. The contract is signed, the last sigil graven into stone. Red King Consolidated and Heartstone will be one."

A round of applause began, perhaps spontaneously or perhaps a junior executive's attempt to curry favor. Either way, it spread from the front rows through the auditorium. The King in Red was watching. No one wanted to be the only person not to clap.

"I present Alaxic, Chairman of Heartstone, and his Chief Craftswoman Ms. Kekapania, to seal the pact between our firms."

Caleb shouldered at last to the front of the standing crowd, stopped, and stared. Teo tripped and fell into his back, but he did not notice.

Three hundred feet away, the King in Red commanded center stage, his robe bloody, his arms outstretched. Crimson sparks burned from his eye sockets. Shadow cloaked Alaxic beside him.

Mal stood between them.

She wore a charcoal suit, not a cliff runner's leathers, but the cant of her chin and the defiance in her gaze had not changed. Her short hair swept up and back from her head in frozen waves. She looked upon Red King Consolidated, and smiled.

"Mal," Caleb said, and realized that he had spoken out loud, in the silent auditorium. Kopil paused, and searched the audience for the speaker. Mal's smile widened. Had she heard? Did she recognize his voice?

"Malina Kekapania," said the King in Red, "has been my primary liaison with Alaxic throughout this process."

The old man raised his head and moved papery lips. His voice passed over the audience like crumbling windblown leaves. "My blood is shed upon the contract, and signing it, I am quit of Heartstone Holdings." He bared long white teeth in a ghastly grimace of what Caleb hoped was pleasure. "Ms. Kekapania will seal the bargain in my stead." He clutched his hands behind his back, retreated a step, and watched the stage with glittering black eyes.

"What's wrong?" Teo whispered.

"That's her."

"Her who?"

"Mal."

"Some of you," Mal said, to Caleb and to the crowd, "may be surprised to see us here."

No kidding, Caleb thought.

"This deal," she continued, "has hung for months on technicalities and minor disagreements, but its end was never in doubt. Heartstone prides herself on knowing what she wants. The question we've had through these negotiations has always been: what can we do together?" Her eyes scoured the room. "Now we're here. What's next is up to us."

"Yes," Kopil said. Caleb's mouth formed the same word.

The light faded, and Caleb's mind opened to the universe. He fell a hundred stories and did not smash or splatter when he hit bottom, but spread like a drop of water through thin cloth.

A silver-blue gossamer net connected the audience. Caleb breathed, and two thousand pairs of lungs breathed with him. Two thousand hearts beat in two thousand breasts.

He sank into the ocean of Red King Consolidated. Blood rushed in his veins and water rushed in pipes under the desert. Lightning danced down his nerves, crackled along glyph lines across the city. Octopus arms of Craft wove through sea and stone, binding RKC to Deathless Kings and giant Concerns in cities across continents and oceans: to Alt Coulumb, to Shikaw and Regis, to the metropolitan sprawls of the Shining Empire, the mines of Koschei, the gear-bound desert cities of King Clock.

The King in Red shone crimson. A million contracts wove through the iron bars of his spirit, and bound him. Caleb could not see where his soul ended and RKC began.

Mal stood transfigured, a figure of adamant edged with razor blades. Space bent with her breath.

In the dark behind them both, Alaxic lurked half-visible, avuncular ghost to their glory.

The world doubled: Caleb saw the King in Red on stage, doll-sized by distance, a puppet of the cords that bound him, and saw himself also through the King in Red's eyes, caught in webs of silver. They were all at once themselves and not themselves, human and Deathless King, mortal and immortal, bound by dread pact and mystic pledge.

The King in Red turned to Mal, the blazing anchor of the world.

"I stand embodied representative for Red King Consolidated, as majority owner of my soul and Chief Executive of this Concern." Caleb's lips did not open, but his mind echoed the words. The King in Red spoke for him, for all of them. "I accept the terms of our contract and the privileges and responsibilities stipulated there."

Mal, or rather Heartstone Holdings overshadowing her, stared into Kopil's burning eyes and said through dagger teeth: "I stand embodied in this my servant; as Heartstone, I accept the terms and conditions of our pact, and the responsibilities and privileges therein. What we forge today never will be sundered."

"What we forge today never will be sundered," Kopil repeated and the audience with him.

Mal drew close, walking six inches above the stage as if the air was solid ground. The King in Red embraced her, and she returned his embrace with arms of fire; their worlds tilted toward each other, and they kissed.

It was not the kiss Caleb remembered from the night of the blackout. That had been soft and harsh and strong, but a human softness, a human harshness and a human strength. This was a god-kiss, skeletal teeth touching lips cool and strong as marble, two colossal powers driven by a need that was not desire, an eagerness that was not passion. One was the shadow cast by the other, but which was which?

Or was each the shadow cast, and neither one the caster?

Thorns pierced the King in Red and Heartstone-in-Mal, and spread, weaving through Kopil's bones and coursing in Mal's blood. Barbs curled out of Kopil's eye sockets and burst Mal's eyes from the inside, flowered between his teeth and ripped her throat and tongue as they tied, and tangled, and became one.

Seventy-thousand-page contracts sitting in the RKC archives

erupted with unearthly light. Blood signatures burned into reality; silver glyphs appeared on stone circles and obelisks throughout Dresediel Lex and in cities around the world, as if etched in an instant by giants with diamond chisels. The pacts built by hundreds of Craftsmen over thousands of billable hours were loose strands of rope, and the kiss one pull tightening them to a knot.

Seconds passed, grains of sand falling down a well deep as forever. Through ticks of agony Caleb wondered how Mal could bear the pain.

The deed was done. The thorns joined. Heartstone Holdings was itself no longer, subsumed into RKC; Red King Consolidated was itself no longer, transformed by consuming Heartstone.

Mal's lips clung briefly to Kopil's teeth, so gently did he pull away. Before she fell, she clutched him tight, leaned in until her cheek brushed the side of his skull, and whispered into his ear-well: "Still interested?"

She sank to the stage. The lightning frame of Heartstone left her and wound about the King in Red, a separate form at first, then a swelling within the firestorm of his being, then merged entirely and gone.

Caleb collapsed into his own skin. Others glanced about in confusion, wondering at the significance of Mal's last words. Some code between her and the King in Red, a joke or dare: speculation whispered through the awed hush.

Caleb did not wonder. He turned to Teo.

"I have to go," he said, and fought toward the door.

18

Caleb sprinted through twisting halls and passages, all alike. By intuition and dumb luck he soon found an iron door fitted with latches resembling eagle's claws—a former fasting chamber that served visiting speakers as a green room. Mal would be there now, resting. Caleb touched the door, the latches gave, and he tumbled into a small room hung with yellow-and-black tapestries. Ghostlight danced in iron braziers on the walls.

Mal, Alaxic, and the King in Red sipped sparkling wine around a stone basin in the room's center.

She would be resting, yes. Or else celebrating the deal with two of the city's most powerful Craftsmen.

"Mister Altemoc?" The King in Red sounded shocked, even amused. Caleb backed toward the door.

"Hi," he said. "Sir," and "Sir," again to shrunken Alaxic, who regarded him with narrowed eyes and a thin, warped smile. "Excuse me. I should, um. Go."

Don't say anything, he begged Mal with his eyes.

"Caleb! What a surprise!"

"Ms. Kekapania." Kopil's skull revolved from Caleb to the woman beside him. "Are you and Mr. Altemoc acquainted?"

She raised her glass to Caleb first, then to the Deathless King and Alaxic. She drank. "We're dating, actually."

"Dating?"

Caleb and his boss spoke at the same time. They looked at each other, then back at Mal. She shrugged. "I wasn't convinced at first, either, but he's persistent."

The blood red sparks of Kopil's eyes winked out, and returned. Caleb had never seen the King in Red blink before.

"I didn't know she worked for Heartstone when I met her," he said.

Mal raised an eyebrow. "You wouldn't have come after me if you knew who I was?"

"It would have changed the way I approached you. Yes."

She raised her glass in a salute and downed its contents.

Kopil's shoulders shook. A noise like grinding gravel issued from somewhere below the hinge of his jaw.

The King in Red was laughing.

"I'll leave," Caleb said, and reached behind him to open the door. He did not want to take his eyes off the three Craftsmen. "I'm so sorry I burst in. I didn't expect anyone would be here."

"Sure, sure, sure." Kopil nodded three times. "Take the day off." He spun his finger bones in a circle above the basin. Water droplets took the shape of miniature nymphs, who skidded over the surface like skaters over ice. "Let us all celebrate Alaxic's retirement."

"The pleasure is mine. I leave you to inherit the rising salaries and health-care costs of my employees, my tempestuous engineering department, and my other bureaucratic diseases. I, meanwhile, will retire and find a hobby. Gardening, perhaps."

"Lord Kopil," Mal said, "may I escort Caleb out?"

"Of course. Go. Get out of our hair. Metaphorical hair, in my case. Try not to kill him. Hard to replace good people these days."

"Lord Kopil, Lord Alaxic." Mal said as she bowed to each. "It's been a pleasure. Let's do this again soon." She grabbed the sleeve of Caleb's jacket, and pulled him into the hall after her. Behind them, the water nymphs began to scream. Their high-pitched cries pursued Caleb and Mal through the maze of passages.

"What is going on here," Caleb said when he thought they were safely out of earshot. She turned on him with a finger to her lips, and said nothing more until they reached the front door of the pyramid and stepped out into sunshine.

"How's this?"

"Not far enough. Why don't you buy me a drink?"

Mal raised her hand. A four-foot-long dragonfly fell from the sky with a whir like a thick book's pages being fanned, and landed on Mal's outstretched arm. Translucent wings split sunlight into a rainbow haze. Another dragonfly landed on Caleb's shoulder, bowl-sized eye inches from his face. He flinched, and resisted the urge to brush the insect away.

Mal laughed at his shock, and stroked her opteran's thorax. Broad wings twitched in anticipation. "You don't take fliers often?"

"Isn't the airbus good enough for you? These things," he said with a flick at his opteran's exoskeleton, "are expensive."

"They are expensive," she allowed. "And your Concern just closed the largest deal in its history. Celebrate."

Her teeth gleamed in the sunlight. The creature perched on her forearm regarded him with many-faceted eyes, each facet quizzical.

Optera were descended from smaller bugs the gods and priests had used to ferry packages across the city. After Liberation, Craftsmen swelled the creatures' size, gave them unnatural strength, and changed their diet. Instead of other bugs, fliers fed on the souls of those they bore aloft. "There are stories," he said, contemplating its feathery proboscis, "of young Craftswomen riding these things drunk."

"I've heard them."

"They get so caught up in the flight that they forget to land. The opteran brings a husk back, or nothing at all."

"Some girls don't know when to quit," Mal said. "Same for boys."

"Where to?"

"You choose. Last time I made you follow me. I don't want to seem unfair."

"Emphasis on the 'seem.' You're happy *being* unfair."

She lifted the opteran to her shoulder. Joints clicked as it crawled over her. Two long limbs latched under her arms. Two circled her waist, and two her thighs. Translucent wings spread from her back. She wore the creature as a mantle, its monstrous head rising above her own.

"See if you can catch me," he said, moved the opteran to his own back, and flew.

19

They landed on one of the balconies that bloomed like flower pet-
als from Andrej's penthouse bar. The optera buzzed off, leaving
Caleb and Mal alone with sky and city and declining sun. An
airbus drifted past between them and the light.

"What do you think?" With one sweep of his arm Caleb took
in the view.

"It is wonderful," she said. "You could watch the world end
from here and be happy for it."

"I don't often come to Andrej's when the sun's up. The games
start late."

"You gamble," she said.

"I play cards. Poker, mostly."

"What else?"

"Bridge, when I was a kid. Not so often these days."

"Why'd you stop?"

"I lost my partner."

Wind and surf filled the silence between them. She turned
from the city and leaned against the railing, arms crossed, head
lowered, waiting for the question Caleb did not know how to ask.

"Who are you?" was the best he could manage.

"What do you mean?"

"When I met you, you said you were a cliff runner. You said
you broke into Bright Mirror Reservoir because it was good exercise."

"It was good exercise."

"And your being a senior Heartstone executive had nothing
to do with it."

"I'm hardly senior," she said.

"I put myself at risk for you, and I don't mean just chasing you over rooftops. I didn't tell the King in Red about you, or the Wardens. I could be fired for that—hells, I could be tried and convicted. I trusted you."

"Not smart, trusting someone you've only met once."

"I never claimed I was smart. I don't know if you owe me an explanation, but I want one. And I think you'll give it to me."

She walked from the railing to the balcony door. It was locked. "They don't open for another twenty minutes."

"You planned this, I see."

"Didn't you?"

She frowned, turned from him, and paced the balcony, weaving between tables and chairs. He did not move, but followed her with his eyes.

At last, she wheeled on him, feet wide-planted, hands on her hips. "Alaxic told me he didn't trust your security. Not with the Serpents at stake. He knew I ran, and he asked me to run a penetration test. Not to break anything, just get in if I could, and out again."

"He wanted leverage against the King in Red."

"Of course. He had to send someone he could trust. But he couldn't give me anything to help, in case I was caught. So I found a Quechal glyph-artist in the Skittersill who made that pendant. Claimed it would hide me from anything."

"It did more than hide you."

She crossed her arms and turned away. Caleb waited.

"I know," she said at last. "I didn't realize until after you took it from me. I've never dealt with Quechal glyphwork. If the tooth was made with modern Craft, I would have seen right away. I was blind, and I guess I deserve to suffer for it. The blackout, the Tzimet, your dead guard, my dead friends—the cliff runners who died at North Station—those are my fault. So you're safe. I can't turn you in, because you'd do the same to me. For all I know, you'll do that anyway."

"I won't," he said.

"Why not?"

He sought the dry blue sky for an answer, finding none. "I need a drink," he said at last.

"I'll buy."

He walked to the balcony door and rapped his knuckle against the glass until the bartender heard, and opened the door to ask their business. "Drinking," Caleb said, and Mal added, "Dancing." The bartender regarded them both skeptically, but she recognized Caleb and, after a few thaums changed hands, she let them inside.

Chairs stood on tables. The marble tiles were clean-swept. A quartet tuned on the stage by the dance floor—drums, bass, piano, and trombone, dinner jackets immaculate white. Caleb ordered a gin and tonic, Mal single malt on the rocks; the bartender set the glasses in front of them and busied herself stocking the icebox for the evening.

"To you," he said. "Whoever you are."

"That's hardly a fair toast." She pulled her glass away from his.

"You know me—my job, my family, or at least my father. I only learned your full name today."

"Well." Her whiskey cast golden light on the bar. "My name doesn't get you much. My parents died when I was a kid. My aunt and uncle couldn't support me, but a scholarship sent me to a good school, and after that to the Floating Collegium." Caleb recognized the name: an academy of Craft a hundred miles farther up the coast and inland. Classy place, good sports teams. "Once I graduated, I drifted back to the city. Heartstone was new then, and growing. Alaxic was one of the sponsors of my scholarship, and he offered me a position. How's that?"

"It's a start."

"A start, he says. It's not as though I know much more about you."

"You know more than most of the people who work with me."

"You mean, they don't know who your father is."

"I don't exactly spread it around. Like you say—Temoc's a pretty common name."

"I don't care about your father," she said with another sip of whiskey. "He's no mystery. Unlike you."

"What do you mean by that?"

Mal left her drink at the bar, and walked to the band's dais. She spoke briefly to their leader, passed him a sliver of silver. Half-formed melodies and scales cohered: the bass the spine, the drums ribs, the piano and horn meat and sinews of music.

Her hips rolled to the beat as she returned. She held out a hand, and said, "Let's dance."

He let her lead him onto the floor.

Caleb was not a good dancer, but Mal was. She matched his steps, and by her body's alchemy transformed his unfinished movements into gold. His hand fit below her shoulder blades as if sculpted for that purpose, and her fingers rested warm against his palm.

The walking bass line quickened, and with it Caleb's steps and Mal's. Caleb could not tell who led whom. He lifted his arm, perhaps in answer to a suggestion from her wrist, and she spun, white skirt flaring with the force of her revolution. Stepping through, he turned, too, her arm falling to his waist and his to hers.

Drums beat in syncopation with Caleb's heart, one two quickstep. Their turns swelled and sharpened as cymbals clashed and the drums took their solo.

Mal's fingers slipped from Caleb's hand. He lurched, too slow, to catch her, but as she started to fall, invisible cords caught his arm. Her Craft lines snapped taut and Mal stopped in midair, rigid as a plank, her left arm extended toward Caleb. Beneath the skin of her arms and fingers, glyphs glowed silver. With a snap of arm and shoulder, she pulled herself back up, and spun toward him once more.

He let momentum carry her past him. His hand moved in a swift half circle, and he grabbed at empty air. He caught her Craft line, solid, invisible, and cold, and Mal stopped.

Pale light streamed from the scars on Caleb's arms. He pulled her back to him.

Sweat beaded on her forehead and her lip. "I didn't know you had glyphwork."

"I don't."

She didn't ask him to explain. They danced, touching and not touching, bound by invisible cord, each in accelerating orbit of the other. Her glyphs left tracks of shadow in the air, and his scars trailed light.

The band played three songs, a small set, before breaking to prepare in earnest for the evening. Neither Caleb nor Mal objected. Leaning against each other, they staggered to the nearest table and called for the bartender. Waiting, Caleb watched Mal. She hugged her shoulders and shivered. The Craft devoured heat, life force, soulstuff. Combining Craftwork and physical exertion—no wonder she was cold.

"You're a great dancer," he said.

"You're not bad yourself." Her hands traced a cat's cradle in the air before her. "What are those scars?"

He turned away from her, to the empty dance floor.

"Tell me."

"It's personal."

"Okay," she said. "Fine."

Caleb ordered soda water and Mal a mug of hot tea when the waiter drifted past. After she left, Mal said: "It was an excellent dance. I'm sorry if I was too curious. All the Lords and Ladies know there are parts of my life I don't like to talk about."

"Okay." Caleb rolled down his shirt cuffs, and buttoned them. "It's a sensitive subject. I'm sorry."

"I can live with that." Their drinks arrived. Greedily, Mal drank her tea, both the liquid and the heat inside it: she touched the mug, the glyphs on her hands sparked, and frost spread from her touch. By the time the mug reached her lips, dew clung to its sides. Color returned to her cheeks.

She set her empty mug down. Ice crystals encased the tea leaves within. Strange future, for someone. "Where do we go from here?"

"What do you mean?"

"I told your boss we were dating, to keep you from saying something stupid and ruining our careers. I don't find the idea of dating you repellant, of course."

"Gee, thanks."

"My point is, we have a choice. We don't need to keep up the illusion. I can walk out of here now, never look back. Our paths probably won't cross again. Your boss never needs to know I spied on him, or that you hid information. Either that, or we could try to make this work."

"What do you mean?"

She leaned across the table toward him. "Are you . . . interested in me?"

He remembered her eyes, black and endless, in his living room, in the dark, after the explosion.

He tried to speak, but could not. Across the room, the bass played a slow, deep scale. "Yes," he said, at last.

"Good. Me too." She stood and placed a silver coin on the table to cover her drinks.

"You're leaving?"

She smiled with one side of her mouth, like a crack in a stained-glass window. "Last time we were together, I gave you an invitation, and you declined. I can't just come to you because you want me now."

"I'm serious." He stood, so she could not look down on him.

"So am I. But I don't want to rush this." She revolved around the table to him, eclipsing the world as she approached. "Do you trust me?"

"You saved my life."

"Say it."

"I trust you."

"I'll come for you in my own time. Find someone else, if you're not comfortable waiting; plenty of girls out there wouldn't mind you. If you'd rather have someone who wants you, someone you want in turn, then wait, and let me claim you when I claim you."

"You enjoy this."

"Making you suffer? Maybe a little." She held her hand up next to her eye, thumb and forefinger an inch apart. "You can handle it. You're a strong young man. Loyal. Brave." She slapped him on the shoulder, hard. "And a good dancer."

"I'll wait. Not forever, but I'll wait."

"I know."

She turned from him and left. Doors opened without her touching them, and drifted closed behind. Her afterimage burned in the dark behind his eyes, dimming from gold to red to purple to colors deeper than black, an invisible brand on his brain.

He lifted her coin from the table, felt the piece of her soul worked into it, and walked her down his knuckles and up again.

If he could have seen through the bartender's eyes when she came to refill his drink, he would have recognized his grin—though he had only seen it on Mal's face before.

He ordered his dinner and sat alone while lovers, dancers, and gamesmen drifted in to Andrej's bar. Deep in thought. Laying plans.

20

Two weeks later, the water ran black.

Caleb and Teo were sharing dinner in her apartment over a game of chess. Sam lay supine on the couch. A glass of cold white wine dangled from her fingers.

Every year, when spring evaporated into the punishing heat of desert summer, Teo stole a few bottles of old wine from her family's cellar and held a private bacchanal. Caleb was a usual guest on these occasions, but this year he had not expected to attend—Sam harbored sharp, serrated feelings toward him after his interruption the night of the Bright Mirror disaster. She caved to Teo's pressure at the last moment, though, and Caleb received an invitation the day before the event. Sam was friendlier in person than Caleb expected—which was to say, cold and gratingly radical, but she had not yet opened outright hostilities.

Their games proceeded in triangular fashion—Caleb lost to Teo, who loved chess though she did not study it, and Teo lost to Sam, who was too busy railing against the hierarchical relationships encoded in the rules to notice how blatantly Teo let her win. Sam lost to Caleb, and the cycle repeated.

Teo's bishop scythed across the board to complete Caleb's most recent humiliation. He stood, swayed, and surrendered his seat to Sam, then excused himself to the kitchen.

High and far back in Teo's cabinet he found a clean mug, placed it in the sink, and touched a glyph on the dragon-headed faucet. The glyph glowed, ripping away a fragment of soul so small Caleb barely felt it, and the faucet vomited black water over his hand into the mug.

He cursed, dropped the mug, and reached for a towel. The black sludge kept flowing, and a rancid, rotting odor filled the kitchen. When he slapped the faucet glyph, the flow stopped. He touched it again, testing. The dragon disgorged three more drops into Teo's sink, retched, and died.

"Teo?"

"Did you break something?" Sam called back.

"Teo, does your building have any trouble with RKC? Anything wrong with the water?"

"No. Hells, if there was trouble I'd be the first one with a torch and pitchfork." Noise from the living room: Teo pushing her chair back from the table. "What's wrong?"

"The water's black."

"What do you mean?" Before he could answer, she reached the kitchen door and saw, smelled, for herself. She blanched. "Gods. What is that?"

She sounded more shocked than a broken sink would warrant. Caleb began to turn, to see if he'd missed something.

Several small, sharp knives struck him in the back at high speed. He fell, cursing. Hooked claws tore at his skin. Groping over his shoulder, he felt a shell of slick, curved chitin, cold as ice. Small legs scraped his hand. He ripped the creature from his back and threw it across the room. A black, sharp blur, it struck the wall and splashed into a hundred fat droplets. Caleb bent forward, and panted. He heard Teo swear, and looked up.

The droplets had grown legs, pincers, snapping mandibles, multifaceted eyes. Sprouting from the wall, they skittered across the floor toward him.

Tzimet.

In the water.

"Shit!" He staggered back, flailing for a weapon. From the sink he heard a clatter of claws and teeth. His clutching fingers found Teo's knife block. He drew a cleaver and whirled to face the sink, from which reared an insect the size of a small dog, mandibles gnashing.

The cleaver passed through the creature's head, struck the sink, skidded and sparked. Caleb slipped and fell, still holding the knife. The creature hissed, and the droplet-bugs advanced. Teo grabbed a broom and struck the little bugs with its bristles. The sink-thing flopped onto the counter, and thudded to the floor a few inches from Caleb's leg.

"What's going on in there?" Sam, approaching from the living room. "You two better—" She cut off, and drew a heavy breath.

Caleb raised the knife as the sink-creature scuttled toward him, recovered from its fall. Not that the knife would do much good. He needed a broom of his own, or a stick, or—

A frying pan slammed down onto the Tzimet, pulping shell, claw, leg, and staring eye, and shattering ceramic floor tiles. Sam raised the pan and brought it down again. The wet black smear stopped moving.

Sam extended her hand to him. Blond hair frizzed into a halo about her head.

"Thanks," he said, his voice heavy with shock.

"No problem," she replied. "I can't believe that worked."

Teo had given up sweeping the bugs away in favor of spearing them with her broom's bristles. She struck, and the creatures popped into tiny, inert puddles. "What are these things?"

"Tzimet," Caleb said as Sam pulled him to his feet.

"Like at Bright Mirror."

"But smaller."

Caleb heard a scream from the apartment next door.

"What in all hells is going on?" Teo asked, but Caleb was no longer in the kitchen to answer her.

He ran out of Teo's apartment toward the neighboring flat. The door was closed; he knocked, and wished he were sober. The woman inside cried out again, and he struck the door with his shoulder and all the strength his scars could give him. The door burst off its hinges, and he stumbled into a grim gray living room heavy with the stench of sulfur and burnt metal and old blood. A gray-haired woman in a bathrobe swung a thick pillow against a horde of animated shower-droplets, spiders carved from black ice. Caleb grabbed towels from the bathroom, and tossed them to Sam and Teo as they ran in through the front door after him. Together, they smothered the little evil things with the towels. The towels, at least, did not rise up against them.

The neighbor stared dumbfounded at her stained rug and linens, at her traitor bathroom, at Caleb.

"Water inspectors, Ma'am," Caleb lied, and flashed his RKC identification. "Reports of hard water in this area. I have to take a sample; do you have a small bottle I could borrow?"

The neighbor was an amateur chemist, and from her back room workbench (alchemical sigils shed dim light on glass retorts, phials of quicksilver and phosphorescent dye; a dead mouse, arms and legs pinned to the points of a triangle), she produced a small test tube with a rubber stopper, which he filled with water wrung from the towels.

Placing the tube in a pocket of his blazer, he made a quick excuse—"more apartments to see, sorry for the inconvenience, please direct any questions or concerns to customer service"— and backed hastily through the front door, urging her not to open her taps until further notice.

In the hall, he exchanged harried looks with Sam and Teo. Sam's skin flushed red with action and anger; Teo tried three times to speak and at last stammered: "What the hell, Caleb?"

"I don't know. We locked the Tzimet in Bright Mirror. They couldn't get out." But his mind betrayed him with images of Mal's necklace, of the white-winged woman burning in the sky over North Station, of his father. The Tzimet could not escape unaided, but there were forces more pernicious and persistent than demons working against the city. "We need to get to the office."

From down the hall came another cry, deeper, a man's. Teo glanced from him, to Sam, then back in the direction of the scream.

Before she could say anything, Sam interrupted. "I'll take care of it. You two get to work. Fix this." Before either of them could object, she sprinted down the hall, a towel clutched in each hand.

"She's a keeper," Caleb said when Sam was out of earshot.

"I'll get my coat," Teo replied.

Pedestrians shuddered on the sidewalk, wearing housecoats and trousers, crying or shouting, clutching cuts through clothes and skin. Wardens clogged the sky. One broke a high window in the Seven Stars, and jumped inside. Glass shards rained down, and Caleb took cover under his jacket.

Caleb and Teo caught a driverless carriage across town. Sky-spires drifted in the evening clouds. Crisscross ribbons of traffic coursed through the heavens along lanes marked by hovering lanterns: west to the suburbs, east or south toward the nighttime carnivals of Monicola Pier and the Skittersill. Buses of day labor-ers floated back to their tired camps in Stonewood amid the skel-etons of trees. The sky was mostly empty of Wardens.

"Looks like the Tzimet haven't spread far," Teo said.

"Not yet."

The carriage turned onto an elevated road, and streets sank out of view as the horse surged to full gallop. They had the road to themselves. Few carts or wagons crossed the city's center so late; the densest traffic was farther south, near the port, where trucks pulled by oxen and giant lizards bore freight from the oceangoing ships docked at Longsands to warehouses in Skitter-sill and Fisherman's Vale.

They descended from the elevated road to surface streets. A fight boiled outside a busy nightclub: girls in short spangled dresses and young men in wide-brimmed hats flailed at one an-other. Water sellers hawked refreshment to the drunk and disor-derly. Those carts would have long lines in front of them soon. For sixty years, the city's need for water had been satisfied without fail by the taps, pipes, wells, and dams of Red King Consolidated. That chain was broken.

At last the darkness of the 700 block closed around them. No streetlamps here, where they would wash out the starlight great Concerns needed for their Craft. The pregnant moon shone over-head. Pinprick stars winked in distant mockery.

Caleb shivered. In Camlaan and Iskar and Alt Coulumb—across most of Kath, for that matter—poets wrote odes to the beauty of the stars. The Quechal knew better. Great demons lived between the stars, and in them, beings immense in power and size, who sucked the marrow from suns and sang songs that drove galaxies mad.

There were demons on earth, now, too.

He watched the skies, and thought about death, riots, and Tzimet. To full-grown, healthy men and women, creatures like the ones he and Sam had fought presented little danger, but not everyone was full-grown and healthy. Many would fall, and die, tonight. The stars would watch, and hunger.

The usual protesters chanted outside 667 Sansilva. Teo and Caleb left the cab and shouldered past the crowd toward the pyramid. A squad of RKC employees had erected complaint booths in the parking lot, in front of trucks stacked high with pipes and wire. Good. They already knew. Some emergency policy, gathering dust in the archives beside deals with dead gods and distant autarchs, must have been wiped clean and consulted. He hoped the customer service scripts were not decades out of date.

The lobby stank of cigarettes, despite the no-smoking signs. Stress drove men and women to long-unopened packs stored in the backs of drawers or at the desks of trusted friends. They congregated beneath bas-reliefs of the Red King's triumph, and smoked and whispered in tight clutches. Caleb and Teo crossed the lobby and listened, taut as antennas. They did not speak until they reached a blissfully empty lift.

"Sounds like the attack is limited to downtown," Caleb said when the doors rolled shut. "And pieces of Sansilva."

"No gods anymore," Teo commented as the lift began to rise.

"No."

"Then who do we thank for small favors?"

He closed his eyes and melted into the lift wall. "Shit. This is all my fault somehow."

"We don't know if it's anybody's fault, yet."

"Can't be an accident. Tzimet before, Tzimet now. We have an enemy."

"If so," Teo said, "we'll find them."

The elevator rose through their silence.

"You'll be up all night," she said.

"You, too. Your office will be flooded with messenger rats."

"Don't remind me. Thousands of notes of desperation, and nothing I can do but pass them along to the service department, who will be even worse off than either of us. Do you think people are okay, out there?"

"I hope so." A bell chimed, doors rolled back, and Caleb stepped out. "Good luck with the rats," he called to Teo as the elevator resumed its ascent behind him.

Most of the offices and cubicles in risk management were dark. Even workaholic Tollan was gone: visiting her mother in the farthest recesses of Fisherman's Vale, where bungalows bordered on orange groves.

She would be back, as would the others, but in the meantime that left Caleb in charge. And the King in Red would want answers, soon.

Light streamed under the door of a conference room down the hall, the department's only sign of life.

He thrust the door open, and it struck the wall with a mighty noise. Mick and the few other actuaries that constituted his army looked up from the documents sprawled on the conference table. Paper fluttered in the draft; ghostlight shone from Craft circles scrawled onto slate walls. A young woman hunched over a gutted chicken on a silver tray. The room stank of fear and auspices.

He saw himself through their eyes: hair wild, eyes wide, clothes shredded. Blood seeped from the wound in his shoulder.

"Ladies," he said. "Gentlemen. Tell me what you know. And someone, please find me a bandage."

21

Forty-five minutes later, Caleb stood in a dark and spacious room, addressing figures wrapped in shadow. "The black sludge is basically water." He removed the test tube from his pocket and placed it on the long mahogany table. "Laden with muck, heavy metals, and particulate refuse, obviously unsafe to drink, but water nonetheless. Water, infested with Tzimet."

"We are fortunate it appeared so unappetizing," said Ostrakov, the Chief of Operations, from a seat to Caleb's left. "Imagine if someone drank Tzimet water. We are doubly fortunate that only the wealthiest districts were affected. The Skittersill would have rioted by now."

"Do not underestimate the number of disturbances we have put down tonight," said gray-faced Chihuac of the Security Bureau. She wore a Warden's badge and number, but no mask: the public, human face of Dresediel Lex's police. "Seventy-three arrests in the last two hours, for public brawling, disturbing the peace, arson, assault, and second-degree sedition. That's aside from the injuries caused directly by Tzimet."

"And why is our water no longer safe to drink?" Lord Kopil leaned forward from his throne at the far end of the table. Darkness rippled around him like a cloak, and the fires of his eyes flared.

Caleb's throat was too dry for him to swallow. Tollan sat at the table beside Chihuac, but there had been no time to bring her up to speed before the meeting. This was his play.

He tapped a Craft circle on the table. On the wall behind him, a wriggling colony of glowworms flared to display a map of the west coast of Northern Kath. Dresediel Lex strangled a giant bay in the continent's southwest corner. Blue lines wound from the city across the blasted desert, north and east into mountain ranges and south into the jungles of the Fangs. "Most of our water comes from Bay Station." He gestured to a glowing dot at the harbor's mouth. "But we haven't been able to expand its production since the mid-eighties, while the population of Dresediel Lex has grown three percent a year. More people means we need more water—for manufacture and agriculture as well as drinking and bathing. The native water table is already too depleted to support the city. We've contracted with other Concerns to pump water from springs, lakes, and rivers in the wilderness. Heartstone was one of the most productive of these contracts; that's why we subsumed them." It was not precise to say devour, though that was the word Caleb used in private to describe the process: Heartstone lived on within the hideous, many-limbed organism of RKC.

"One of their main projects was Seven Leaf Lake, a natural reservoir in the northern Drakspine. Eighty square miles of surface area, and deep—a hundred twenty eight million acre-feet, fed by snowmelt and mountain springs, with a refresh time of about two hundred years. Seven Leaf has enough water to sustain our growth for another decade at least. Over the last two years, Heartstone has bound the local spirits and opened an aqueduct between Dresediel Lex and Seven Leaf. Three days ago we began mixing Seven Leaf water with the DL system, specifically in Sansilva and downtown. We chose those districts to limit unrest in the event of any, ah, problems."

When he said "we," he spoke figuratively. No one had asked his advice about these decisions. But he was a part of something larger than himself—one limb of a reeling beast.

"The Seven Leaf water is tainted." Caleb removed a second phial of black water from his pocket. "Maintenance tapped this direct from the Seven Leaf aqueduct half an hour ago." He removed the phial's cap and poured foul black liquid onto the table.

It landed on the lacquered wood with eight legs sharp as scythes, an exoskeleton lacking guts or soft tissue. Mandibles clashed in the air. The tiny Tzimet screeched with organs that were not quite vocal chords, and pounced at Ostrakov, who vaporized it with a backhand wave.

Kopil's red gaze turned to Alana Mazetchul, head of the Pipeline group—draped in robes, her face fallow and lined as if she had not slept in months. "Were there any signs of contamination in Seven Leaf Lake before tonight?"

"No," Mazetchul replied. "None of Heartstone's water came to us tainted, nor do their projects have a history of Craft trouble. We performed extensive tests on Seven Leaf Station before Heartstone was subsumed."

She left that sentence hanging, and Caleb recognized his cue. "The corruption could have two sources: either the aqueducts and pipes are faulty—unlikely considering the number of wards that would have to malfunction—or the problem lies at the source, with Seven Leaf Station or the lake itself. Seven Leaf Lake contains about a hundred and a quarter million acre-feet of water. It could not have become this corrupted in a few weeks. Trouble at the station is the likely cause: accident, assault, act of gods. We can't raise the station by nightmare telegraph, which supports this theory."

"An attack using Tzimet," Tollan added, "would fit the pattern established by Bright Mirror Reservoir."

Caleb waited for someone else to speak. When no questions or objections rose, he continued.

"Until we fix the problem at Seven Leaf, we'll have to meet the city's water needs somehow. Conjuring water out of thin air, or purifying the ocean with evaporation, is expensive. To subsume Heartstone, we issued private bonds, and borrowed funds from other Concerns including First Soul of Alt Coulumb, the Collective of Iskari Faith, and Kyrie Thaumaturgics. If we borrow more, other Deathless Kings will doubt our creditworthiness, which leaves us open to attack. Unless we find a major source of soulstuff, our only other option will be to adopt rolling droughts within the city."

Kopil shifted in his chair. Hidden snakes rubbed scales against scales in the darkness around the table. "There will be riots, if we institute a drought."

"There will be riots anyway." That was Chihuac. "Sansilva and downtown may be more easily cowed than the Skittersill, but the limits of the people's patience have been tested. Rolling droughts will manage social unrest."

"Exactly," Caleb said. "We can't afford to appear weak, especially if we are: a lack of confidence will make it even harder to borrow the soulstuff we need to survive this."

"Why not use the Serpents?"

An opening door shed light into the dark conference room, and Mal stood on its threshold. Caleb's first impulse was to run toward her, but he suppressed the urge, and watched.

Mal's words rippled through the room. Ostrakov swore in a language Caleb did not recognize. Chihuac and Mazetchul turned to the King in Red, either for reassurance or to watch his reaction. Tollan grimaced.

Kopil spoke, his voice heavy with death and time. "I summoned Ms. Kekapania to this meeting. I am glad she has chosen to attend. If Heartstone has exposed us, Heartstone should stand to account."

The door closed behind Mal. "Sorry I'm late. The crowd's grown outside." Her footsteps approached through the dark. Stripes of lamplight revealed and concealed her by turns as she circled the table. "I'll do better than stand to account. I can fix this."

"Explain."

"The Serpents have all the power we need. You've wanted an excuse to draw on them for months."

Caleb glanced down at his notes, turned a few pages, and found the figure he sought. "We'd have to spend more power keeping them asleep than we can draw from them."

"Much more," Mal said. "But over a longer time. The Serpents grant you a reprieve. Think of it as a loan to yourself, with interest."

"That doesn't make sense. We can't loan soulstuff to ourselves." He expected others to join in, but no one spoke. All eyes had turned to Kopil.

The King in Red's eyes burned in shadow. "Your people have caused this chaos. Why should we trust you to fix it?"

Before the dread lord of RKC, Mal looked smaller than he remembered.

"Because I can imagine what you'll do to us if we fail," she said.

"Can you."

"I have a powerful imagination."

"It will be worse than you imagine. For you not least of all."

"Give me a chance. Use the Serpents to preserve the illusion of your strength. In three days, I can fix Seven Leaf Lake." She held so still the world seemed to spin around her. "If all the demons from all the hells stand in my way, I will break them."

In the ensuing silence Caleb heard the breaths of the four people in the room who still breathed: Tollan, Chihuac, Mal, and himself. Most of RKC's executive board had discarded lungs and blood on the thorn-paved path to their current positions.

"So let it be," Kopil said. "We will send Caleb with you."

The number of breaths reduced by one. Stunned to strangulation, Caleb looked up at his boss. Bony hands rested on the table beside Kopil's mug of cold coffee.

Mal bore the King in Red's gaze, and Caleb's, and the board's, as if they were the stares of frightened rabbits.

"Alone?" Caleb asked.

"Of course not." The King in Red struck his teeth together, and Caleb heard laughter echo up from a deep well. "You'll travel with an escort of Wardens, on our fastest Couatl. Leaving tomorrow morning, you should reach Seven Leaf early the following day. Assess the situation and determine what aid you require. Fix the problem within three days; if you cannot do so, whisper my name thrice before a mirror in darkness, and I will send aid."

"I understand," Mal said.

The conference room stretched cavernous about them. Mal turned from Kopil to Caleb, and smiled a cliff runner's smile.

"This should be fun."

22

Mal excused herself to prepare. Caleb wanted to follow her, but he could not snub the Directors in their power. They wrung information from him: captives in a hot, dry cell, fighting for a drink from the same mangled sponge.

"How much water can we cut back from manufacturing and agriculture in the next week without damaging crops?" asked Alana Mazetchul, who had little love for RKC's industrial business. Ostrakov, whose department served farmers, makers, and builders of things, cut in before Caleb could answer Mazetchul: "How many souls are lost every minute our manufacturing plants stand dead?" More questions followed that, each one pointed, though Caleb could not see the purpose of every barb. He answered in raw figures with no commentary. He could not allow himself to be torn between these fanged eminences. He had problems enough already.

For thirty minutes they grilled him, and as each minute passed he felt Mal retreat further into the night.

The King in Red listened, and made occasional notes on his yellow notepad with a quill pen. He did not speak.

At last, Caleb exhausted the pool of questions. The meeting adjourned with a solemn incantation: "We wait, and we rise; we move, and the earth trembles." They stood as one and left the room severally—somber, disturbed, and determined not to betray their exhaustion as they retreated into shadows. Sixty years ago, these men and women broke the heavens, and made the gods weep. They had spent the time since learning how hard it was to run a world.

Tollan joined Caleb at the front of the room. "Well done," she said, with a ghost of a smile. "Don't die up there."

"I'll try not to."

She left.

Two others remained in the conference room. Chihuac waited by Kopil's throne; in the crook of one arm she carried a scroll as long as a sword. The King in Red leaned on the table and levered himself to his feet. The sparks of his eyes dimmed, and Caleb heard something like a cough rattle where his esophagus once had been.

"Sir?" Forgetting his notes, he moved to the King in Red. "Are you okay?"

"Of course," the skeleton said. "Thousands cry out to me that they thirst, that they are wounded; thousands more will join them soon. Their need tears at my soul. I could die, satisfying them, and if I die, so will they. Yet if I do not satisfy them, they will also die, and the city will die, and I will die at last. I am, in short, a perfect image of health. Someone will carve me on a monument."

"I've drawn up figures," said Chihuac, "for increased Warden deployment over the next week."

"We will discuss them in my office in ten minutes. I must speak with Caleb. Alone."

She withdrew. Her shoes were soft-soled, her step light. She walked into shadow and disappeared. He heard no door open or close in her wake.

"What's your plan?" Caleb said when they were alone.

"What do you mean?"

"Why are you sending me north? I won't be able to help."

"Your mere presence will suffice." Kopil lifted his coffee and his notepad and walked into the unbroken black. Caleb followed.

The last trace of light failed. Cloak and King were different textures of darkness. Caleb blinked, and with eyes closed he saw a hallway outlined about them in silver-blue fire, and the King in Red a lightning mosaic, a many-limbed spider with a thousand slavering mouths.

He opened his eyes, and saw nothing.

Liquid shadow welled about his legs. Viscous, palpable, it rose from his ankles, to his knees, to his waist. The tips of his fingers trailed over the surface of the shade. Shadows covered his chest, his neck. When they reached his mouth he expected to choke, yet when he inhaled they sat sweetly in his lungs. The dark enclosed him. He could not see the red of Kopil's cloak. His body was ice. He closed his eyes.

His next step pressed him against a cobweb wall. His heart quickened, but he strode forward. The King in Red did not mean to kill him. Dead, he could not go on this mad mission to the north.

Except as a zombie, of course.

He wished he'd thought of that earlier.

The shadows parted, as if he were floating upward through a subterranean lake and suddenly breached the surface. He blinked cobweb from his eyes, and clutched at the retreating liquid dark. He caught a handful, black and quivering like mercury in his palm.

He glanced over his shoulder, expecting to see the conference room at the end of a long hall, but saw only a closet of red: crimson robes, scarlet suits and ties, shirts the color of blood both fresh and dried.

"Can I get you a drink?" asked the King in Red.

Caleb wheeled around. He stood in a bedroom, large, elegant and sparsely furnished, walled on two sides by smoked windows. Thin metal pillars supported a high, unfinished rock ceiling that glimmered with ghostlights. Bookcases lined the walls, stuffed with red and black leather volumes polished by age and use. The room's opulence was almost obscured by mess: books piled on desk and floor and furniture, a stack of scrolls collapsed by the chair, a crimson duvet rumpled and askew on the king-sized bed. In an adjoining kitchenette, the King in Red poured reposado tequila into a lowball glass.

"Nothing for me, thanks."

Kopil emerged from the kitchenette. He snapped his fingers twice and two cubes of ice fell into his tequila.

"You don't live here," Caleb said. As he watched, the duvet straightened, books floated to the shelves of their own accord, and piles of scrolls snapped to order. "You have a mansion at Worldsedge. I've seen pictures."

"I have a mansion at Worldsedge," Kopil acknowledged. "And one in the Skeld Reaches, and a penthouse in Alt Coulumb, and three extensive estates on this coast alone. Plus the occasional island. But do you have any idea how long it takes to commute from Worldsedge? Even flying, I'd waste an hour every day, and I have no interest in spending all morning lurching through a crowded sky. Not to mention the expense, which I assure you would be considerable. Easier to sleep where I work. This room isn't large, but the whole building belongs to me, so I don't feel cramped."

"Not much good for work-life balance."

"I haven't been alive for more than seventy years."

"I see."

"It's not so bad." Kopil swirled tequila and ice. "RKC is a part of me, literally and figuratively. I built this Concern, and I have become a gear moving at its heart—a larger gear than many, but a gear nonetheless. When I sleep I see in my dreams the beast to which I have given birth. Thousands of miles of tunnel and pipe. Millions of people drink of us and live. Billions more spread throughout this mad world draw strength from Dresediel Lex. Men on the other side of the globe, in the southern Gleb, borrow our might to fight their wars. Ignorant children on six continents eat our grain and rejoice, though they do not know our name. So much depends on us. On me. Even at a time like this."

He didn't know how to respond, so he tried, "That must be stressful."

"It's no more than I asked for—than any of us asked for." He sighed. "There is one thing you must understand about destroying gods, boy."

"Only one?"

"You must be ready to take their place."

"I was thinking something like that myself, at the end of the meeting." Caleb glanced around the room, wondering how to change the subject without offending his boss. He blinked. "This room doesn't have any doors."

"Who needs them?"

"Most people."

Kopil shrugged, and sipped tequila.

"Sir, why are you sending me north? Lives depend on this mission. But you're sending a handful of Wardens, a Craftswoman, and a mid-level risk manager. Why not specialists? Why not an army?"

"If we send an army and we didn't need one, we'll have left Dresediel Lex weak for no reason, with an enemy loose inside our gates. If an army is needed, an army will be sent. The dead travel fast."

"In that case why send Mal—I mean, Ms. Kekapania? I doubt she knows anything about pipelines and Tzimet that Ms. Mazetchul doesn't. Or any of a hundred other Craftsmen and Craftswomen."

"I'm sending her because I trust you." The King in Red placed special weight on the last word in that sentence.

"You trust . . ." Caleb blinked. "Oh."

"You see the outlines of my design."

"You trust me. But you don't trust her."

Kopil could have been dead indeed for all the reaction he betrayed: a corpse arrayed in funeral red with a cup of sacrificial liquor in his hands. Beyond the windows, Wardens circled above Dresediel Lex.

"You're sending her because you want to give her a chance to betray you. You think Heartstone sabotaged its own project, and you want to give Mal a chance to fail, or turn on us."

"Those are two possibilities."

"You know she and I are romantically involved."

"I do."

He saw the rest of it, and cursed himself. "It's a long journey on to Seven Leaf by Couatl. Lots can happen on the way."

Ruby stars glimmered in endless night.

"If Ms. Kekapania is a traitor, any observer you sent with her might not reach Seven Leaf Lake. Even their death would tell you nothing. Accidents happen. So you send an observer you think she likes, someone she would hesitate to destroy."

"You are far too comfortable with conspiracies, Mr. Alte-moc."

"Comfortable isn't the word I would choose."

The skull shifted to one side, considering. "Say, in theory, that you have the following problem: the perfect woman for the job at hand was trained by an enemy so bitter that you devoured his Concern so he would no longer trouble you. Say he feels about you the way you feel about him, and say also that he is given to laying long plots and deep plans."

"Do you really think Alaxic might be involved?"

"Al was always more of your father's party than of mine."

He thought of the old man's face, cast lava red by the Serpents' light. "Can I speak frankly, sir?"

Kopil waved him on.

"You're playing long odds. Mal won't betray the city."

"If you trust her, why are you afraid to travel with her?"

Caleb had no answer. "I should sleep," he said at last, turning away. "And prepare."

There was no exit, so he walked toward the closet again.

"Let me get that for you," the King in Red called after him.

Caleb did not stop. He tossed the liquid shadow cupped in his palm through the closet door. The shadow spread, like ink spilled in water, to obscure robes and suits and shoes. He stepped through; the black parted for him, and he was gone. Two steps, three, brought him out of the ink and into the boardroom.

In the crimson flat, Kopil watched the darkness recede from his closet.

"Interesting," he said. If he had eyes, they would have narrowed. After exhausting the few seconds he could spare to puzzle irrelevant mysteries, he snapped his fingers and one of his kitchen walls swung open. Chihuac waited in his office with stacks of paperwork. The night was, unfortunately, still young.

23

Caleb could not sleep in his soulless room. RKC kept emergency quarters at 667 Sansilva for visitors and workers too busy to travel home: efficiencies with all the comfort and warmth of a grain thresher. He tumbled on the hard bed for an hour before he gave up, dressed, and rode the lift down to the street.

Stars menaced the silent city. Even the protesters were mostly asleep, coats bundled to serve as pillows: bow-backed men and broad-shouldered women, young and old, poor and middle-class. Children slept in a clutch on the sidewalk. Ancient men huddled near a flickering portable fire.

Zombies in burlap jumpsuits shambled among the sleepers. They swept the street with broad stiff brooms and speared garbage with rakes and pikes. RKC contracted with a minor Concern to keep the local streets clean, and the revenants came every evening, rain or sleet, protest or riot, earthquake or conflagration, to do their duty.

Sea wind bore the scent of fish and salt off the shark-infested Pax. A few blocks in from shore, the stench of crowds, pavement, and livestock mugged the wind in a dark alley and took its place.

The Wardens guarding RKC's perimeter shifted to let Caleb pass. He stepped over an unconscious child and turned left toward Muerte Coffee.

The shop's windows were beacons in the bruised night. Caleb bought a cup of spiced chocolate from a clerk no livelier than the street sweepers, and retreated into grave-cool darkness. He sat on a sidewalk bench and watched dead men move among the sleeping. Chocolate sank a plumb line to his core.

Fifty years ago, at the God Wars' height, Craftsmen had used a terrible weapon to bring the Shining Empire to its knees. Skies shattered, sand turned to glass, men and women and trees burned so quickly not even their shadows could escape. Those shadows lived still, travelers whispered—pinned to the ruined city by day and wandering at night, wailing after their lost flesh.

He felt like one of those shades, nailed to the city walls, the bench slats, the stone beneath his feet, the cup warm in his hand.

"Hello," said Temoc beside him.

Caleb let out a strangled squawk and spilled chocolate over his hands onto the sidewalk. Temoc passed him a handkerchief. He dried himself off, returned the sodden cloth, and took another sip before he faced his father.

Temoc sat like a statue on the bench. A coat the size of a tent swallowed his massive body, and a long scarf concealed the bottom half of his face. In the last few weeks he had even let his hair grow, to cover the ritual scars on his scalp. A passing Warden would see only a large, amiable derelict seeking conversation in the small morning hours.

"What are you doing here?"

Temoc sighed and leaned back. The bench sagged with his weight. "Why shouldn't a man visit his son?"

"Dad."

"You know, from time to time, see how he's getting on."

"Dad."

"How else am I supposed to brag about you to my friends in the old freedom fighters' home?"

"Dad."

Temoc stopped. The corners of his eyes smiled.

"This is a huge risk, coming here," Caleb said. "Even in disguise."

"What disguise? This is how I look now. I wander from safe house to safe house, avenging wrongs and fighting the State. It's not a bad life."

"You're a bum, is what you're saying."

"A fool, perhaps. In the old days we had holy fools. Madness claimed a few of those who saw the Serpents, and their madness made them sacred. Now the fools are all that's holy." He patted his chest. "My life could be worse."

"Meaning, you could be me, I suppose."

"What are you talking about? You're my son. I love you. You work for godless sorcerers who I'd happily gut on the altar of that pyramid"—he pointed to 667 Sansilva—"and you are part of a system that will one day destroy our city and our planet, but I still love you."

"Thanks, I suppose," Caleb said. "You realize that if you actually killed the King in Red, this place would be a desert in days. Water isn't free."

"It used to rain here more often."

"Because you sacrificed people to the rain gods."

"Your system kills, too. You've not eliminated sacrifices, you've democratized them—everyone dies a little every day, and the poor and desperate are the worst injured." He pointed at one of the street cleaners. "Your bosses grind them to nothing, until they have no choice but to mortgage their souls and sell their bodies as cheap labor. We honored our sacrifices in the old days. You sneer at them."

"Yeah? If being sacrificed was such an honor, tell me: how many priests died on the altar?"

They retraced their old arguments without rancor, knife fighters circling one another out of habit, armed only with blunt sticks.

Revenants shambled down the street, sweeping though no dust remained to clean. Silver studs on their wrists glinted in the streetlamps' light.

"How did the Tzimet get into the water?" Temoc asked.

"Like you don't know."

"I've spent all night fighting small demons. Saving lives. Do you think so little of me as to imagine I'd do this?"

"It has your signature in foot-high yellow paint. Yours, or one of your friends'."

Temoc chuckled.

"I missed the part where this was funny."

"The King in Red's unholy systems have let demons into the world, and you blame me."

"Is that why you're here? To send another message to the King in Red? He almost killed me last time you tried."

"I knew you would be safe. Besides, if Kopil tries anything, you can defend yourself."

"Dad," Caleb began, but he could think of nothing more to say that he wouldn't have to scream. He stared into the dregs of chocolate at the bottom of his mug. "I couldn't defend myself against him."

"You don't know the strength in your scars. Kopil and I fought each other for days at a time, in the God Wars."

"He's grown stronger. He almost crushed me without meaning to."

Temoc shrugged.

"Why are you here, Dad?"

"To wish you luck."

"How do you know what I'm about to do?"

"You sleep like a stone most nights. But now you're fretting over a mug of chocolate. You're worried about something big. You have a task ahead, and you don't know whether you'll be good enough, strong enough, smart enough."

"You came, defying Wardens and Deathless Kings, to tell me everything will be all right?"

"No."

"What, then?"

"Everything won't be all right. I didn't turn the water black, but someone did. Likely the same person who blew up North Station, and poisoned Bright Mirror. The Wardens are so busy hunting me they haven't found a trace of their real enemy. A dark force moves against Dresediel Lex with strength and subtlety. You aren't safe. No one is. I came to wish you good luck, and warn you to be careful."

A gust of hot wind stung Caleb's eyes. He knew even as he blinked that when his vision cleared, Temoc would be gone.

He sat for a while on the empty bench, then set his cup on the curb and shuffled off to his cold bed.

24

Gray dawn brought Caleb bleary and blinking to the pyramid's parking lot. The previous night's protesters had swelled to a crowd. Men and women across Sansilva and downtown woke to find their showers would not shower, their faucets would not run. Some sent angry letters by rat. Others came to 667 Sansilva and complained in person.

A line of Wardens separated the crowd from the parking lot. RKC golems and revenants waited behind the Wardens, clanking and moaning whenever a protester staggered too close.

Cheery, middle-aged customer service reps staffed complaint tables just outside the Wardens' line, listening to those customers who could explain their troubles, and suffering verbal assault from everyone else. No violence yet, so far as Caleb could see. The crowd still shied before the gaze of the dead, and the Wardens.

Mal elbowed toward him through the press of humanity. A golem lumbered to block her way, but she struck its chest with her palm; the air around the golem rippled, and it stumbled aside to let her pass.

Once through the line, she sauntered over to him, smiled, and thrust up her chin in greeting. "Great complaints department you have here. I especially like the guys with the melty faces. Way to make your clients feel at home."

"Life is hard, undeath is harder. We need someone to keep us safe."

"I'll watch out for you."

"Who will watch out for you?"

"You'll think of something."

"You have an exaggerated sense of my abilities."

"In that case, I'll have to trust them." She pointed up.

Caleb's chest thudded with the approach of massive beating wings. A scimitar shadow passed over him, and another. Couatl circled in the sky, sharks pondering their prey. These were larger than the common Warden's mount, beasts bred for distance and battle. Baggage studded straps around their bodies: tents, supplies, weapons.

Eight Wardens, come to bear him north to war.

The Couatl swooped lower. Mal frowned. "Our ride's here."

The Wardens slung a wide, flat gondola under the largest Couatl for Mal and Caleb, who reclined inside as they flew north. The rising sun burned off the morning fog, but factories and foundries had already lit their fires. An industrial haze cushioned sky and earth, and did not abate until the flying caravan cleared the northern reaches of the suburbs.

Their course curved west over a broken-scab carpet of farms: acres of orange groves, miles of avocados, artichokes, tomatoes, peppers, garlic, grass pasture and waving wheat, all green, all growing, in defiance of the desert two hours' flight away. Eight-tenths of the fresh water from Bay Station went directly to these fields, where revenants and colossal machines planted and harvested the food that fed not only Dresediel Lex, but cities across the continent and beyond the Pax. A few sapient men and women lived on these farms, tenants for the Concerns that owned the land, but for the most part the fields belonged to iron and the dead.

After three hours of northward flight the farms gave way to rolling hills, the hills to mountains. Rather than follow the First Highway up the coast toward Regis, they curved inland and soared between snowcapped peaks. The air grew cold; Caleb wrapped himself in an alpaca blanket, and Mal produced a long, fur-lined leather jacket from her backpack and draped it over her shoulders. Wind whipped the jacket's tail behind her as they dove into a ravine.

"I've never seen the mountains from up here before," he said as they flew past temples hung from sheer cliffs by forgotten sages.

"Have you seen them at all? I thought you were a city boy."

"When I was too young to live in town by myself, Mom brought me out here on her business trips."

"She raised you alone?"

"Temoc sure didn't help. You know how it is," he said, though he realized with a pang of guilt that, being an orphan, she might not. "Mom's trips into the Badlands took months at a time, but she brought me along anyway. Better than leaving me in DL to get into trouble."

"What did she do out there?"

"Research, mostly. Interview people, take notes. She works for the Collegium, studying nomadic Quechal tribes in the mountains and the desert."

"Exciting."

"I don't know," he said. "For the most part that meant wandering through the Badlands, following a bunch of people with a host of diseases any doctor could cure with a handful of pills and halfway decent nutrition. Life out there is a tapestry of danger: Scorpionkind and snakes, desert wolves, trickster spirits and wandering godlets who'll burn you if you don't worship them. Then she'd come back to the city and write books about deep truths the tribes know that the rest of us have forgotten. Seems silly to me. I always thought we had life better in DL than they do in the desert—at least as far as the lack of constant danger is concerned."

She rolled onto her back, laced her fingers behind her head and looked up into the scaled belly of the beast that bore them. "Maybe that's what the tribes know. The danger, I mean. How often do we really feel close to death anymore? Everyone in Dresediel Lex is wrapped in cotton: ladies worry about a patch of sagging skin, pale women want to be darker, dark women want to be paler. The men are no better. You live in Fisherman's Vale; you must see them jogging shirtless in the mornings, bodies sculpted for no purpose grander than vanity. In the Badlands nobody has the luxury to worry about stupid shit like that."

He struck his own stomach, which was flat but hardly sculpted. "I thought that way until I saw my fourth person die of a blood infection."

"What about the five hundredth person dying on the streets because they don't have a job, or can't afford a doctor, or water?"

"Those same people wouldn't last two weeks in the desert."

"And you would? If you think we should kill everyone who can't survive in the wild, you want a lot of blood on your hands."

He stilled the dozen sharp replies that rushed to his tongue. "No, that's not what I meant," he said. "I'm sorry. I've fought this stuff over and over with my father. It's hard to talk about it without getting emotional."

"It's a sensitive subject. There are no easy answers."

"No," he said after a long hesitation. "I guess not." Their Couatl rose toward and through the low thin layer of clouds. Water vapor flecked Caleb's face and lashes and wet his hair. Three wing-beats, four, and the clouds gave way to unbroken sky. The sun warmed them; it cast Caleb half in shade and left Mal in light.

She gathered her legs and stood, slowly, gripping a gondola cable for support. Her coat flared like wings. She wore a tan shirt open at the collar. A row of short scars marred the skin at her collarbone. "Here," she said, "let me show you what I mean."

He realized what she was about to do an instant before she released the cable and tumbled off the side of the gondola.

With a wordless cry he leapt for her; his stomach wrenched and his hand shot out. He reached, grasping, desperate, into the clouds.

Too slow, he knew in his bones, too slow, even as a firm grip clamped around his wrist. The sudden weight almost tugged him from the basket. He looked over the edge, and laughed in relief. Mal dangled from his arm. Her coat whipped and snapped with the speed of their passage. Sharp joy gleamed in her eyes.

"See?" she said, unperturbed by the open sky and the mile's drop. She shouted to be heard over the rush of wind. "Don't you feel alive?"

"I feel terrified," he shouted back. "And angry."

"Your heart's beating, you're breathing deep, you're desperate. Have you ever felt that way in Dresediel Lex, except when you were running after me?"

"What would you have done if I didn't catch you?"

"It's a long way down. I would have thought of something."

"You're crazy."

"You're not the first to say it."

He pulled her back into the gondola. When his arm trembled and his grip almost failed, she grabbed a rope and pulled herself the rest of the way aboard.

"All things considered," he said when they were both safely reclining once more, "I think I prefer the cotton-padded life."

She shrugged. He remembered chasing her across rooftops, and the chill in his heart as he flew.

After a silence, he said: "What do you think went wrong at Seven Leaf?"

She didn't answer at first, but he refused to change the subject again, and she relented. "Animals, maybe, or a raid from the Scorpionkind, though there aren't many of them in the mountains and it'd take a larger clutch than I've ever seen to hurt Seven Leaf Station. Could be a spirit rebellion, but we bound all the local ghosts and gods in the lake before we started pumping."

"Treachery?"

"Possible. From within, or without."

"So what's our plan?"

"Fly north. See what awaits us. Deal with it." She leaned back and let her eyes drift shut. "No sense worrying about the game before we see the cards."

Caleb didn't agree, but neither did he argue. Mal's breath settled, and she slept. He sat a few feet away from her, and tried to think as the world passed below.

25

An hour before nightfall, the Wardens guided their mounts down to survey a broad forest clearing. A brook bordered the clearing to the east, and the forty-foot-wide stump of a magisterium tree towered in the clearing's center. The Couatls' approach set resting deer and small birds to flight. The Wardens saw no danger, and made camp in the fork of a spreading root, between stump and water.

Magisterium grew in deep mountains, at glacial speeds. The living wood was strong, and stronger after death—its sticky sap set fast, and dried smooth and hard as stone. Only lightning and Craft could topple such trees, breaking them before the sap stiffened. Felled magisterium was valuable: carpenters could shape the wood into the bones and masts of ships, lighter than metal, tougher, and resistant to most Craft. Prospectors combed the mountains every year after winter storms, seeking fallen wood to sell.

Too old and weathered for the most desperate prospector, the stump by which the RKC team camped was well into its third century of wind and rain and insects' futile attempts at tunneling. The Couatl nested on the stump's flat top, and rubbed their hides against splinters sharp as steel nails.

Caleb built a fire, which Mal lit with a glare, and they cooked and ate a simple, hearty meal, tortillas and cheese and dried meat heated over the flame. They did not talk much. No local beast or bird dared return to the clearing—afraid of the campers, or more likely of the Couatl. Caleb swatted a couple mosquitos at sunset, but even those made only a halfhearted effort.

After they ate, Caleb leaned back, patted his stomach, produced a coin and walked it up and down his fingers. "I'm bored."

"I'm sorry," Mal said, "that our covert mission isn't exciting enough for you."

"Oh, I'm paralyzed with fear. But I don't like paralysis." He produced a deck of cards from his jacket pocket. "What do you say to a game?"

"A game?"

"Poker."

"With only the two of us?"

"What about you guys?" He called to the Wardens across the campfire. Their quicksilver masks warped and reflected the flames, transforming blank features into the gates of hell. He raised the cards. "A game?"

The leader of the Warden band, a blocky young woman whose badge numbered 3324, was the first to speak: "We're on duty, sir."

"You aren't all planning to stand watch at the same time, are you? A few can play while the others guard."

"We have to remain on duty in the field." She raised one gloved hand and tapped the spot on her mask where her cheek would have been. Her glove disappeared into the silver. "It wouldn't be fair."

"I don't need to see your faces to take your souls," he said as he slid the cards from the pack. "And don't call me sir." The rattlesnake shuffle of card against card sounded small and alien in the clearing.

3324 acquiesced without further prodding. Three of her squad mates joined, for a table of six, while two slept and two more stood guard. All the Wardens bore the same initial numbers on their badge.

"Does that mean something? The thirty-three?"

"We're an extraterritorial unit," said 3324.

"Arrest authority, but no responsibility to arrest," added the Warden beside her.

"Soldiers," Mal said, with a sour voice.

"No," she replied. "We're Wardens who don't always have the luxury of bringing our suspects home to trial."

"A fine distinction. I'm sure your victims respect it."

If 3324 reacted, her mask gave no sign. "Sometimes we have ugly assignments. Sometimes the world is ugly. I'd be overjoyed if all I had to do was direct traffic."

"I doubt it."

She shrugged. "Doubt what you like. But until that day, we're stuck with jobs like this—in the forest, riding to confront an unknown threat, probably outgunned, with two civilians in tow. No disrespect."

"You chose this life," Mal said. "You'll excuse me if I don't believe you when you say you'd be happy to give it up."

"I chose to serve. Turns out this is what I'm good for. What we're good for." She motioned to her men, who sat statue-still and did not acknowledge the statement. "We wanted to serve our city, and we have talents for last-ditch action, and violence. The jobs that no one wants to do, but must be done. So here we are. Serving."

Mal opened her mouth, and Caleb almost interrupted her, afraid of what she might say. But he did not, and she settled for: "So you serve." And, "Let's play cards."

"Let's."

"We can't keep calling you all by numbers," Caleb said, relieved at the opportunity to change the subject. "Thirty-three twenty-four is a mouthful."

"You may call me Four. Within our team, the final number is enough."

"Pleasure to meet you." Caleb removed a folded silk cloth from his jacket pocket, and spread it over a flat span of earth. He dealt the cards first into eight piles, one for each of the eight directions, then stacked the piles atop one another and shuffled the deck eight times. His heart stilled, and he forgot that he sat in the middle of the Drakspine, hundreds of miles from the city of his birth. He set aside Mal's argument with the Warden, and his own fear. The cards carried a world with them. "Three-faced goddess, we call you to us." The formula burned his tongue; the cards stung his fingers as they ripped pieces from his soul. Quechal designs covered the cards' backs: the Twin Serpents twining a woman with a threefold face, a goddess without a name. As he shuffled, the designs began to glow.

He laid the deck in the center of the silk, and Four touched it with the first finger of her right hand; the Warden beside her followed, and after him another, and then Mal. With each touch, the designs brightened. The players gave shreds of themselves, their hearts, minds, lives, loves, patches of the dust and lightning that formed them.

The light detached from the deck, and, rising, assumed a woman's form, half-turned away: a tempting and inviting figure, a face that would be beautiful if Caleb could see it fully. The goddess sprinted beyond her worshippers' reach, teasing them with gifts withdrawn at their moment of greatest need.

She hovered over the makeshift table in the wilderness, small and perfect as a porcelain doll. At Andrej's late in the evening, where kingdoms were won or lost at hazard, she towered, glorious, a green light at the end of a long pier that he might pursue and embrace to drown.

Caleb dealt the first two cards to each player, and waited as the betting began with Four. He glanced at his cards—two of swords and eight of wands. Just as well. A bad hand was a fine way to open the evening. Ease in.

The goddess assumed their features as they bet: Mal's taunting smile, the square solidity of Four's shoulders, one Warden's back, another's delicate wrist, a third's laugh. Caleb folded, and watched.

Four won the first hand, with twos full of jacks. Mal had a nine and a seven, and grinned as the power left her. Had she meant to lose the hand, to make the Wardens bold?

He shuffled and dealt again.

Time stopped for them, though the blue sky darkened to black and a jeweler's dusting of stars emerged. The goddess grew, all things in turn to her worshippers, demanding, cajoling, reprimanding. The fire burned so low Caleb had to squint to see his cards.

Play was a simple matter of calculating odds and finding tells:

Four touched her chin when a card turned to her advantage. Eight, jovial and immense, flexed his cards between his fingers when he held a strong hand. Mal was hard to read. She played with reckless abandon, yet seemed to win important hands and lose meaningless ones.

Once he crossed with her, riding king-queen in swords, and she followed him in a rising spiral of raises. They pressed against each other with the game as a thin cotton sheet between them, disguising nothing though it covered all.

He won, with a straight to her two pair. She laughed savagely as the goddess ripped her from herself.

They all had won and lost enough for one night. The game broke, and with a sigh the goddess dissolved, relinquishing the scraps of her divinity to the players.

Caleb closed his eyes as she entered him. Lightning danced through his blood, burned through his nerves. He would live forever, deeds resounding through legend.

He opened his eyes as if for the first time in years, so fresh did the world seem, and so raw.

The cards lay like inert slips of stiff paper on wrinkled silk.

Silence echoed in the mountain heights—not an absence of noise, but a presence in itself, a medium that endured human intrusion as the sea endures the passage of a ship. Before the ship came, there was the sea; as the ship passes, the sea rolls against the hull. When the ship is gone the sea remains. Without the sea, there could be no ships. Without the ships, there could be no sea, Caleb thought, not knowing what that might mean.

He listened to the silence above the Drakspine in the dark, beside the dwindling fire.

The players wandered off. The Wardens relieved the watch or took their rest, and Mal faded into the night while Caleb stowed and purified the cards.

Searching the campsite after his rituals were done, at first he could not find her. The Wardens stood guard or slept; those who acknowledged him did so with curt, quiet nods. He thought about Four, by the fireside, and about duty.

He was about to call Mal's name, when he looked up.

She sat on the edge of the magisterium stump, her profile lit by campfire and stars. She watched the sky.

She must have heard him climb the tree's gnarled roots. But when he stood beside her, hands scraped and arms aching with exertion, she did not look away from the stars and mountains. Couatl slept behind them in a coiled heap, wings furled over winding bodies. Long crocodile-toothed heads rested against cold, pliant scales.

"I never took you for a religious man," she said, lost and faint as if she wandered beyond the horizon of a dream.

"I'm not." He waited for her to turn, but she did not. "My father's the last of the Eagle Knights, a priest of the old gods, and I work for the man who kicked his gods to the curb. More religion is the last thing I need in my life."

"Yet you follow a goddess."

He laughed, but she did not, so he stopped. "I wouldn't call that a religion."

"What would you call it?"

"The Lady of the Cards," and he heard the capitals and wished he could unsay them, "lives between the players of a game. She's their souls mingled, and has no power save over the game. The game ends, and she leaves. Not much of a goddess."

"Yet you worship her."

"Not really."

"You observe her rites and rules in the dealing of a hand or the shuffling of cards. You worship her, sure as a ballplayer sixty years ago worshipped the Twins or Ili of the Bright Sails or Qet Sea-Lord or Exchitli. For you, at least, the card game never ends. You're an occasional priest—pledged to a goddess who only exists occasionally."

"You're philosophical tonight."

"Maybe I am."

She faced north, toward a palpable darkness on the horizon, where the curtain of stars faded and failed.

"Looks like Craftwork," he said.

"That's Seven Leaf Lake. We'll reach it before noon tomorrow." She spoke with a measured tone that could have been excitement or fear or anger masquerading as control.

"Good." Starshine was a potent source of power for Craft, rawest of all raw materials: starshine filtered through human mind became the stuff of souls, and Craftswomen could use it to accomplish wonders and great blasphemies. Whatever force had seized Seven Leaf, it would be less powerful at noon, with the stars hidden, than at any other time of day.

"That blot must be miles across. Is Seven Leaf supposed to pull down so much light?"

"No. The station's drawing more power than it was designed to use. That narrows the possibilities. Narrows them down to one, actually: someone is inside, working against us."

"Not someone," he said after a while.

"Excuse me?"

"Our enemy isn't faceless, is he? Pushing the station beyond its limits like that takes real Craft."

"There are many trained Craftsmen in the world. They're not all good people."

"Sure." The dark spot bled into the sky, growing as he watched. "But this one took over your station without raising a single alarm. This is an inside job. I'd wager a tenth of my soul you know who did it, or can guess."

Her legs dangled over the edge of the stump. Her feet were bare, long and narrow, their bones slender. She looked back over her shoulder at him. "What if I do?"

"Tell me." He sat down beside her. Tree frogs sang a senseless throbbing song.

"I tell you, and you tell the King in Red."

"I won't."

"You will."

"Fine," Caleb said. "Trust me, or don't. I'm going to bed."

He was about to climb down and abandon her to the stars and sleeping serpents, but she put out a hand and stopped him.

"Her name is Allesandre Olim," she said. "Allie. She was the strongest Craftswoman at Seven Leaf. She was eager for the assignment. I guess now we know why."

That name floated back to him through time, from tunnels and caves and a lake of lava. "Allesandre. Alaxic's aide?"

"Yes."

"I met her once. She didn't seem insane at the time. Precise, dangerous, yes. But this . . ."

"I know." She pointed again to the corruption of the stars. "But there it is. She was the best Craftswoman at Seven Leaf by far. A genius. No one else in the station could have overcome her, or done this."

"Can you reason with her? Talk her down?"

"I doubt it. She's gone too far. That blot's larger than a living Craftswoman could handle without going mad. If people want to use more, they have to die, like your boss."

"Maybe she died."

"Death takes time. There are classes, support groups, premortem exercises. Allie's alive, but her mind is a splinter caught in a tornado. She'll tear through anything in her way, but she has no control."

"That doesn't sound good for us."

"We'll be outmatched when we reach Seven Leaf, and overpowered."

"So we call for backup. The King in Red's forces can be here by morning."

"No."

"Why not?"

"You heard your boss, in that meeting. If I succeed, Heartstone's safe. I'm safe. If I call your boss, I admit failure, and everything that goes with it. He already blames us for this mess. He'll take his revenge, scour Heartstone from the foundations up. None of my friends and colleagues will survive." She tore strips of moss from the trunk, and threw them over the side: centuries of decomposition undone by a fingernail scrape. "It's better this way. I succeed, if I can. If not, the King in Red and his armies can be here in hours, and ride to the city's rescue."

"But you'll die."

"I don't care," she said in a monotone as striking as a scream.

"I do."

In the dark her eyes deepened.

"Yes," she said. "You do."

"You're not worried for yourself. You're worried for me."

"Worried," she said, and laughed at the word's poverty. "The Wardens knew what they were getting into when they took the job. You heard Four down there. I know why I'm here. But you didn't ask for this."

"I knew what I was getting into."

"Whatever you thought chasing me would bring you, this is worse. I don't know what weapons Allie will throw against us. The Wardens are scared. I'm scared. You've never been in a war of Craft before. You'll die, if you're lucky, and dying hurts." She looked away from him. "I don't want you to die, Caleb."

"You don't have to sound so surprised by that."

The uncertainty left her voice. "If it were up to me, I wouldn't have let you come."

"I can handle myself."

"Oh," she said with a small laugh like bells. "Can you."

Blue flames flashed from her eyes, and he froze. His hand refused to twitch, his chest to rise or fall. Sweat stung his eyes, but he could not blink.

"This is a taste of what she'll use against us tomorrow," she said. "You see why I'm worried. I want to protect you. If I must, I'll knock you out and leave you here, warded and sleeping, until this is settled."

His starved lungs spasmed. Time beat slow. Air pressed against his palms: air subtly ribbed like the surface of a plank of wood. Her Craft had bound him in strong cords woven spider-fine.

But he could feel the cords. What he could feel, he could touch, and what he could touch, he could seize.

A chill spread through his scars. He closed his fists, and the paralysis broke. He held two fistfuls of stinging nettle, but the relief of being able to blink and breathe was so strong he forgot the pain. Her Craft glimmered in his grip.

He looked up. Mal had recoiled into a fighting crouch, her eyes wide.

"What" was all she could manage.

"Well," he said, "did you expect me to let you strangle me for my own good?"

"You," she said when she tried to speak again.

"I'm coming with you. I might die. I'm okay with that." As he spoke he realized he was not lying. "I like the thought of standing beside you. Whatever happens."

"You," she repeated.

"I have your Craft, yes." The scars on his fingers bent the blue light of her power like lenses. "I didn't think you would be surprised. I've done it before. Remember the bar? Dancing?"

"You're glowing."

He looked down. Cerulean lines twisted about his torso. They shone through his shirt like moonlight. "That's a hell of a lot of power to use just to knock someone out."

"Those aren't Craftsmen's glyphs."

"They aren't glyphs at all. Like I said at Andrej's. They're scars."

"High Quechal."

"Yes."

"You're an Eagle Knight." He heard awe in her voice, and it sickened him. "Your father—"

"My father's an Eagle Knight, and a priest, and a terrorist, and a bunch of other things I'm not." He unbuttoned his shirt. Scars glowed from his skin, curving and intricate: Qet Sea-Lord bleeding the oceans, Exchitli the Sun falling into the Serpents' fangs to seal the bargain that made the world. The Hero Twins blazed above his heart.

He released her Craft.

Darkness bloomed purple. He closed his eyes, and waited alone in the dark for a slow count of ten. A warm pressure settled against his chest. He recognized her calloused fingers, and the hiss of her breath when she touched his scars.

"Eagle Knights," he said with eyes still closed, "used the gods' power in battle. My father's the last. When he was ten, he knelt at the peak of the pyramid where I work today, and carved the symbols of their order into his skin. Last step of the initiation. Some of his blood's still in the altar stone there."

"Gods, Caleb. What did he do to you?"

"When I was ten." He opened his eyes. Her face was inches from his, but distant as the moon's. "Well—" He tried again, and again stopped. Words laced with acid formed in his stomach. They hurt rising to his tongue. "When I was ten, he left my mother and me. But he didn't want me unprotected." He grimaced. "So he gave me the most powerful gift he knew. He drugged me at our last dinner, and came for me in the night with a black glass knife. Mom found us as he was finishing. Blood everywhere."

One of her hands clutched his shoulder; the other cupped his ribs. She did not draw him to her, but her strength creaked his bones.

"He thinks he did right by me. I think he's a fanatic. But the scars give me strength. They let me touch Craft, grab it, bend it. I've never liked to use them in my work, because I didn't want to owe him anything. Until now. Until you. My father's madness has never brought me anything, but at least it'll let me stand at your side."

The river rolled south. Sentinel stars stared down.

"Say something," he whispered.

She could have walked away, as she had done so many times before, as he might have himself under the same circumstances. He wouldn't have blamed her. Worse was for her to stand, hands on his shoulders, watching him with that wasteland expression between concern and fascination and terror, as if he were a traffic accident or a shark-gnawed carcass on a beach.

But terror receded, and fascination. Her mouth closed, her shoulders sagged, the corners of her eyes and her grip on his body grew soft. He saw himself in her eyes; she saw herself in his.

A shell closed over that silence, sealing it away. She stepped back, cupped her chin in her hand, and said, "I have an idea."

26

Morning was cold and overcast, the trees mist-haunted. A caul of fog covered river and earth, transforming the black magisterium stump into a dour promontory. Couatl woke and stretched their wings.

The Wardens moved in simple, straight lines, breaking camp, packing tents and bedrolls. They hung weapons near their saddles: wicked hooks on long chain, barbed javelins, automatic crossbows, razor-edged silver discs of many sizes. The weapons whispered sharp words when Caleb drew near: *flay, flense, shatter, twist.*

Even Mal was grim this morning. "Are you ready?" he asked her as they settled into the gondola. She shook herself back from a distant lonely place to answer: "As ever." She gripped his arm through his jacket. He set his hand on hers; at an unseen signal from Four, the Couatl surged skyward.

The morning pall did not retreat before the rising sun. The shadow dome, their destination, grew larger on the horizon with each wingbeat.

All morning they traveled up a narrow ravine between snow-edged ridges. Two plates of the earth's crust jutted against each other here, buckling and crushing down slow generations. A river ran along the cleft, fed by the falls from Seven Leaf Lake, and their flight traced the river to its source.

The shadow-dome was miles across and just as high. It curved immense ahead, surface mottled like different oils mixed. Dark currents twitched within as they approached. "Why does it look different colors?" Caleb asked.

"Allie can't watch everywhere at once," Mal said. "She sees

her world in pieces. When she peers at a section of the dome, it darkens."

"You still think she's the one we're fighting?"

"Yes."

After a pause, he asked: "Why do they move randomly? It'd be safer for her to have a system."

"She probably thinks she does. Her mind's warped, trying to contain all that power."

"So we're fighting a mad, almost omnipotent sorceress."

"Yes."

"Great."

"For what it's worth, madness tends to be a disadvantage in this sort of thing."

"Glad to hear it."

She sat in fierce profile, watching.

Caleb pondered his current predicament. A beast sacred and profane bore him north, with a beautiful, terrifying woman, to defend a city wonderful in its horrors. He lived in contradiction, and in fear.

His father would not approve.

The night before, Mal had knelt beside him in her tent and painted figures on his skin with silver ink that burned when wet, but cooled as it dried. Even now he could trace the outline of her sigils on his chest and arms and shoulders and back, the ink cold as Craft, a pattern to complement his scars. His war paint, his mark as her protector.

He laughed.

"What?"

"I've gone from manager to knight in two days. I think I deserve a bump in salary."

"I'll recommend you if we pull this off."

"I don't think you're allowed to write your boyfriend a recommendation."

"You're my boyfriend now?"

"This is our second date."

"Some date. Fighting for our lives."

"We'll be fine," he said, without conviction.

"Yes." She sounded no more certain. "Next time, we'll go someplace nice."

"Sure," he said as they passed into darkness.

The world changed, like walking on a tidal beach: one step dry and warm and yielding, the next wet, cold, firm. The pleasant sunlit world faded. Mountains surrounded them, crags old as the frame of the earth. Trees shivered in the wind of their passing, restless shades rising from hungry sleep. This was the world immortal. It would endure man's scrabbling on its surface, and rejoice when the last city crumbled.

Was this how Craftsmen saw the universe? So pitiless, and dark?

Shadowy cords throttled the air overhead as the Couatl dove for the tree line. Where the cords passed, they left silence solemn as the halls of an ancient tomb.

The Couatl threaded through magisterium trees toward the falls: water rushing in torrents down an indomitable cliff. Up the bare rock they flew, until with a final surge of tired wings they crested the ridge and reached the lake.

Seven Leaf stretched before them, twenty miles at least from western to eastern shore and mountain-ringed.

Caleb had never seen so much fresh water in one place. Dresediel Lex was a desert city, no matter how it pretended to temperate ease. In his childhood he had played among cactus spines, and the forest he knew the best was the Stonewood, eons dead. An embarrassment of wealth lay below him, fresh water from horizon to horizon, salvation to his thirsty city.

The black lightning of Allie's mind flickered and lanced above the waters. The sun was a pale ghost. Sickly blue-green luminescence shone from everywhere and nowhere at once, casting no shadows—undigested remnants of light, vomited up by their adversary.

Shade-wrapped Seven Leaf Station shimmered atop the water: a silver dome in the lake's center, surrounded by a metal superstructure in the shape of a six-pointed star. Three rings of Craft circled the entire station, crackling with flame. Domes and towers blurred and flexed, sprouting annexes, buttresses, and arches that crumbled in moments, shining upside-down through time.

The Couatl sped toward the station. Their pinions carved vicious arcs in the gloom. When they crossed the outermost of the three Craft circles the world flashed white, and before the light faded they crossed the second and third in quick succession, a flare of black, a strain of music calling Caleb down a deep tunnel beyond which unfamiliar stars glared into a desolate abyss. Wards on the Couatl's scales popped and hissed and sparked, and gouted smoke that stank of ozone and burning flesh.

They landed on a flat stone platform at the station's edge. Four was the first to hit the ground, followed by One, Three, and Seven; Mal followed, as did Caleb, and the remaining Wardens reared the Couatl back into the air.

No sooner were the Couatl airborne than tentacle arms a hundred feet long burst from the lake. Most grabbed for the Couatl and missed, but two carved deep trenches in the stone platform where Caleb, Mal, and the Wardens stood.

Caleb stumbled back, slipped on the slick stone and fell. A tentacle curved overhead, dark against the gray sky. It struck, and Caleb flinched, but when he opened his eyes he was still alive. The tentacle twitched on the landing platform, severed halfway down its length. Four stood above him, ichor dripping from a long black blade she sheathed again at her side.

Three more tentacles rose to replace the fallen limb. Mal pulled Caleb to his feet, and they ran, following the Wardens down a long catwalk toward the central dome.

Couatl wove and rolled through the sky, dancing amid a storm of tentacles. Caleb had seen his share of human brawls, brutish and brief: breaking, snapping, tearing, that was how man fought man. The Couatl and the shadow-arms were made things, perfect mechanisms. They dueled with an artist's precision.

Tzimet scuttled out of the water onto the catwalk, slick curved claws scratching metal. Four and her comrades struck them like a hammer, so fast their forms were lost in movement. Four's hands burned with green flame as she punched through a Tzimet's abdomen; Seven tossed a silver ball down the catwalk, and the ball shed thin rays of light that shredded shadow and black water.

This is what we're good for, Four had said across the camp-fire. Last-ditch action, and violence.

They carved a hole in the horde, and running, Caleb and Mal followed.

The world warped: a phantom of Sansilva Boulevard lay under Caleb's feet, broad and pyramid-flanked, and he would have run down that road into the lake had he not fixed his eyes on Mal and followed her instead. He fell a thousand feet from a sky-castle onto a blasted desert, but he followed Mal and the desert melted.

The dreams that nipped at Caleb's mind turned ugly as he neared the dome. Demons gnawed his entrails, and peeled Mal's skin in long strips that unraveled as she ran.

Footsteps rang on steel.

Light scattered Caleb's illusions. Overhead, Wardens loosed lances of flame, spinning discuses of silver, and brilliant hooks against Allie's tentacles. The dome's surface twisted the firefight into a funhouse hell.

Four reached the dome and rushed through without pause, leaving only a ripple in reflected flames—the walls were not made of glass or chrome, but water.

Caleb grabbed Mal's hand, and they stepped inside together.

Water enclosed him, and let him pass. When he opened his eyes, he was dry, and alone.

Darkness illuminated a wrecked room: broken tables, up-turned chairs, scattered consoles and implements of Craft. A web of twisted wire and bent pipe filled the chamber, and a woman sat in the center of that web, cradled like an idol in an old priest's hand. Caleb recognized her.

At their last meeting Allesandre had been clipped and precise, level as a frozen river. Her ice had thawed into a flood. Glyphs burned from her skin, marred her face with talon patterns, ringed her brow like a crown of knives. Tatters of a dark wool suit hung from her body. Eternities wrapped around themselves in her eyes.

Misshapen lumps of human flesh hung from her metal web, and corpses sprawled beneath her on the floor.

His gut turned, and he almost turned with it, almost fled back through the water curtain. Fear, more than bravery, prevented him. She would not spare him just because he tried to run. His only chance at survival lay ahead.

Her mocking smile cracked open. Blue light sparked between dagger teeth. "It's been a long time."

"Allesandre," Caleb said. "Stop this."

"Why?" the Craftswoman said pleasantly. "You put me here, asked me for this. You and your master."

He shook his head. "I didn't ask you for anything. I've only seen you once." She did not answer. "Where are the others?"

"Your companions are dead. I let you live."

Caleb heard flesh crisp to ash. Mal screamed. Craft-born hallucinations. Witchcraft. "You're lying."

"I'm not."

"I'm here to fix the water. Don't try to stop me."

Fire burned in her eyes. "Come, if you dare. Wrap your hands around my neck and kill me."

A trick. Of course. Yet he felt her throat in his right hand, flesh and tendon and bone. Squeeze. Kill. No. He hadn't moved. His hand was empty. He was alone in the dark.

"Come," she said. "I'm waiting." A flash of lightning cast her and the web of wire and the corpses in chiaroscuro. Four silhouettes hovered in the air about her, shadow cutouts contorted in pain.

Four shadows. Why four? Why did those silhouettes seem familiar?

"Where's Mal?" he asked. He tried to look away from Allesandre, but his eyes remained fixed on her.

"You have no power here," she said.

He ignored her, and focused instead on the feeling in his right hand. Skin, yes, but too hard and calloused for a throat, bones too thin for a spine. He recognized the meat of a palm, and slender strong fingers wrapped around his own.

"Mal," he said, louder this time.

"No one can help you. We two are alone, the only human beings for miles. Face me and fight, or I will destroy you as you look away."

Look away. His nerves locked against him. Air froze in his chest. Waves of blood beat on the shore of his body. His scars ran cold.

The foundation of the world shook, or he did, or both. Cords bound his mind. He gripped them, and they fell loose.

Mal stood beside him, holding his right hand, her gaze fixed on Allesandre. Glyphs burned from the open collar of her shirt. "You presume to dictate terms to me?" Her voice was sharp and fearsome. "He was no part of this. I will end you for killing him."

She thought he was dead. Overhead he heard a rustle of motion, smelled ozone as claws of Craft ripped through empty space. He recognized the Wardens by their speed. They darted between pipes and wires; one leapt at Allesandre only to be swept aside by an invisible force. Their attacks were out of joint, uncoordinated. A pair struck at once and a single wave of fire threw them back. A tangle of black arms snared Seven, who fought free, and the same trap caught Three seconds later.

They fought with courage and desperation. They fought as if each one, alone, was the last bulwark between Dresediel Lex and doom.

Caleb closed his eyes, and saw the barbs of Craft sunk into the Wardens' minds, and Mal's.

Mal stepped forward and became inhuman, tall and lean and sharp, an eidolon of smooth spiked bone. Her fingers almost slipped from his grasp.

Almost.

He pulled against her with his scars. Allesandre's illusion bent. Mal fought him, her hand a knife's blade that cut his palm, a flame caged in his grip, but he pressed harder. The pain grew. He cried out, but before he could let go, the illusion broke.

Mal froze. Blood dripped from the cuts in Caleb's hand. A drop at the curve of his smallest finger welled, swelled, fell.

She turned to him. Her eyes had been open, but now she saw. "Caleb," she whispered, and the bone and crystal melted from her. Her look of surprise changed first to joy, then to predatory confidence. Her skin chilled to his touch. She closed her eyes, and turned on Allesandre.

"Allie," she said, "that was clever. But not clever enough."

She advanced, and Caleb followed her.

A hissing serpent of frozen flames encircled them, but it shattered at a wave of Mal's hand. Sweat and condensation gleamed on her forehead. Her slow and shallow breath turned the air to fog. They walked into the jaws of a shark with jagged crystal teeth the size of men. Mal frowned, and, closing, the teeth melted to raindrops and splashed cool on his face.

Skewering thorns blossomed into roses, which fell upon them heavy and suffocating only to take wing and rise as butterflies, which became a swarm of bees swept away in a rush of wind.

The world ran taut as a violin string.

Lightning-haloed Allesandre blazed with hidden fire.

The night before, Caleb sat in Mal's tent naked to the waist. Her brush tickled the back of his neck.

"Duels of the Craft," she said, "are fought on many levels. Mind and soul are two battlefields, the body another, time a fourth, and most of the others make little sense if you're not a Craftsman. The world is an argument, and like any argument there are many ways to win or lose. You can force your opponent to contradict herself. You can point out her fallacies, her false dichotomies, her exaggerations and distortions of reality. Our authority from the King in Red threatens Allie's control over the station. She'll attack the bond between Seven Leaf and RKC, claiming independence. The contracts between the station and RKC are strong, though. I can turn them against her."

"And once you do that, you win."

"Ordinarily." Her brush slid silver along his neck. "If this were a case before a judge, in a Court of Craft, supported by precedent and dread command. Out here . . ." She trailed off, and drew a spiral at the base of his spine. "There's an easy way to win any argument, no matter the quality of your position—you kill the person with whom you disagree. When she sees I'm about to win, she'll strike with every thaum of her power. I won't be able to stop her. I'll have fought my way to exhaustion already. A simple, blunt attack will go through me like an arrow through a paper wall." Her brush spun in place to articulate a dot. The ink dried cool on his skin, and in his soul. Closing his eyes, he saw the night inside his skull painted with her diagrams. "That's where you come in."

Allesandre swelled with rage. Wires twisted like octopus arms around her, and her mouth shaped words in demonic tongues. She reared, serpentine.

Lightning poured down upon them like water from a height.

The lightning slammed into Mal's protective wards, and would have burned through if its power had nowhere else to go.

Lines of silver paint flared on Caleb's skin, and the scars on his chest and back and arms flared too.

Thunder riveted his mind. Power battered the cords of his being. His heart stopped.

Caleb held Allesandre's might as a rider holds reins.

He knelt, and touched the lightning to the metal deck of Seven Leaf Station.

The bottom dropped out of his soul, and he fell into the station, into the water, into and through Allesandre's defenses. She threw her head back. Her skeleton sparked through her skin; she screamed, long and high-pitched, until her own throat strangled her and the world collapsed in rushing water.

The dome, built to withstand storm and earthquake and divine wrath, gave way. Thousands of gallons of water fell on Caleb and Mal, on the Wardens, on Allesandre in her wire web.

Caleb collapsed to the deck. Time disappeared in the roar and rush. Gravity failed, and he grabbed for anything firm. His hands closed around a hot water pipe, scalding but stationary, and he held his breath through coursing dark.

The universe righted itself in noon brilliance. Caleb doubled over on the deck, coughing up sweet water. The sky spread blue above. He blinked at the fierce sun.

For months he knelt, years, gathering the pieces of his mind into a working whole. When he looked up, he saw the knotted pipes and wires in tangled disarray, Allesandre limp at their heart. Wire circled her head like a crown, and her neck like a collar. It was difficult to tell where she ended and the machines began— metal slipped smoothly beneath her skin.

Corpses lay on the floor, flood-tossed against consoles and raised altars. Two Wardens had fallen overboard, and Four and Eight were lowering ropes to rescue them.

The torrent had not moved Mal, who crossed her arms and canted her head to one side like a governess regarding a trouble-some child. She walked forward. Her legs trembled with each determined step.

Allesandre looked up. Her face was Quechal dark, Caleb's own color, and her hair streaked red. Ruined, she resembled the woman she had been months ago, the woman who ushered him into the burning foundations of the world. Her chest heaved. Her mouth was slack and her eyes set, exhausted and defiant.

"Mal," she said so soft that Caleb barely heard: desperate, despairing. "What now?"

Mal did not answer. One hand rose to the hollow above her heart, and twisted. The sun dimmed, and above the wind and the waves' soft roll, Caleb heard a sound like cloth being torn. Mal drew her hand from her breast, and she held a sliver of night-mare in the shape of a knife. She raised the blade.

"I'm sorry," she said.

"Mal," Allesandre repeated. "How did we get here?"

Mal moved her knife in a smooth arc that began on one side of Allesandre's neck, and ended on the other. Allie's eyes went soft, and she slumped forward with a wet gasp. The wires would not let her fall. Blood unfurled from her throat down her shred-ded blouse. She blinked once, and mouthed a word Caleb could not hear—it might have been Mal's name, again. Pain twisted her, and she died.

Mal stood like a lightning-struck magisterium tree: solid to the eye, but the leaves and furthest branches quivered as the trunk fought to stand. The tremors traveled inward from her fingertips, and when they reached her shoulders she collapsed, curled over her knees, head down. The nightmare-knife vanished. Blood fell to the deck and mixed with water.

Caleb moved to her side and stopped, uncertain. Mal collapsed was more fearsome than Mal girded for war. He had staked his soul on games of chance, confronted the King in Red, jumped off buildings into empty space. Kneeling beside her and placing his hand on her shoulder was the hardest thing he had ever done.

He wondered if she had killed before, and wondered, as he had last night, what he would have felt if their situations were reversed, leaving him with the knife and her to watch. Alessandre was dangerous. He tried to think of Dresediel Lex dying of thirst, tried to justify the blood at his feet, and could not.

Sixty years ago, his father stood atop the pyramid at 667 Sansilva. As cantors sang, he raised his knife. It glinted black in the sun. The obsidian edge reflected the naked sacrifice. The blade fell, the murder was done, and that, too, had saved the city.

Silent, he stared into the dead woman's eyes. But for the blood, she might have been lost in thought, or prayer.

His hand hurt. Mal had gripped it, hard. After a while, when she stopped trembling, she looked up.

"That was worse than I thought," she said.

A distant lake bird called.

She tried to speak but choked, and stopped, and tried again. "Come on. Let's get this place running."

27

Caleb left Mal alone as she worked. He lacked enough Craft to help her, and she seemed happier without him. No. Not happier, exactly. She worked in a brittle silence that he feared to break.

The Wardens cased the scene. Four and Six draped the corpses in evidence shrouds, capturing pictures of each victim for later analysis. Three's thigh was broken in the battle, and he rested next to twitching, unquiet One, whom Allie had trapped in a recursive nightmare. Four said she would wake soon. "If not, we have people who can bring her to her mind again."

Seven walked around the station at a measured pace, forming detailed memories that specialists in Dresediel Lex would retrieve.

Couatl flew above. Four's green-crested mount swallowed an unwary lake bird in a single bite. Feathers drifted down on the breeze.

Allesandre hung from her wire crèche.

Caleb followed Seven, listening to his footsteps and the water. Broken glass glinted at his feet. Kneeling, he lifted a shard and threw it into the lake. It disappeared in reflected brilliance. Light pinned him down and made even his shadow feel small.

He turned back to Mal, who was stripping cables from Allesandre's skin. He approached her, but she didn't look up. "Are you okay?"

She stopped, mid-incision. Blood sizzled on her knife. "What do you think? Go kill a friend and tell me how you feel after."

"I'm sorry."

She kept working as if she hadn't heard him.

"I'd like to help. But I don't know how."

She didn't respond, so he shrugged, grabbed one of the wires at her feet, and closed his eyes. A brilliant network charged the blackness, extending from the station in all directions: the system that pumped and treated Seven Leaf water, and sent it south to Dresediel Lex.

The web was sick. Thick threads hung limp; slender strands knotted and tangled. The wire twisted in his grip like a living thing. He reached for a loose thread and pulled it tight.

Seven Leaf Station convulsed. Mal swore, Couatl roared, and Caleb's eyes snapped open. The Wardens had drawn their weapons and faced the lake, as if they expected a host of Scorpionkind to rise from its depths.

Mal grabbed his wrist. "What are you doing?"

"Helping, I thought."

"Allie almost destroyed this place. Pull the wrong thread and everything might unravel. We could sink. Or the spirits bound in the lake could break their chains."

He released the wire. Its falling tip scraped the deck.

"Good. Thank you."

"Is there any way I can help?"

"Well," she said, softly, considering. "Pick up that wire again, and close your eyes."

The web hung in darkness. She touched his shoulder. "See the red lines?"

Faint solar afterimages shadowed the blue and silver strands. "I do."

"Those threads tie the station to the Serpents back in DL. Without them, we'll have to spend another week rebuilding the local generators. Using the Serpents, we'll have water flowing in a few days at most. Help me link them to the system."

"How?"

"Touch one of the red lines, first—only one."

With his free hand, Caleb clutched the nearest line. Fire shot up his arm, crisping nerves, singeing muscle.

Mal caught him as he stumbled. "You'll get the hang of it," she said as he recovered his balance. "You're not being damaged; your soul's just reacting to the Craft. All you need to do is merge the red lines with the blue."

He grabbed another thread, and this time he was ready for

the pain. When he touched the red line to the blue he felt a movement in his heart like shuffling cards as the two strands melded
into one.

He opened his eyes. The wire he held was the same color, the
same weight, but something had changed about the way it gathered and reflected light.

"That's it," Mal said. She examined the wire. "Do the same
wherever you see a red and a blue line twinned. You'll save me a
day at least. I'll focus on the hard stuff."

She turned to a tangle of bent metal, closed her eyes and furrowed her brow.

He left her to her work, and went about his own.

They paused for a brief lunch around three. Sweat soaked
Caleb's shirt. Mal had discarded her jacket and rolled up her
sleeves; her arms quivered as she lifted the canteen to her lips.
She tore her meat with her teeth. They ate without speaking.
When Caleb was only half-finished with his lunch, she stalked
back to work.

Later he remembered that afternoon as a series of images,
mostly of Mal: she knelt atop a Craft circle cut into the steel platform with the blade of her knife. She stripped Allesandre's body
from the web, cleaned the wires of blood and meat, and replaced
the dead woman with a cold iron ring. She leaned against a con-
sole, shaking. A handkerchief tied over her hair kept sweat from
her eyes.

Sunburnt, exhausted, five hours later, they stepped back to
examine their handiwork. The station was clear of human refuse,
and Allesandre's web re-strung. Smashed crystal screens stared
from control kiosks. Gears and levers, frayed wires and mystic
diagrams protruded from broken panels. But when Mal said,
"That's it," Caleb did not challenge her.

The setting sun cast the station's shadow long upon the water, and their shadows with it: the Wardens, Caleb, and Mal.

"It's working?" Caleb asked—the first words he had spoken
since lunch.

"No." She moved her hand in a swift circle. "Now it's working."

At first, nothing seemed to change: a stretching, still span in which he wondered if Mal had fixed the station at all, or if she had snapped when Allesandre died, and spent the afternoon drawing ineffectual lines in metal. He waited in silence. Four's feet scuffed the deck as she shifted. Caleb slid his hands into his pockets, and the sound of fabric on skin was louder than the waves.

Louder, because there were no waves.

The waters of Seven Leaf Lake lay flat and even as a pane of glass from horizon to horizon, reflecting the universe aflame with sunset. Caleb's breath stopped. The slightest exhalation might shatter this perfect mirror of the world, and with that mirror the world itself.

Then the screams began.

At first he felt them in his stomach, but they rose in volume and pitch to fill his ears, the insensate fury of a Skittersill mob, rage so strong it broke into despair. The screams came from nowhere and everywhere at once, rising to crescendo as the sun fell.

Mal's arms remained outstretched. The Wardens did not move. They stood sentinel.

The setting sun spilled its blood on the water. Night crept in from the edges of the world. The first stars appeared, puncture wounds in the sky from which darkness spread. Glyphs burned at Mal's wrists, around her fingers, beneath her collar.

Caleb felt the screams in his teeth.

When the sky deepened to the rich purple of a king's robe, he saw light in the lake.

Phosphorescent fish, he thought, or invisible creatures too tiny to be seen. In deep caves, as a child, one of his mother's native guides had shown him underground eels, skin slick with green radiance.

He was wrong.

Gods writhed in the water.

Starlight sank into Seven Leaf Lake and branched into rippling, multicolored thorns. Figures thrashed, impaled upon the light: humans, deer, wolves, snakes, mice, great-winged birds,

Scorpionkind, all wriggling like caught fish. The smallest was three times the size of Seven Leaf Station.

The screams came from their open mouths.

He remembered, back in Dresediel Lex, telling the King in Red that the local spirits of Seven Leaf Lake had been subdued. He said this without emotion, because that was how it was written in the report.

Caleb's knees struck the metal deck. His hands rose to block his ears, but he forced them down, and forced his eyes open. He had been to Bay Station, had seen gods entombed and tortured. These were nowhere near so grand: remnant spirits, that was all, lesser deities that grew with the tribes that once roamed these mountains. When the tribes died or moved on, their gods remained, living off scraps of wonder and remembrance, barely conscious.

Conscious enough, though, to realize when someone came to take their land, their water. Conscious enough to fight. Conscious enough to be a threat—and Dresediel Lex would tolerate no threats.

Mal clapped her hands twice. Machines clanked and Craft hummed its sphere-music. A curtain of water, reflective as mercury, curved over Caleb and Mal, the Wardens and Seven Leaf Station, blocking their view of the lake and the tortured beings within. Above, the water closed the sky in a shrinking circle, a hundred feet in diameter, fifty, twenty-five. A red star gleamed in the circle's center.

The circle closed, and cut off the cries like a guillotine blade. The water blocked out moonlight, stars, sky, and lake, and cast the station in a bloodless light. The air smelled of rain and burnt metal.

Caleb realized he was still kneeling. He stood, using a nearby chair as a prop. Beside him, Mal sagged.

"Those are gods," Caleb said. "They're in pain."

"They're not gods. Not exactly. And when someone comes to salve the world's pain, those things can take a number like the rest of us. Meanwhile, Skittersill and Sansilva and Stonewood and North Ridge and Central and the Vale will have water to drink."

She turned a wheel on a nearby altar, and a hatch telescoped open in the floor, revealing a flight of stairs down into the station. "I'm going to bed." She took the first and second steps slow, but on the third her strength failed her and she steadied herself against the wall. "You should get some rest."

She descended out of sight. A closing door cut off the tap of her footsteps. Caleb remained, alone, on deck with the Wardens. For a while, he watched his own reflection distorted in the water, and listened. He heard nothing. He was used to that.

He followed Mal into darkness.

28

Seven Leaf Station was not designed for comfort. Below the surface, between banks of slowly revolving Craft circles and humming soul catchers, Heartstone architects had added as an afterthought a few bare rooms for the station's staff. The Wardens split four chambers among themselves. Caleb chose a cold bed in a room with a writing desk, a few pictures of a dead man's family, and a chessboard set with a problem involving knight moves. He glanced at the board but didn't mull over the problem. He had enough of his own.

Troubled by the thought of sleeping in a corpse's sweat, Caleb stripped the bed and remade it with fresh linens. He lay down to rest, but sleep evaded him. He saw blood and water flow from a cut throat, surging in time to the beat of the machines that drained the lake.

He stood at last, slipped on his shoes and jacket, and left the room with the chess problem still unsolved. Turning through a maze of corridors he found the Wardens' larder; he poured a cold glass of water, assembled a plate of rice and meat and tortillas, and bore them back into the twisting halls.

There was no mystery as to where Mal slept. When Caleb and the Wardens followed her into the under-station, they found all the doors open save one, marked "Manager's Quarters" in thick block letters.

The door was still closed. He knocked, waited, and heard her muted by steel: "Go away."

"I brought you food. You didn't come to dinner."

"I'm not hungry."

"It's not for your sake. What if we hit bad weather on the

way back and I'm thrown out of the basket? I want you strong enough to catch me."

"Who says I would catch you?"

He opened the door and stepped inside.

The manager's suite was larger than the other rooms, but still small. It smelled faintly of incense, and contained an overstuffed bookcase, a desk, a nightstand, and a large bed.

The far wall was transparent. Beyond it writhed the gods impaled on thorn-tree contracts, larger underwater than they had seemed from the surface. Currents and passing fish distorted their features. Their cries did not penetrate the walls.

Mal sat in silhouette, cross-legged on the bed with her back to Caleb. She was naked from the waist up, the curves of her neck and ribs and the swell of her hip lit blue and green and red by light from the window. As he entered, she lifted her shirt from the bed and slid it on, one arm at a time, without hurry. She fastened one button at her breast, but did not look back at him. "I thought I told you to stay out."

"You didn't. You told me to go away."

"And you listened so well." She set a slender object down on the nightstand. In the dim light he could not tell what it was.

"I'm a good listener." He set the plate of food on the desk, turned the desk chair to face her, and sat, watching her back.

She seemed so still, a statue in contrast with the fluid pain beyond the window. He focused on her outline.

"Allie was a colleague," she said. "She left for Seven Leaf soon after the Bright Mirror thing. This would be her big break into management. She wrote me, at first. Her letters stopped coming a month ago, but I was too busy to check."

"It must have been hard for her," he said, "so far away, no friends."

"Nothing but the work, and what work." Mal waved at the water and the things inside it. "Subdue these spirits, torment them. Even if they aren't conscious the way we are, they feel."

"It's worth the price," he said, though he was not certain.

"For how long?" Her voice was hollow. "Ten years from now,

or twenty, this lake will be a dry and cracked bowl in the mountains and we will turn to the next, and the next after that. One day it won't be mindless gods who suffer for our thirst, but other cities, other people. How long until we decide Regis doesn't need its wealth of water? The cities of the frozen north, surely they don't thirst like we do. Shikaw, next. We could drink this continent dry, from the Pax to the World Sea. Water is life, and life is worth any price, even life itself."

He didn't say anything.

She sighed. In the depths of Seven Leaf Lake, the trapped gods screamed. "This is the world we live in."

"Why not try to fix things?" Even as he said the words they felt small. A broken window or a broken promise you could fix. The scene in the lake was beyond fixing.

"How?"

"I don't know."

She laughed, a sour, sad sound that hung on the station's dead air like a corpse on a rack. "Everybody needs to make a sacrifice sooner or later, to survive. I guess this was my first—or the first one to hit me so close. I prepared for this moment years ago. I told myself I had."

He didn't ask what "this moment" was. In the flickering light, he could barely recognize Mal. Maybe she couldn't recognize herself. He moved to the bed, which gave slightly under his weight. The mattress was a firm lie: the world beneath was only water. He slid next to her and touched her shoulders. Her muscles were knotted steel cables. He pressed into those knots with his thumbs and the heels of his hands. Mal stifled a cry as he began. He tried again, with a lighter touch. "Thank you," she said this time.

The cropped fringe of her hair feathered against his fingers. Small, downy hairs trailed down the nape of her neck, an arrow pointing to her back and shoulders. He had expected her skin to be cool to the touch. Everything down here was. She was warm though, feverish.

So close, he studied her: smooth skin a shade lighter than his own, shoulders and neck dark and freckled by sun. He could not feel her glyph-marks—the Craft left no scars, unless you knew how to look for them.

He studied her to capture her, to capture the moment, but also to distract himself from the tortures outside the window. Why would she choose to face that? Maybe she felt it was a part of her sacrifice, or Allesandre's. He pressed against her skin, and thoughts of sacrifice faded. He worked her shoulders until the steel melted and became almost human.

Sitting on Mal's bed, massaging her back, Caleb felt time stretch and transform. This moment was a door ajar.

He leaned into her, silent, and she leaned into him. His arms drifted around her. Mal's breath fluttered like wings. The tips of his fingers explored her jaw and throat, the slim even lines of muscle and the gently pulsing vein. She clutched his arms. He felt the line of her collarbone, the skin above the swell of her breasts.

It was wet. In surprise he lifted his hand from her and held it up to the light of tortured gods. His fingertips glistened dark and red.

Later he could not recall whether he recoiled from her, or she from him. One of them moved, or both, and seconds later she sat a foot away from him on the bed, in profile like a temple statue. Beneath the open collar of her shirt ran two long cuts, one on the left side and one on the right. Other cuts, long healed, lay below them, parallel to her collarbone: a necklace of scars. Her eyes glittered.

"Mal. What the hells, Mal." The object she had placed on the nightstand was a knife—not the Craftwork blade that killed Allesandre, but a length of black glass with a handle of beaten gold and silver wire.

The half of her that faced him was in shadow. The half that faced the gods reflected the bitter green glow of their pain.

Behind her, on the windowsill, sat a stone carving, three inches tall and no broader than a woman's arm: a hollow cylinder formed by the bodies of two serpents intertwined. Twin trails of thin gray smoke wisped from a coil of incense at the idol's center. Rising, the wisps wound around each other and faded into air.

"It's called—" she began.

"I know what it's called," Caleb said before she could finish. "Autosacrifice. Bloodletting. Cutting."

"It's not cutting."

"What's the difference?"

She wiped the blood with a handkerchief, folded the handkerchief and set it beside the knife. "I told you to leave."

"Don't change the subject."

"Hells, Caleb. You saw what I did up there. You see what's happening outside. I need to atone."

"Atone?" The bed shook with the force of his standing. He reached around her and grabbed the idol off the windowsill, leaving the incense and its excrement of ash behind. "Aquel and Achal." He threw the statue onto the mattress beside her. It bounced, and rolled to rest with Aquel facing down and Achal snarling up. "These are bloodthirsty creatures. We have them locked up, and I'm glad for it. We killed people for them. Cutting yourself before that statue—do you know what it stands for?"

"Of course I do!" Metal walls reflected the force of her shout. Caleb stepped back. She stood, her half-open shirt flaring like the robes of a Deathless King. "The priests killed. Sure. But are we any different? Am I, after what I did today? You've seen Skittersill, and Stonewood, what our city does to the people who lose. Your father—"

"Don't bring him into this. My father's a criminal. A madman."

"Your father led the Skittersill Rising! He tried for years to make peace between theists and Craftsmen, and when that failed he tried to protest. And they rained fire on him. They burned his followers by the hundreds."

"He wanted to kill people. That's the freedom they were fighting for, him and his followers. Freedom to kill people."

"Freedom from persecution. Freedom to practice their religion. Freedom to sacrifice volunteers—people who wanted to die."

"That's murder! It's murder when you carve someone's heart out of their chest, no matter if you're doing it because a god tells you to."

Muscles on the side of her jaw twitched. "Fine. But what I just did was murder, too. When we sin, we shed blood to atone. That's what my parents taught me."

"Then they were crazy."

He said the words before he knew them: they sprang to his mind, slithered down the spine to his lungs, infested the air, and burst out his mouth. Mal's eyes widened, and her lips pressed thin together. Caleb opened his mouth to say something, anything, to apologize or explain.

The gods' light faded, and it was too late.

Night filled the room. A great hand seized him, and threw him like a stone. He struck the wall, or perhaps the floor or ceiling. Directions no longer met in his mind. Weight pressed against his chest, the weight of thousands of miles of water. His ribs creaked and he fought to breathe.

"You don't get to say that."

She was talking. Good. Talking meant she wouldn't kill him straight off.

Blood and silver, he thought, when did her killing me become a possibility?

He remembered her standing over him goddess-like on the border of the Skittersill. Deities kill those that follow them. He opened his mouth, but only a dry croak escaped his lips.

"My parents were good people." Her voice was an anchor in his whirling world. "They were faithful, and they were angry, but they were good. They stood against the Red King in the Skittersill Rising, and fell. And burned. My mother took a week to die."

He struggled against her Craft, but his arms did not move, his scars would not wake. Blood pounded in his ears. His lungs ached for air.

The Rising had been his father's fault. When Temoc decided to walk a path, fools always followed in his footsteps. A peaceful demonstration, they claimed, and it was at first, but as weeks rolled on his control of the mob wavered. On the tenth day, some idiot threw a stone, a child died, and the Wardens moved in.

Battle lines were not drawn. There were no heroic struggles. Those who resisted, fell.

Caleb was ten. Mal could not have been more than twelve.

After the bodies cooled, the King in Red issued a public call for peace, and Temoc became an enemy of the state.

Caleb's father had already gone, leaving his scars behind.

Caleb was also, in his way, an orphan of the Rising.

Mal's parents lay burning in the streets in Skittersill. No amount of water could quench those flames, and their bodies would never fall to ash.

Mal, too, took power from her scars.

"I'm sorry," he said as spots of black deeper than black swelled behind his eyes.

The weight lifted from his chest, and darkness drained away down the hole in Mal's mind. He slumped, but though his legs felt like stretched and fraying rubber, he did not fall.

Mal stood between him and the gods, blanched and wan as a crescent moon. The draining dark had taken something from her.

"Sorry," she said. "Yes." And: "You should go."

He reached blindly for the door, opened it, and backed out without looking away from her. He had to say something, but there was nothing to say.

She grew smaller as he withdrew. When he crossed the threshold of her room, she was the size of a statue. Three steps more, the size of an idol.

The door closed between them, and he turned away and ran.

INTERLUDE: DREAMS

Snow fell on Dresediel Lex for the first and last time, covering the bodies of men and gods that littered the streets. Where the snow fell in fire, it hissed and burst to steam. A falling god had cracked the face of a pyramid with one flailing hand, and rubble covered the broad avenue below. Rage and sorrow burned in the mottled sky.

Blood-slick, Alaxic stumbled through the city's doom. Cold air stung his throat. Pain from the wounds in his chest, and arm, and leg, pierced and beggared thought. At dawn he had ridden into battle on a feathered serpent, bedecked with the blessing of the gods. The serpent lay dead two blocks away, and he was tired.

"Hello, Alaxic," someone said behind him.

The voice was deep and familiar, but alien to this time, this place. He turned, fast as his wounds would let him.

A skeleton in a red suit stood in the road, between the burning corpses of two demigods. He bore no weapons save a cup of coffee.

The snow did not fall in the coffee, or accumulate on the skeleton's robes.

"What are you doing in my dreams?" Alaxic asked.

"At the moment," the skeleton replied, "I am pondering why of all the places and times you might choose to dream, you would select the Liberation of Dresediel Lex. This was not your finest hour."

"It was a noble struggle."

"You fought us and we crushed you."

"You besieged and blockaded us. We had no choice."

"Your people tore out my lover's heart. What did you think would happen after that?"

"I had no part in that decision."

"As the inquest found, or else we would have sunk you into solid bedrock, or trapped you in the corridors of your own mind, or tied you to a mountain somewhere with a regenerating liver and an eagle that likes *foie gras*." A band of skirmishers ran past, bound to nowhere. "So, why do you come back here?"

"My friends died in this battle. And we do not all choose where we dream."

"You are a strange person," Kopil said. "You were a priest, but became a Craftsman. You do not control your own dreams. You refuse to leverage your soul, though it means you won't survive the end of that slab of meat you call your body."

"The Craft," replied Alaxic, "is a tool. Not all of us let our tools rule our life."

Kopil sipped his coffee. "Tell me about Seven Leaf Lake."

"I heard there were problems."

"One of your employees went mad. Killed everyone on the station."

"Horrible," Alaxic said. "I don't know what I'd do if I were in your shoes. Makes me glad I'm retired."

"Are you really?"

"Glad?"

"Retired."

He exhaled fog into the cold. "You've watched me for the last few months, you and your spies. What do I do?"

"You drink tea, and you read."

"I drink tea, and I read. I don't plot, I don't scheme. I don't want the old world back any more than you do."

A winged serpent flew overhead, and was transfixed by arrows of light. It shrieked, and fell in bloody pieces to the street around them.

"Yet you still dream of old battles."

"And you haven't forgiven me, in five decades, for surviving this one. You resented my success in the Hidden Schools. You opposed the Wardens' decision to set me free after the Skittersill Rising. You plotted against me as I built Heartstone, and took it from me when you had the chance."

"You were a rebel. An anarchist."

"I am a populist." He looked up to the sky, where Craftsmen clad in engines of war tore gods asunder. Heavenly blood fell, mixed with snow. "At least I only dream about old battles," he said. "You're still fighting them."

A wave of night rolled over the world. When Alaxic looked again, the King in Red was gone.

Book Three

∎ ∎ ∎

HEARTSTONE

29

Caleb left Seven Leaf Lake soon after dawn, with an escort of two Wardens. He told Four that the King in Red wanted a report on their success, that Mal would stay until reinforcements arrived. This was not, exactly, a lie. Mal could have stopped him, but she didn't.

They took flight as the first rays of sun glanced off the long flat plane of the lake. Sleep had haunted him all night, ambushing from the darkest corners of his mood. Sharp-fingered devils charged his fitful dreams, demons with his own face devouring the flesh of screaming gods.

He shaded his eyes against the sunrise, leaned back into the gondola, and drowsed.

The Couatl carried him south. Lake gave way to waterfall and smooth-flowing river. Every few miles, stone circles protruded from the forest, their centers thick with shade. Silver glyphs glowed against gray granite. The standing stones bled Seven Leaf Lake south, to slake his city's thirst. Soon the falls would cease to thunder, and the river shrink to a stream.

One hundred twenty eight million acre-feet of water. After a decade or so, the city's growth would outpace the lake's ability to refill itself. The forest would feel the effects long before then.

After three hours they stopped for lunch on a cliff overlooking a deep valley, and ate bread and cheese and drank stale canteen water and agave liquor.

The Wardens napped on the cliff after lunch. Caleb, restless, walked a hundred feet into the woods, found a sturdy birch tree, and struck it with his palms, with his feet and the sides of his hands, scaring away broad-winged birds that roosted in the canopy. He ripped his knuckles' skin, and left a smear of blood on the white bark. He pushed against the trunk until his shoulders, arms, legs, belly all convulsed and he let out a long, low cry.

A roar answered from the valley, larger, deeper, a sound made by no human throat.

Shaken, he returned to the Wardens, who stood with weapons bared, roused by his cry or the valley's answer. They packed quickly, and flew south.

By day's end the Drakspine peaks mellowed into farms and bare hills. Here, amid long dry rows of wheat, the Wardens kept observation posts, small adobe buildings beside barn-sized hutches where Couatl warmed their eggs. Caleb's escorts spent most of the evening writing reports; afterward, he challenged them and the other attendant Wardens to a quick game. As he played, he did not look the goddess in the eye.

Talking over cards, he listened for news, but heard little more than farmers' gossip, rumors of Scorpionkind raids on outlying settlements. When he asked about the city, the Wardens glanced at one another and claimed they had heard nothing certain.

They reached Dresediel Lex the next morning. Serpents of smoke tangled in the air above Sansilva. Caleb's heart leapt, but when they crested the Drakspine he saw the damage was limited to the 700 block. Some shops burned, that was all, a few lives destroyed. Wardens circled above emptied streets.

They landed in the pyramid's parking lot, strewn with broken bottles, rocks, clapboard signs, all the detritus of a protest turned riot. Two Wardens met them and rushed Caleb across the lot into the pyramid. Glancing over his shoulder he saw Muerte Coffee, empty, its front window webbed with cracks.

His escorts bore him wordlessly across a lobby manned with guards and security demons, into a waiting lift. By the sixtieth floor, he stopped asking questions.

The foyer of the Red King's office was empty save for dark leather furniture, a grim portrait on one wall, and Anne, Kopil's secretary, at her desk. She acknowledged Caleb with a curt nod, and turned a stone desktop idol counterclockwise; the double doors behind her, marked with deaths-heads, opened without sound. The Wardens thrust him into the shadow beyond, and the doors slammed shut.

"Caleb."

The voice was weak, a bare suggestion of wind. For a confused moment he thought it belonged to his father, captive, tortured, and he turned in slow terror of what he might see.

He stood in Kopil's office, beneath the crystal dome on the pyramid's peak—the office without entrance or exit. There was no sign of the doors through which he had come.

A hospital bed rested near the altar-desk. The carpet was rolled back, and someone had drawn a mandala around the bed with white and purple and yellow sand. Red sheets clad the mattress, and a red robe wrapped the skeleton who lay upon it.

The shadows that clung to Kopil looked light and insubstantial. His gestures were weak, the sparks of his eyes dull and rust-colored. The Kopil who confronted Caleb in this office months before had been a river in flood, and here he lay at ebb.

Caleb stared. Everything he could say seemed wrong.

The King in Red beckoned Caleb with a twitch of his fingers. He approached.

Bare jaws worked silently until the Deathless King could speak. "What happened?"

"You look different," he said, and wished he had said something else.

"I am different," Kopil replied with a low, grating laugh like a snake's rattle. "I lie reduced, and the water flows. It has been half a century since I last felt weakness. Do they appreciate what I do for them, I wonder."

"There are people who have sacrificed more," he said, though he didn't know why, "and lived less comfortably, with death their only promise of release."

Kopil did not seem to understand what he had said, or if he understood, did not care. "Is Seven Leaf Lake ours again?"

"Yes."

"Tell me."

Caleb did, though he left out many details. He did not

mention his scars, or Mal's acquaintance with Allesandre, or her bloodletting and their fight beneath the lake. Dates, times, names, these he related with precision. Four and her team deserved commendations for their service. Seven Leaf was safe again, and the water flowed.

He spoke of the agony of the gods in the lake, and shuddered when Kopil said, "Good."

"The riots should stop now," he said, but the King in Red waved the subject away.

"They were barely worth the name of riot. A tussle with the Wardens. Someone knocked over a few fire barrels, and the coals ignited a line of Sansilva shops. We couldn't use tainted water on the fire—some Tzimet might survive the heat—so we flew saltwater in from the ocean."

"The Vale looked quiet when we passed over."

"Not much trouble there. Wardens arrested a few agitators, prophets proclaiming the Twin Serpents' return, that sort of thing."

"Do you think," Caleb said, but stopped himself.

"What?"

"Do you think they knew we're drawing the Serpents' power? Do we have an information leak?"

"One of the men we arrested was a salesman from Centervale with three children and a pending divorce; another, a minor landowner; the third, a junior league ullamal coach. Their wives, husbands, children claim none had any religious history, not even the coach. They dreamed of the Hungry Serpents, and when they woke, they prophesied in tongues of flame."

"A thousand people must go mad in Dresediel Lex every day."

"Three thousand. But the visions here were all the same. They saw Aquel and Achal, waking."

"We only have six weeks to the next eclipse."

Kopil sighed. "I know. RKC has already volunteered to pay for the fireworks. Fifteen thousand souls for simple merriment. We could buy everyone in the city a cup of decent coffee for that. And yet the revelers must revel."

"The Serpents are on peoples' minds as the eclipse nears, is my point. When they go crazy, their madness takes a form to fit their fears. It's just dream stuff. Nothing serious."

"Have you ever read Maistre Schatten?"

"Who?"

"Schatten wrote about dreams and myths and the unconscious: *Sleeping Giants, The Shadow's Refuge, The Ends of Time.* Did you ever read them?"

"No."

"I knew the man," Kopil said. "Old in his fifties, shaken and shattered by a life of delving under the placid surface of his clients' minds. Do not ignore dreams. They are a line from the past to the future. All nightmares are real."

"You're worried."

"I'm worried," the King in Red replied. He crooked one finger, and a brown paper envelope floated from his desk to Caleb's hand. Caleb opened the envelope, and slid Mal's shark's-tooth pendant into his palm. The closed-eye glyph and the tracking pattern were cracked and blackened. "Yesterday, the sigils and enchantments on this pendant burned themselves out—around noon, when you struck down Alaxic's aide."

Caleb pursed his lips. Allesandre had spouted no True Quechal rhetoric, no promises of the gods' return. Then again, she had been all but a goddess herself, at the end. And when she usurped Seven Leaf, she had let Tzimet into the water. She would have been a logical poisoner's agent—she knew Mal was sneaking into Bright Mirror and North Station. As Alaxic's aide, as Mal's friend, Allesandre could have set Mal up, pointed her toward a dealer in Quechal artifacts who would give her the tracking amulet. Only the faintest strands of the deal would lead back to Allesandre herself. "Interesting," he said.

"Are you still in contact with the cliff runner from whom you took this amulet?"

He blinked. "I could try to track her down. I don't know if she'll talk to me." Both statements were true.

"The talisman is dead. Even the tracking signals have ceased. Only broken glyphs remain. My people copied the glyphs, studied the tooth down to its component atoms, and found nothing.

This supposed link between your cliff runner and Alaxic's aide is our only lead. Find the runner. Ask her if she recognizes a woman of Allesandre's description. You may offer to return the talisman, if she requests it in exchange. Report back to me on your success."

Caleb slid the tooth into his jacket pocket. "I'll try." No need to say more than that.

"Do." Kopil clicked his teeth together three times, and rested his skull back against the pillow. "Weak, I feel something like fear again."

"I don't understand," Caleb said.

"We've built a world in the last six decades, but it has not endured the test of time. We inhabit the gods' abandoned buildings like spiders in an old house. Madmen flock to worship departed lords and dead ladies, to tear down all we have built. They seem to hate me. Perhaps they're right to do so."

"No."

"Gods perished at my hand half a century ago. Was that for any purpose, beyond satisfying my vanity, my lust for vengeance?"

"Yes."

"Yes?"

Caleb pointed to the altar stone. "It's been sixty years since the last death on that altar." He saw Mal again, blood black against her dusky skin. "Our city is cruel. It exploits its children. But it does not corral those it fears and hates, does not kill them to appease bogeymen. There's a lot wrong with this world you've made, sir, but that much is right."

Kopil lay still beneath blood-colored sheets and blood-colored robes.

"I take it your time with Ms. Kekapania did not go well," said the King in Red, after a time.

"No," Caleb replied. "It did not."

"I'm sorry to hear that."

"Thank you."

"You are right, of course. About the sacrifice, and the value of our creation. But do not underestimate the power of dreams."

The red sparks in his eye sockets blinked out. "I see the Serpents when I sleep, too."

Caleb said nothing.

"You may leave."

A Warden flew him home over the Drakspine. Dry heat sucked his blood and spirit. Yet, standing for the first time in days outside his own house, in full sunlight, he could not shake the chill from his bones.

30

Zolin, the finest ullamal player in the world, tore down the narrow court. She dodged defenders, juggling the heavy rubber ball from knee to knee. It struck her flesh with a thick sound. Ten thousand onlookers watched from the stands, and did not breathe.

For two hours Zolin's squad had lagged behind, but in the last thirty minutes, through a haze of exhaustion, the Dresediel Lex Sea-Lords had closed the gap in score through luck and grim determination. In ordinary games, the audience laughed, cried, shouted obscenities at the stripe-robed, monstrously masked referees; tonight, they waited and hoped for a moment of magic.

Zolin spun clear of the last blocker and struck the ball with the crown of her head. It flew over the opposing team toward the gaping mouth of the serpent statue at the arena's far end. That serpent was Aquel, the Creeping Hunger; across the field coiled Achal, the Kindled Flame.

For two thousand years, this game had been a cornerstone of Quechal religion. Play mimicked the Hero Sisters' sacrifice to the Serpents, at the beginning of the world. Modern fans cared little for mythology. Neither did Zolin. But if there was an afterlife, and she met ancient players there, she would play circles around them all.

The ball soared, a blur of black and bone, struck the inside of the serpent's mouth, and disappeared down its gullet. A bell rang.

Roars of triumph filled the arena. Beer and wine showered like rain onto the sand; torn programs and strips of cloth joined the deluge. Zolin raised her arms and leapt into the air. Sweat flew from her skin. Her teeth gleamed like pearls. She was immortal.

"Dammit," Caleb said from his seat far up in the stands.

With vicious pulls he tore the bookie's receipt to shreds. Swearing felt good, so he tried again. "Godsdammit."

"I warned you not to bet against the city," said Teo as she tallied her winnings. The crowd thinned, making for the exits. Sam, in the aisle, cupped her hands around her mouth and hooted in triumph. "Especially when Zolin's playing."

"If she's sober."

On the court, each team saluted the other's serpent-goal. Zolin's teammates lifted her onto their shoulders and ran a slow circuit around the court. A band struck up a bassy triumphant tune, and Sam thrashed to the music. She waved to Teo, who waved back but did not leave her seat.

"She has a face full of powder off the court, but it's never hurt her play. This is religion to her."

Caleb winced, and Teo noticed.

"What is it with you?"

"I just lost a decent chunk of soul. Give me some space."

"Whenever I mention religion, you get this look like you're about to stalk off and beat your head against a wall somewhere."

"I told you what happened with me and Mal."

"You told me what happened. You haven't told me what you're going to do next."

"I don't want to talk about it."

Again Sam waved, and this time Teo smiled, and stood. "Fine." She slid her receipt into a pocket of her white linen jacket, and joined Sam in the aisle. They danced as the band played, hands on each other's hips.

Fans filtered out into the dark, hot night. Caleb sat alone in the empty row, save for a small Quechal man, silver-haired and slump-shouldered, who rocked in his seat, muttering a half-remembered prayer.

Sam whispered in Teo's ear. They drew apart, glanced around at the empty stands, laughed. "You want to grab a drink with us?" Sam asked.

"Sure," he said.

They extricated themselves from the labyrinth of halls and

shops and parking structures that adjoined the stadium, and found a bar with a crudely painted, misspelled sign and a muscular young woman guarding the door. Teo gave the bouncer a wink as they ducked inside, and the woman shifted, unsure whether to smile back. Teo and Sam joked about her confusion as they found a booth. Inside the bar, Caleb drank gin and listened to them argue about art, faith, sports, and alcohol. Sam picked up the tab; her *Urban Grotesquerie* had sold at auction, and while she was still an artist, she was no longer starving.

After an hour, the bar's air grew stagnant and they staggered out onto cool streets. Teo hailed a driverless carriage and the horse pulled them across town through traffic toward Andrej's. As they rolled through the night together, Caleb remembered their last carriage ride, the rush and terror of the evening when the water ran black.

Sam didn't like Andrej's. She sat uncomfortable in their corner booth, eying the brokers in the dark elegant suits, who drank expensive cocktails and laughed moneyed laughs. "How can you relax in this place? You think anyone here's ever seen anything real?"

"What's real?" Teo asked, swirling her drink.

"Don't you know?" she replied with a smirk, and touched the side of Teo's face. A small scar ran next to Sam's eye, new since the riots. Caleb had not asked how she was wounded. He did not want to hear the answer.

After an hour he excused himself and climbed the spiral staircase to the roof. He looked out over the city to the sea, and to Bay Station barely visible on the horizon. The city gleamed below and above, skyspire lights reflected on the belly of the clouds and on the harbor's black surface. Salt spray mixed with the bitter quinine taste of his gin and tonic.

"You should go to her," Teo said when she found him.

"Are you sure you should leave Sam in there alone? She might burn the whole place down."

"She'll be fine. And you should apologize to Mal."

"I don't want to talk about it."

"You haven't talked about anything else all night."

"I haven't talked about anything all night."

"Exactly."

He leaned against the balcony railing, and hung his head over the drop: four stories to the next step of the pyramid, then another four stories, and so on down. Windows glowed from the sandstone blocks: other bars, or people late at work, lost in paper mazes.

"She should apologize to me," he said, though he knew it wasn't true. "I didn't do anything wrong." That, also, sounded like a lie. The air up here, fresh and cool and open, would not admit falsehood. He drank. "What would I say to her, anyway?"

"Say you're sorry for being an idiot, to start. Maybe you add: I was under a lot of stress. We'd just saved the city from a mad necromancer, and I have issues with religion, but those don't give me the right to pass judgment on you. You could plea the fact that your father's a lunatic, which makes you sensitive about the subject."

His next sip of gin lingered too long in his mouth, and when he swallowed he shivered as it slithered into him. "Yeah." Turning from the world he leaned back against the railing and followed Teo's gaze to the altar in the center of the roof. "Apologize," he said, testing the idea. "Even if I'm right."

"Do you want to be right, or do you want to be with her?"

"Can't it be both?"

"Later, maybe. From her point of view, you've insulted her, insulted her dead parents, and left her in the Drakspine Mountains with no one to keep her company but a bunch of the same Wardens who killed her family. This is throw-yourself-at-her-feet-and-beg-forgiveness time."

"I do sound like a jerk when you put it that way."

"Yes."

They watched the stone.

"Hey," he said at last.

"Yes?"

"You've been a real friend to me about this, for the last few months."

She shrugged, and sipped her single malt.

"I'm glad it's working out, with you and Sam."

"Is it? I mean." She examined the constellations reflected in her whiskey, in the ice. "She's wonderful. Wild. Too wild for me, I think. She went out in the riots, when you were gone. I couldn't get her to stay. She said she had to be where the people were fighting."

"Artists."

She didn't reply.

"Do you love her?"

"I think. I don't know. Shit. Maybe I'm just giving you all this advice because I'm desperate, and I can help you, even if I can't help myself."

"To desperation," he said, and raised his glass. She raised hers as well, toward the altar.

"And to bleeding hearts," she added, and they drank.

31

An apology was easier to conceive than to compose. He tried
writing the words he would say. He tried all the sales tactics—
delivering his speech to a mirror, to an empty room, to a picture
of her drawn with charcoal and tacked to his wall. Nothing
worked.

At the office, instead of processing claims or helping prepare
for the eclipse, he began and abandoned countless variations on
an apologetic theme. Drafts formed a crumpled mountain in his
wastebasket. In the end he settled on a paragraph cribbed from a
classic play. "The problems of two people don't amount to much
in this crazy world," it began. He felt foolish reciting another
man's words, but he couldn't think of anything better.

Once he abandoned his search for the perfect words, he realized he didn't know where to deliver the imperfect ones. Mal had
never brought him to her home. He could find her office without
trouble, but the conversation he wanted to have with her was not
fit for a place of business, and dangerous besides. Walls could hear,
and Red King Consolidated was not a religion-tolerant workplace
as such. Finding her home address from payroll would attract too
much attention.

Better to meet her on neutral ground, he thought, and returned
to the border between Stonewood and the Skittersill. Seeking
runners, he found an indigent circle of them sharing a pipe
with Balam in a shattered statuary court. The tattooed trainer
sported a new scar over his brow, and his right arm hung in a
sling. Caleb did not ask what he had done in the riots. Balam took
the pipe from a girl to his left, breathed in deep, held smoke in
his lungs, and exhaled; as a dragon it rose, circling through ru-

ined statues. Balam's eyes fixed on a point beyond the sky. "Haven't learned enough to let her alone."

"I owe her something. I want to pay her back."

Balam examined Caleb, passed the pipe, set his free hand on top of his cast. "Maybe you do. Been weeks since she last ran with us. She's keeping herself to herself. You'll find her when she wants to be found."

The runners did not offer Caleb their pipe, and he left alone. No wonder they were suspicious. Their circle was reduced. Many must have died at North Station, or been wounded in the riots.

He set those thoughts aside.

Mal was back in the city—a team of technicians had relieved her at Seven Leaf a week before—but where?

How much did he know about her, really? A few chance encounters. Chemistry. They had saved each other's lives. They were both wounded. Was that enough to build on?

The public address books were useless: eighty M. Kekapanias to choose from, assuming she was listed at all. With his other options exhausted, he bought a box of pastries at Muerte Coffee and went upstairs to beg Anne, the King in Red's secretary, for help.

She drank the coffee and ate two bear claws, and when Caleb told her a bowdlerized version of his fight with Mal, she clicked her tongue and smiled. Conversation turned to mystery plays and sports—Anne was an ullamal fanatic—and when Caleb left the Red King's foyer, he had the address. A calculated risk: if Anne believed his story of a lover's quarrel, she would protect his privacy. Not that he was lying. This was a quarrel, even if he and Mal were not precisely lovers.

Apology written, address in hand, he should have gone to her at once, but for three days he did not.

He walked at night. Aimless steps wound him to Skittersill. He kept to the light, walked well-traveled streets, and soon reached a patch of red earth between two brick buildings, bare of rubble, weeds, or insects. Twenty years ago, Temoc's temple stood on this barren plot.

Caleb remembered waiting in the pews, aged seven or eight,

knees drawn to his chin, as Temoc stretched out his arms and chanted the story of the Hero Twins to solemn men with faces made from wood and stone. He made mock sacrifice, brought his knife down handle-first on the chest of a prostrate disciple. Half-formed godlings crawled from the altar and licked the living sacrifice's skin for drops of unshed blood.

The Wardens burned Temoc's temple after the Skittersill Rising. They draped it in a silver net with lines as fine as dream, and the net burned down through brick and metal, plaster and rock and concrete. In thirty minutes the temple fell. The silver net sunk into the earth, leaving a crosshatched scar on bare red dust. Nothing grew there to this day.

Caleb threw a pebble into the empty lot. Green light flashed where the pebble landed. When Caleb's vision cleared, a fine white dust lay against the red.

Mal lived in a skyspire on the west side. Caleb took the airbus over, transferring three times. Most of the people who lived in Mal's spire, in any spire for that matter, flew on their own rather than take the bus.

Leather-winged drakes roosted in an iron aerie beneath the skyspire. Their wings twitched as the airbus approached, and they followed the passenger gondola with hungry yellow eyes. Caleb was the only one to dismount at the stop. He staggered along the catwalk, hands clasped to guardrails, not looking down. The drakes watched him.

The catwalk ended at the skyspire's crystal wall, without any sign of a door or entrance. He waited outside at first. The sun set over the Pax and the roosting lizards roared their dusk roars. Night fell, and he felt ridiculous standing on the doorstep with flowers tucked under his arm.

Reluctantly, he pressed against the crystal wall with his scars, and bent its Craft to let him pass. A familiar tingle washed over him, and he entered the arctic chill of Mal's spire.

Craftsmen and Craftswomen preferred the cold. Dancing elementals of air and ice cooled their buildings to the edge of sanity. Shivering in his thin jacket, Caleb climbed three flights of stairs. Mal's room was one of four on the spire's third floor. A mailbox on the wall bore her name engraved on a silver plate.

He knocked on the door, but received no answer. Waited, knocked again—still nothing. He set his ear against the door, but heard no movement. Working late, most likely. She was a busy woman.

Fine, he thought, and turned to go. He forced himself to stop. The next bus wouldn't come for another hour. If he left and returned, he'd arrive at midnight; his apology would not go over well if he had to wake Mal to deliver it. Better return the next night—but what if the same thing happened? And the night after that?

A bead of sweat trickled down the back of his neck. His hands shook for reasons unconnected to the cold. He touched the doorknob, turned, found it locked. A deadbolt, no Craft for him to pry apart or bend. Of course. In a flying tower full of wizards, who would trust an enchanted lock?

He paced, and counted slowly to a hundred. She did not appear. He cursed, and she did not answer that summons, either.

Caleb sat beside her door, and laid the flowers on the carpet. He drew a deck of cards from his pocket and dealt a hand of solitaire.

The denizens of Mal's tower all worked late, or else came and went without recourse to the hall. Minutes ticked by to hours. Caleb played every variant of solitaire he knew, four times, then won and lost three fortunes to himself at poker. No human presence relieved his isolation. Every quarter hour, regular as clockwork, an elemental eddy whisked by, trailing frost, and he clutched his jacket tight across his chest.

Midway through his fourth fortune, he heard a sound like a champagne flute crushed to sand: an inhuman approximation of the clearing of a throat. He paused, hands hovering above the cards, and looked up. Two demons—he thought there were two, invisible save as impressions in the air, glass scythes and scissor mouths, spiked fangs of crystal and eyes upon eyes—stared down at him.

He started to gather his cards, but they seized him before he could finish.

Either the demons could not talk, or they chose not to. They twisted Caleb's arms behind his back and thrust his head down. He staggered through white-walled halls, until they arrived at a dark, small room with a table and two chairs. The demons threw him inside, and closed the door.

He sat under a punishing spotlight, and wondered if the Wardens would come, if there was any law against lingering outside a woman's door and waiting for her to return.

Probably.

He would have played more solitaire, but half his cards remained on the floor outside Mal's apartment, with the flowers. Instead he practiced palming the cards that remained, sleeving them, sliding them into and out of his pockets. He did not cheat, but even an honest player should know how. When sleights of hand grew dull, he placed his feet up on the table and tipped his hat down over his eyes.

He woke to the click of an opening latch.

He blinked, blinded by light. Exploding galaxies faded into a dim mess of purple and red.

Demons stood in the door.

He did not struggle when they took his arms in their scissor-grip and marched him out.

"Where to now, gentlemen?"

No answer. He hadn't expected one.

When they did not steer him down the stairs toward the exit, he started to worry. Not handing him over to the Wardens, then—unless the Wardens used a different landing structure than the spire's residents. But he had seen no such structure from the air. If they didn't plan to hand him over or let him go, why move him from the cell?

Unless they had other uses for him. What powers ruled in a skyspire? The city's law, or the law of the Craft, or no law at all? And what if the demon guards had not in fact reported his capture, and were only waiting until the rest of the spire would be too fast asleep to hear his screams?

Demons, he recalled, kept peculiar diets.

As they marched him up a winding stair, he searched for opportunities of escape. None suggested themselves.

When they turned onto the third floor, he began to look more intently. They brought him to Mal's door, opened it, and thrust him in.

He stumbled, and caught his balance on a hardwood floor.

Shadow soaked the small bare room. Moonlight filtered through the large rear windows, illuminating gray carpet, a leather chair, a small coffee table, and a machine designed for either torture or home exercise.

The city burned below.

Something moved to Caleb's right, and he turned, expecting to see Mal.

Instead, he saw snakes: a wall of them, writhing.

He swore, jumped back, and after a panting, panicked moment, he recognized *Urban Grotesquerie*. Sam's piece. Sold at auction. "Seven hells."

Demon laughs sounded like spider legs skittering across a steel floor.

"Give us a few minutes." He recognized Mal's voice, from the corner beside the exercise machine. He turned to her as the demons withdrew and closed the door behind them.

He pointed at the snakes. "I know the woman who made this. Girlfriend of a friend of mine. I'll tell her you put it on display."

Mal moved between him and the city, and pointed to the ceiling. Recessed ghostlights glowed, and details filled in the room. Closed doors led off the main chamber. A photograph, framed, hung on the wall opposite *Grotesquerie*: a girl, a man, and a woman, in front of an adobe house of the kind that had been common in the Skittersill twenty years before. "You're lucky I saw the cards," she said. "And the flowers."

"I thought they'd have cleaned up after they grabbed me."

"Demons don't clean. Another hour, and the maid would have come by, and who knows how long you'd have been stuck there."

She looked much as he remembered her: hard and elegant. She wore a dark suit and a pencil skirt.

"I don't think I've ever seen you wear a skirt."

"Formal dinner. Dress to impress."

"Looks nice."

"I thought about leaving you in that cell, for the Wardens. I thought about throwing you off the top of this spire. Tell me why I shouldn't."

He opened his mouth, but no words emerged. His rehearsed, stolen speech would not fit through his throat.

Mal started to turn away.

"I'm sorry," he said.

She waited.

"I didn't mean to hurt you."

Still, she said nothing.

"I didn't think. It's hard to live in your parents' shadow. Believe me, I know. I don't want you to forget them. Even if I disagree with them. Even if I disagree with you."

"What do you want?"

"You," he said at last. "If you'll have me."

She turned away. "You don't have the first idea of the trouble you make for yourself, wanting me. Go. I'll persuade the building not to press charges."

"No," he said with more conviction than he felt. He walked to her, placed his hand on her arm. Her skin was tawny and soft. She did not pull away. Traffic surged through the streets and skies beneath them. "Without you, there's no race. I'm just running, in the dark, alone. And so are you. Burdened, with no one to share the burden."

"This won't work."

"I'll take that risk, if you will."

"I'll destroy you."

"Possible."

"I destroy everything I touch."

"I don't care."

"I wish I could believe that."

"Do."

Leaning in to her felt like leaning toward a cactus—every second swelling with the promise of pain. Her lips were round, and close, and still the pain did not come.

He kissed her, and did not die. He was so shocked by this that he pulled back, but she followed him, and kissed him in turn.

A minute passed, an eternity. A scythe-claw rapped on the door, and Caleb heard a muffled voice like the death of something beautiful. Mal replied in the same language, and stepped back. He shivered from her absence.

"I need you to leave," she said. "I have documents to review, and work tomorrow."

"Now?"

"Now."

"But—"

"Sorry."

He tasted her lips on his lips. "See you next month, I guess?"

"We don't have that long." She hugged herself, looked down at the city, looked back. "I'll wait for you in the foyer at RKC, tomorrow night, at five."

"You'll wait for me?"

"For you," she said, "and no one else. Now go, or else the demons will eat your soul and I'll have to take a husk to dinner." She snapped her fingers, and the door opened.

He almost left without kissing her again.

Almost.

32

The next day Caleb worked like a man possessed. He tore through stacks of memos, processed claims and ran figures, outlined complex deals and hedges against failure. Her fire would devour him if he let it, so he buried his mind in news and risk reports.

The nightmares had not stopped after Seven Leaf. Madmen crowded hospitals, crying the Twin Serpents' names. An itinerant philosopher in Stonewood immolated himself in a public square at noon, ranting about Aquel and Achal. When others rushed to douse him, he fought back with burning flesh, melting skin, crisping meat. A mother in the Vale nearly threw her two young children out of a second-story window, before her husband stopped her. She claimed to doctors and reporters that she had seen snakes of flame coiled inside her babies.

Somewhere, Temoc was laughing. Caleb felt sure of it.

Incidents of madness clustered near Heartstone installations. Caleb wrote a memo, a call to discontinue the Two Serpents project, with the frankness of a man certain he would be ignored. The Serpents had come to the city's aid in its hour of need. If their use entailed risk, well enough—they required more study before they were used again. The first investigations into the Craft had transformed kingdoms to deserts. This was no different.

At four forty-five he closed his books, capped his pens, cleaned his quill, sharpened his chisel, and walked to the lift. As he descended, he ran through an inventory of doom.

The doors rolled back, and he saw her across the hall, ablaze in a white linen dress. Arms crossed, one eyebrow raised, Mal looked inviting as the emptiness beyond a cliff's edge.

He didn't run to her, but he walked quickly. She kissed him on the lips.

"You're wearing a dress."

"I do that sometimes," she said. "Come on. Let's get something to eat."

"Something to eat" turned out to be dinner at an Iskari restaurant named Esprit, on the lowest level of a skyspire overlooking the ocean, the kind of place a wealthy couple in a mystery play might eat. At first the eremite decor, the silver place settings and expensive porcelain and sunset view crushed Caleb into insignificance. Then he looked across the table at her.

They discussed ephemera: the color of the sky, the sharp bright bubbles of the champagne, the transgressive thrill of spending so much on a single meal.

"We don't have much time, when you think about it," Mal said. "I want to appreciate as much as I can before it's gone."

"Morbid," Caleb replied. "But I won't argue."

As tuxedoed waiters served course after airy, delicate course, Caleb and Mal spoke of wine, of ullamal (Mal was not a fan, and Caleb found himself defending the conduct of players he would have condemned to Teo), of childhood games, and art. A string quartet behind a curtain played a gavotte he didn't recognize. At first Caleb thought it strange that no one danced, but the entire evening was its own kind of dance, with subtle steps and pleasant turns. He blundered through, cheerful as a child at a waltz, and laughed when Mal recounted the story of their first meeting back to him.

"You had the most serious expression I've ever seen on a human face. I would have laughed, but I thought that might make matters worse."

"You did laugh, if I remember right." He sipped a dessert cordial, and felt it go down slow. "I've been thinking a lot about the Tzimet in the lake, and the Serpents."

Her smile faltered. "What do you mean?"

"I spent all day doing damage control. When we draw power from the Serpents, their, I don't know, their hunger bleeds out into the city. A woman almost killed her kids, a guy burned himself. More people going mad all the time. We're responsible."

"What choice did we have?"

"I don't know. But I can't stop thinking about Hal, the guard who died at Bright Mirror. We took reasonable precautions against Tzimet. No one can blame us for what went wrong—but maybe they should. We could run a perfect operation: a Concern that hurt no one, every risk sorted and managed, each contingency accounted for. It would cost hundreds of millions of souls even to come close. Too much. So he died." The ocean rolled green and gray as slate below them.

She wore a string of tiny pearls at her throat. The pearls smiled even when she did not. "There are always risks. The world isn't safe."

"Why not feed the Serpents? If they weren't so hungry, they wouldn't drive people mad."

"We can't feed them without killing people."

"You can't give them soulstuff because . . ."

"Because the Craft is built on exchange. We give, and receive something in return. That's the reason we can't just magic ourselves food or water: use Craft to force a field to grow, and you'll wear the earth to desert in a year. If we funneled souls into the Serpents, their power would flow back into us, and they'd get hungrier. All we can do is keep them sleeping, and that's only if we're careful." She toasted him with cordial. "Here's to being careful."

"Here's to that." He drank. "Why not leave the Serpents alone? Let them sleep."

"And one day they would wake, whether we called for them or not. Our grandparents feared Aquel and Achal. I think we should use them, not cower from them."

Caleb didn't know what to think. Sunset burned in her eyes.

"Maybe you're right."

They saw more of each other, though Caleb hesitated to call their meetings dates. Yes, they kissed, but they did not melt into romance. Mal studied the world around her, broke it into pieces. On their walks together, every mystery play or advertisement or empty storefront signified something about life or Craft, religion or politics or poetry. Being around her was a rush of genius and expectation. They danced, and talked, and danced again.

Their meetings were a welcome respite from the business of the coming eclipse: insurance bargains to be signed and sealed with demonic agencies, water rights secured, Warden patrols doubled in case of accident or unrest. He swam every day through end-time prophecies, waiting for night and Mal to save him.

He kept the shark's-tooth talisman in his pocket, but every time he thought to mention it, he remembered Allie's death, and their fight under Seven Leaf Lake, and decided to wait.

Mal returned to the cliff runners as a goddess in white leather, offering no explanation for her absence. Caleb did not run with her, but waited beside Balam, and watched.

She soared on currents of air, leapt and turned, rolled and ran. She was a monkey, a flame, a flash, an angel, a demon in flight. Caught between sky and earth, she was most herself. When she touched down, she stood lightly, as if one wrong step might break the ground beneath her feet.

A week before the eclipse, on Monicola Pier beside the rolling Pax, he showed her the tooth.

It hung from her fingers, caught by sunset, swaying.

"Kopil says it burned when Allie died."

"And you think it means she wasn't mad. That she betrayed me. Betrayed us. Poisoned Bright Mirror Reservoir, and all the rest."

"It seems likely. Doesn't it?"

"You have one explanation for the facts," she said. "Perhaps she was working against you all along. Or she was only recruited after she saw the gods at Bright Mirror and decided she could not be a part of your world. Your adversary would have bound her to his purpose with subtle cords and bargains. When we turned her power against her, some might have flowed back through those bonds, and destroyed this tooth."

"I don't buy it. She must have been a radical from way back."

She smiled sadly. "Why?"

"She was only at Seven Leaf for a few weeks. People don't change so fast."

"Maybe you don't know people as well as you think. You didn't handle Seven Leaf Lake well. Neither did I. What would we have become if we remained?"

"What we do there is ugly, sure, but it didn't make me want to set demons loose on the city."

"I doubt that was her goal." She lowered the tooth.

"What do you mean?"

"I think Allie didn't want to cause harm. I think she wanted to recover something she'd lost. Seven Leaf confronted her with that loss, and she responded in the only way she knew." When he looked at her uncomprehending, she tried again. "She saw spirits in pain, and wanted to stop their pain. That was the seed. Everything else—the power, the madness, the betrayal—followed."

"Their pain is horrible. But we need that water. She must have known that."

"Does our need justify our methods?"

He remembered the torment beneath the lake, and did not answer.

"We were born together," she said, "men and gods: our first cave wall scratches let them into the world. We miss them. Allie missed them, I think. I sympathize with her."

"You miss our gods?"

"Why shouldn't I?"

"They're soaked in blood."

"So am I. So are you. So's this city. You seem to think it's different if we kill for gods or for water; either way the victim dies at the end."

"Why not find another pantheon? Iskar still has gods, and they get along fine. Orgies and existentialism, the occasional burnt aurochs, once in a while a tentacle or two. Seems better."

"Iskar's gods aren't ours, though."

"Oh, I see, we need to preserve our heritage. Will you burn the pale skins out of Stonewood next?" Barges shifted on the water, pulled by broad-backed sea turtles forty feet across: firework ships moving into position for the eclipse. Their burning arrows would frighten hungry stars away from the wounded sun.

She laughed. "Our economy would collapse. Every tie to the

rest of the world would be cut. We must be cosmopolitan, without sacrificing our identity. Walk our own path."

"Isn't that what we're doing now?"

"How many of the Craftsmen and Craftswomen in this city are Quechal, do you think? Twenty percent? Thirty, at most?"

"Something like that."

"In a city that's eighty percent Quechal."

"I don't see your point."

"We're occupied. We don't talk about it that way, but we are."

"We're not occupied. We're a world city. There's a difference."

"Are you sure?"

A cold breeze off the ocean shivered her, and he placed an arm around her shoulder. From the sidewalk an observer might have thought them man and wife, or lovers. Caleb didn't know what they were. No words seemed to fit. Children ran down the beach, volleying a ball back and forth. "You loved your parents. You value the things they valued. But our gods killed people. They're gone, and I don't miss them."

Mal stopped shivering, but she did not remove his arm. "You don't get to choose your parents. Why should your gods be any different?"

"What do you suggest? We should bring back the altar and the knife? People will fight you if that's what you want, and I'll lead them. We can't do those things anymore."

"Of course not," she said. "That's not what I meant."

"What did you mean, then?"

"Think about your father. You don't live the way he lives."

"No. I have a roof over my head, and I don't have three quarters of the city out to kill me."

Waves lapped the thick pylons of the pier. Caleb watched the barges and thought about sharks moving underwater.

"But you have something of him in you, anyway."

"Scars."

"Those, yes. But that's not what I meant. You have his determination. You know a few things in your marrow, and you will never compromise on them. You took parts of your father into yourself and reinvented them. Your mother's in there, too: contemplative, independent, solitary, strong. You made yourself out of what they gave you."

"What does this have to do with sacrifice?"

"We used to know that everything ends, and it is better to give one's death than accept it. The first corn sprang from a dead man's body. Qet's blood makes the rain. Beasts give themselves to the hunter; kings give themselves to their people. Sacrifice was the center of our world. We defended that world from Iskari invaders four hundred years ago, but then the Craftsmen came, and here we are."

"Here we are: better fed, better protected, more justly policed than ever in history."

"I don't think the Wardens are just."

"I know."

"We're better fed, I'll grant, but so what? Cows on a farm are fed. As for 'protected,' Dresediel Lex only ever fell to one adversary: the one who rules us now. My problem isn't that we no longer sacrifice, it's that we're no longer conscious of the sacrifices we make. That's what gods are for."

"What do you suggest?"

"We should bring them back, on our terms. We form a society with sacrifice, but without death."

"Sacrificing what? Shreds of cotton, clods of earth? A bit of wine, stale bread? Gods are hungry, thirsty creatures."

"I don't know what they would accept. But we need them."

"People don't miss the gods."

"They do. You do."

"I don't know what you're talking about."

"You've been chasing me for months. Half the things you've done should have killed you."

He laid his hand over the back of hers, on the railing. A ridge of scar tissue ran below her knuckles.

She looked at him through the black sway of her hair. "You didn't know me. You saw something in me you thought was worth your blood." His expression must have changed, because she frowned, and shook her head. "You saw something you could

chase, something for which you could bleed. You wanted to sacrifice yourself, and you've never been given the chance. I know
the feeling. Desperate for duty. For purpose. Direction. It's why I
saved you, when North Station fell." She handed the tooth back
to him. "I'm sorry I can't say more. Allie was a friend, and I
think I understand her—but I can't help you with this."

He took the tooth from her, and slipped it back into his jacket.
His grip on her hand was so tight that his forearm trembled. Mal
raised an eyebrow. He released her hand, and chose his next
words carefully. "We do sacrifice. We pay bits of soul every time
we use a faucet."

"It's not the same. Those are payments, not sacraments. What,
really, do we sacrifice to live the way we live?"

Children sprinted along the waterline. Rising tidewater
dulled their footprints, filled them with eddies and sand. By the
fourth wave, the footprints vanished as if they had never been.

The last child paused every few strides to lift a shell from the
beach and throw it into the Pax. She mouthed a prayer with each
throw, an offering to Qet Sea-Lord in payment for her passage
along the shore. Caleb's mother had taught him the words to that
prayer, when he was young. After the Skittersill Rising she
never mentioned it again.

Caleb followed the arc of a thrown shell, imagined it drawn
out past the barges and their harnessed sea monsters, through
the deep toward Bay Station.

"I know what we sacrifice," he said. "But I don't have the
words to tell you."

"What, then?"

"I can show you, if you'll let me. Do you have plans for the
night before the eclipse?"

Calculating eyes watched him. "I do. What do you have in
mind?"

"Come with me to Bay Station."

"I can't."

"It won't take all night. We'll be ashore in plenty of time for
fireworks."

Her weight shifted from left leg to right. One hand slid down her dress to rest against her thigh.

"Where should I meet you?" she asked.

"There." He pointed to the little girl, still throwing seashells. A battered lifeguard chair stood beside her, covered in peeling paint and weathered Quechal glyphs.

"Ominous."

"We'll be safe."

"Fine," she said. "It's a date."

She cupped his chin in one hand, guided him to her, and kissed him. Her mouth was cooler than the twilight. Her kiss danced like a spark down his neck and through his limbs. It quickened in his scars. He wrapped an arm around her waist, and pulled her closer. The vibration inside him built to shiver them both apart.

She slipped from him, and walked away.

Teo had once claimed that human history began with a storm: the interval between lightning and thunder, between the flash and the rumble felt in the body's core, was primitive man's first experience of time—the awakening of consciousness, the birth of the gods.

As Mal receded down the pier—quick strides, long for her body—Caleb believed Teo's theory. Godhood began with watching her leave, and feeling her still present.

When she reached the road, she hailed a driverless carriage and disappeared into the evening traffic up the Pax Coast Carriageway toward the hills. Caleb bought a churro from a street vendor whose cart bore the brand of a winking skull, and walked down to the beach. He lifted a shell from the tidal sand, and poured out the water within. He tested the shell's weight, and threw it into the advancing tide.

33

Dresediel Lex bled for the coming eclipse. Red banners draped skyspires. Streamers of crimson paper, ribbon, and rope hung from lampposts, and every storefront sported red splatters of decals and paint. Fake blood dripped down walls. Imitation entrails, veins, viscera dangled from fire escapes in the winding back streets of Skittersill. Even the migrants of the Stonewood slums added a splash of red to their tents and battered lean-tos.

Before Liberation, the red decorations had been bought from temples: nothing could match the cardinal dye brewed in holy vats beneath the pyramids, for no one possessed the sheer quantity of blood available to Quechal priests.

Times changed. Simple alchemy mimicked the many colors of blood, and Craftsmen sold their cloth more cheaply than priests.

Teo had tickets to the Eclipse Games, but Sam refused to come—the contest was part of the commercialization of a sacred holiday, she said, though she lacked a trace of Quechal blood. Caleb came instead, and said he was sorry Sam couldn't make it.

"Yeah," Teo said, with a tightening of her lips that warned Caleb to drop the subject. "It's a shame."

The Sea-Lords played Oxulhat, a rare match-up since the desert citadel was part of a different ullamal conference from Dresediel Lex and seldom made the play-offs. The Eclipse Games were an exception: a relic of centuries past, before the Twin Serpents destroyed the horn of land that once joined Northern and Southern Kath, before refugees fled north to transform the village of Dresediel Lex into a metropolis. Oxulhat had been a frontier outpost of the old Quechal empire, and survived its doom. The cities' teams played at each eclipse, in memory of what was lost.

Oxulhat scored a string of goals at the top of the first quarter.

Zolin replied with play brilliant in its ferocity but sloppy in its execution, and earned herself a penalty. Anticipation swelled. Moans of fear and joy accompanied the rubber ball's impact on skull or limb or girded hip. The players' cries rose like mountain peaks above gasps, curses, and threats from the audience.

Caleb followed the game with morbid fascination—not the players, but the game itself, the story upon which it was founded: the balls, the Hero Sisters' hearts, the players, gods or demons or both. Thousands of feet below the city, Heartstone's engineers and Craftsmen chanted to bind the Serpents in sleep, no hearts or deaths required. Yet still the people of Dresediel Lex gathered in this stadium and watched their players strive to save the world.

The teams grappled on the narrow, frieze-lined court. The Sea-Lords wrung points from Oxulhat like water from a sun-dried rag. Teo gripped Caleb's arm through his jacket, hard enough to break skin. She shouted, she swore, she twisted her black small-brimmed hat in her hands as if to rip it into pieces.

A drift of fog with a familiar face hovered above the court, ragged and almost invisible. The goddess of games alone survived to consecrate the contest. All the other gods were gone.

Victory arrived at last, and with it hunger. Teo, who had spent the last quarter standing on her chair screaming at the players, dragged Caleb to a downtown bar where they met Sam, already drunk. For the festivities she'd twisted her golden hair into a bun and painted her face red and blue. Together they roamed the broken streets, staggering from trouble to trouble until they arrived at a battered nightclub packed with Sam's artist friends. A swinging band welcomed one and all to the dance floor.

Caleb, drunk, danced with two women whose names he promptly forgot, then settled at the bar with a gin and tonic and watched Teo and Sam dance closer, closer as horns cried golden in the smoke. Teo led, and Sam spun a series of turns so sharp her flowing skirt wrapped tight around the muscles of her legs. The heat of their proximity burned the air around them white. Caleb watched until Teo kissed her, hard and full. He took his drink to a game being dealt at a corner table, bought in and played loose, not caring how much he lost. The goddess fled him, and he pursued; embraced him, and he tumbled through space wrapped in a net of jewels.

He woke the next morning swollen with the stolen souls of other men, a dull ache where his head should have been. Rolling to his feet he found himself in a dark hotel room, blackout curtains pulled. He left the curtains alone, not wanting to see what time it was, knowing he had risen early. His body never let him sleep off a hangover. He identified the hotel by its faded harlequin wallpaper: he was three blocks south of Teo's apartment.

Confronting the wreckage of his face in the bathroom mirror, he decided against going to work. He sent a rat to Tollan, apologizing and claiming one of his many unused vacation days. Little point visiting the office at any rate. No business would be discussed. Half the staff was on vacation. RKC could mind itself.

In the shower, he thought of Mal.

He remembered Temoc's stories of the old days, of priests bleeding themselves to the edge of death before a full eclipse. Their howls must have echoed through the pyramid, down to the pens where sacrifices trembled in their chains. The Red King's lover had been one of those wretches. Caleb remembered his smile in the sepia picture.

Screw it. Had he been sober, he would have lain awake all night tormented by ratiocination and self-doubt, like one of those Iskari novelists who could unpack world history from the taste of a cookie. He had plenty of time to recover from his hangover before sunset.

Clean, he slid one finger down the showerhead glyphs. Angular symbols ripped pieces from his over-full soul, and the stream of hot water ceased. Wrapped in steam and thought, he stepped from the stall, groped for a towel, and prepared his mind against the day.

34

Caleb waited on the beach at the turning of the tide. Families and couples crowded the sand; toddlers built pyramids and older children played catch or tag, or ullamal with buckets for goals. Wave by wave the water advanced, bearing ropes of seaweed and sticks, trash and dead fish: the ocean threw the city's refuse back to shore. Edged against sunset on the bay, barges waited to unleash the fireworks that slept within their hulls.

People gathered at the shore and in the city's parks and fields, watching a night sky their myths said festered with bogeymen and many-armed devils. Tonight, DL's citizens faced those demons, armed with ritual, comradeship, and explosives. They drank, danced, cheered. On the beach, a wandering chorus sang the Death Hymn:

> *Dreaming, dying, counting time*
> *We wait upon the days sublime*
> *Living edge of dooméd earth*
> *We wait for joy of bloody birth.*

They skipped the second verse, which named the Twin Serpents, and the fourth, which described the sacrifice: the flick of blade that parted skin, the strike that broke the breastbone. Rather than chanting god-names for the chorus, they sang nonsense syllables, *la ne she la te la ta.* Caleb realized he was mouthing the original words, and stopped.

"Couldn't you have picked a less crowded place to meet?"

Mal's voice at his side. He whirled on her, and almost lost his balance. "You startled me."

"At least one of us is discrete." She was dressed sensibly: gray slacks, flats, a loose white high-necked blouse belted at the waist, a leather bag slung over her shoulder. Sunset caught her skin in burnished bronze. "Shall we go?"

A black sliver detached from the sky, plummeted, and stopped above Caleb's outstretched hand, hovering on long dragonfly wings. The opteran's proboscis brushed his skin, tasting his soul.

She called another flier to her. Multifaceted eyes glinted sunset red. Caleb guided his own insect to his shoulders. Its legs wrapped beneath his arms, around his stomach, about his thighs. He fell forward, gave himself to gravity and the surge of lifting wings. Mal followed.

He flew up and out, over the gunmetal gray Pax, high enough that neither spray nor leaping sharks nor the springy tendrils of gallowglasses underwater could catch him.

From above, he saw the ocean's wounds: four stripes of water six feet broad and half a mile long, transparent from the sea's surface to its floor. No fish moved in those channels, nor any other living thing. The God Wars had been fought over the oceans of Dresediel Lex, as well as the land and air. Even the sea bore scars. Ships sailed around the clear water, which rusted metal, warped wood, and rotted flesh.

The city retreated at their backs. Skyspires fell toward the horizon, spears to skewer the world. Left and right the Pax opened beyond the harbor's shelter. Miles to the south, hidden from Dresediel Lex by a spur of rocks, the port of Longsands bristled with triple-masted sailing vessels and the superstructure towers of Craft-sped container ships. Few sailors would join in the evening's revel. Shipmasters from the Shining Empire and Koschei's kingdom knew better than to let their crews make landfall on Dresediel Lex during an eclipse. True Quechal gangs would roam the Skittersill tonight, in search of victims with the wrong color of skin or hair.

Bay Station swelled like a pustule on the horizon. Walls of Craft surrounded and protected the atoll and its tower. He drifted through them like a ship through sharp coral and jutting rocks. Dark shapes long as boats and sinuous as serpents circled under the water.

Caleb guided his opteran down toward the ocean.

Mal followed, but when he stopped five feet over the water's surface, she balked, and shouted: "What are you doing?"

"Don't worry. We're safe."

"Do you know what lives in this harbor?"

"Deaths-head coral, sharks, and gallowglasses. Maybe a star kraken, though I doubt one could get past the wards."

"A gallowglass could grab you from there."

"Barely."

"One sting and you'd claw off your skin to stop the pain."

He reached back to his neck, and brushed the opteran's proboscis away. His dull sucking depression ceased, the creature's arms unclenched, and he fell, arms pinwheeling, to the ocean.

He had made this trip many times, but experience did not dull the monkey panic of falling toward a sea full of teeth and poison. A strangled cry escaped his throat. Gray water struck him in the face and body. Pressure and pain illuminated his ribs, his right hip and cheek, shoulder and thigh. He inhaled through the pain, groaned, and lifted himself off the water.

The Pax gave beneath his hands like a firm bed covered in silk. Testing one leg, then the other, he worked his way to a crouch and stood. Ocean stretched behind him to the city, ahead to Bay Station and beyond. A wave nearly pitched him off balance, but he recovered. "Come on down," he called up to Mal. "The water's fine."

"I remember a story," she replied, "about two brothers who tricked a Tzimet king into killing himself, by pretending to cut off their heads and daring him to do the same."

"Trust me."

"That's what they said in the story." But she closed her eyes, released her opteran and fell, twisting through the air like a cat. She landed lightly, and rolled with the waves to her feet.

Standing, stable, Mal pressed her toe into the water and watched the ripples when she lifted her foot. Eyes closed, she repeated the experiment.

"Wild," she said. "I can't see anything keeping us afloat, with my eyes open or closed."

"A club back east figured it out," he replied. "One of those weird sensory deprivation tricks, for clients who happened to be Craftsmen, or Craftswomen."

"What kind of club would want to blind its clients?"

"It has a particular clientele." He bit his lip, wondering how to explain without going into detail. "The place calls itself Xiltanda," which was one of the High Quechal names for hell.

"Ah." She walked toward him unsteadily, shifting her weight to remain upright. "Why isn't this in mass production? I've never heard of anything that could make Craft invisible to Craftswomen."

"No sense mass producing a system that's not cost effective. Soul for soul, this is the most wasteful piece of Craft in RKC. Lord Kopil likes it, though. Who am I to argue?"

"And so you walk on the water."

"Not quite." She pitched forward and he caught her outstretched hand. "If you're not the right sort of person, you fall through into the ocean."

"Disturbing."

He didn't disagree.

She turned west. An island lay two miles out, and from that island rose a matte black tower, like an arrow drawn to pierce the sky. A shadow crossed her face. "Bay Station," she said, resigned. "I think I know what you plan to show me. I'd rather not see it."

"I thought the same thing, the first time someone took me here."

She drew back. A cool wind blew salt spray against his face.

"You need to see this," he said.

"They'll show me when it's time."

"I want to be the one who shares it with you."

"Let's go back to the shore. Watch fireworks. Have a nice evening."

"Yes," he said. "Let's. But first I want to show you what I mean about sacrifice."

Her eyes met his: black mirrors reflecting the passion of the sunset.

"Okay," she said.

He bowed to her and walked toward the station. Out here, away from the shore, the sea no longer smelled of dead fish. "Have you spent much time on the water?" Caleb asked after a while.

"Some friends and I kayaked through the Fangs once, after graduation."

"I didn't know you could kayak in the Fangs."

"Some of the bays are still tainted by the Cataclysm, so the kraken and sea serpents and the other big monsters stay away. Wards on the kayaks deal with little ones." A tall wave rolled beneath their feet. "The ocean between the Fangs is warmer than the Pax, shallower. On calm days you can see all the way down to sunken Quechal cities overgrown with coral." She sighed. "Why do you ask?"

"The path is sensitive to intent. The more I think about the station, the more it strays. If I don't distract myself, we could walk all the way to Longsands, or into the center of the Pax."

"Oh."

"So," he said. "Tell me about your trip to the Fangs."

"We splashed around for two weeks; I was almost eaten. That was the end of the vacation, at least for me."

"Eaten?"

"I was bored with the stars one night, and the ocean looked placid, inviting, rippled soft as molten glass. I took off my clothes, warded myself, and swam out."

"Gods."

"It wasn't a good idea."

"Wasn't a good idea," he said. "There are things in the Fangs that would eat you in one bite, wards or no wards."

"Most of those don't swim close to shore. I thought I was safe. The water was cool, the ocean dark. I've never felt such wonderful solitude."

"What happened?"

"A riptide."

"Oh."

"I looked back and realized I was farther from our island than I thought, and no matter how I tried to swim back, the current bore me out. Panic took over. I forgot everything I knew and tried to swim against the tide, splashing and pulling and kicking, but it didn't work. I tried to call for help, but I was too far away." Her grip on his hand tightened. "It's strange. You talk about something like that and the moment rushes back."

"So, what did you do?"

"I was about to die. I remembered that riptides are strongest near the surface, and don't extend far from side to side. I dove down and tried to swim parallel to the island's shore, but I was tired. Then the gallowglass struck."

"Qet and Isil," he said, not realizing that he had sworn to gods.

"The water around me glowed green, and I was caught in a tangle of burning wires. Even with my wards, some of the poison made it through. For weeks afterward I looked like I had been flogged from head to foot with a barbed whip. I screamed, I'm not ashamed to admit, and the winding wires drew me up to the surface, toward the beast's mouth. Which was lucky, in a way."

"I think we have different definitions of lucky."

"I was tired. If it hadn't reeled me close to what passed for its brain, I couldn't have struck it with the Craft. I drank the creature's life, and used the strength I stole to guide me back to the island. My classmates found me the next morning, lying on the beach, passed out and wound with the stinging tendrils I hadn't been strong enough to tear away. They launched a flare, and a nearby settlement soon sent help. I spent the rest of the vacation in bed. I don't go to the ocean much anymore. I like the land. You can see what's creeping up on you most of the time."

Sand crunched beneath Caleb's shoe, and he realized that they stood on the eastern beach of Bay Station, in the black tower's shadow. As always on this journey, he had missed the moment of transition, when the island ceased to be a distant goal and appeared beneath and before him.

Watchmen waited atop a grassy bank overlooking the beach—burly, armed, the air around them thick with Craft and threat.

"Friends of yours?" Mal asked.

"No," he said. "I'll handle this." Raising his hands, he strode forth to meet them.

35

Caleb and Mal descended into the island, paced by silent guards. The stair was long and winding, and pristine, like everything else in Bay Station. Every light was sun-bright, each corner swept.

"They keep house well," Mal said.

"Dust can hide things," Caleb whispered. The wide halls and open spaces made him nervous. "One of my father's associates once tried to sneak a goddess in here, lodged in the dirt of his boot. She nearly took over the station before the King in Red stopped her."

"I see."

Their descent continued. Down side corridors, Caleb glimpsed the other station staff: academic Craftsmen in white laboratory robes, junior initiates arguing about thaumaturgical theory or professional sports, gray-shirted janitors living and undead, mopping floors and polishing windows.

On Caleb's previous visits Bay Station had resembled the inside of an anthill, but tonight it was almost deserted. Everyone who could request time off for the eclipse had done so. The unlucky remainder would gather tonight in the observation tower to watch the fireworks and miss their families.

The staircase ended in a broad landing and a thick double door of cold iron, so wrought with wards and contracts that Caleb's eyes refused to rest on its surface. The guards stood on opposite sides of the door, and placed their hands on the featureless white wall. Their wrists twisted at a particular angle, and silver-blue light shone around their fingers.

A glyph in the center of the doors blinked three times, and the world dissolved in darkness. Out of the darkness flashed a brilliant claw that pierced Caleb's body and soul. The night broke, and the door ground open.

Beyond, white walls gave way to unfinished rock. Crude, primal symbols marked their path through the stone labyrinth.

"How old is this place?" Mal's voice sounded small in the winding, echoing tunnels.

"There were Quechal colonists here before the city was founded. Since they lived so close to the Pax, they worshipped ocean-gods, predator-gods, rain-gods. Qet Sea-Lord was the center of the pantheon. After the Cataclysm, when so many Quechal moved up here, their heresy became dogma. We built new temples on land, Serpent-temples, sun-temples, but the old sacred caves remained out here."

A rhythm resounded in his chest: a twinned concussion, two building-sized hammers beating against granite. Rocks shifted on the floor of their rough-hewn path.

"There's still a god here," she said.

"Yes."

"We can go back. You don't need to show me this."

"I do. For my sake."

The rhythm drew nearer. Caleb heard a rush of breaking surf.

The tunnel widened into a cavern. Stalactites hung like rotten teeth from the arching roof. Dark rock glittered wetly in the ghostlight.

The path split to circle an enormous pit. The percussion and the rolling ocean swell emanated from within.

"Is that what I think it is?" Her voice was so soft he could barely hear her.

"Yes."

She stopped, mouth half open, tense as a scared cat. She closed her eyes and breathed deep, mastering herself. Chin high, she strode past him to the pit's edge, and looked down.

Caleb waited. He examined the thick pipes that lined the cave walls, the glyphs ancient and modern carved into stone. Too soon, he ran out of objects for his attention, and approached Mal, walking heavily so as not to startle her.

She stood straight, and still. He touched her arm and felt tension beneath the envelope of her skin. Her nostrils flared.

A god lay in the pit. No statue, no graven idol could compare to this imperial thing. Spread-eagled, suspended in dark water, he was the size of a mountain. His massive lips, softly parted, bared teeth as large as carriages. His eyes were sails, his chest broad as a pyramid. Legs and arms thick and long as magisterium trees hung limp in the dark water that lapped at his sides.

Unconscious, his silence was the silence of the sea. His slow indrawn breaths were the rolling tide, the sleeping twitch of his hand a hurricane. Eons past, in deep time, the first Quechal had looked out over the ocean, seen chaos, and given it form, and name, and life.

Qet Sea-Lord was not dead, but not alive, either. His closed eyes did not move like the eyes of a dreaming man. Thick metal pipes protruded from his arms, his chest, his neck, his corded thighs, to join the hive of plumbing below the surface of the water. Silver bands circled his chest. Before each breath, the bands glowed with unearthly light, and after each breath the light faded.

Caleb said the god's name gently, knowing Mal would hear.

She recoiled from the pit. Her eyes flashed white, and shadow cohered about her skin. Her teeth grew long, pointed like fangs and gleaming. She towered above him. Ghostlights flickered and shattered on the walls; Mal hissed, and lightning cracked between the fingers of her outstretched hand. She swelled like a cloud of smoke above an erupting volcano.

"This is what I wanted to show you, Mal," he said. "I'm sorry."

The magnesium flames of her eyes burned into him, but he stepped forward and extended his hand, palm up and open. She glanced from him, to the pit, and back.

In a black blur, she fled up the long hallway. A guard barred her way, but she struck him and he fell. Caleb ran to the guard and knelt beside him, felt his pulse. Still strong. Good. He rose to follow Mal, but another guard blocked his path.

"Get out of my way," Caleb said.

"Who in all the hells was that?"

"My girlfriend," he almost said, but stopped himself. "My

boss." That was also true, technically, and confused the guard long enough for Caleb to brush past.

"We'll head her off at the beach," the guard called after him.

"No," he shouted back. She might hurt someone before the guards brought her down. "No. She's just confused. This is her first time to Bay Station."

"Oh," the guard said. "That explains it."

Caleb began to run.

He found her on the starlit beach. Silver waves lapped the sand, and the calm sea reflected the fat full moon. No halo of Craft clung to her, no ichorous claws tipped her fingers. Lit by the night, she resembled a cave drawing: a life defined in five lines of ink. He could almost ignore the guards surrounding her with weapons raised.

She turned to face him as he approached through the cordon.

"Hi," she said.

"Hi," he replied. "Shall we go?"

"Yes." She held out her hand. Her skin was cool to the touch, colder than the night air. She stepped onto the water. The ocean buoyed her up, and he walked beside her away from shore.

"Don't look back," he whispered. "The guards are hair-trigger tense. They won't relax until you're gone."

"I can't believe I did that."

"It happens. Everyone takes their first sight of Qet in a different way. I've seen grown men kneel; one Craftsman I know wept."

"I can't— I mean, I knew, or a thought I knew. I thought I could handle it. The expectation, and the shock, and everything at once—I can't believe I let you take me. I'm an idiot." She spat the last word.

"Don't talk that way."

"Don't tell me what I can and can't do."

"I should have listened when you asked me to stop, when you asked me not to show you. I'm sorry." A rising swell shifted his weight sideways, into her. She kept him from toppling. "I'm a bit of a jerk, I guess."

"It's not your fault."

"It was a stupid thing to surprise you with."

"Yes," she agreed. "Stupid." The sound of surf faded into rolling ocean silence. Dresediel Lex burgeoned on the horizon, a tumor of light that dulled the stars and blunted the moon. No ships passed them in the dark. Barges stood at anchor beyond the harbor's mouth. "Think it's safe to look back yet?"

"Yes."

She glanced over her shoulder. "The island looks bigger from this distance. Less human."

"It camouflages itself with Craft. If you could see the real island, you would know where it was, which would make it easier to attack."

"Elegant system." She stopped walking. "Can we stop here?"

She sat cross-legged on the water, and he sat beside her. The ocean surrounded them like a meadow.

"I thought it would be like the Serpents," she said. "But it's worse."

"Yes."

"They're beasts, however big they are. Terrors. But that's a God. Not a half-conscious spirit like the ones we bound in Seven Leaf. Qet ruled us, once. Loved us. And we loved him."

"Yes."

He traced ripples in the water in front of them.

"He's not . . . dead."

"No. Not exactly."

"I heard he lived somewhere, in chains." She sounded strangled and slow, as if every word had to be won from her throat by single combat.

"Those are chains," he said, "of a sort. Qet fought the King in Red during Liberation. The Sea-Lord was broken on his own altar. But he didn't die."

"He didn't survive, either."

"Yes. He's not strong enough to have a mind anymore. Flashes of awareness at most, on high holy festivals. Once in a while, he cries out, or babbles nonsense. But his power remains."

"And so you use him. In pain."

"We use what's left of him. He was the bringer of rains from the ocean, Father of the Green Beside the Desert. We pump saltwater into his heart, and as the water runs through him, he removes the salt. He didn't have such a physical form, before—like most gods. What you saw was a salt statue grown in his image. Pipes and pumps draw purified water back into the reservoirs of Dresediel Lex. Whenever a tap is opened or a glass raised in this city, Qet is there. Or what's left of him."

"Why did you show me this?" Her hands rested in her lap, one inside the other. Her thumbs pressed together, their tips white.

"I wanted," he began, but he could not complete his sentence. The false serenity of her face terrified him: still as the surface of Seven Leaf Lake before the gods began to scream. "You asked what we sacrifice, to live the way we live. This is our sacrifice."

"This isn't a sacrifice," she snapped. "This is abuse. Exploitation."

"We drained the water table around Dresediel Lex a hundred years ago, maybe more. We suck lakes, rivers, streams dry like a starving leech. Even Seven Leaf won't last long. Ten years, twenty at the most, before we have to reach further afield. We've studied Qet day and night for five decades and no Craftsman has been able to duplicate his methods. We can take from him, though, and we do, and so we survive."

"Why don't you show the people what you've done?"

"Think how you reacted when you saw the truth. Can you imagine that magnified through an entire city?"

She did not answer.

He leaned back, unfolded his legs in front of him, and thought for a long while.

"The sacrifice," he said, slowly. "We come out here, learn the price of our world, and we go back convinced it's worthwhile, because we don't have any choice. Whenever I pass a beggar in Skittersill, when I hear about riots in the Deep Vale, when I run afoul of True Quechal punks or when some fool like my father tries to start a revolution, I know that they're all of them party to Qet's torture. Spend long enough with that in your mind and you can't fight for anything anymore. You wander through this city, and wonder if anything you do will make up for the horror that keeps the world turning. To live, you rip your own heart from your chest and hide it in a box somewhere, along with everything you ever learned about justice, compassion, mercy. You throw yourself into games to mark the time. And if you yearn for something different: what would you change? Would you bring back the blood, the dying cries, the sucking chest wounds? The constant war? So we're caught between two poles of hypocrisy. We sacrifice our right to think of ourselves as good people, our right to think our life is good, our city is just. And so we and our city both survive."

She rocked beside him, or else the waves rocked her. Her gaze rested in the cup of her hands, like a statue of a monk from the Shining Empire. Their sages claimed that all was nothing, or nothing all. For a moment, he understood.

"It's funny," he said. "The first time I saw Qet, I couldn't handle it either. I didn't call upon dark magic or anything like that, but I tackled my boss, demanded an explanation. You did the same to me tonight."

"What's funny about that?"

"We have a lot in common. We both keep secrets, and maybe we don't even know we keep them. When we try to share ourselves with other people, we don't know how to begin."

"Is that what drew you to me?"

"No."

"What, then?"

"Everything I said just now—about Qet, and sacrifice, and what it does to us—it's not an answer. It's an escape. The question remains: how are we supposed to live? The world can't be a war between the too-certain and the bankrupt, between my father and the King in Red. But what else is there?

"It took me a long time to figure out why I chased you. You're beautiful, and compelling, but I've known beautiful and compelling women before, and none of them caught me like you did. I think, somehow, I decided you had the answer. Maybe you don't. Maybe no one does."

She placed a hand on his shoulder, and he fell silent.

She leaned back and lay on her side, body rolling softly with the sea. Her lips opened. Inside them he saw a waiting darkness.

"I don't know all the answers yet," she said. "I think I will, though. Someday soon. I'm working on it."

"I can wait."

"Dangerous, to trust someone else's answers more than your own." Her fingers traced the curve of his collarbone, finding a nest for the heel of her hand. "You might not like what they have to say."

"I think I will."

From the ocean behind them came a dull pop as if a cork had been pulled from a giant wine bottle. A needle of sparks knit through the night, apexed, and burst into a brilliant blue sphere.

The second explosion came faster, a red globe within the blue, and the third faster still, a mist of yellow-white stars that twisted and schooled like fish made from light. The fireworks, he thought, were as tall as the Serpents would be if they reared above the city.

"Look," she said.

"I see them." Her eyes mirrored the explosions, and the stars behind.

She kissed him, and drew him toward her. He gave himself to the kiss, wrapped an arm around her curving back, and pulled her toward him in return.

The fireworks above Dresediel Lex that night cost thirty million thaums. A grown man earning a decent wage could work for four hundred years and still not earn that much. The Nightflower Collective, owners of the barges and their explosive cargo, conducted similar events every few weeks around the world: always there was a High Prince's birthday to celebrate in the Shining Empire, some Iskari ritual that demanded dramatic accompaniment. Once, the Empire of Deathless Koschei ordered a solid month of festivities to celebrate the construction of the Dread

Lord's golem son. The Collective ordered its affairs with an army's precision and an artist's skill, each flood of light succeeded in rushing crescendo by the next.

Caleb and Mal rolled together on the waves in grand confusion. His hands tangled in her shirt; she ripped a button from his cuff with a sharp pull and it flew through the air to sink. Her pants slid off easily. Explosions overhead battered hearts and lungs as he gripped the curve of her hips, the taut muscles of her legs. When they kissed, the sky erupted in reflection of their minds, and they kissed often, lips finding arms and shoulders, stomach and sides as often as each other's mouths.

A precisely timed sequence of blasts formed a pyramid in the sky, two serpents rising above with mouths flared. The ocean was smooth against Caleb's skin, and it warmed beneath him as he scrambled among heaped clothes for the condom he had placed in his pocket before he left his house. She bit his neck, he clutched her, they fell together. The chill of Craft faded from her skin. Reflected flame burned in her eyes, and as they lay with each other, on each other, in each other, the flame built. She was a single purpose crafted into flesh, and as Caleb grappled with her, he forgot terror, forgot fear, forgot himself and became a single purpose too.

A great wave rolled from below, and a shark's maw enclosed them. The solid sea surface shielded them from the beast's teeth, but for a moment they were wrapped in the cave of its mouth. Mal let out a laugh that was a scream, her teeth gleaming white, her mouth red, surrounded by many ranks of fangs. Her laugh shook the world.

The shark released them and fled to safer depths. Caleb and Mal remained, set large upon the surface of the water. Mal panted, skin slick and bright as she crouched astride him. They breathed in unison, and clutched each other forever.

Fireworks burst and burned, flared and retreated. The sky broke open time and again only to reclaim its darkness. All was subsumed in flames, which were themselves dancers, singers, beaters of drums, flowering on the infinite to die.

The universe faded back into view, and found Caleb and Mal sleeping on the dark ocean.

Hours passed. She shivered and pulled him closer. A slit of pink tongue wet her lips. She swallowed.

"I'm sorry," she said, but only the ocean heard.

INTERLUDE: TEA

Alaxic sat on the balcony of his villa in the Drakspine, and watched the sleeping city. His skin was thin as parchment, his bones twig-slender and brittle. An autumn leaf of a man, a cicada husk, he waited in his chair. He raised a steaming mug of tea to his thin lips, sucked hot liquid into his mouth, forced himself to swallow.

"You have not aged well," said a shadow from the balustrade.

The old man fixed his gaze on the tea, and the reflections within: reflections of starlight, of the candle flame beside his chair, of the ghost he did not recognize as himself.

"The Craft," he croaked, "does not reward one with a long and healthy life, if one wishes that life to end someday. I will not permit myself to be trapped within a skeleton for all time."

"You will not find true death pleasant." The shadow advanced. Candle flame chiseled out rocky muscles, massive fists, black eyes, scars that glowed on the dark skin. "You are a traitor to gods and man. Demons wait hungrily for your soul."

"Nice to see you again as well, Temoc." His voice wavered and cracked. "I'm glad you received my letter."

"Such as it was. What did you want with me?"

"To pass the night before the eclipse with another priest. Is that too much to ask?"

Temoc hesitated at the light's edge. "Perhaps."

"And perhaps I am not so afraid of the world to come as you believe I should be," Alaxic said, and drank another sip of foul tea. His face contorted, and he set the cup on the small table. "An annular eclipse tomorrow. The first in more than a century. Occlusion for fifteen minutes. What a celebration this would have been in the old days."

"Much work for the priests. The gods would have feasted well. The Serpents, too."

"Yes." Alaxic motioned to the teapot, and the empty cup beside it. "Share a drink with me, in memory of what was."

Temoc regarded the tea, and the cup from which Alaxic drank. At last he shrugged, poured himself a cup, raised it to the moon, and shed three drops with the tip of his finger. "Water in the desert," he said.

"A glorious gift."

They drank.

"We are the last, you know," the old man said. "The others have lost their minds, or died, or languish in prison."

"Yes," Temoc replied.

"Do you have a sacrifice planned?"

"I will spill my own blood." Temoc's voice soured with distaste.

"That is not enough."

"Of course not. I would have kidnapped a Craftsman, made the ritual preparations, and drawn his heart, but since North Station I have not had the luxury of a permanent base from which to plan. The Wardens' eyes are everywhere. I would not need a scheme of any kind if I had one of the great altars at my disposal, but few survive, and all those are watched."

"So the old ways pass," Alaxic said. "As they should. There are new times ahead."

"The old ways will not pass while I live."

"Nor while I live," Alaxic said, and laughed a dry-leaf laugh, and tapped his teapot. "Fortunately, we are neither of us long for this world."

Temoc regarded his empty cup, and swore.

"I apologize for the deception." Alaxic drained his mug. "I thought it was better this way. You and I, the last two priests of the old Quechal, gone. Life belongs to those younger than ourselves."

Temoc's scars burned. He staggered back, and dropped the cup from fingers already numb. He turned to run, but his limbs would not obey him. The old man raised one finger. Craft crackled in the night air.

Alaxic's grin widened. Breath rustled in the hollow chamber of his chest. Stars spun overhead. Temoc bared his teeth. Knives of moonlight pressed against his skin. Sweat beaded on Alaxic's face, and on Temoc's; their eyes met, and the world turned like a key in a lock between them.

The rattling leaves paused, and Alaxic slumped in his chair, still.

Temoc staggered for the balustrade and leapt into space, landing in a desperate roll that sent rocks and gravel scampering down the hillside scree. Behind him, an alarm sounded, as servants discovered Alaxic dead.

Temoc crawled to a bush, bent double, and was violently ill. He threw up four times, gasping in between for air. His nerves were brambles lodged inside his skin. With shaking fingers he clutched at his belt, found a roll of leather marked by holy symbols, and pulled from within a green jade disk that shimmered faintly in the moonlight.

The disk broke between his teeth like porcelain. He chewed it into sand and forced himself to swallow. The sand coated his throat and sat in his stomach like ice.

Some time later, his shivers subsided, and the brambles withdrew. Unsteady, he rose to a crouch.

Behind him, hunting dogs howled.

He ran.

Book Four

■   ■   ■

RISING

36

Caleb drowned in dreams of fire, death, and lust. He tumbled from the sky, stretched out to ribbons that floated in blissful agony on the air. He was a tower, falling to an unseen foe. Bodies struck stone and broke into disconnected limbs, like bundles of sticks dropped from a height. Skin bubbled from bones, and the bones too burned.

In a cave at the world's heart, two sleeping serpents writhed with expectant hunger. Their mouths opened. Tongues long as thoroughfares whipped out to taste sulfurous air.

He lay prostrate and paralyzed under a descending knife. As the blade pierced his flesh he recognized the woman who held it.

"Mal," he gasped, and woke coughing. He sat halfway up and collapsed onto the yielding ocean.

The ocean. Gods, devils, and everything in between. He had slept on the open ocean. He opened his eyes, slowly and with much protest from his tired body.

Midnight-and-milk sky hung overhead. Dawn threatened to the east. He sat up with a groan, and found himself alone and naked on the water. His clothes lay a few feet away, pants and shirt and jacket folded beside sock-stuffed shoes. Mal must have folded them before she left.

He didn't wonder where she had gone, nor did he blame her for leaving: what would they have said to each other, waking on the Pax? The normal script, the "I had a good time last night"s and the "should I make some coffee"s and the "let's do this again soon"s, seemed flimsy and insincere. Gods, did he remember a *shark*? What was real, and what was dream? His memories beggared reality, and ran together like mixed paint.

Bruises lined his ribs, legs, and arms in triple rank, sized and spaced correctly for the points of a shark's teeth. The shark was real, then. Judging from the scratches on his back, and the half-moon marks of human teeth on his arm and shoulder, so was Mal.

Fumbling with laces, buttons, and buckles, he clothed himself and stood. Gorgeous day for an eclipse: blue skies without a shred of cloud. The first rays of sunrise gleamed off Dresediel Lex. No ships moved on the water. Only a thin column of smoke from the tower on Bay Station marred the morning.

Wait.

The smoke rose from a broken tower. And the island looked no different from any other island, bereft of the Craft that should have sheltered it.

Bay Station sat squarely in front of him, undefended, ordinary. He slipped into a rolling, pitching jog, each step rippling the ocean. He tripped on his own waves, floundered. After a few minutes the pain in his ankle subsided and he could stand again. He limped the last half mile to the island.

Disaster unfolded in the gloaming. The black tower was cleft from pinnacle to foundation. Piles of rubble jutted from sand and grass, fallen masonry amid turned earth and broken trees. Ruined walls laid bare the tower's inner chambers: office chairs splintered, conference tables overturned, a chalkboard shattered, its diagrams in pieces.

Black-clad guards lay in a semicircle around the beach where Caleb made landfall. Some bled from wounds in chest or arms or legs, some were crushed or tangled horribly around themselves, others burned until their skin was a charred cracked crust. One scarred, burly man had vanished from the waist down. Ropes of his guts coiled on the sand.

Further up the beach, Caleb found what remained of the marksmen: piles of dust nested in the shreds of uniforms. There had been archers and spearmen, bullet-throwers and lightning-callers, in the tower. They must have died when the building fell.

The odor of burnt meat filled his lungs. He should have cried out, torn his hair, thrown up in a nearby bush, but his stomach refused to turn. He staggered toward the tower with a revenant's uncertain gait.

Caleb found them next, the revenants, the zombie cleaning force marshaled as a last line of defense. In pieces, they still moved. A hand clutched the stub of a wrist. A head tried to roll upright by clenching its jaw.

The tower's double doors, fifteen feet tall, nearly as broad, and half as thick, were crumpled on the broken lobby floor. Dawn shone sharp through holes in the wall. Caleb picked past rubble and potted ferns and the empty reception desk, to the winding stair that led down to the caverns.

He descended.

Char blackened once-white walls. A spiderweb made from acid had bored into, or out of, the stone. He slid down steps melted to slag. The doors at the foot of the stairs were torn to metal splinters.

A man lay impaled on those splinters. His white coat marked him as a Bay Station Craftsman, a researcher studying the comatose god. The skin of his face had melted away. Eyeballs, somehow intact, stared unblinking from the skull. Metal spikes poked through his chest to dimple his bloodstained jacket.

Caleb would have closed the dead man's eyes, but there were no eyelids left to close. He stepped over the corpse and into the labyrinth.

There was less damage here, probably because there had been less to destroy. The station used little Craft around the divine body: even unconscious, gods bent structures and systems around them, like taproots growing through cracks in concrete.

He ran down the long hall. Cave-paintings watched him go.

He soon reached the island's heart. The walkway around the vast pit was empty. Caleb stood alone in the dull amber silence of dying ghostlights.

The silence told him everything he feared, but he walked to the edge of the pit anyway, and forced himself to look.

Qet Sea-Lord floated still upon the water. His eyes stared at the ceiling, open and blind and so large Caleb would have been a mote had he stood upon them. Pain had twisted the god's features into a grimace; emergency lights painted his teeth orange.

Qet did not breathe. The silver bonds that sustained him were gone, sunk beneath black water. His chest had been sliced open from the continental shelf of his ribs to the mountain range of his collarbone: folds of crystal skin peeled away, ropes of glassy muscle slick with rainbow blood, the rocky breastbone split, ribs pulled back. Tumulose lungs swelled in the god's open chest cavity.

His heart was gone.

On the cave's far wall, someone had painted the hundred-foot-tall silhouette of an eagle, wings spread, in blood: the sigil of the Eagle Knights. His father's sign.

Caleb staggered to the cave wall and threw up, bowed and shivering. The sight of the dead god let him collapse. Arms the size of hills, limp. Vast eyes stared, open, black. You could swim in those eyes, or drown.

He sobbed sour breath.

The pumps did not pump. The pipes were still.

He backed away from his refuse.

The god was dead. Bay Station could no longer strip salt from the ocean. Someone must have noticed. Where were the Wardens? The King in Red should be here. What was going on?

Leaning on the passage wall, he climbed back to the surface.

Rising, he let his mind race. He would be blamed for this somehow. No. Even the King in Red would not leap to that conclusion. The night before, Caleb would have laid his soul that no army could break Bay Station—not Deathless Kings or gods, certainly not a kid with no Craft to his name. Kopil would see that.

Was this Temoc's doing? Other groups used the sign of the Eagle Knights these days, True Quechal terrorists mostly. Caleb's father was on the run. An attack so brutal, so destructive, so successful, took time to plan and resources to execute. Temoc might have found a hole in the island's defenses, though, and passed word to others.

But this wasn't his style. Liberate Qet, yes. Free him from bondage, deliver him to his few remaining worshippers. Return him to health, and power. Temoc would never kill a god.

Bodies sprawled on the beach amid rubble and surf-tossed debris. Searching the sky, Caleb saw no Wardens flying westward from the city. He heard no wingbeats.

Where was everyone?

Where was Mal?

Safe. She had folded his clothes, a sign of care: she hadn't left in a hurry. What if she was about to leave when the attack began? She would have gone to fight. Woken him, surely. Unless not: unless she'd seen the attack, and decided to let him sleep.

I don't want you to die, Caleb. Frozen atop the magisterium stump, eyes burning with starlight. *I'll knock you out and leave you here, warded and sleeping, until this is settled.*

She wouldn't have done it. Couldn't have left him. And anyway he hadn't seen her corpse.

Not that there were many corpses left.

No. She was alive. Back in the city, sleeping, safe. If safe had any meaning, now.

At the eastern edge of the ocean path, he held out his hand and called for an opteran. None came.

Some fliers always waited over Bay Station, kept by contract with RKC. If they were gone, something must have so shaken the firm that its routine contracts failed. Even Qet's death should not have done that much damage.

Or else the god's murderer had killed the fliers, too.

He walked back to the island, and paced along the coast. Gulls cried and waves spent themselves on sand. In a small artificial bay, he found a pier. A few coracles and a supply barge rocked in the water. Had the attackers been so shortsighted as to leave the boats seaworthy? Then again, why torch them if no survivors remained to sail home?

Caleb had never felt comfortable on the water. The ocean was a terrible thing, domain of creatures greater than man. Brave souls plied its surface, geniuses and madmen driven by the promise of foreign wealth. There were few Quechal fishermen anymore—with Qet gone, the ocean grew restless, and not even the King in Red could tame all the creatures of the deep.

Caleb stepped into a coracle, untied it from the dock, and dipped the oar into the water.

Glyphs on the coracle's hull glowed silver, and the oar grew heavy in his hand. When he paddled, a swell rose behind the tiny boat to bear it up and forward.

Caleb's first stroke carried him ten feet from the dock, his second ten feet farther. Paddle by paddle, spray on his face and fear in his heart, he guided his craft into the open harbor and rowed toward the city, leaving island and ruined tower behind.

He rowed east, on the breast of the tide, and tried not to think about Mal.

37

When he neared the docks, he heard nothing. Eclipse or no, by six in the morning the city should have twitched into grudging motion: horses neighing, optera buzzing, airbuses wallowing through the sky. Seventeen million inhabitants of the urban sprawl should be murmuring, cursing, muttering good morning over coffee.

Waves broke against the beach.

Smoke rose from the Skittersill, and Wardens swarmed in the smoke, more than Caleb remembered ever seeing in flight at once. The sky belonged to them. No optera, or airbuses, or commuter drakes flew this morning. Skyspires glimmered silent, and watched.

Caleb quickened his stroke, and soon approached the shore north of the shops and Ferris wheels of Monicola Pier. Revelers littered the beach, unconscious mostly, wrapped in surf and their own hangovers. Couples slept tangled under blankets, arms and legs and ropes of black hair trailing out from under cloth. Kegs of corn beer squatted on the sand beside smoldering barbecue pits.

Not everyone was asleep. A few dark heads peeked up to stare at the smoke rising from Bay Station and the city.

His coracle stuck in wet sand ten feet from shore. No flailing with the oar would drive the vessel nearer to solid ground. Caleb untied his shoes, removed his pants, folded the one around the other, and barefoot, clad in boxers, shirt, and jacket, stepped into the knee-deep water. On one shoulder he held his bundled clothes, and over the other shoulder he carried the oar. A weapon might be useful. Or not.

Wardens turned in the sky. Was Four up there, with her squad?

The water chilled his legs. A jagged shell—he hoped it was a shell—scraped the bottom of his left foot. The few inebriates and revelers awake gaped at him as he walked out of the water. He wondered why they stared, then realized that the scars on his legs were glowing. Why, he didn't know.

The onlookers kept their distance as Caleb dried his legs on a discarded towel and donned slacks, belt, socks, shoes again. He slung the oar over his shoulder, and waded through sleepers to the road.

"What's going on?" asked a woman covering herself with a red blanket.

"I have no idea," he said, and walked past her into the city.

Empty streets greeted him. Down alleys and narrow footpaths he heard cries of pain. Staved-in restaurant windows gaped with jagged glass teeth: their shadowy mouths held broken furniture, shattered plates, plants and statues overturned. He saw a man in a ripped coat stagger down an alley, and called to him, but he recoiled and fled.

Some stores were destroyed, others untouched. No graffiti anywhere, nor any fire he could see, and riots bred flame, especially in the absence of water.

Chaos was not due for hours yet—not until the eclipse, around noon. But chaos seldom stood on ceremony.

None of the people he saw responded to his approach, to his questions. They shrank from him, eyes wide. Nervous clutches of men and women clustered at the intersection of empty roads, but they fell silent when he neared. Clanking steel golems staggered drunkenly down alleys. Golems did not require water as such, but they loved coffee, and without water, coffee was hard to find.

He reached the Monicola Hotel after thirty minutes' walk: an ornate tower that would not have been out of place on a fancy boulevard in Alt Coulumb. Caleb hadn't come to see the hotel, but rather the perpetual waterfall that formed its facade.

The water no longer fell. He had not expected it to.

Men, women, children, stood at the plaza's edge, clad haphazardly in bathrobes, pajamas, suits. They watched the dead waterfall, the silent fountain, and did not speak. "Hey," Caleb called to a nearby woman. "What's going on?"

She shook her head. He shrugged, and walked toward the hotel.

Someone ran at him from behind, and he swung around, raising the oar. The woman and two men stopped moving. Their eyes flicked from Caleb to the oar and back. He retreated slowly, holding the oar between them. "Watch it."

"You're not safe," the woman said. "Come away from there."

"First, tell me what's going on."

She reached for him.

He took a step back, and another, toward the gurgling fountain. The fountain, which moments before had been still.

He dove to one side, and the instinct saved his life. Black ice scythed overhead, and water roared in frustration. He turned, scrambled back, fell. A black plume towered above him, lit from within by scintillating starlight. Claws curved like spray. Fanged whitecaps gnashed.

The Tzimet struck again, four ice-pick claws in a blurred swift arc that tore trenches in the pavement where Caleb had lain moments before. He rolled away, feet scrambling on stone. The creature screamed. Barbed claws descended, and he raised his hands in a vain effort to defend himself.

He did not feel the claws enter his body. At first he thought he was dying, that his mind had numbed him to the pain, but he was not numb. Blood sang in his veins.

The Tzimet staggered back, flailing, a beast of shadow and sharp edges. A wet black puddle lay on the ground at Caleb's feet.

He held the oar between himself and the Tzimet. Its glyphs glowed. Panicked, he had raised the oar to defend himself: a length of wood worked with Craft to move water at high speed. And the Tzimet was, on some level, a pattern imposed on water.

The creature struck again, and Caleb parried with the oar. His second frantic sweep connected. Six of the creature's arms ripped from its body and dissolved to spray.

The Tzimet recoiled, reared, and roared. Caleb stepped back, holding the oar at ready. A tendril of water tethered the Tzimet to the pool in front of the Monicola Hotel. The creature was bound to the fountain; having lost so much of its bulk, it could not reach him.

The Tzimet's next attack slashed empty air, raked bare stone. Frustrated, furious, lessened, it slunk back to the pool, and sank into its shelter.

The crowd around the plaza did not meet Caleb's gaze— except the woman who had tried to stop him.

"Thank you," Caleb said.

"You're welcome," she said. "Stay away from the water."

"All the pipes?"

"Everything that ran. If you open a tap, they're waiting for you. Like it was a few months back, but everywhere."

"When did this start?" he asked, though he bet he knew.

"In the night, I think. After the fireworks."

"Has Red King Consolidated said anything?"

"No."

Paralyzed. Or worse.

The woman pointed to the oar he held. "Is that a weapon?"

"No," he said, and laughed bitterly. "I should go. I need to find someone."

She did not protest as he turned to leave.

After the Monicola Hotel, he noticed Tzimet in the shadows, hiding from light. That explained the broken restaurants, and the untouched bookshops and hardware stores: the first busboy arrives to brew a pot of coffee, and demons spew from the tap.

He walked on, as the city's stolen water rebelled against it. Serpents of ice wavered over fountains. Jellyfish tendrils spread from sprinklers. Soon he heard his first Warden pass overhead, augmented voice rattling from windows and walls: "Stay away from running water. Do not attempt to shower, or bathe. Drink bottled liquids only."

Caleb imagined spiders falling from showerheads, and shuddered.

He walked by scared men and women, golems and snakelings and skeletons. He kept to himself. They all did.

Caleb traveled surface streets. He passed grocery and convenience stores with shattered windows and ransacked stock. Refrigerators gaped, empty of water, juices, beer, even bottled chocolate. Fresh bread rested untouched on racks.

Vibrant lawns hid barbed networks of wriggling Tzimet. The sun hung warm in the sky. He was thirsty. So was everyone else.

The oar weighed on his shoulder. Sansilva was several hours' walk away. No airbuses overhead.

The panic would grow worse over time. The city was quiet still, nursing its festival hangover. Those citizens who were awake had barricaded themselves in their houses, or started looting already. Riots in the Skittersill, though. That would account for the smoke.

More people would wake in the next hour. The Tzimet would feed, and the riots grow.

He called for an opteran, but none descended from the sky.

Of course. The fliers came when they smelled need, and the city was need-drenched this morning. Caleb closed his eyes and focused. Dresediel Lex was falling apart, and only he knew why. He imagined the madness of crowds, children crying for water, clashing fangs. Mal, and Teo. He needed to find her. Find them. He had to reach RKC, and help.

A black buzz grew on the edge of hearing.

Like a fisher-bird the opteran plucked him from the ground and swept aloft. Broken shops and quiet houses cohered into streets, lanes, and blocks. He felt a demonic pull on his soul; the creature's touch chilled his skin, and color drained away, as if the world were a sun-blanched painting. The opteran was hungry.

They followed Monicola east and inland; shopping centers and row houses gave way to modern buildings, which bowed in turn before the pyramids of Sansilva. People crowded the streets here, ant-sized and boiling in their masses.

Even from such a height, at such a speed, Caleb heard the crowd's cries—a relief after the unnatural quiet of the morning city. Couatl soared above the mob, but did not strike. The Wardens had not yet declared war.

Black heads bobbed below. Upturned faces showed as small tan circles; someone pointed at Caleb and shouted something he could not hear. A few angry protesters threw rocks. The first volley fell back to earth well short of him. The second whipped past his head with the force of a crossbow bolt, and he veered to evade. There were angry Craftsmen down there, or else toughs with rock throwers or black powder guns. Swearing, he shifted course to fly over buildings rather than the street.

When he turned, he saw the Canter's Shell.

A smooth blue sphere enclosed the pyramid at 667 Sansilva. A bubble, Caleb would have called it, if bubbles could curve out as well as in. Buildings reflected back on buildings on the blue surface, leering over the crowd like distortions in a magician's mirror.

A Canter's Shell was a weapon from the God Wars: infinite space compressed to finite dimension. Passing through the shell consumed an eternity of subjective time. Enter the shell, and you emerged as a haze of subatomic particles, if at all. Craftsmen used Canter's Shells in the Wars to fend off priests and mortal followers while they wrestled with gods.

Caleb had never seen a Canter's Shell used. It was a lethal defense, overkill against any force less than gods or armies. RKC was more scared than he had thought possible.

Optera darted among the Wardens near the shell; several swarmed one Warden's mount, only to be batted aside by mighty wings. Protestors taking flight—their attacks angry and erratic.

One dove toward the shell, and through. Caleb winced. Creature and rider stretched out and compressed in the reflection, and were gone.

Caleb turned from the pyramid.

Breath came shallow in his chest. The world retreated down a long, dark tunnel as the opteran drained his soul to the lees. He had to find somewhere safe, somewhere with water. He had to find Mal.

He remembered a golden afternoon months before, when they stood on a balcony and looked over the city toward the ocean.

"You could watch the world end from here," she had said, "and be happy for it."

Stupid idea, latest in a string of stupid ideas, but at least he would have a place to sit and think. There might even be water.

Shivering, unsure, he flew south to Andrej's bar.

38

Mal waited on the balcony. She shone with the risen sun.

She looked up as Caleb neared, and waved as he landed—or collapsed, rather, in a gasping heap on the balcony tiles. The opteran took a final sip of his soul, released him, and retreated to the sky.

"I didn't expect to see you here," she said as he struggled to his knees. The universe was a lovely indigo. Demons tangoed between his temples. He groaned, swooned, and fell. She pulled him to his feet. Her touch burned like hot metal.

She tried to help him toward a chair, but he shook his head and pointed into Andrej's. Someone, presumably Mal, had melted the balcony doors. They stepped over a glass puddle into the empty bar.

With Mal's aid, he stumbled to a circular silver glyph inlaid in the wall by the card tables. Caleb produced a pin from his pocket, stuck his finger, and smeared a drop of blood on the glyph's center. Behind the wall, counterweighted machines swung into motion, and the glyph began to glow.

"It won't work," Mal said. "The bank's dead. RKC's frozen, and everyone else in this city is sitting on their funds. You won't be able to withdraw anything."

And so the crisis would spread through the world. In the Skeld Archipelago young fishermen begging Deathless Kings to back their latest venture would receive no aid; a soup seller who heated his soups on morning credit would find none to hand.

Dull milky light seeped into Caleb from the glyph. "Andrej," he tried, and found his voice steady. "Andrej keeps his own credit, for the tables." His blood flowed, his heart beat. Color charged the world. His legs straightened and steadied.

"Better?"

"A bit." He glanced at the glass puddle near the entrance. "Better than the door, at least."

"I was thirsty. It was in the way."

"Thirsty." His head swam. "Gods, do you have water?"

Mal held him up, and together they returned to the balcony, to the breeze and open air.

A blue pitcher stood on a table near the banister. Mal fetched him a glass from the bar with a tine of levitation Craft. Hands shaking, he poured himself a cup of water, wet his finger, flicked three drops to the ground—"water in the desert"—and swallowed the rest so fast he choked and spent an undignified minute coughing into his arm. He poured a second cup, which he sipped like wine.

"You never appreciate things so much as in their absence."

"Hells. Mal. Do you know what's happened?"

She sat across the table, black leather bag in her lap. She clutched it as she watched him. "Tell me."

"Qet." He had to stop for breath. Saying one word felt like running a mile. He took the rest at a sprint. "He's dead."

Mal pressed her lips together into a pale line, and bowed her head.

"There's no water."

"Yes," she said.

"Tzimet loose in the streets. Riots in Skittersill, I think, and near RKC. True Quechal, probably."

"Or else normal people, scared and angry."

"The King in Red's closed himself behind a Canter's Shell. I don't know if he's even still, ah—" He stopped before he said, "alive," and considered. "Awake."

"I expect he's collapsed," Mal said. "His contracts to provide water bind deep. Every faucet in Dresediel Lex, every toilet flushed or factory trying to fill its boilers, is a claim he can't ignore. Not to mention the strain of keeping the Serpents asleep. He might as well be dead. The rest of the board, too. The more they were tied to RKC, the weaker they'll be."

"It doesn't work like that. I know those contracts. There's an escape clause, for emergencies. You don't want the person most qualified to fix the water to collapse if it breaks."

She shrugged, which he thought was odd. Then again, the entire situation was mad. How did he expect her to act?

He continued: "But the boss wouldn't have raised that Canter's Shell unless something was wrong inside the pyramid, as well as outside. We can't count on his help."

She nodded, and waited for him to speak.

"You have to reach Heartstone. We'll fire up the Serpents, use their power to get the water running, kick out the Tzimet, calm everybody down. Once that's done, one of the big Craft firms should be able to resurrect Qet, or a part of him at least. RKC will have a rough year, but we should survive, and so should the city."

Mal watched him through half-lidded eyes. He poured himself more water, drank, licked stray drops from his lips. "What do you say?"

"Why?"

"What?"

"Why," she repeated, "should we save Red King Consolidated?"

The marble tabletop was cool and solid. "Because the city needs water. Because people are dying, and we can help."

"We will."

Her voice was flat, as it had been on Seven Leaf Station, when the gods writhed beneath the lake. "Are you okay?"

"Never better."

Mal was intensity restrained, so still the air seemed to shake. *I have a secret*, her body screamed.

"If we're not going to save RKC, what do you think we should do?"

"Caleb." She closed her eyes, and massaged them with her hand. When she opened them again, they looked soft, and red. "We have to wait."

"That's it? That's your plan? Wait?"

"At first."

"The riots will get worse."

"They must. When the eclipse comes, we'll use the Serpents to grant water to the city. They will rise, and we'll chase the Tzimet from our land—and the skyspires, too. Craftsmen will flee rather than face the Serpents." She said it as if reciting the bids in a round of bridge. "We can start fresh."

He leaned back from the table, and from her. "Mal. What are you saying?"

"If the King in Red recovers, he won't let Qet's death go unpunished. He'll destroy the old religion and everyone who follows it, snap the spines of the last gods and goddesses, break their bones and feast on their marrow. But only if he recovers. If he doesn't, we have a chance to take a different path."

"You're talking as if this is an opportunity."

"It is. You asked me for an answer, last night. This is it. RKC is dead. Let it rot. Build something new."

"No."

"When the cards are dealt, and the players go all-in, what do you do if you hold the winning hand?"

"But you don't hold the winning hand."

"We do," she said.

The world chilled. Caleb forced himself to speak. "Who's 'we'?"

"Me, and people like me. People who care about fixing our city, our world. You, too, if you'll join us."

He licked his lips. To the south, fires spread. "Mal." He didn't, couldn't, say anything more.

"Caleb." She leaned across the table, laid her hand on his, gripped tightly. Long hours of climbing had left her fingers smooth and hard. He thought her running, a goddess in flight.

"You're talking about rebellion. Regime change." He exhaled. "I get it." Gods writhing in the lake. Qet Sea-Lord dead in a sea of filth. Burning nets fell from the sky to snare her parents, his father, the thousands of the Skittersill Rising. The Rakesblight Center slaughtered twenty thousand pigs every day, turned animals to meat with hooked blades and spinning diamond wheels. "Not today. Please. Not now. Even if you chase the Craftsmen out of town, where would that leave you? In the middle of a desert, without any water. Qet is dead. Without the firms you won't be able to bring him back to life. Let's save the city first, then talk."

"I've taken care of that." She released his hand, placed her leather bag on the table, and undid the brass buckle. Her shoulders slumped, and her hands trembled.

She opened the bag and turned it toward him in the same motion.

He fell.

Falling, forever, into a sky without stars. Silent colossi moved through limitless space, invisible presences whose immensity built the world. He was a speck of dust, a leaf drifting down a cave chimney.

A misshapen planet of meat and rainbow blood hung below him. Severed arteries and limp veins the size of skyspires dripped ichor.

He fell through nothingness toward the heart of a god.

Caleb caught the table's edge and pulled himself upright. The bag gaped. The heart filled the space within, yet was somehow swallowed by that space, too, a single bright spot in blackness deeper than the deepest cave, longer than the longest tunnel.

"What is this?" he said, though he knew already.

"His heart," she replied.

"Where did you get it?"

She closed the bag. "I cut it from his chest with a knife of lightning. I would have used obsidian, but I couldn't lift a blade that large. Lightning is less traditional, but easier to handle. And the effect's the same."

"You . . ."

He trailed off, hoping she would finish for him, but she didn't.

"You attacked Bay Station. While I was asleep."

"Yes."

"I saw what happened there."

Pain flickered across her features. "I'm sorry."

"Sorry for what? Sorry for what you did, or sorry I saw it?"

"Both. The attack had to be last night, because of the eclipse today. Bad luck. I tried to get you to turn back. I should have insisted. But. I didn't want to be alone before it happened."

"You're lying. You couldn't have done all that. You're not powerful enough. No one is."

"The Serpents are with me. I am weak, but they are strong." She opened her hand, and fire blossomed in her palm—not the cold fire of Craft, but a hungry inferno, a burst of heat that blew desert wind in his face. She closed her hand, and it stopped. "Nothing can stand against them."

"Gods. You're serious."

"I am."

"But drawing power from the Serpents makes them hungrier."

"Which weakens RKC, and Kopil. Alaxic insisted on that condition. You remember? RKC has to keep the Serpents sleeping. When I attacked Bay Station, everything I threw against them weakened their defenses. The more RKC fights, the more it's caught."

"And once Bay Station cut out, RKC tried to draw water from Seven Leaf, but . . ." He remembered his own work: melding red wires with blue, splicing the Serpents into the system. "Hells."

"Your people audited Seven Leaf with a magnifying glass and sharp calipers before you bought us; we couldn't tie Seven Leaf to the Serpents until the deal was done."

"Oh," he said. "No."

"So we broke the station, knowing we could rebuild it later. Allie started the work. You and I finished it. Now, when RKC tries to pump water out of Seven Leaf Lake, it draws power from the Serpents, and the King in Red fades further."

"The True Quechal didn't poison Bright Mirror."

"Of course not. They can barely paint graffiti without misspellings. Their hearts are in the right place, but they've had nothing to guide them for eighty years. No sacrifice. No transcendence. They're small, and petty, and mean."

"Your entire Concern was a sham."

She laughed bitterly. "Have you ever tried running a Concern? You need people to do the work. People to manage those people, and to manage those in turn. The Concern is a dumb god and human beings are its cells. After his defeat in the God Wars, Alaxic studied the Craft. He started Heartstone to beat Kopil at his own game. We made contact with the Serpents in their slumber. And when we were ready, Alaxic showed the King in Red what he had found. Kopil raced to acquire us—he couldn't let Alaxic control the Serpents. Out of two thousand employees, only a handful knew the full plan. Alaxic. Allie. Me. A few engineers, a few Craftsmen. The True Quechal—even if they're small and petty, they have their uses. When you need someone to take a suicide run into North Station, for example, why not use a premade band of zealots, any one of whom would gladly die at a Goddess's side?"

"That was you."

"Once Kopil knew we had the Serpents, we had to convince him he was under attack, which made him more desperate to acquire us, to control them. He wanted insurance. Security."

"You played me all along."

"No." Mal pushed her chair back and rose. Her expression was earnest, desperate. "I didn't plan for you to see me that night. At first I was scared. I wanted to get rid of you." Her heels tapped on marble as she rounded the table toward him. He stood and retreated, not fast enough to escape. "But you chased me, through death and pain and fire. You chased me, devoted, suicidal, scared—and I saw you wanted more than me. You wanted to give your life to something. To change the world, only you'd forgotten how."

"Yes." The word fell heavy from his lips.

"Well, here we are. Let's change. Let's change the world. Together."

"You sound like my father."

"Your father wants the gods back on their pedestals. I want us working as one: humans with Craft, gods with divine power, priests with Applied Theology. But we need space to build that society. We need the time and the power to change, and we'll never have that time or power with Craftsmen crushing us. We need freedom, and I can win that freedom. Not in a decade or three. Today. In one stroke."

"You want a moderate revolution. You just need to kill a few people first."

"A few people. Yes. To free a city. To save a planet. Dresediel Lex will be a model for the world."

"I kind of like it the way it is."

She reached for his hand but he drew back. They circled the table, and each other.

"This city bothers you as much as me. I've seen the way you look at the long streets, the empty-faced men and women. You hold back when you talk, when you think, because you know thinking too deeply will drive you mad. I've dragged the madness out into the open. There's no need to hide anymore."

He slowed, despite himself, and she caught him in her orbit. She gripped his arm, and through his jacket he felt the feverish warmth of her fingers.

She pressed against him. One hand slid up his arm to cup his chin, curve around the back of his neck, and pull his head to hers, his lips to her lips.

They kissed, atop the pyramid, as the world crumbled.

The kiss was a collision. Hunger shot through them both, and need. They kissed violently, and violently they broke apart, each stumbling from the other.

Caleb looked at her, and imagined years beside her, leaping from rooftop to rooftop above blood-soaked streets as two serpents reared in the sky.

He grabbed the bag off the table, and cradling it in his arms ran from her toward the door.

"Caleb!" she cried behind him, which was all the warning he received before a curtain of flame blocked his path. Glass and metal melted. Recoiling from the bloom of heat he skidded on marble, nearly fell, and ran again, this time toward the banister.

"Caleb, please!" The air thickened to slush and ice, but he opened his scars and the ice thawed. The world inverted, directions twisted, but his scars bore him forward. The marble balcony became an ocean of clashing stone waves and he pressed through. Blind, staggering, he struck the railing, and threw himself over the edge.

He fell ten feet, and stopped, arms jerked nearly out of their sockets. His scars protected him from Mal, but did not guard her bag and the heart it held. Closing his eyes, he saw the silver cords of Mal's Craft binding the leather. He flailed at those cords, but they rewove themselves faster than he severed them.

The strap warmed in his hand. He gripped it tighter, teeth bared. Heat seared his skin. He held a length of molten metal.

With a cry, he released the bag, and fell again.

After five feet he struck the side of the pyramid, bounced off stone, and slid, accelerating down the incline. Rock tore his pants and jacket. His fingers scraped for handholds, found none. The bag floated back to the balcony and Mal's waiting hand.

He reached the step of the pyramid and tumbled into emptiness. Out of reflex his eyes closed. Silver-blue cobwebs whipped past his face. Desperate, he clutched at them.

The Craft lines slowed his fall; unlike the cords around North Station, though, these were too thin to support him. They ripped free of the wards that cocooned the pyramid, and those in turn unraveled; an avalanche of Craft followed Caleb down, sparking off pyramid stones.

He shattered the skylight of the pyramid's next step. Impact rainbowed his world in pain.

He stood, slowly, favoring his left leg. His ribs hurt: bruised, he hoped, not broken. He was alive. He brushed glass splinters from his face and clothes with his jacket sleeve.

Opening his eyes, he found himself in a gray office beside a desk glittering with skylight glass. Thick books filled shelves on the office walls; a three-ring binder lay open on the desk.

Caleb waited for Mal to follow him. She did not.

She would not. He'd made his choice.

But what had he chosen?

When he trusted his legs to carry him, he limped out of the office toward the stairs.

39

Caleb walked, bleeding, down Sansilva Boulevard. He needed a drink. He needed rest. He needed to scream. The first two options were unavailable, and the third would be no help, so he pressed on, limping. Retreating floodwaters of adrenaline revealed new vistas of pain to his battered body.

The distant mob cried rage. A group of ragged young Quechal ran past him down the sidewalk, laden with loot: jade amulets, hammers to drive any nail through any surface, speakers with demonic symphonies trapped inside. A long-haired girl turned cartwheels in the road.

Lighthearted looters, glorying in brief anarchy. No danger.

Tzimet swarmed behind the broken windows of restaurants, jaws clattering. They crawled over a chewed corpse in a busboy's uniform, who grinned with bloody teeth. Sentient spikes jutted from sewer grates. Demons scuttled down desolate alleys.

Caleb walked south, and east. Blood dripped from his cut face onto his torn shirt. Blood seeped from the slice on his right thigh into his shredded pants. Blood was his point of contact with the world.

He found the building without trouble—could have found it blind. He had walked this path many times before, drunk and nearly dead. Caleb walked through the front door; it flowed away from his scars. The lift rattled him up seven floors. He lurched through opened doors and down the bare hall, to apartment C.

He tried to knock, but collapsed instead. His cheek pressed into the pale wood's grain. A heartbeat rhythm pulsed in his ear.

Halting footsteps from within: slippered feet approached.

"I have little water, less food, and a blast rod pointed at the door."

"Teo," he said. "Glad to see you're . . . hospitable as ever."

"Caleb?"

He grunted.

Chains rattled. Locks unlocked. When the door opened he stood straight for three seconds before slumping into her arms. She shouldered the door closed and latched it with one hand.

"Caleb, gods. What happened to you?"

"Gods happened."

She sat him in the chair beside her coffee table. The cubist war scene taunted them both from her wall.

"You look like you went ten rounds with the bastards."

"Only one. That was enough."

"I didn't take you for such a pushover." She disappeared into the kitchen, and returned with water. "Drink it slow. There's not much left. Three quarters of a pitcher, and the ice in the icebox."

"Water in the desert," he said wryly, dipped his finger and flicked a drop onto the floor.

"What's happened?" she asked as he drank.

He wiped his lips with the back of his hand, then sucked the moisture from his skin. "What do you know?"

"I woke up and saw the shell from my bedroom window. I thought it was a joke before I heard Sam scream from the bathroom. She'd turned on the shower, and they were all over her."

"Is she—"

"I got them off. The tap shut down pretty quick. She was cut, bruised, one bad tear in her shoulder where they dug in." Teo exhaled. "We went door to door, telling people not to use the water. They understood pretty quick. Nobody here's forgotten when the demons came from the taps, during the Seven Leaf crisis. Most of the building's trying to wait the trouble out, for now. Some went to Sansilva to complain. I stayed here, lucky for you."

"Good idea." He savored the water. "The city's dangerous." Doomed, he almost said. "Where's Sam?"

"I don't know."

"Oh. Seven hells."

"She said we had to do something. I said, yes, hide, and wait.

She called me all the things you call someone who says a thing like that at a time like this. Coward, and the rest." She laughed like a razor scraped over piano wire. "My girl loves a riot. She'll be in the thick of the mob, next to all the other fools."

"You've been drinking."

"Screw you. There's a woman out there killing herself for no reason, in the middle of a city killing itself for no reason."

"I'm sorry," he said.

"So I repeat: what in the hells is going on?"

"The water's bad."

"I noticed, thanks. And if that's all you knew, you'd say so, rather than trying to dodge the question."

"Qet Sea-Lord is dead."

She sat down. Her face went blank. "Oh."

"Yes."

"I can't, I mean." She ran her hand through her hair, gripping strands that slipped between her fingers. "What happened?"

"Mal happened."

"Mal? Your Mal?"

"Not my Mal. Nobody's Mal but her own. She's been behind it from the beginning. Her, Alaxic, her friends and coconspirators."

"Behind what?"

"Everything. From Bright Mirror to North Station to Seven Leaf, to this. They poisoned Bright Mirror and blew up North Station to speed RKC's merger with Heartstone. They turned Seven Leaf against us. And this morning, Mal attacked Bay Station, broke in, and killed Qet Sea-Lord."

"She would have been slaughtered. She's, what, mid-thirties? No way she could have taken Bay Station on her own. Armies couldn't do it."

"She's using the Serpents somehow. They feed her power."

"No."

"She shattered Bay Station, Teo. I've never seen anything like it. Killed the guards, broke the tower, ripped Qet's heart out of his chest."

"Caleb." She shifted her chair back from the table, back from him. "How do you know all this?"

Meaning: you're crazy. Or worse: are you on their side? Is that terror or eagerness I hear in your voice?

He told the tale from the beginning, as far as he knew it, from the Skittersill Rising when Mal's parents died to Alaxic's discovery of her, his tutelage, and her decision, on that naked swim in the Fangs, to strangle life rather than be overcome. He outlined her plot.

Teo interrupted when he mentioned Seven Leaf Lake, Mal cutting Allesandre's throat—"Because she would have talked. If she survived I mean. The King in Red would have pulled the truth from her somehow." Caleb did not answer. He finished with his fall from Andrej's pyramid, and turned to her for solace, for comfort.

"What the hells, Caleb?"

This was not the reaction he expected. "What?"

"You came to me with this? Out of all the people in this city? Not to a Warden, or the King in Red, or any of the board members."

"The pyramid's locked in a Canter's Shell, and I have no idea how to reach the board. Ostrakov, Mazetchul, the rest of them, they're probably as bad off as the King—comatose, or close to it. They're as tied to the system as he is. Even if some of them are still moving, they're probably low on power, and in danger— fighting Tzimet, trying to fix the water, save their own skins. I had to hide and catch my breath. Decide what to do next. Maybe that is looking for the board. I don't know."

"You could have died on the way over."

"Or as I wandered through Monicola on foot with Tzimet loose. Or when I tried to steal the heart from Mal. Or when I jumped off the pyramid. My life isn't the point now."

Teo stood and paced. She thought best in motion. "How could we have missed this?"

"You never knew her. Nobody did. She was careful. I got closest, and I was in love. Or thought I was." The past tense hurt.

"What's her plan?"

"Take over the city, it sounded like. In the short term."

"We need more detail. She wants to wake the Serpents up. Use them to chase the Craftsmen out, set up a new government, hail the glorious revolution, whatever. But the Serpents wake up on the eclipse. She'll have ultimate power for, what, half an hour, maybe less, until the Craftsmen move back in."

"The eclipse wakes the Serpents up, I think. The sacrifice is supposed to send them back to sleep. Maybe they'd normally sleep once the eclipse ended, but Mal's used a lot of their power. I bet they're ravenous. Have you ever tried to sleep with an empty stomach and food in the next room?"

"So we feed them."

"We'd need a sacrifice."

"So we find a sacrifice."

"No."

"I'm only saying, if we can—"

"We are not going to sacrifice anyone. To anything."

"Even if it would stop Mal? Fix all this?"

"Hells."

"I'm just saying."

"No."

"Okay. Fine." She cradled her forehead between her hands. "Why did she let you go?"

"She didn't let me. I jumped, remember? Off a building?" He indicated his wounds and his ripped clothing with an angry wave.

"She grabbed the heart. I'm sure she could have caught you, if she wanted."

"I don't know. Maybe she wanted to let me go. Maybe she still has feelings for me."

"Feelings." Teo strangled a laugh. "Sorry. This situation is absurd."

"It's serious."

"Absurd and serious. The worst kind of joke." She tapped her lower lip with a curled finger. "RKC's out of commission because it has to spend all this soulstuff keeping the Serpents asleep. That's the problem. If we could get into the Sansilva pyramid, maybe we could break the contract binding RKC and Heartstone."

"Won't work. Craft is more than words on a page."

"But words on a page are important. Without a contract, without a signature, RKC could weasel out of the deal. We might have a chance."

"A deal's a deal, though. Can we really just cancel the contract without Heartstone's consent?"

"Cancel, no. But weaken, sure, enough for someone as strong as the King in Red to ignore it for a while. If Heartstone had Craftsmen and Courts on their side, nothing we do would matter, but I imagine their Craftsmen are all busy right now, and none of the Courts are open."

"Fair point."

"But if that's so, you're the only one alive who knows what's going on, and how to stop it. If I were Mal, love you or not, I'd hunt you down and make sure you didn't tell anyone."

"Good thing she doesn't think the way you do."

"Maybe she hasn't caught up with you yet."

There was a knock on the door.

He and Teo exchanged a brief, deep glance. She picked up her blast rod.

There was a second knock, like the beat of a funeral drum.

Is that her, Teo mouthed. He did not answer, but tiptoed to her kitchen and returned bearing a long, sharp chef's knife.

The third knock, the fourth: thick, solid sounds.

Teo edged down the hall, blast rod leveled at the door. Her hands shook. He followed her. "Sam?"

She received no answer.

"I'm angry, and I'm armed. Tell me who you are or get away from my—"

The latch snapped and the door burst from its frame. Black, sharp-edged shadow boiled through. Teo's blast rod flared twice. A clawed hand grabbed her wrist and twisted. The wand fell from her limp fingers; the shadow figure spun her around and pinned her against the wall.

Caleb stabbed the shadow, and felt a dull thud as if his knife had struck solid wood. Before he could react, something hit him in the stomach. He sunk to his knees, swallowing air.

The blurred world resolved into outline. Teo's knife lay on the ground beside Caleb, its blade melted. Their attacker was human-shaped, broad-shouldered and massively muscled, clad in darkness and gleaming light; the air about him thrummed with ancient chants. One huge hand held Teo's wrist. A forearm thick as a column pressed against her throat. Teo's free arm clawed at her attacker's face. Her nails drew sparks as they skidded over the steel-smooth dark.

Caleb recognized him.

"Father," he said. "Put Teo down, or you'll have to hit me again."

Temoc released her and stepped back. Teo coughed, and straightened, cradling her wrist. Anger flushed her face.

Shadows passed from Caleb's father like flowers closing for the night. His scars dimmed, and the man himself stood in Teo's hallway: naked from the waist up, dark skin distended with muscles and old wounds.

"Son," Temoc said. "I need your help."

Caleb blinked. "What?"

40

"A group of fanatics is about to destroy the city," Temoc said.

"I know."

"They intend to use the Twin Serpents as a weapon. The last time Aquel and Achal were used this way, they broke the continent in half. I need you to help me stop them." He blinked. "Wait. What do you mean, you know?"

"Mal, the woman who's planning all this, she and I. We're dating, I guess. I mean, we were." Temoc's eyes widened. "I'm not a part of the plan. I left as soon as I found out what was going on. About an hour ago."

"You did not tell me you were seeing anyone."

"I didn't know I had to clear my romantic choices with you."

"Caleb," Teo said, massaging her throat, "I've never met your father. Please introduce me to this man who just broke into my apartment and tried to strangle me."

Temoc looked at her. She glared back.

Caleb counted to ten and down. "Teo, this is Temoc, last of the Eagle Knights, high priest to All Gods. Dad, this is Teo. She's a contract manager at RKC, and my friend." He laid special emphasis on the last word.

"I apologize for hitting you." Temoc bowed his head. "I do not relish striking women."

"Thank you," Teo said with a cold edge, "for your condescending, sexist apology."

Temoc clasped his hands behind his back and raised his chin, and waited, like a statue staring into the glorious future.

Teo knelt to reclaim her blast rod. "How can we trust you? You're a theist, a murderer. You tried to kill the King in Red. You could be part of this whole plot."

"I could have killed you both if I wished. I have not done so. Nor did I break your wrist when you shot me. These are signs of my good faith."

Teo bared her teeth. Caleb stepped between them. "Swear you're not part of this, Dad. Pick a god, and swear."

"I speak truth, on the bones of Ili of the Bright Sails. Your woman and her comrades have betrayed us all. They have abandoned the keeping of the days and the marking of the hours."

"Add deicide and murder to those charges."

Temoc drew a deep, rumbling breath. "Then Qet is dead."

"Yes. And some people, too."

"Your woman's master was a priest once. A good man turned sick. I discovered this planned blasphemy too late, when he tried to kill me, and killed himself. I recovered, broke into his house, found his journals, learned the truth. We must stop his student before others die."

"Yes," Caleb said. "But how?"

For a time, Temoc did not reply. He should have been a poker player, not a priest. He was immutable as a mountain. Eons could pass about him, civilizations rise and fall, without Temoc registering the change.

"First," he said, "I would like you to tell me about this woman. Second, I would like a glass of water."

Temoc, Priest of All Gods, sipped water from a blue coffee mug emblazoned with the words "World's Best Daughter" above a picture of a goddess suckling a serpent. Caleb shifted in his seat. His wounds hurt, talking hurt, not talking hurt, sitting at a table across from his father hurt. Teo paced, tapping the tips of her blunt fingers together. She scowled as Caleb repeated the story of his relationship with Mal.

Temoc considered for a long, silent time, head downturned, shoulders sloped over the table like a rocky hillside. Since the Skittersill Rising, Caleb's father had become a myth, to his son as much as to the rest of the city: a name shouted from newspaper headlines and whispered in dark corners. He was a legend, and a legend could not be a father. Nor could a legend sit in Teo's white living room, surrounded by sensible Iskari furniture, drinking from a World's Best Daughter mug.

"The Serpents are the great danger," Temoc said at last. "If all she had were her Craftswoman's tricks, we could defeat her. We cannot stop the Serpents while they are hungry. We must feed them with sacrifice—feasting, they will be sated, and sleep. The great altars are all destroyed, or under heavy guard, but lesser altars remain, used before the Fall for simple sacrifices, goats and cows, rarely touched by human blood. Two priests, working together, could purify one of these lesser altars and make sacrifice there. Caleb, you are not a priest, but you bear our marks." The old man touched the scars on his arms. "You can help me."

"I won't sacrifice anyone," Caleb said.

"Why not? No doubt one of the True Quechal will give his life for the city. Many would count it an honor to be asked. I will find one for us."

"If your plan involves murder, walk out that door now."

"You will not let one person die to save an entire city?"

"I won't kill anyone. Teo and I covered this already."

Temoc raised an eyebrow. "It is the only way. The Serpents wake when they are called, and will not sleep until their hunger is assuaged."

Caleb searched the walls of Teo's apartment, blank white, hung with paintings, but found no help. "There must be another option."

"There is not."

"Caleb," Teo said, carefully. "Maybe you should listen."

"No."

"You are not being reasonable," Temoc said.

"And you're being disgusting."

"Disgusting." He laughed. "You are comfortable when violence is done by others on your behalf—when gods are imprisoned, when men are slain or reduced to slavery, you do not blink. But faced with the need to dirty your own hands, you shudder."

"That's not what bothers me." He pointed to the battle-scape above Teo's couch. Jewel drops of blood rained from an infernal sky. "People fought a war to keep us from doing this sort of thing. If we sacrifice someone to stop Mal, she's won."

"Sophistry. If we sacrifice someone to defeat her, she has lost. This city holds seventeen million people—surely one of them can assuage your wounded conscience in the aftermath."

"You refuse to even try to think of a better way."

"Do you not think that if a better way existed, we would have found it somewhere in three thousand years of history?"

"I could say the same about, oh, dentistry. Anasthesia."

Teo leaned against the back of an empty chair. "Caleb, you're not helping. Your father knows the Serpents better than we do. If he says this is our only choice, shouldn't we believe him?"

Caleb's bruised ribs and burned hand radiated pain.

"The Serpents," Temoc said, "feed on the souls of our people. The human heart is a focus—the nobler, and more innocent the heart, the better, hence the preference for altar maids and altar men, who are pure in their own bodies. The ritual binds the soul into meat and blood. Death focuses the spirit, heightens its awareness."

Caleb did not listen.

He stared at the painting of the battle.

Gods fought and died over the pyramid at 667 Sansilva. Temoc and Kopil wrestled in midair, figures wreathed in flame. The flayed body of Qet Sea-Lord sprawled upon a black glass altar stained red with blood.

"Dad," he said.

"Without that moment of death, without the moment of transcendence, we cannot—"

"Dad."

Temoc stopped.

"I have an idea." He pointed to the pyramid at the painting's center. "This is 667 Sansilva, right?"

"It is Quechaltan. Yes."

"And this is the altar on top of it. Stained with blood. Three or four drops from every person who's died there."

"Yes."

"I've seen it. The whole block's red-black."

"What is your point?"

"Thousands of people were sacrificed on that stone. They've left their blood behind—their souls, their deaths. Let's feed them to the Serpents again. Let's feed Aquel and Achal so much death they'll sleep for five hundred years. Let's feed them the altar."

Teo straightened. "Would that work?"

"It is mad," Temoc said, "this thing you suggest."

"Thousands of sacrifices. There has to be some way we can use that. If the altar itself won't work, pull the souls out and feed them to the Serpents directly."

"Impossible."

"Impossible," Teo said, "or just difficult? Why don't we try it and find out?"

Temoc shook his head. "Even if we were to attempt this madness, you would not accompany us."

"I'm not staying behind."

"You are not—"

"Don't talk down to me!" She struck the table with the palm of her hand. Glasses rattled on glass. "My girlfriend's out there, in danger. I won't cower here if there's a chance I can help her."

"Girlfriend?" Temoc said.

"Do you have a problem with that?"

"No," he replied. "You would risk your own death to save the city."

"Of course."

Temoc turned to Caleb. "But you will not permit me one sacrifice."

"That's different."

"How?"

He did not answer.

"Perhaps you think no one else would volunteer themselves?"

"I think," Caleb said, "there's a small chance we might survive."

"There is."

"So, death isn't certain."

"Nothing is ever certain." Temoc cracked his knuckles, and his neck. "It may be possible to do what you say—the altar atop

Quechaltan, 667 Sansilva, whatever name you give the building, is old, and well-seasoned with death. There are ways, rituals, to extract spirits bound to a place. But I cannot guarantee this method will succeed. Do you understand?"

Caleb blinked. "You're serious? You think this might work?"

"If we fail, there will be no time to try again. The city will be destroyed. The danger will be great."

"Never mind the danger," Caleb said, though he minded it plenty.

"Can we even get to the altar, though?" Teo asked. "There's a Canter's Shell in the way. The grounds are crawling with security demons. The altar's in Kopil's private office, and gods alone know what kind of wards he has."

Temoc glanced out the window. "Canter's Shell. That is what you call the Curtain of Endless Span?"

"I think so." Her hands described a sphere in the air. "Translucent blue ball, lots of reflections. Looks wrong in space. Walk through it and you turn to dust."

"It poses no obstacle."

"Since when is turning to dust not an obstacle?"

"The gods will shroud us."

"I thought a shell was supposed to keep gods' servants out."

"There are servants," said Temoc, "and then there are servants. A priest ridden by a god is immortal in most senses of the word."

"I'm not a priest. I'm not even related to one."

"A god may ride you nonetheless."

"I don't like that image."

"It is the only way through the shell. The feeling is of ecstasy, not violation."

"That depends on how you feel about gods."

Temoc shrugged.

"Well," she said, "if we can get past the demons, I can take us up, as far as the thirty-second story. I have clearance to reach my office, even during a lockdown."

"If I bring us through the curtain, and you grant us access to the building, can we then reach the altar?"

Silence.

"Teo can take us to the conference room on the twenty-ninth floor." Caleb spoke slowly, uncertain what he was about to say until the words left his mouth. "I think there's a back door, a sort of tunnel, into Kopil's apartment. He brought me there during the Seven Leaf thing—he was on his way to meet an aide in his office. So there's probably another path from his apartment to the top of the pyramid."

Temoc bowed his head, and raised it again. Some religious sign, Caleb thought at first, before he realized his father was nodding.

"We can do this." Caleb heard the wonder in his own voice. He had almost believed Temoc, almost given in.

"We can." Teo smoothed the front of her shirt. She walked to the coat rack beside the door, and donned a short-brimmed hat and a leather jacket. "Let's go. We'll figure out the rest on the way."

41

Mal stood at the edge of the world. Smoke and flame and cries of riot rose from Dresediel Lex. New life swelled within the urban shell, ready to break the ground, burst upward, fly.

She tried not to think of Caleb. He didn't understand, yet. He would, she hoped. He was a good man, and almost wise, even if this city had warped him into a mess of indecision.

She could remedy that, given time.

The wind shifted. She looked up from the streets, from the riots, and smiled.

The skyspires were moving. They retreated from Sansilva and downtown, floating east toward the Drakspine and Fisherman's Vale. Reflections of rising smoke slid over their crystal walls.

The Deathless Kings that ruled those spires had caught her scent. Blind prophets trapped in silver cages, card-laying soothsayers and elder augurs, saw her face emerge from the dim confusion of probable futures, framed by fire, laughing. They saw death come to Sansilva, and decided they should leave.

That was the problem with the Craft. A Craftswoman's power derived from deals with great Concerns, with devils and demons from beyond the stars, with the secret powers of the world. These pitiless masters did not permit their servants the easy relief of death. A Craftswoman grew great in power, age, and wisdom, but she was bound to the systems that gave her strength: averse to risk, hesitant in action, a cog in a machine beyond her ken. A slave.

Mal was no one's slave.

But watching the spires leave, she felt their loss. Until this moment, she could have stopped. Turned herself in. Claimed Alaxic had controlled her somehow, or the Serpents had. She could have returned to her job, her apartment, her life, her moonlit runs. To love.

But the spires knew the future, and they were leaving. She had made her choice, even if she didn't know it yet.

She took her silver watch out of her pocket. The watch had five hands, and six concentric dials marked with letters, glyphs, numbers. A black hand swung from one letter to the next, and spelled out a message from Heartstone's head cantors.

Serpents restless. Please advise.

No sense answering. They would understand soon enough.

The moon climbed as a silver sickle toward the sun.

She poured more water, drank, and set the empty glass on the table. Bending, she shouldered the bag that held Qet Sea-Lord's heart. Power radiated through the leather, rhythmic as rolling waves.

She walked toward the balcony's edge. The railing exploded, and stone splinters rained onto the city.

Mal stepped out into empty air. Fire quickened within her, and in the black spaces of her soul, she was no longer alone.

Caleb, Temoc, and Teo walked down Sansilva Boulevard, past upturned carriages and carts. Tzimet quivered and recoiled when Temoc turned his gaze upon them. They feared the Eagle Knights of old. Unfortunately, the Tzimet were not the only obstacle between the trio and their destination.

Caleb heard the mob first—bellowing terror, voices cracked with thirst. Then he saw it. Heads and bodies pressed together, rippling and roiling like the sea at storm, overflowing the boulevard to spread out down side streets. The Cantor's Shell curved above them all, bluer than the parched sky, taller than the tallest pyramids. Its reflection captured world and crowd.

Approaching from the ground, Caleb found the protesters both more and less intimidating than they'd seemed from the sky: less, because the black mass of hair and clothes and noise resolved into individual men and women, and more, because those men and women were near enough to hurt him.

Teo stopped on the sidewalk. "Can we go around?"

"No," Caleb said. "I flew by here earlier. The crowd surrounds the pyramid."

Temoc removed a pouch from his belt. Coils and claws pressed against the leather from the inside. "The Gods' power will cow the masses."

Caleb thought he heard the pouch growl. He shook his head. "You'll attract the Wardens. They're almost as scared as the mob, only they're armed. Give them something to shoot at, and they'll shoot."

"We will fight them, and they will fall."

"If the Wardens open fire, they'll hit the crowd, too, and we'll be trampled in the panic—unless you plan to burn through all these people. We're here to avoid killing, right?"

Temoc did not reply, but he returned the pouch to his belt.

"Okay," Teo said. "Optera?"

"The bugs are unclean. Their existence offends Gods and man."

"Don't the ends justify the means?"

"A sacrifice demands purity of intent and form. If we use the bugs, we will have neither."

"You just suggested we fight our way to the pyramid."

"Battle is holy. Craft-twisted beasts are not."

"You can't be serious."

No response.

"Caleb?"

"Crowd's thick. Dangerous to force our way through. Unless." He groped in his jacket pockets until he felt something smooth and fiercely pointed, which he drew out into the light. The shark's-tooth pendant lay dull in his palm, its surface broken and burned. "I took this off Mal months ago. It helped her sneak into Bay Station, and Seven Leaf. Hid her from anyone without a priest's scars, including Wardens."

Temoc took the pendant from Caleb, turned it, lifted it to the sun. "Broken."

"I know, but the glyphwork is old Quechal style. Can you see what's wrong?"

"The bonds between the two symbols, here, the seeing and the not, were burned away. Overtaxed."

"Can you fix it?"

"I would require a week of fasting, preparation, meditation, to repair this link. In four days I could make a new talisman on the same model."

"We don't have a week. Or four days."

"Or four minutes," Teo said. "I don't like the looks the crowd's throwing our way."

"A glyph-combination like this consists of two pieces: the seeing-not and the not-seeing." Temoc drew a line from each end of the negation glyph to each corner of the stylized eye. "The first link directs attention from the wearer. The second suggests to others that the area where we walk is occupied. Without the one, we will be seen. Without the other, we will be crushed by those ignorant of our presence. These links are severed now, but I can re-forge them in my mind, using the amulet as a focus."

"Great."

"But I cannot do so and extend this protection to all three of us at the same time."

"So much for that idea." Teo tipped her hat brim down over her eyes. "Do we fight our way through?"

"Dad," Caleb said. "You can't hold the links alone. Could we do it together?"

Temoc looked from the amulet, to Caleb, and nodded.

They advanced, and the crowd parted before them.

Caleb's left hand, and Temoc's right, wound through the amulet's leather lace. Caleb's right hand clasped Temoc's left wrist, and Temoc's left clasped Caleb's right. Teo walked in the circle of their arms.

Seeing not, Caleb repeated to himself. Look anywhere but here. A closed eye shone in his mind, surrounded by billowing clouds. No, not closed—stitched shut.

"You must empty this space in their minds," Temoc had said. "We become a moment of distraction, a daydream. I will fill the gap that remains."

Look elsewhere. Keep your head down. Nothing new about that. Kopil had been right, months ago. Caleb did not want the world to notice him. Everyone the world noticed, it burned.

Poker worked this way. Bet aggressively, and others will respond in kind. Play as if you have nothing to loose, and you will lose everything. Play quiet, play calm, and win.

Men and women stepped aside for them, and closed after they passed. In the heart of the crowd, someone struck up a chant, and a few hundred others joined: "Hear us! Hear us!"

The shark's tooth glowed blue. Caleb gripped a line of ice, of fire. His scars cracked and burned, casting shadows into the crowd, and onto Teo.

Don't look. Don't see.

They closed half the distance to the Canter's Shell, and half that distance again.

Hide. Live a good life, safe. Guard against disaster. Wrap yourself in cotton.

Mal's voice in his ears, flying north to Seven Leaf Lake.

We cushion ourselves against death. We live in ignorance.

The closed eye in his mind pulled against its stitching.

Twenty feet.

Ten.

The crowd thinned as they neared the shell. Only the strongest protesters had reached this point: thick men and determined women, daring to approach eternity. On the other side of the blue shell lay piles of ash that had once been human.

In the crowd near the shell's edge Caleb saw a yellow smiling face tattooed onto the back of a shaved scalp. He looked again, and saw Balam, the old cliff runner scowling and shouting at the pyramid. "Cowards hide! Cowards run!" Of course. Where else would Balam be as the city fell apart? Sam was here somewhere, too, or else rioting in Skittersill. He did not mention this to Teo. She knew already. She had to know.

They passed within feet of Balam; his drill sergeant voice boomed in their ears. Caleb shivered as the man raged at him, and through him, unseeing. He did not break stride. "Cowards!" Fair enough.

Temoc stopped beside the dome, and released Caleb's wrist. Caleb did not let go of Temoc's arm. His father took a leather ribbon from his belt and draped it around Teo's shoulders like a stole. The leather stank of herbal unguents.

"Dad," Caleb whispered, as Temoc produced a second ribbon. "What is that?"

"God-bearer," Temoc replied, and reached for him. Caleb pulled back.

Gods lived beyond the mortal world, beside, above, below, permeating it with their presence. Yet deities had anchors: statues, idols, prayers, and god-bearers, relic holders made from cured human skin.

He tried to find a better way to phrase the question, but settled for: "Who was it?"

"One of the lesser corn gods."

"I wasn't talking about the god."

"Caleb, put it on. We don't have time to argue."

Seeing. Not. Seeing.

"Cowards!"

"Caleb," Teo said. "Do it."

Stitches strained, burst. The shark's tooth burned blue.

"He died centuries ago. A sacrifice. This is the only way to pass through that shell. You must carry a god within you."

"You could have told me before."

"I hoped to avoid this conversation."

"Excellent job you've done."

"I have set this city and all our souls at risk out of respect for your reluctance to shed blood," Temoc said. "Do not balk at a millennia-old death."

"My *reluctance*?"

"Caleb," Teo whispered. "Can we have this conversation when we're on the other side?"

"Put it on."

"Fine," Caleb said, and grabbed the stole.

Temoc stiffened. Teo swore.

Caleb froze with his hand on the leather. He had let go of Temoc's wrist.

The amulet's glow guttered and died.

Silence fell over the crowd. A hundred thousand eyes fixed at once on Caleb, Teo, and Temoc. Caleb's half of the link had failed, but Temoc's had not—and so the crowd looked upon them, and saw something greater. An immense impossible presence filled the space where they stood.

Couatl screamed overhead, and their wings beat closer. Green light flickered about the serpents' claws: weapons of Craft, building, burning.

Caleb grabbed Temoc's wrist, but panic gripped his mind, and he could not blur them to insignificance again.

The burly men and broad women nearby had stopped shouting. Balam curled his massive hands into fists. He saw, they all saw, a target for their rage. He took a step toward them, and another.

The Wardens dove to attack. The green light in their Couatls' claws sharpened to barbed spears.

Caleb grabbed the god-bearer, wrapped it around his neck, and dove into the blue. Teo and Temoc followed.

42

Imagine a cerulean field that stretches to the farthest star. Plummet through that field. Close your eyes. Forget them. Forget the body that falls, and leave only the sense of falling.

He could not see Teo, or Temoc. Were they near? What did that term mean? Between any two points stretched infinity. Could one infinity be larger than another?

He fell, but he was not alone. Another mind woke within his, powerful and still. Caleb gibbered at empty time, endless space. The stranger did not.

Let me in, the stranger whispered.

At first Caleb shrank from the voice, fleeing across forever. The stranger did not need to pursue. All space and time were equal before it.

You will fall, screaming, through ten thousand ages until your mind breaks and body crumbles, and nothing will endure but a scream. Listen and you can hear them, cries that outlast the throats that gave them voice.

Listen, and let me in.

Caleb heard: high-pitched and low, screams of women and men and children, unending.

He opened his mind.

Sensation pierced him, charring synapses, wiring his body to an engine of pain. He remembered he had lungs, for they spasmed in agony; his flesh shriveled and his mind burst and he *was*—

Was golden sunlight on the tip of a blade descending, a knife's edge drawn over flesh, a spurt of blood and a relieved sigh from upturned faces. Red droplets fell in rain, as a dragon vomited up the sun. The people wept and prayed and interned his corpse in soil to decay and be reborn in wriggling worm and fruitful seed, in the first brave green spear that pressed through the hard earth and swelled into corn.

He was gathered, he was burned, he was beaten and pounded into thin flat bread. Teeth tore him and he became flesh once more, breathing, sighing, loving in a million bodies until the dragon swallowed the sky, the raven stole the sun, and he lay again upon the altar. He writhed in drugged futile struggle against his chains; in his eyes he gathered the world, concentrated its wasted pieces into a perfect image of the universe—and in his death that world grew again from corn.

Death and rebirth became him, a cycle of time stretching back past Dresediel Lex to the Quechal homeland sunk below the sea, and further still, to men and women weeping over a grave in a trackless wilderness, bedraggled creatures with bedraggled gods, haunted by ghosts of language and ceremony.

Time was a ring, the cosmos a cycle. Space itself was curved, the Craftsmen claimed.

Spinning in emptiness, he gave his blood to the world, and the world cracked open to receive him.

Caleb struck the gravel hard and skidded. Rocks tore his shirt and the skin of his back. The impact jarred, the gravel stung, but the pressure and pain were gloriously real. He laughed in relief. The shark's-tooth pendant fell beside him. He slid it into his pocket, patted the pocket, and stood, turning back toward the Canter's Shell.

Teo fell into him out of the blue.

She was limp, and heavy, and made no sound. He staggered beneath her weight.

He set her back on her heels. She trembled, eyes closed, and did not move. Her chest rose and fell. Quechal symbols glowed from the god-bearer draped across her shoulders. Her lips moved, and she whispered in High Quechal: praise the mother who bears the twins, praise the father risen in the corn, praise the twins who die and rise again, on and on.

"Teo," he said. She did not respond. He touched her cheek.

Her eyes flew open, and they burned. No trace remained of

her pupils and iris. To stare into her was to stare into the sun. She chanted, louder. "Praise the mother and the father. Praise the mother who bears the twins. Praise the father risen in corn."

He tore the god-bearer from her neck, but she did not wake. The leather coiled on the ground, and twitched as if alive.

Temoc stepped out of the Canter's Shell, and approached Caleb. Walking over gravel, he made no sound. He regarded Teo as if appraising her for purchase. "She was not ready to host a god. Without scars, without training, the experience can overwhelm."

"Wasn't ready? You knew this wasn't safe for her. You knew, and let her come anyway."

"She insisted on accompanying us, though she knew the dangers. She claimed she could open the pyramid. She may still serve that purpose."

Caleb looked back at Teo, and closed his eyes. A twitching ruby spider spirit hunched in her heart, preening with each repeated syllable of her prayer. A small god, feeding.

Caleb opened his scars. The spider in Teo's body twitched as if it could smell him.

He bent to her ear and whispered in High Quechal: "I cast you out."

The spider twitched. Teo spoke, and he heard another voice, like brushing cobwebs, paired with hers: "By whose authority?"

"My own." His words were ragged with rage. "Leave her, or I will break your legs. I will blunt your fangs and blind all your eyes and you will die."

The spider wavered, as if about to fight, then faded into darkness.

Teo stopped her prayers. Her eyes closed.

Caleb waited.

When she opened her eyes again, they were dark, and human. "Hi," she said.

He hugged her, and she embraced him weakly in return. "I appreciate the sentiment," she said, "but I don't swing that way."

"You're back."

"Did I leave?" She stepped forward, swayed, and almost fell. He grabbed her by the arm, and she recovered her balance.

She shot her cuffs and straightened the shoulders of her jacket. Her hat had rolled to the ground, and she knelt to retrieve it. "I've never felt anything like that. The King in Red has been inside my soul once or twice, but . . . I lived a thousand years. I could hear time."

"If you lived a century ago, you would have been prepared for the experience," Temoc said. "Gods are not so common today as once they were."

"Fine by me," she replied.

Mal stood on air like a bride on an empty dance floor, waiting for the groom to emerge and the band to play.

Most days, downtown airspace was a muddy mess of airbuses and optera, Warden mounts and skyspires and flying machines. Every few hours a dragon passed overhead, beating three-hundred-meter wings on its journey to the Shining Empire. Dresediel Lex had an anthill for a sky.

Today, though, the sun shone at the apex of a bare blue vault, cut with smoke. Optera retreated to their nests. Skyspires fled. No private citizen would fly today, and the Wardens were busy.

She closed her eyes and saw Dresediel Lex as a sprawling web of power and Craft, the human stain wiped away to reveal the bent lightning at the city's root. But this too was a mask, a deception—a way she had been taught to see.

She touched glyphs at her wrist and temples, and looked down, through basements, pipes, sewers, tunnels, caves, to the beating, blinding red heart of the planet, where two serpents quaked with unpleasant dreams.

Her pocket buzzed: a warning from the Craftsmen back at Heartstone. The Serpents' hunger outstrips our power to contain them.

She opened her hands and waited for the eclipse.

Caleb, Teo, and Temoc approached the pyramid. No one challenged them. Teo glanced about, wary of security demons, but they were not attacked.

They left the parking lot and walked down a paved path flanked by topiary. Unconscious revenants sprawled in the loam between sculpted trees, sheers and clippers fallen in the shadow of shrubbery globes and pentagrams. When Mal attacked, the undead workers would have been near the night shift's end.

He touched Teo's hand. "Hey." His voice sounded small.

"Hey," she answered. Their footsteps were the only sound in the garden, beneath the Canter's Shell.

"Are you all right?"

"All right?" She laughed. "No. What do you think?"

"I'm sorry. I was an idiot back there, in the crowd."

"Usually you only hurt yourself. I don't like being part of your collateral damage."

"Hells."

"Relax. I was kidding."

"I deserve it," he said. "This is my fault. All of it. If I hadn't got mad at Temoc, I wouldn't have let go of his arm. We wouldn't even be here if I'd put the pieces together about Mal. If I'd pressed her about that pendant, about Allesandre. I think she was trying to tell me, but I didn't listen. I spend my life evaluating angles, but as soon as my feelings get involved, it all goes to hell."

"Don't think like that. Blaming yourself for everything."

"Why not?"

"Because Mal's crazy. And your father, he's helping us, but he's crazy, too. We all are. You can't hold yourself responsible for people's actions. Even if Mal made you a bit stupid, you aren't the one who came up with her plan. You aren't the one who set her on this road. She's her own woman, and she did this for her own reasons. It wasn't your fault."

He put a hand on her shoulder. "Sam will be okay."

She didn't answer.

They reached the wide, flat front steps of the pyramid. Caleb's gaze swung to Temoc, and kept swinging. "Where's my dad?"

"I thought he was behind us."

The grass rustled in a light breeze, but there was no breeze.

Bushes to their right crashed and parted. Temoc stumbled out, wearing a gardening zombie's jumpsuit. The revenant had been

296 ■ *Max Gladstone* ■

shorter, and larger around the waist, than Caleb's father. Cuffs of trousers and shirt rode up on his calves and his thick wrists.

Temoc lurched as he walked, and held one of his arms akimbo. Light twisted in his grip, and trailed on the ground behind him. Caleb blinked, and the rainbow confusion resolved into many-jointed limbs, a barbed tail, and a chitinous body. A triangular head with serrated mandibles lolled at a broken angle from the neck clutched in the crook of Temoc's arm.

Temoc let the demon fall. It struck earth, twitched once, and blurred to match the grass.

"I thought," he said, "a uniform might let the building recognize me as one of its own. It seems your lawn is well defended." He joined them at the steps, and ushered Teo toward the revolving door.

She climbed the steps, extended her hand, and touched the door. Glass glowed red beneath her fingers. She pulled her hand back. Nothing happened. She did not die.

She touched the door again, and this time it recognized her. She pressed, and it moved.

"Follow me," she said, and stepped into shadow.

43

Crystal lamps hung lifeless above RKC's dark lobby. No sun shone through the doors. Faint ghostlights set into floor and baseboard runners were the only source of illumination; they traced a branching red labyrinth that connected elevators and stairwell to the entrance. Bas-reliefs glowered from the walls—gods in agony, the King in Red triumphant, hearts torn from chests and altars split to shards.

Demons wandered through the foyer, their footsteps like glass on stone. They took many forms: a looming silent shade whose five arms ended in scalpel forests, a spider with legs six feet long. A bus-sized centipede tasted the air with tremulous antennae.

Caleb's lungs and stomach tried to squeeze into his throat. Teo cursed in High Quechal.

The demons did not attack, or seem to notice them. Nor did they intrude on the labyrinth. A giant spider crossed one crimson path, but it lifted each leg well clear of the red lines and did not step between them.

Simple enough. Stay on the path, and remain safe. Stray, and be devoured. Strange to have a security system that posed no danger to any intruder with eyes.

Caleb stepped forward, but Temoc gripped his arm like a vise. "Don't."

"What?"

"There are demons here."

"I can see that."

"They haven't attacked yet. We don't know what might set them off."

"It looks like we'll be fine if we stick to the path."

"What path?"

"That path." Caleb pointed to the floor, to the red ghostlight lines—the red ghostlight lines, which cast no shadows. Oh. "You can't see any light on the floor, can you?"

"I see a small red circle around us. You were about to cross the circle's edge."

"Ah. What about you, Teo?"

"I see green lines."

"Damn."

"Exactly. My lines turn left after five feet."

Caleb's red path remained straight for ten feet, then curved sharply to the right. "So there's a safe path for you, and a safe path for me, and none for Temoc."

"Makes sense. It can tell that we're supposed to be here, and he isn't."

"RKC has fed upon both of you for years. The beast knows your taste, and hungers for fresh meat."

"You're a creepy man," Teo said.

"This," Temoc said, indicating the demon-filled room with a wave of his hand, "is your office building."

Caleb tried not to think about teeth and claws and legs and pincers. "Dad, I don't suppose you can fight them off?"

"This would not be a battle," Temoc said. A thing like a crystal mantis scuttled up to the edge of the red circle, and stared at them with mirror eyes. "I would disappear under claw and fang."

"Can you climb the pyramid from outside?"

"Perhaps. But there will be defenses outside as well."

"Okay. Then I'll carry you."

"You'll carry me?"

"If the demons can't cross my path, we have to make it so they can't attack you without attacking me."

"Your carrying me will not solve that problem."

"Do you have a better idea?"

Another silence of legs and claws. "No."

"So we do it this way. Straight to the lift."

"Not the lift," Teo said. "The stairs."

"You want us to take the stairs up twenty-nine floors?"

"If the lobby looks like this, do you trust the lift?"

"Stairs it is." He bent his knees and surveyed his skeleton. "Watch my ribs. I think I broke one earlier, or bruised it. Breathing hurts."

Temoc grunted, grabbed Caleb's shoulders, and lurched onto his son's back.

In that first moment, struggling to balance Temoc, Caleb almost stumbled into demon-haunted dark. The world pitched and righted itself, heavier. Temoc was muscle, sinew, and bone, nothing light or soft. Caleb's first step fell so heavily he feared it would break the marble tiles. Temoc kept his muscles tight, at least, which made him easier to balance.

They crept into the labyrinth.

The first ten steps were the hardest, except for the next ten, and the ten after that. His father's living weight pressed him into the floor. Demons writhed half-seen about them, enraged by Temoc's scent, repelled by Caleb. In a paradox of obligations they gathered, champing teeth and flicking long tongues. Teo walked her own path with ease. Caleb felt a pang of envy that broke his focus, weakened his arms, bent his knees. The horrors of the night drew close.

The floor was dark as the inside of Mal's mouth.

Caleb shook.

"You know," Temoc said with a conversational air, "there's a Telomere legend about this."

"About—" Caleb sucked in breath. His arms burned, and his back trembled. "About what?"

"The Empire of Telomere traced its origins to a city near the mouth of the Ebon Sea. When that city was destroyed, the future founder of the Empire fled his enemies through the burning wreckage, bearing his father on his back. That father, too, carried the gods of their people."

Two more turns, and ten feet. "Nice story, Dad." Gods, how

much did this man weigh? Did being a priest-king make your bones more dense? Were outlaws' muscles heavier than those of normal people?

"Take strength from the story. Stories give us direction."

Turn. His hip twitched, and his hand slipped on Temoc's left leg. He lost time struggling for a better grip. "This hero's father—did he weigh as much as you?"

"I do not think so. The man in the story was old, and frail."

"Encouraging, thanks." I bet his gods were more helpful, too, Caleb thought, though he didn't say it. If Temoc started an argument about religion, Caleb might buck him into the demons, and to hell with Dresediel Lex and the Serpents.

He took the last curve with arms and legs of molten rubber. His lungs ached, and his ribs felt as if they might break through his skin. Mal—no, Mal wasn't there, that was Teo, opening the stairwell door. Blinding light streamed through. The concrete steps beyond were free of demons. He lifted a silent prayer of thanks for office health and safety rules: in an emergency the stairs had to be safe to travel, no matter the security risk.

He staggered the last three steps across the threshold, tripped, and fell to his knees. Temoc pitched to one side and slammed into a wall. Caleb's burned right hand struck the floor. The world shimmered with pain. He tried to breathe, and choked.

Teo closed the lobby door. The scuttle of demon claws dwindled to a crinkle of torn paper. Caleb sank against the wall, let his lungs fill with air, expelled it all, and let them fill again.

Time passed. How much time, he did not care. When the world settled, Temoc was waiting. Caleb read no sympathy on his face.

"Are you all right?" Teo asked.

"Yeah," he said, more to reassure himself than her. "I'm fine."

"Good." Temoc glanced up the gap at the heart of the turning staircase. "We have nine hundred steps to climb."

"Hells."

"The trouble with atheism," Temoc said, "is that it offers a limited range of curses."

Caleb ignored him, and started climbing.

Heavy footsteps echoed up and down the stairwell. No doors opened or closed. Caleb, Teo, and Temoc climbed alone.

After the tenth story, they rested, though not for long. Teo's watch read quarter past eleven. The eclipse was due shortly after noon. Temoc claimed he could draw fossilized souls from the altar in ten minutes. On schedule. Barely.

Caleb swayed. Teo draped his arm over her shoulder. At first he tried to walk on his own, but around the fifteenth floor he trusted her with his weight. She bore it without complaint or comment, and they climbed together. Temoc sprinted each flight of stairs alone, and waited at the landing for them to catch up.

"Not much of a team player, is he," Teo asked when Caleb's father was out of earshot.

"He had a team," Caleb replied. "Most of them died."

"He could at least act like we're on the same side."

"We're not."

"Maybe you're not." Teo grunted as Caleb's leg gave out and she took his full weight. "He's trying to save our lives, which puts him on my side."

"No. It puts you on his side, for the moment."

At the twentieth floor they allowed themselves another short rest. Caleb sat on a step and leaned against the cool railing. He had slept in beds less comfortable. Teo crouched beside him. Temoc did not sit. Tensed like a spring, he scanned walls, ceiling, and lower floors for threats.

Temoc broke the silence.

"You know," he said, "these stairs weren't a part of the original pyramid design."

"What was here earlier?" Teo asked.

"An empty shaft descending into the sub-basement."

Don't ask what they used it for, Caleb begged Teo with his eyes.

"How would they use something like that?"

"We threw bodies down the shaft," Temoc said, "after the sacrifice. There was a fire at the bottom, for the corpses."

Teo looked as if she might reply, but did not. Caleb stood, and turned from Temoc to the steps.

They climbed the rest of the way without speaking.

44

Potted ferns lined the broad dark hallway on the twenty-ninth floor, like soldiers supervising an execution. Faint inhuman laughter hung on the still air.

"If we survive this," Caleb whispered to Teo, "I am never coming in on a weekend again."

They reached the conference room's mahogany doors without incident. Caleb's skin wanted to crawl away and leave his meat and bones to fend for themselves. Veins popped on Temoc's thick forearms and the backs of his slab hands; he squared his shoulders and stood strong, but his eyes flicked restless about the passage. Teo waited by the doorframe, lips tight, silent.

Caleb opened the doors, and light flooded the hall.

"Hello," said a voice like honey poured off a razor.

A many-legged horror filled the doorway: thorns and thin-spun glass, steel and barbs and blue lightning, clustered multi-faceted eyes, and a mouth like a child's, above a maw that brimmed with ichor-wet fangs.

"Hello," the demon repeated with its child-mouth. Its maw shrieked torn metal.

Temoc punched the demon in the face.

It tumbled backward, arms flung out for balance. One of its eight hands slammed into the conference table; knife-claws gouged long streaks from the wood. The child-mouth wailed.

Temoc did not wait for the creature to recover. He became a silvered shadow and leapt on his adversary. The demon swatted him to the ground with a flailing paw, and followed with a kick. Falling, Temoc grabbed the demon's knee and barbed ankle and wrenched the joints in opposite directions. Chitin cracked like crystal. Temoc struck the floor, and rolled between scrabbling claws to his feet.

Caleb pulled Teo into the room, and closed the door behind them.

"What are you doing?" she shouted.

"The fight might draw others. You think we can hold off more of those things?"

Caleb's father danced with the demon. A talon slashed Temoc's side, and he staggered but did not fall. He had grown large in shadow, scars shining. He wrenched one of the beast's arms sideways, and tore it from the shoulder. Two mouths screamed, and scythe-claws swung, but Temoc was already moving.

Crystal limbs and teeth clashed. Liquid light dripped from the demon's wounds, and smoked where it fell. Temoc was a dark blur, leaping from table to floor, taunting his opponent in High Quechal. The demon cursed him in its broken tongue, all pretense of human speech gone.

They circled each other around the table, slow enough at last for Caleb to comprehend the demon's shape: a round scorpion-jointed back, six clawed legs gripping the floor, one of its eight arms gone and two more limp.

Between cries of pain, the demon laughed like thunder.

"I think it's enjoying this," Teo whispered.

Temoc was the first to slow, and the demon pressed him until it slowed in turn and Temoc fought back with maniacal ferocity. The silver scars on his face twisted, and by their light Caleb saw, for the first time in sixteen years, his father smile.

The demon leapt onto the conference table and landed with a heavy, hollow sound. Temoc circled, and it scuttled to face him. It hissed, and he was silent; roared, and he showed no fear.

The beast sprang, a storm of teeth and sharp edges. Temoc dove into and through the claws, and wrapped his arms around its body. Knives scraped the corded muscles of his back; jaws snapped inches from his face. His grip tightened, and cracks appeared in chitin. Temoc stepped under his opponent's center of gravity, and swiveled his hip to the left.

The demon's left legs gave way, but Temoc did not let go. As it fell, he twisted its torso back to the right.

The snap of the demon's spine should have been too soft to hear. Somehow, it overcame all other sound.

Thorned legs went limp, but the upper body fought on. Temoc rolled with the demon on the floor. Soon, they lay still.

Temoc rose. Fading shadows hung from him in tatters. His skin was a mess of welts and bruises. Thin, shallow cuts crisscrossed his back and legs and arms, broken by the protective network of his scars.

He retreated from the demon's corpse, and slumped against the pitted remains of the conference table.

Caleb ran to his father. Temoc held up one hand, motioning him back, but Caleb ignored him.

"You're hurt."

"Don't worry about me," Temoc said between breaths. "I'll be fine."

"I'll worry about you if I want."

"No time. Others have heard the fight. They will come soon. Find the door."

Caleb wrapped one arm around his father, counted to three, and lifted him off the table. The old man swayed, but steadied on his feet, and spat blood to the floor. "Find it."

"Fine." Caleb stepped back, and examined the room. There was, of course, no door in the wall through which Kopil had led him on the night of the Seven Leaf crisis. No door, and nothing that could hide a door: no bookcase, no trophy stand, no glyphs Caleb could see. The room was blank and featureless, its walls an even grey.

He closed his eyes, but saw no trace of Craft. "I walked through this wall."

Teo prodded the blank stone with her hands, and struck it with a broken chair leg. The wall did not sound hollow. "Nothing's hidden here. You're sure this is the right place? I can think of twenty rooms in the pyramid that look just like this."

"Of course it's the right place."

"I'm not calling you a liar. Relax." She paced around the demon's corpse, over puddles of sizzling blood. "It must be here. Otherwise why set a demon to guard this room? To defend the table?"

"More demons are coming," Temoc said. "Up the stairs."

"They can use the stairs," Caleb said, then checked himself. "Of course they can use the stairs. Do you see any controls anywhere?"

"Only the usual ones, for the lights. You say you walked through this wall? In this conference room?"

"Yes." In the hall outside, he heard a sound like the world's largest centipede crossing a tile floor.

"The door will hold them," Temoc said. "But not for long."

Could Kopil have opened a gate between two points in space, and closed it, just to disorient Caleb and save himself an elevator ride?

No. Kopil was a miser. He didn't like to fly—too wasteful. He barely left the RKC pyramid. He wouldn't go tearing holes in the world for his own amusement. Any passage he built for himself would be reusable.

"We should leave," Temoc said. "There must be other ways to the altar."

Something much larger than a dog scraped at the conference room door.

Caleb's mind caught the end of a thread. "Teo, what did you just ask me?"

"I asked you if you were sure this was the right room. If that was the right wall."

"I don't think it is. I don't think there was a wall there to walk through."

"What?"

The scraping grew louder and insistent. Wood splintered beneath hooked claws and bladed fingers.

"You said this looked like any other room in the pyramid, but it doesn't. Even my little office has carvings and decorations all over the place. These walls are blank stone."

"So they redecorated."

"They did more than that. When I was here, I never saw any walls. And no one but Mal entered or left by the door."

Temoc's eyebrows rose.

"Teo," Caleb said. "Turn off the lights,"

"What?"

"The overheads. Turn them off. There should be one light on the center of the table, that's all. One light so bright you can't see the walls."

"Caleb—"

"Do it. Please."

A heavy weight struck the doors, which shuddered but held firm. A demon's cry scoured the air.

Teo ran to a bank of dials on the wall, and turned them at random until the lights dimmed.

"More!"

Lights flickered, flared, cut out. Caleb could still see the wall. "Make the center light stronger."

Her fingers flew. Twice more demons struck the doors. Wood splintered near the latch. "Here!" Teo spun the second-smallest dial clockwise. The table's spotlight brightened to surgical brilliance. The world twisted.

The walls vanished.

The doors broke open. Beyond, ranks of eyes burned with ruby fire.

"Teo!"

She leapt over the dead demon's claw, sprinted toward him, and grabbed his hand as he grabbed Temoc's. Together, they ran into the dark. The fiends followed after.

45

The demons pursued on many legs—distortions in darkness, closing at an insectine gallop.

Caleb, Teo, and Temoc fled through shadows beneath the universe. They should long since have reached the King in Red's apartment, but the farther they ran, the closer night drew around them.

The path was closed, apparently, on the far end. Caleb tried to remember what Kopil had done to open the way on the night the water ran black, but his memories blurred together.

The conference room's walls existed as long as he could see them. Maybe the other door could not open while he knew it wasn't there.

The demons' footsteps grew louder.

"Close your eyes," Caleb shouted.

"What?" Teo snapped back.

"Close them. Close them, or we're stuck here."

Their grips on his hands tightened.

Caleb closed his eyes.

Space was a net of flame; universes hung like water droplets at its intersections. The net spun and warped. Worlds merged, broke, reformed in fractal patterns.

Caleb let go of his father's hand, reached out, and touched a smooth brass doorknob. He turned the knob, the latch gave, and he tumbled onto a red carpet.

Temoc and Teo staggered into the room after him. Demon footfalls pursued from the darkness beyond the door.

Caleb slammed the closet shut. He waited for a few heartbeats, then opened it again. Suits, robes, shirts, ties and expensive shoes had replaced the void.

"So this is where the monster sleeps," Temoc said.

The room looked as Caleb had last seen it: round bed unmade, books stacked beside the armchair, piles of paperwork teetering on end tables.

"This doesn't look like a monster's room," Teo said once she found her breath. "Doesn't look like his, either. I don't know what I would have pictured. Something cleaner."

"He's a busy man," Caleb said. "Skeleton. Thing." He wiped sweat from his eyes. "You want him to spend his days cleaning?"

"Or get maid service. A team of zombies could scour this place in five minutes."

Temoc pursed his lips, and turned away.

"What?"

"You would rather exploit another's body than dirty your own hands with work," Temoc said. "I find that interesting." He wandered away into the kitchen.

"Caleb," Teo said, when Temoc was out of sight.

"Hm?"

She had flushed red, and her brows drew low over glaring eyes. "Your father."

"Trust me, I know."

"He's a jerk."

"And a murderer. And he just saved our lives, which, I know, doesn't excuse the rest of it." He leaned against the door, fighting exhaustion.

"Are you okay?"

Kopil's empty unmade bed looked more comfortable than any he had seen in years. He wanted to lie there and vanish. "I'm tired. And I keep thinking about Mal."

Teo sank into the red armchair. Neither of them spoke. She wove her fingers together, unwove them. "If she comes, and tries to stop us, what will you do?"

"I . . . I'll fight her," he said. "And I'll die. She's stronger than you can imagine. She'll kill me."

"What if she doesn't, though? What if you win?"

He looked away.

She walked to him. In her eyes he saw himself reflected, a cutout shade, barely human.

In the kitchen, wood splintered, china broke, cutlery clattered on stone. Temoc appeared at the threshold, dignified and calm. "I have found the entrance to his office."

The moon rose, and rising lost its light. Black sphere in a dusky sky, it stalked the sun.

Mal sat cross-legged above the city. Her mind moved with the serpents, turning in uneasy slumber. They whispered to her in High Quechal and tongues older still, brutal cries from the birth pangs of the world. Their dreams surrounded her like gallowglass tendrils, and they burned.

Where was Caleb? Somewhere safe, she hoped, and doubted. He was not the type to hide.

At Andrej's on the day of the Heartstone acquisition, the day Kopil betrayed himself with a kiss, she had danced with Caleb on an empty floor. They danced without touching: she wrapped him in Craft and he grabbed her by those same ties. They were dancing now. How he thought to stop her, she could not imagine, but he would try.

She hoped she was wrong—hoped he would hide and wait, and she could find him later, when the battle was won, and explain herself, and all would be well.

And she hoped she was right. She hoped he was marshaling forces against her even now.

She felt the familiar lightning thrill of touching knifepoint to skin, before the small sharp movement of the wrist that let blood flow free.

Craft threaded through the Serpents' diamond brains, through their pulsing hearts of molten rock. By itself, each of Heartstone's systems served a purpose: channeling the Serpents' hunger, dulling the edge of their sleeping minds, drawing them to the surface of the lava to be tamed.

Together, those strands wove the reins of the world.

With a small sharp movement of her wrist, she called the Serpents to her.

The stairs from Kopil's kitchen were long, straight, and rough-hewn, so narrow Temoc had to climb them sideways.

"That apartment," he said as they rose, "was once a vestry room. Priests prepared there for the ceremony. Divining stones were cast, chants sung, days named. They shed their own blood and prepared to shed the blood of others."

"And that," Teo said, "is why you broke the King in Red's cabinets?"

"There used to be beautiful murals on those walls, depicting the triumph of the Twins, the sacrifice of Ili. Gone now. Replaced by porcelain and cutlery."

The gray sliver at the top of the stair grew, and through it Caleb saw the curve of Kopil's office dome.

They emerged through a thin opening that vanished behind them. The office had changed little since his first visit: carpet, plants, low bookshelves and chairs, and of course the altar-desk. The hospital bed was gone.

Kopil lay sprawled atop the desk, a mug of spilled coffee by his hand. His skull rested on a thick sheaf of papers.

Caleb ran to him, Teo close behind.

The King in Red did not move as they approached. Caleb knelt and lifted the skeleton's hand. Somehow his bones clung together, as if bound by invisible rubber strings. Hand and arm were lighter than he expected, and clattered as he set them down.

"He's gone," Teo said, wondering.

"Can't be. He'd have taken most of the pyramid with him. Deathless Kings go out in flames." He rolled up the red robe's sleeve. Glyphs glowed blue and silver against bone. "He's alive, or whatever they call it. Unalive. Must be sleeping."

"More like comatose." Teo slid the papers out from under the King in Red's head. His skull struck glass with a dull, dark sound. She fanned the pages, and froze. "Caleb. This is the Heartstone contract."

"What? The original? The one that's seventy thousand pages long and carved into stones from here to Alt Coulumb and back?"

"This is the signature page. The keystone. See, here. That's his signature, and Alaxic's, and the witnesses'. If this is destroyed, the contract starts to unravel."

The King in Red must have woken early that morning, if he ever slept. Sipping his coffee, he felt Qet Sea-Lord die, felt the Serpents suck the marrow from his bones.

"He knew what was happening. And he tried to stop it." Caleb laid Kopil on the floor beside the altar, arms crossed over his chest.

"This changes nothing," Temoc said. He circled around the altar toward them. "We have no time. We must begin."

"It changes everything. If we break this contract, the King in Red might wake up. RKC could break free of Heartstone. The board—"

"Their heathen Craft will be useless against the Serpents, as would your master's if he wakes. Besides, he would see me, and try to kill me. We have no common cause."

"You do now." Caleb took the signature page from Teo, and held it up so his father could read the scrawled ink. "If he wakes up, he'll see that you're not part of Mal's plot, that you've risked your life to stop her. You have a chance to make peace with him—to keep him from blaming this madness on every religious Quechal in the city."

"What I have done today will change nothing in his eyes. We are old enemies, he and I."

The picture in the silver frame stood on the desk, two men smiling, their eyes sepia-black. Caleb remembered Kopil's voice: everyone thinks they're on their own side, until the time comes to declare war.

"He might not like you, but he'll fight beside you." Caleb searched the desk, and found a letter opener, three pens, a coffee mug long since dry. Nothing that looked like it could dissolve contracts. "Teo, do you know how to break one of these things?"

"There's usually a mess of protective Craft, but it looks like Kopil got rid of that already. Rip it. If that doesn't work, try fire. Here, let me . . ."

"No," Temoc said.

Teo's shoes scraped against the floor, and Caleb looked up to see if she had tripped.

Temoc stood behind her, squeezing her throat in the crook of his elbow. Her eyes screamed. She clawed at his father's arms, his hands, his face. Her mouth gaped for air. Her hat fell to the floor. She jerked her head back, but Temoc tightened his grip.

Her eyes rolled white, and drifted closed. Her body hung limp in his father's arms.

Caleb leapt at Temoc.

His father turned faster than Caleb's eye could follow. One fist swept around in a blurred half circle.

Darkness consumed the world.

46

Temoc looked down on his fallen son, and shook his head. He was a brave boy, to bear his father on his back, to grow to halting manhood with only a mother's hand to guide him.

He was weak, but he lived in a time of weakness. The God Wars flayed the world and hung it on a cross. The strong fell and the craven thrived. No wonder Caleb's generation retreated into despair and compromise. No wonder the children of the Wars drank and fornicated, gambled and danced and wondered, after long days smeared drunkenly into night, why their lives seemed meaningless.

An obsidian knife hung from Temoc's belt. In seventy years he had used the blade twice. Ten years old, at his initiation into the priesthood, he carved the gods' signs into his chest with hands blood-slick from the wounds his teachers gave him. The second time was the night the barricades rose in Skittersill; he knelt over his son and cut the same symbols into his flesh.

Temoc had never wondered about his purpose. His purpose was the point of that knife.

He lowered his son to the floor beside Teo, and turned to the King in Red. Kopil's round skull glistened. Six decades before, peals of laughter had rung from that grinning mouth as he scattered the Quechal priesthood and broke their gods. He had impaled Temoc on a thorn of ice, and left him writhing to die.

Temoc set his foot on the skull and pressed down. The bone did not yield.

He stomped. Bone bounced against the floor, but did not chip or shatter. He roared and leapt on the skull with both feet, but it rang like iron and he stumbled back. The shadows of Kopil's face mocked him.

Above, the moon broke the circle of the sun. Time enough for vengeance—later. He had a world to save.

Temoc lifted his son's friend, the girl who had never known a man's touch, the altar maid, the offering who confessed her willingness to die. He placed her on the altar.

He bowed his head, and drew his knife, and began to sing.

Mal and the moon opened their mouths and breathed in fire. The moon swelled and darkened as it consumed the sun's body. Mal too devoured flame and was transformed.

Shadows fell upon the earth. She worked her Craft through the slumbering course of the Serpents' minds. From deep dreams they whispered to her. They knew her name. The eclipse came, and the stars called them to battle.

"Come," she whispered, taking hold of the Serpents' reins. "This is your moment. Rise, and be my weapons."

The earth trembled. Buildings shivered, pyramids shook. Another tremor came, stronger than the first.

Wake, she willed. The sun dies. Stars circle like starving vultures, and sup on the light that bleeds from its husk. As it dims they shine.

Come forth.

A stillness passed over the surface of the earth. Mal's eyes snapped open.

Beneath the world's shell, the Serpents stirred, and stretched, and woke.

Balam laughed at the first earthquake. Other protesters screamed, farther back in the crowd on Sansilva Boulevard before the Canter's Shell: newcomers to the city's struggles. The masters and Wardens of Dresediel Lex used their power to cow resistance. They shook the ground and burned the sky to spread fear, but they rarely killed. Hardened protesters trembled only at Couatl claws and lightning. Or they feared nothing, for Craftwork weapons moved faster than human eyes could follow or human ears detect, and to fear those was to live in fear.

Balam did not fear. Decades of cliff running and riots had burned the emotion from him.

And if this was no plan of the Wardens', and the ground was trembling of its own accord, well, then, Dresediel Lex was a city on the ocean's edge, and sometimes the earth shook beneath its weight. The crowd surged against him, acres of sweaty skin, stinking of meat and leather and rage.

"Is that the best you can do?" he shouted at the sky, at the pyramid sheltered behind its shield.

When the second earthquake came, he did not laugh.

Bedrock and packed earth did not stay the Serpents. Slithering upward they carved tunnels that caved in as they passed. The land rolled. Glass broke in skyscraper windows. Towers swayed and bowed their heads. Only the pyramids stood strong: they were built to outlast the world.

Sansilva bisected Dresediel Lex from east to west. Foreign visitors often wondered why the ancient Quechal had built so broad a road through the center of their city. Little freight passed through Sansilva, and few commuters—the priests had lived on their temple grounds.

They wondered on a false premise. The road had not been built for human use.

The second quake began like the first, shaking pitching ground, men and women crying out in alarm and pain, but rather than receding it built. Balam and his comrades stumbled against one another. They thrashed and pitched like froth, and this too was normal—but over their cries Balam heard another note, a high creaking cascade, everywhere at once, scraping against the pate of his skull.

In the surge and thrust of angry limbs, at first he could not find the sound's source. When the screams began, he saw: broken glass rained from skyscrapers and pyramids all around. Shattered panes fell from shaking towers. Transparent knife blades tumbled, sparked by the dying sun. Striking, they severed flesh. Screams cut short before others took their place. Bodies pressed against Balam from all sides: ten thousand people simultaneously forced themselves toward the center of Sansilva Boulevard, away from the glass and blood.

This was not Wardens' work. They would not break the buildings they were sworn to defend. Real estate was sacred to them. Above, their Couatl wheeled, wings beating rapid, roaring with jaws unhinged by panic.

Couatl feared nothing—not fire, not death, not the shifting earth. No mere earthquake would make them cry. But if not Wardens, and not an earthquake, what was happening?

The groans and cries changed tempo and tenor, rising, gaping, higher. Hot wind blew across Balam's face, and the crowd convulsed again, pressing him not toward the center of the road this time but forward, toward the lethal blue border of the Canter's Shell.

He turned, straining against the tide, and saw fire.

Asphalt glowed like broken coals. Mal flailed in flame, in hunger. She strained against the weight of stony sleep. Air melted to plasma. Below, demonstrators fled, screaming.

In the old days, the rooftops had boiled with spectators, risking their sanity to see.

The fleeing protesters thought the quakes, the flames, were the Craftsmen's vengeance.

They would understand soon.

The world held mysteries more worthy of their fear than human Craft.

Tar bulged, rippled, burst. A forked fiery tongue spouted from the molten flow, and retreated into a blunt mouth a hundred yards across. Two eyes of white flame flared from an immense arrow-shaped face. Aquel bared fangs the size of trees. A thousand years of sacrifices stared out from the diamonds that lined her gullet, Quechal faces trapped in agony. She roared a volcano roar.

Her sister too broke free, and they rose together, sinewy, strong, hungry. They cried doom.

The city shook. Elders trembled as nightmares wormed from the rotten timbers of their memory. Madmen shouted prayers in High Quechal, though they did not understand the words spilling from their lips. In hospital coma wards, patients silent for years opened their mouths to speak:

"Blessed Be They."

In the Skittersill a burning building collapsed around a three-year-old girl and left her unharmed. A Warden's mount plummeted from the sky, dead; the Warden's partner swooped to save him from a bloody landing.

From Fisherman's Vale to Monicola, from the Pax Coast Highway to Stonewood, Tzimet exploded into steam. In the fountain of the Monicola Hotel, the beast of water and black ice shattered. Insect-sized demons popped like blisters. They fled the approach of greater monsters.

In Balam's childhood when his grandmother lay drunk on corn beer on cool dry winter afternoons she had told him tales of old gods and heroes. Beyond these he knew no sacred signs, no holy chants beyond those repeated before an ullamal game. But he recognized the cobra-hooded coils above Sansilva, the house-sized scales slick as water if water burned, taller than the pyramids, tall enough to eat the sun, or kindle it aflame again with the darting forked lava spouts of their tongues. Shining in every color and none, cored white as alabaster: Aquel and Achal, greater than goddesses, fiercer than demons, the world's first children.

He almost froze in awe and wonder, and if he had, he would have been lost. The crowd saw, and whatever they understood, whether they recognized the Serpents or thought them Craft-born terrors or demons run loose, they knew to flee. Desperate they stumbled away from the Serpents: down alleys and into swaying buildings, despite the rain of glass. But most ran along the path of least resistance, down Sansilva Boulevard, and their tide carried Balam toward the Canter's Shell and forever.

Balam pushed against the crowd, with muscles built down decades of cliff running and decades more of teaching runners. A

stone statue stood fifty feet upstream, some robed Iskari goddess, a break in the human tide. Fifty feet might as well be miles.
He thrust himself into spaces between people, he struck men in
the stomachs, he tore free from clawing fingers, and pressed toward the statue.

Heat passed over him, raised rivers of sweat on his arms: the
heat of the Serpents' gaze, or else their distant breath.

His legs ached. A flailing elbow caught him above the eye
and tore his skin. Blood ran down his face. He growled, and fought
harder, in and down, gripping cobblestones with his feet, desperate not to lose the slim scrape of traction that bound him to the
earth and kept him safe from pounding feet and pulsing legs.

Men and women died around him. They fled the Serpents
like ants flee the beam of a magnifying glass. Those too slow
were crushed, or burned.

The air stank of panic and sour sweat.

Ten feet left. An eternity. He could not cross the distance. He
could count his wounds, and weaknesses: a finger broken when a
woman he was fighting past shifted left instead of right. Blood in
his eyes. A back twisted by too much running, by a youth spent
sprinting over rooftops. Forty years of fat.

Damn the crowd. Damn the Wardens for circling above the
damage. He might not make it, but for one more moment he
would fly.

Six feet. He released his hold on the ground, but rather than
let the tide carry him forward he grabbed the shoulders of the
men pressed against him and pulled himself up, onto them, over
their bodies, through the forest of arms and heads, a cliff runner's last leap—

Too short. He landed a foot shy of the open space around the
fountain; his weight pressed bodies beneath him to the ground,
but others surged over him, over them, dragging him back. He
roared in frustration, reaching toward that stone Iskari goddess
to strangle her promises of victory.

A hand closed around his: a steel grip, slender but implacable,
a rock against the tide.

He pulled with strength that could tear stone, and the hand

pulled back, and in a tumble he lay panting in the statue's shadow beside his savior, a woman, not even Quechal: blond hair in tangled braids, a scar on her temple. Her eyes were wide with terror, and she sucked in breath like a horse after a sprint. So did he. He swore, and cursed, and spit.

"Thank you."

She nodded.

"Balam," he said, and tapped his chest. He could not raise his hand to offer it to her.

"Sam," she said. Around them, the world continued to end.

Mal tossed, spun, caught inside the Serpents.

"Stop," she said, in High Quechal and then in Low: "Stop."

The Serpents swayed, brighter than the dying sun. She hovered level with round crystal eyes a hundred feet tall. Heat scored her skin. Sweat ran down her face—altar sweat, the sweat of the bound woman who sees the knife. The Serpents' scales pinged and hissed and cracked as the air tried and failed to cool them.

They waited for her.

A smile crept across Mal's face.

The Serpents twitched, and her smile faltered.

The smell of sacrifice rose from the pyramid at 667 Sansilva. The serpents smelled it, and so did she.

Temoc. No other priest remained to make an offering. Alaxic had killed the others, one at a time down the decades, with poison, blade, and Craft. Temoc should have been the last. Somehow, he must have escaped, and reached the altar with a victim.

No matter. She would burn him from his place of power.

She flew down Sansilva toward pyramid, sacrifice, and victory. The Serpents slithered after her.

Sea was the word for world, rocking, rolling, turning. Sea, and Caleb floated upon it beneath a woman who laughed knives and kissed with steel. His pain floated up toward a sun like a burning ring in the heavens: a hollowed sun, a hallowed sun.

Caleb followed the pain up, toward the light.

He blinked at the gray arch of the crystal dome. His skull throbbed. So did his hand, his ribs, and the rest of his body.

Incense coiled in the air.

"Qet Sea-Lord, Exchilti Sun-Shaper, Seven Stone, receiver of offerings. The Twins gave of themselves when the sun their father died. Yes, they gave of themselves—suckled the Serpents on their blood and heart-flesh. In innocence they suckled them, and we give innocence in their memory."

The words were High Quechal, spoken in the vocative of address to the divine, with a priest's conjugations and declensions. The voice belonged to Temoc.

He remembered: the blow to his head, Temoc's arm around Teo's neck, the rage and fear in her eyes as she went limp.

His vision cleared.

Temoc bent over the altar, his back to Caleb. Shadow flowed silken over his skin, wreathed his body from head to foot in a darkness like priestly robes.

Mounds of copal incense burned at the altar's head and foot. In one large hand Temoc held a hook-bladed obsidian knife.

Blood dripped from the knife's tip, and from the gargoyle mouth in the altar's side.

Caleb's world chilled, and drained of color.

"Let me go!"

Teo. Still alive. Gods. Temoc was bleeding her before the sacrifice.

"Each age is called to give of itself," Temoc chanted. "We fortunates are called to give our hearts."

Caleb rose. His father rocked with priestly fervor. Teo lay spread-eagled on the altar, hands and feet locked in obsidian cuffs. She pulled against her bonds, and shouted obscenities. Blood ran from her left wrist down grooves in the glass, and dripped from the altar's mouth into a coffee cup.

He searched for a weapon, but saw none. The King in Red was more partial to deep magic from before the dawn of time than to up-swords-and-sally-forth. Nothing useful in the office clutter, either. Books, few large enough to do damage. Chairs too heavy to lift or swing. Temoc had pushed the detritus of Kopil's desk onto the floor to make room for Teo: papers, a coffee mug, the picture of Kopil and his dead lover.

The picture, in the heavy silver frame. Caleb hefted it, testing its weight and the sharpness of its corners.

Teo's stream of invective paused for breath. Her head lolled to one side, and she saw Caleb. Her eyes widened.

Caleb swung the picture frame with both hands into the side of his father's head.

"We have to go," Sam said.

Balam shook himself back into the world. "Go where?"

"Anywhere. That pyramid over there, on the left. Those things are coming." She peeked over the lip of the fountain, and ducked again. "This way."

"The Serpents."

"What the hells else do you think I might be talking about?"

"We'll die. We can't fight through the crowd like this."

"They're headed for RKC. We're in the way. We move or melt."

"We move and die."

"I'm going."

He shook his head. "Wait."

"No."

"Wait!" He put all his anger and his trainer's authority into the shout. She paused halfway to her feet. "When they're nearer, the crowd will thin out. Then we go. And hope."

She sunk back onto her calves. The air around them swelled with heat.

Temoc staggered; Caleb struck again, harder, and the priest sank to his knees.

He jumped over his fallen father onto the altar.

"Caleb." Teo was hoarse with shouting; Temoc had cut her shirt open, and drawn a charcoal cross at the base of her sternum to guide the knife. Wet streaks ran from the corners of her eyes. Blood pulsed from two precise cuts in her left wrist.

"I'm sorry." He tore at the manacle on her left hand. "Gods, I'm sorry." Scars flared on his arm. Obsidian pulled and snapped like taffy. He reached for her right.

An arm strong as an iron post circled his waist and flung him to the ground. He hit, skidded, and staggered to his feet.

Blood streamed from a deep cut on Temoc's scalp, over his ear and down his neck; rivulets ran to his chin. "Caleb," he said, kneeling to retrieve his knife. "Do not stand in my way."

"Why are you doing this? We had a plan!"

"Your plan will not work."

"You didn't even try!"

"I do not need to try. Aquel and Achal hunger for life. There is only one way to feed them. This is better, surer, than I thought possible. An altar maid's heart offered by a high priest atop Quechaltan, as of old."

He had loosened Teo's right manacle enough for her to pull both hands free. Blood gouted from her wrist. She clasped her palm over the vein, and tugged against the bonds on her feet, but they did not give.

"What would you have done if Teo didn't come? Kill me?"

"Even had we barred her way, she would not have remained behind. She is well-suited for a sacrifice. Noble intentions, and noble blood, too, if I do not mistake her features. Unsullied by man. Strong of spirit, strong of heart. She must have sensed my plan, known her fate."

Teo slumped to one side. Her arm and head hung over the altar's edge, and her outstretched fingers brushed the floor.

Caleb rushed toward the altar, and once more Temoc threw him. Falling, Caleb dug his fingers into his father's shadow, and it tore. Cold strength rushed into him. He spun in midair, and landed on his feet. Darkness clung to him like a halo, and his scars glowed from within.

A bright light rose to the south.

"See," Temoc said. "The Serpents wake. They smell their meal. Our time is short. I will save this city, with you or in spite of you. I will take her heart."

"I'll stop you."

Caleb ran forward; Temoc swung the dagger's pommel around to where his son's temple had been a moment before.

Caleb ducked, grabbed Temoc's leg, and pulled up. Temoc sank his weight against Caleb's pull, and did not fall. He kneed Caleb in the ribs, scattering shadows and knocking him to the floor.

The world swam as Caleb stood. He tried to raise his fists, but could not move his right arm.

"I don't want you to lose," Temoc said sadly. "You put up a good fight, for an untrained boy. You have shown courage. I'm proud of you."

"Thanks." Caleb panted. He heard something tear.

"But I can't let you win. I hope you understand."

"I wasn't . . ." Exhale, inhale. Take the moment slow. "I wasn't trying to win." The dome darkened. He smelled ozone and the pits of hell. "I just had to distract you long enough for Teo to rip up the Heartstone contract."

Temoc blinked. A cold gust of wind blew over them. Somewhere, heavy velvet curtains swayed.

Teo sat upright on the altar, holding a torn, bloodstained piece of parchment—one half in her right hand, the other half in her teeth. Sparks trailed from sundried silver glyphs. Her shirt hung from her shoulders. Blood leaked through the fingers she'd clasped over her vein. She spat out the piece of parchment, and it drifted to the floor, landing signature side up.

Incense flames guttered and died, and with them light and life.

The dark of deep space devoured all. There was no pyramid, no dome, only emptiness, and at its core, immense, astride the husks of dying stars, the King in Red. His eyes flared like the birth of the world.

He smiled.

"Temoc," he said. "It's been a long time."

47

As Mal advanced, the sky turned against her.

Wardens swarmed her on Couatl-back, black serpentine streaks striking with arcs of lightning, with silver spears and nets of green thread. Wingbeats and thunder thickened the air. A golden lasso caught Aquel's neck; the Serpent hissed in frustration.

Of course the Wardens had come. Lapdogs of the King in Red and his brothers, murderers, servants who did not ask why they served, who let themselves be shaped into weapons against their own people. The Wardens had burned her parents in the Rising, had unleashed fire on screaming crowds. They had missed Mal in their cull, and now they realized their mistake.

She smiled, and her teeth were pointed as the Serpents' fangs. Let them come.

Aquel pulsed sun-brilliant and threw a wave of plasma against the Warden who had caught her. The golden line snapped, and the Warden who threw it fell in smoking pieces to the ground.

Mal laughed, but in her joy an emerald net snagged her limbs, her mind. The world collapsed to a projection inside a nutshell where she hung suspended, bounded empress of space. She lived and died in the net, lived and died again, infant with every indrawn breath, growing, swelling to maturity with the filling of lungs, dwindling as she exhaled to a fragile age, arms and legs thin as mast-cord, skin taut and dry, dying to inhale and be born again.

No. She was more than this. She was rage, dying, and born again she was vengeance. The Wardens would not bind her.

Fire burst from Mal, and she was free. Spears of flame lanced in all directions, burning holes through pyramids, reducing Wardens to ash. She felt each death. She was Dresediel Lex. She was

Quechal. They were her children, though twisted and deformed. She wept and moved on.

More Wardens rose against her. She broke the wings of their mounts and they fell. Some swooped low above the crowd, catching refugees and winging them to safety; these she did not strike down. Their kindness pleased her.

She approached the Canter's Shell, and pointed toward it. Thin ropes of flame snaked from Aquel and Achal, surrounded the blue bourn and pressed in. The shell's logic, its Craft, its mechanisms strained against the Serpents' power, the weight of history and wrath older than gods.

At first she thought the shell might hold.

Then it began to crack.

Caleb closed his eyes to the billowing dark, and saw. The King in Red wore midnight like a halo. Temoc's skin bled light. Around them, between them, space twisted and gave birth to fever dreams, knives and hooks, grasping claws, chains and webs of iron, barbed tentacles and hideous geometries.

"You will not stop me," Temoc said. "The Gods lived before you, and when you die they will endure."

"I died eighty years ago." Kopil's voice held no trace of humor. "Your gods and I have that much in common."

A blade swung out of darkness toward Temoc's throat, but blunted and burst to steam.

Wings spread from Temoc's back. The hooks and chains glowed with his faith. White light spiraled through space between them.

"Interesting." The King in Red cocked his head to one side. "You are not dead."

"This pyramid was ours for a thousand years." Chains wrapped Kopil's robes. "You have perverted it, but it still answers to me." Spears swung down to pierce the Craftsman, claws to tear and teeth to rend.

The King in Red snapped his fingers.

Spears and claws and teeth stopped. Time's depths hummed.

Kopil stepped forward, feet tapping triple time on glass. Fire burned in his eye sockets. The hum deepened in volume and pitch.

Sweat shone alabaster on Temoc's brow.

"This pyramid was yours," Kopil said. "Now it's mine."

White spirals flickered, flared, and burned red in the night.

Darkness opened three thousand eyes. A fanged mouth gaped beneath their feet. The mouth had always been there, gnawing the world's marrow, unseen. They were standing on its teeth.

Caleb's eyes snapped open, and he fell, blind, shivering.

A cry of frustration split the shadows, and a cold corpse-wind rushed past his face.

Light returned, and the dome was empty save for Caleb, the King in Red, and Teo collapsed on the altar.

Caleb ran to her. Her chest rose and fell, rapid, shallow. Eyes darted behind closed lids. He tore off his jacket, pressed it against the cut in her arm. Blood everywhere. Blood on the altar, blood on the ground where she had reached for the contract.

If he hadn't cut her free, the cuff would have kept pressure on the vein. If he hadn't cut her free, she would have died at his father's hand.

"Caleb."

The King in Red's voice.

He whirled. "Fix her."

Red stars stared from a blank skull. "I can't."

"You can. She saved you. Do something."

"She's too weak. She has lost much blood. If I touch her with Craft, it will drain her."

"Then heal me."

"What?"

"Try to fix me. Do to me what you'd do to her."

"You are not injured."

"No time to explain. Do it."

Shadows flowed from the King in Red, and plunged through Caleb's skin. His heart slowed, his hands froze. Kopil's Craft worked within him. His cuts and bruises and broken bones ached for healing, but he denied them. Pressure built, until his scars felt ready to burst from flesh.

He lifted his jacket from Teo's arm, and touched her wound.

His light flowed into her, and her pain into him. Her wounds closed, faded, and vanished. Her breath deepened, her eyes fluttered, and she woke.

"Hi," he said, and sagged against the stone.

"Hi," she replied. "We have to stop seeing each other like this."

Oven heat pressed Balam down. The road around him hovered silver as a mirage. The Serpents were so close now, rearing less than a stadium's length behind the statue. Their coils slagged asphalt and concrete.

Sansilva was not yet empty. Much of the crowd had escaped, but those that remained were frantic and impassable. Knots of men and women clogged the sidewalks and open spaces, tumbling and brawling in their terror. Still, he saw the beginnings of a path through them, a road over broken glass to the safety of a bank pyramid. Uncertain, and shifting, but a path nonetheless. If they waited, another might present itself. Then again, maybe not.

Sam waited in a sprinter's crouch. She remained, he thought, due more to concern for him than to belief he could actually judge the proper time to leave.

No sense straining her patience. Balam stood, and as one they ran.

Caleb could not stand on his own, but Teo and the King in Red helped him.

"What," Kopil said, "is going on? Why has Heartstone turned against us? Why is Bay Station broken? Why is the city in tumult?" He produced a pipe from the pocket of his robe and lit it with the tip of his forefinger.

"Is my father—"

"Fled. He used some trick, some hidden means of escape built here when this place was still a temple." Kopil took a long drag of tobacco and exhaled smoke. "He has spent the last thirty years running and hiding. He is skilled in that regard. Now. No delays. Tell me what has happened."

"You remember Malina Kekapania?"

"From Heartstone. Your girlfriend."

"Yes." Of all the things to remember. "She attacked Bay Station, killed Qet, and she has awoken Aquel and Achal. She wants to chase Craftsmen out of Dresediel Lex. Alaxic planned it from the beginning."

Kopil took a drag on his pipe and exhaled smoke. The red lights in his eye sockets blinked off, and on again. "I will tear satisfaction from his soul."

"Too late. He's dead. I think."

"In which case I will content myself with his disciple."

"Who has Aquel and Achal at her back. Can you defeat them?"

Kopil shook his head. "Our plan was to preserve their slumber."

"You've killed gods."

"You," he said coldly, "do not understand the Serpents. The more they hunger, the more they burn. Any Craft I use against them will take from them, and increase their hunger. Only sacrifice can assuage them, but I will not give them sacrifice."

Kopil's eyes blazed. The dome overhead wavered and grew transparent. Angry orange cracks split the blue curve of the Canter's Shell above and around the pyramid; to the south and east, along Sansilva Boulevard, rose two distorted columns of light taller than skyspires.

A ring of sun burned around the moon's shadow. Beneath, the city lay broken. Small human shapes ran for cover.

Kopil drew on his pipe.

Nothing could stop the Serpents except a sacrifice. Caleb could have let Temoc do it: feign unconsciousness until the blade descended.

Teo gripped his hand, and he felt sick.

The cracks in the Canter's Shell widened, and the surface of the sun leaked through.

"So that's it?" Teo asked. "She wins?"

"No," Kopil said. Wind rose atop the pyramid, bearing the dry scent of a thousand years of dead sand. The King in Red reared to his full height. The surface of his skull shone. One hand held a curving knife of lightning, and the other crackled with black flame. "Ms. Kekapania holds the Twin Serpents in thrall. If she dies, they will lack direction, and perhaps they can be contained."

"She'll kill you."

"I died a long time ago. I have the might of RKC at my disposal—my own Craft, that of the Board, and beyond them the millions who live in this city. She has weakened us, but we remain strong."

"The last time someone used the Serpents as a weapon, they broke this continent in half."

"In the God Wars, I tore space and time asunder. I made a crack in the world." The King in Red walked toward the pyramid's edge. Air rippled as he moved. His power pressed against the skin of reality. "We shall see which of us is the more fearsome."

Caleb caught Kopil's sleeve. He did not turn or seem to notice. "If you fight her, no matter who wins, the city will lose. I know you're angry. But this isn't the way."

"Do you have an alternative?"

Sacrifice, Temoc said.

"I do."

The shell shattered into mathematical shards. Each spinning splinter reflected the broken, burning city. An eclipse chill blew through the cracks, ruffling Caleb's hair and Teo's shirt. Kopil's robes flared like wings.

Balam felt rather than heard the shell break, as if every joint in his body had popped at once. He pressed on, pounding through the pain, eyes blind to all but their path—until Sam, behind him, shouted: "Stop!"

He looked back, looked up, looked everywhere at once, and saw a spinning blue curve, three hundred feet on a side, slice through the pyramid ahead as if hundreds of years of stone and steel had never existed. The blue boiled away in an instant, but falling, it scooped out a ten-story section of pyramid, and the floors above strained, creaked, collapsed in a rain of steel and spark and tortured metal.

Sam grabbed his arm again, and pulled, and following her he fled back toward the fire.

Mal laughed when the Canter's Shell shattered, and the Serpents laughed with her. She understood Allesandre's madness now. Sanity was the gap between perception and desire, and that gap had closed. The Serpents' power belonged to her: millennia of sacrifice congealed into will and flame. What could she imagine that she could not create? What could she hate that she could not destroy?

Atop the pyramid stood a figure in red.

She remembered the taste of Kopil's teeth, when they exchanged the traitor's kiss.

How to break him? Slowly or swiftly? A simple rush of plasma, or dismemberment—or should she split his body atom from atom?

As she pondered, a weight struck her from behind.

"Give me souls. All the souls you can spare."

"In exchange for what?"

"For nothing. I need you to give them freely. No strings attached, no contract, no consideration."

"The Craft doesn't work that way. I can't give you something without taking."

"Look." He removed his jacket and rolled up his sleeves. The scars on his arms glowed. "This is how I helped Teo. I don't have any Craft of my own, but I can use others' power, and pay the price myself. The old priests bore the gods' power with these scars, worked miracles with them. My father still does. Maybe I can do the same: give the Serpents power without taking anything in return."

"You'll kill yourself."

"Maybe."

"I'm no god."

"And I'm no priest. But we're the closest we have."

Mal spun, searching for her adversary, but the skies seemed empty. Again she heard leathery wingbeats, and claws tore into her back; she responded with a wild jet of fire. A colorless blur crossed the corner of her eye. She spun after it, but saw nothing.

She summoned a whirlwind that swept several hundred pounds of sand from a nearby construction site into the air around her.

A shape flew through the dust: a Couatl, with a woman crouched on its back, medium height, with broad shoulders and thick arms and a Warden's smooth visage.

Mal recognized her, in the instant before the woman's cloak adjusted to the dust in the air and she disappeared again.

"Hello, Four."

The lights in Kopil's eye sockets dimmed. "So, how is this done? I've never had a priest before."

"Give me your blessing, and your power. I'll take it from there."

The King in Red raised one skeletal hand, and placed his palm on Caleb's forehead. The bones of his fingers shook.

Caleb dissolved in light.

Mal sent waves of lava in all directions, roped the sky with lightning; Four and her Couatl rode the waves, and circled to safety. The Serpents struck, but their fanged mouths closed on air.

Four pressed her assault with spear and talon and arrow, with discus and net of despair. The attacks did not wound Mal, but they broke her focus.

Mal swept the sky above her with fire, and heard the Couatl turn sharply and beat away toward the ocean. Not dead, but wounded at least. She returned her gaze to the pyramid. A fountain of light danced on its summit.

She did not notice the whistle of air overhead, but she did notice when a pair of hands closed around her neck.

Balam and Sam ran around the burning corpse of a fallen Couatl, down the few remaining ribbons of intact road. The broken Canter's Shell had scored trenches several hundred feet deep into Sansilva and the pyramid parking lot. They searched for a path through the maze. Steel fell around them, and glass and molten wires and chips of stone.

Sam skidded to a halt: the asphalt ahead had buckled up in the shell-shard's wake. What had seemed a straight road was actually the lip of a deep trench.

Behind them towered the Serpents.

"We can go back," Balam shouted.

Sam didn't hear him. She had turned to the pyramid's peak.

Souls flooded Caleb, a wash of experience and broken memory: a lover's kiss ringside in the swell of victory, a dockhand's sweat after a hard night on the pier, the glint of a butcher's knife in motion, and the shine in a glass of whiskey as a bartender drew off a shot.

Playing poker he had felt other souls collapse into his own, a few at a time. He could not count how many joined him in those few seconds' rush. Lives swelled him and burst his skin.

The world fluoresced and vibrated. Dresediel Lex was a tapestry of life, debt, ownership, dedication, faith, investment. Multicolored light knotted around the fluttering shadow of Kopil's spirit. Teo's shadow was larger, her bonds fewer: to her gallery, to her apartment, to Sam.

To him.

"Caleb," she said, and he wondered what she saw when she looked at him.

"I'm here." Beneath his voice he heard other voices: the chorus that now comprised him.

She stepped forward, hugged him fiercely, and said: "Go all in."

"That's the plan."

She let go. "And come back."

He turned from her, to Kopil, to the Serpents, and stepped off the pyramid's edge into empty air.

"We have to get out of here." Balam grabbed for her shoulder, but she shook her head, and pointed to the sky.

"Watch."

———

Mal struck Four with diamond-tipped fingers, but the Warden squeezed harder. Her silver mask pressed smooth and slick against Mal's ear. "Can't stab you," Four said through her teeth. "Can't cut you. But you can still die."

She twisted Mal's neck, which did not break. The Serpents' power coursed through her. She was their vessel, or they were hers; her bones were metal and her nerves flame. But Mal had not yet lost the habit of breathing. When Four squeezed her windpipe, she gasped for air, and found none.

Spots and sparks swam across her vision.

She could burn Four to ash, but doing so she might burn herself. A foolish way to die.

As foolish as being strangled by a person you can't even see? Oh.

Yes.

The world contracted to a long thin tunnel. She placed her hand on Four's arm, and pulled.

The sky bore Caleb's weight. Scars on his ankles and the soles of his feet woke to grip the air.

He advanced.

Mal pulled, not at Four, but at the Craft that bent light through the air around her. Invisibility required power, and that power came from somewhere. The most likely source was Four herself.

Mal drank deep.

Her vision dwindled to a single gray spot. Too late.

No.

Four's grip slackened. Her legs loosed. Mal heard her adversary groan.

Air sweet as wine filled her lungs.

She caught the Warden by the arm before she fell.

Four's jacket smoked in Mal's grip. Effortlessly, she pulled the Warden up, took her throat in one hand, and bared her teeth. Four struggled, weak. Her flesh burned, seared, smoked. The face beneath her mask was round, with broad eyes—a Quechal face.

Shame.

"Let her go, Mal."

She looked up, and blinked away a wash of light.

Mal had changed.

Her dusky skin was molten stone, her hair a field of ebon flame. Her eyes were radiant jet. Beside her hovered the leather bag containing Qet Sea-Lord's heart.

"Let her go."

She shrugged, and dropped Four.

The Warden tumbled through empty air. Caleb did not move to help her; after a few flailing seconds, her Couatl arrived, grabbed her in its talons, and flew to safety.

He met Mal's gaze.

"You caught me," she said at last.

"You look surprised."

"Surprised, and glad." The Serpents' mouths moved in time with hers. He saw faces in the diamonds that lined their throats: Quechal faces, painted, pierced, tattooed, plain, agonized or rapturous or simply watching. "I thought you might be dead."

"I'm not."

"I hoped that was true," she said, and tilted her head to one side. The Serpents echoed her movement. "There's something different about you. You've picked up a halo, and your scars are live."

"There's something different about you, too."

"Yes." She laughed. "I suppose there is."

"You don't have to go through with this."

"I'm an arrow in flight."

"Arrows don't have a choice. People do."

"What choice?" She smiled, sad, distant. "My choices were made twenty years ago, when my parents died. Or sixty years ago, at Liberation. Or earlier than that. The world's tossed in bad dreams. Someone has to wake it up."

"There are other ways."

"Not for me." She approached. The Serpents shifted to flank him. Three mouths moved in tandem. Who was the speaker, and who the puppet? "You don't have to fight me."

"I do."

"I'm sorry." She reached for his face. The heat of her touch seared his cheek, boiled his skin. He should have recoiled, but did not.

He wanted to take her in his arms, to shrivel to ash, to kiss her with melting lips.

"You don't have a chance. Temoc stopped his sacrifice."

"I know. I kept him from killing my friend."

"You're too sentimental for your own good." Her eyes were an ocean, luminous. "I don't want to hurt you."

"I don't want to hurt you, either," he said, and gave her his soul.

The heart is the spirit's anchor, Temoc had said. Aquel and Achal hungered not for flesh, but for Quechal souls.

When Caleb bet in a poker game, a piece of him flowed into the game, into the goddess. Each player gave her a part of himself, and at game's end she divided her favor among them according to their victories and defeats.

What if the goddess outlasted the game? What if she stretched through centuries, beyond any purpose she might once have served?

Living, she would grow hungry.

Perhaps the myth was true. Perhaps the Serpents existed before the Hero Twins found them, great beasts that broke the world with their madness. Perhaps not. Perhaps the Quechal threw two sacrifices into the heart of a volcano, and the sacrifices endured, and received sacrifices in turn. They clutched one another in the heat of their dying, and survived.

Caleb gave his soul to Mal, and through her, to the Serpents—his soul, and the souls he bore, so many that they carried him on a flood. There was no bargain, no quid pro quo. He streamed into Aquel and Achal, and became more.

In their diamond mouths, in their gleaming teeth, in their molten hearts, they received him. All were received. All lived. No, not lived—all *endured*, sleeping through centuries: every sacrifice, every victim, caught and one with the Serpents.

He felt the stone knife plunge into his chest ten thousand times, and ten thousand times his death cry rose over the chants of the priests, in High and Low Quechal and languages older still. The dying souls rose with their hearts, dreaming last dreams of a mother's smile, of a coyote's laugh at nighttime, a mug of chocolate, a victory dance, a lover's embrace. Dreams fell into the Serpents' mouths, and the Serpents ate them, and became them. Soul, accreted onto soul, accreted onto soul, down millennia.

When the sun died, the Hero Twins gave their hearts to the Serpents, became one with them, to save the world.

The Quechal were the Serpents.

The Serpents were Quechal.

Caleb was a thousand, a hundred thousand. He was the smile of Kopil's lover on Sansilva Boulevard beside the pyramid of the Sun.

Somewhere, he heard Mal scream.

You can't sacrifice other people anymore.

You have to sacrifice yourself.

Serpentine thoughts twined and spun around him, minds linking to minds. Aquel and Achal joined with the souls he had borne. Their hunger ebbed. He opened four immense eyes and stared out on a crystal world.

Mal burned within him, around him.

"Stay with me."

She spoke through his mind, through all their minds. Voices in forgotten tongues cried out at her touch.

"The murderers, the Craftsmen, the rulers of this world, they tempt you with death, satiety and sleep. They will destroy this planet, and all life with it, unless we stand against them."

She called to him, and he ached to follow her. He burned for her, with her, through her. His heat radiated from her skin, his lightning arced between her teeth.

Three thousand years of Quechal sacrifice lived in the Serpents. Dead generations woke to burn, to melt and mold and reforge. They were the world's last defense, its guardians. Death bowed to their fangs.

"Fight," she said. "Do not give in. Do not sleep. Victory is near. See our triumph."

The Serpents' rage flowered as she called, and flowed along channels she prepared. They would not sleep. She was too strong.

But Caleb could use her strength.

Months ago, drawing pictures on his skin in her tent, she had told him: battles of Craft are fought on many fronts. The world is an argument, and there are many ways to win or lose.

He could not fight Mal with her hooks caught in his mind. When she pulled, he would follow.

But he could follow in the manner he chose.

See, he echoed her, a whisper in the Serpents' minds.

Towering over Dresediel Lex, they saw.

The city lay broken around them.

Glass ran like water down Sansilva Boulevard, and blood melted into steam.

There were old souls within the fire, so ancient they spoke in song and rhyme. They did not recognize Dresediel Lex. To them it was a shadow on a cave wall, an echo, a story, a dream.

But the new souls, the ones Caleb brought, they knew. Sun-baked streets wavering with summer heat. Surf rolling against a cold beach at dawn. Dark corners in well-lit bars where a man could drink in peace. Summer nights when skyspires shone with echoed starlight.

Tollan, surly and pacing with her whiskey at midday. Mick, his desk hung with mementos of faded glory. Shannon, biding time with cards in the Skittersill and dreaming of the day when she could dive again off rooftops. Kopil, who broke gods to avenge his dead love. Teo, laughing and drinking, dancing in aisles and toasting with champagne.

Below, on the broken boulevard, he saw Balam, and Sam, staring up, waiting, scared, and hopeful.

All of these, and more. Millions more.

"Make it new," Mal said. "Burn it clean."

The city has never been clean, answered voices old and young. Nor has the world. The people were never clean. But they are worth defending.

Mal pulled at the Serpents' minds with ropes of Craft, and the Serpents pulled back. Her Craft strained, and snapped.

She flared like a star in the sky, and went out.

The ground gaped beneath him.

Caleb fell.

EPILOGUE

Caleb woke in a cold hospital room, under cotton sheets and an unfamiliar ceiling.

The world was flat monochrome. Bandages swaddled the right side of his body. A bell and a parchment envelope rested on the bedside table. He ignored the bell, and reached for the envelope. Pain called to him from the bottom of a deep narcotic well.

The envelope bore his name in an italic hand. It held a folded note and a shark's tooth pendant.

The note read:

> *If you wake, you will be recovered enough for the*
> *healing to begin. Ring the bell.*
> *The rest of your clothing burned. The tooth remained.*
> *Perhaps it will remind you.*

No signature except a death's head drawn in crimson ink. Of what the tooth was meant to remind him, the note did not say.

He rang the bell.

Three weeks later, Caleb stood at the end of Monicola Pier, looking west. He wore a black suit and a white shirt, and walked with crutches.

The merry-go-round wheeled. Children played ullamal by the seashore. A pall hung over the city, the nurses had said. A palpable fear. He couldn't feel it.

He couldn't feel much.

Soul fatigue, they called his condition in Kathic; among themselves the doctors used a longer Telomiri name. When the soul's been too often emptied and expanded, it recovers slowly.

He was near dead when they found him, empty of soulstuff, apperception broken. He didn't know what that meant, and no one had given him a decent answer. Not quite asleep, not quite dead. A little of both. Soulstuff from his savings had revived him, and he woke with vague memories of fire, of Mal, of a battle within the Serpents. Perhaps a part of him survived inside them, inside the world, slumbering and waiting to wake again. This was his afterlife—this, or else the flame.

Behind him the city's masses scrambled in the shadow of broken buildings. Cranes rose. Construction crews shouted from scaffolding. Airbuses slid by silent overhead.

He removed the shark's tooth from around his neck, and held it out over the water.

Mal was gone. The Wardens found no trace of her body. Of course not. The Serpents' heat had burned her to vapor.

The tooth pointed down into green-black ocean. Waves rippled his reflection, and the burn scar on his cheek seemed to disappear. He stared off the end of the pier toward the horizon, but saw no light there, not even sunset.

Bay Station crouched still at the harbor's mouth. He could almost hear the beating of Qet Sea-Lord's restored heart.

"Good-bye, Mal" he said.

The amulet twitched in his hand, and spun, pointing inland, south and west.

He dropped it into the ocean, and left.

Two days later, Caleb visited Andrej's in the afternoon. The bar had long since recovered. The stone railing and the doors Mal melted were easily replaced. Less so the white and black marble tiles, which the heat of her flame had fused and swirled to mottled gray.

The band played, and he tried not to think about the last time he had visited Andrej's around sunset.

He walked with the aid of crutches to a table by the mended bannister. From Four he'd learned the story of his survival—she'd swooped in on Couatl-back to catch him, but broke his bones in the rescue. His plaster cast scraped the floor. He leaned his crutches against the railing, and lowered himself into a chair.

The sun declined toward ocean. Rooftops and skyspires reflected and refracted tawny light. Tendrils trailed from the spires to the city: pulleys, block and tackle, raising steel girders and glass plates to repair crews in the buildings' upper floors. Craning his neck over the rail, Caleb could see road workers repaving Sansilva Boulevard.

A waitress came by, and he ordered a whiskey and water, and savored it, lost in thought.

Teo arrived a little before five, and sat beside him with her drink.

"Hey."

He sipped whiskey, felt it burn in his throat, and turned to her with a weary smile. "Hey. You got my letter."

"I was waiting for it."

"And you came."

"Of course I did. You look." He wondered what she would say next. Wan? Bruised? Shrunken? "Better than you did in the hospital. How are you feeling?"

"Used up." He tapped his cast, propped on a chair. Then he touched his ribs, and his gloved right hand, and the side of his temple. "Hollowed out. The soul doesn't fit the flesh."

"You should have saved more. Your account with RKC barely held enough to keep you alive. Couldn't you have kept some of that soulstuff back?"

"The Serpents needed a whole person, a real sacrifice to give the rest of the soulstuff shape."

"That was you. The whole person, sacrificed."

"Yes."

"So who am I talking with now?"

"Still me. At least, that's my opinion. Same body, same brain, a transfusion of my own stored soul to replace what I lost. Philosophers might argue. I don't know."

Teo drank away that line of inquiry. "If you were all they needed, why not go in alone? Why take power from the King in Red?"

"Aquel and Achal were hungry. One soul might not have satisfied them. We needed to feed the Serpents enough to keep them asleep for centuries. A mass sacrifice, concentrated in one person."

She looked him in the eyes, and he sensed the question forming: did you expect to die? She did not ask it, which spared him the need to answer.

With a grimace, he pointed to crutches and cast. "Now I'm stuck healing the old-fashioned way. At least I'm drawing sick pay."

She waited for him to say more. When he didn't, she filled the silence. "Sam's fine, by the way. Burned her arm, twisted her knee in the earthquakes, but she's recovered faster than you."

"I'm glad to hear it."

"She's lucky. Artists." She pronounced the word like an expletive. "She deserved worse, running off like she did."

"Don't say that."

A crane lowered a steel girder onto the pyramid opposite. Welding sparks cascaded down the structure's side. "Any word of Mal? Or Temoc?" She hesitated before saying his name.

He drank, and thought about the amulet. "Temoc hasn't shown himself since the eclipse, to me or anyone. But he won't stay gone forever."

"Good," Teo said. "When he returns, someone will make him pay."

"Good luck. My father is debt resistant."

Sparks fell like stars.

"It's boring without you. I go to Muerte on my own. A banker tried to hit on me the other day. I told her I already had a girlfriend. Tollan keeps asking when you'll come back."

He checked his watch, and returned it to his jacket pocket. "That's why I wanted to talk to you."

"You're quitting."

"Yes."

"What will you do?"

He lifted his leg from the chair. "Hold on. I don't want to have to do this twice."

"Twice? Who else do you expect?"

"Me," Kopil said from behind her.

Teo jumped to her feet. The King in Red looked the same as ever: forbidding, crimson, skeletal.

"Good afternoon, sir," Caleb said, and touched his cast again. "You'll forgive me if I don't stand."

Kopil crooked a finger. A nearby chair shuddered to life and walked over to him with groans of tortured steel. He sat. Teo shifted from foot to foot, then sat herself. Caleb focused on his drink.

"I have come for your answer," said the King in Red.

"Am I missing something?" Teo asked.

"After he woke, I offered Mister Altemoc a promotion to senior risk manager at Red King Consolidated. He has demonstrated his worth in a crisis."

"That," Teo said, "is an understatement."

"I don't think so," Caleb replied, and raised one hand against objections. "I stumbled into Mal's plot. I barely survived, and I stopped her by luck."

"You were effective. RKC values effectiveness."

"I know." Caleb sipped his whiskey. "That's why I hope you'll agree to be my first sponsor."

Kopil blinked. "What?"

Teo leaned against the table, face grave, and listened.

"The God Wars aren't over," Caleb said.

"I know several gods who would disagree," Kopil said, "were they alive to do so."

"The God Wars never ended on this continent, because nobody signed a peace. The Iskari have a peace, and the Shining Empire, but here we've kept up the war in silence. Craftsmen score victory after victory, but gods are patient. Ideas don't die easily. True believers pass faith, and anger, to new generations."

Kopil scraped a finger bone across the table surface. Iron rusted and stone blackened at his touch. "And each time they rise up, we will defeat them. We will fight until the sun burns to a cinder, and then we will fight among the stars."

"We won't last that long." Caleb pointed north, past mountains and orange groves, toward Seven Leaf Lake eight hundred miles away. "This city has doubled in size in the last decade, and will double again in the next. The Craft makes Dresediel Lex possible: we provide water, food, and shelter. But use the Craft to farm, and the soil dies. Use the Craft to drill wells, and the land itself sinks. We went hundreds of miles north to steal water from Seven Leaf Lake, and we'll drain that dry before long. What's next? War with Regis, Shikaw, or Central Kath? War with Alt Coulumb? Craftsmen against Craftsmen? If you thought the God Wars were bad, just wait. This isn't just our problem. It's the world's problem."

"Our Craft will improve," Kopil said.

"It won't, not the way we hope, not for a long time. The Craft takes as it gives. You can't heal the land with something like that, any more than you could destroy the Serpents. It only makes the problem worse."

"You sound like a theist." In the Deathless King's voice Caleb heard breaking stone. "Or like your father."

Caleb's hands did not shake. He met the King in Red's gaze, and did not look away. "That's not what I mean, and you know it. The old ways are gone, but we need peace with the gods. Their powers don't drain and break the land. They can fulfill their function, and let the world of Craft fulfill its own. A partnership. The pantheons regain power and respectability. The city, the world, gets a new lease on life. People like Mal, like my father, like Alaxic and the True Quechal, lose the authority that fear and oppression gives them."

Kopil scraped a second trench in the stone.

"I'm not a theist, sir. But think about the Serpents. We sacrificed to them for three thousand years, maybe more, because that was how we always conceived of our relationship. We never tried a different approach. That's changed now. I changed it. I think I can do more. I can use power, your power, to fix the world, piece by piece."

"You're proposing your own Concern."

"I don't know what to call it. Something between a Concern and a holy order. We'll take soulstuff from Concerns like RKC and use it to build bridges with the gods. Maybe we can even use it directly, to heal the soil, repair a water table, stop a war."

"You're not a Craftsman. You've never built a Concern. You have little experience, and no skill."

"We'll find Craftsmen. Specialists. And they'll come to us. People understand this problem, even if they try to ignore it. When we give them a chance to help, they will. The business side, relationship building, all that—you're right, it's not my strength. That's why I hope Teo will take a leave of absence and help me." He was gratified to see her eyes widen in surprise, and interest.

"I'd have to think about it," she said, with a note of wonder—at the concept, he hoped, not her own agreement. She glanced from the King in Red beside her, back to Caleb. "It sounds . . . fascinating. Worth a try."

Kopil interlaced his fingers. Bone clicked against bone.

Caleb sat, and the city rebuilt itself behind him. Re-raise. "Sir. I'm not asking for much. Help. Advice. Support. The risks are too high for you to turn me away. We survived this battle, barely, but there's always another. We can't just crush every rebel who wants to sacrifice someone on that altar. We need to build a world where nobody needs to sacrifice. A world that will survive longer than the few more decades we can eke out, the way we're going."

Kopil bowed his head. "Help. Advice. Support."

"And power. Give me soulstuff, without precondition. Like before."

Two points of flame met Caleb's gaze. "To heal the world."

"Yes."

"Where would you start?"

Screams beneath smooth water. "Seven Leaf Lake."

The band played jazz into twilight. The future unrolled like a strip of parchment, so long it narrowed to a point at the horizon. Kopil inhaled over his teeth, though he had no lungs. "Have you thought of a name?"

"No."

"Choose one that rolls off the tongue. Red King Consolidated was a mistake—monolithic, impersonal. How about the Twin

Serpents Group? Catchy, and there's a story behind it. People like stories."

"I'll think it over."

Kopil extended his hand. "Do what you claim you can, Caleb Altemoc. If you don't succeed, you'll probably die."

"It won't come to that, sir," Caleb said.

Salt breeze from the Pax ruffled his hair. The city surrounded him: music from Andrej's band, muffled conversation from the bar, cries of construction workers on the pyramid across the way.

He took the King in Red's hand.

Power struck him, filled him, shone through his scars. The long scroll of history began to write itself.

He did not know what he was doing. But sometimes, when you didn't know, you had to bluff.

He looked Kopil in the eye and grinned.

ACKNOWLEDGMENTS

Many people offered comments on various versions of this book, among them, alphabetically: Alana Abbott, Christopher Ashley, Vladimir Barash, John Chu, Anne Cross, Amy Eastment, Miguel Garcia, Tom and Burki Gladstone, Dan Hammond, David Hartwell, Weronika Janczuk, Kristin Janz, Marlys Jarstfer, Siana La-Forest, Lauren Marino, Sarah Miller, Stephanie Neely, Marco Palmieri, Margaret Ronald, and Marshall Weir. Failures to heed their warnings and advice are, as always, mine. Thanks to all my friends and family for their love, support, and patience.

And especially to Steph, best friend, constant companion, dearest love. She has not, yet, tried to destroy the world, for which my thanks.